Heat smoldered along Jory ~
kept hold of Piper.

Jory pivoted and put her against the wall, covering her mouth
with his before she could scream. He'd meant to subdue her,
to throw her off balance, but shock ricocheted through him.
The second he tasted her, all cinnamon and woman, his
body flared alive. Her smooth, velvety lips softened under
his, and for once, he lost himself in the moment.

Her gasp mingled with his low groan. The second she
pressed harder against him, her mouth curving under his, he
forgot…everything. Who he was, where they were, the fire
and danger. Only the woman against him, warm and willing,
sweet and sexy filled his mind. He clasped her tight, his arm
vibrating with the effort to stay gentle. Even so, he allowed
the man inside, the one so rarely let loose, to take over. To
push deep, to demand more. To take.

And give everything.

Praise for
Rebecca Zanetti's Novels

BLIND FAITH

"Fast paced, suspenseful...an action-packed journey!... This is a unique, intriguing series and *Blind Faith* is another book you won't be able to put down."

—HarlequinJunkie.com

"I loved the writing. I loved the plot...Zanetti is one hell of a writer." —Melimel.Booklikes.com

"A great installment in the series. Everything was upped; the tension, the stakes, the angst, the romance, and of course the shrinking time line for the Dean brothers' chance at survival...I give *Blind Faith* an A."

—TheBookPushers.com

"This book totally rocked. It had me at the edge of my seat and I was totally engrossed in it from beginning to end."

—GuiltyPleasuresBookReviews.com

SWEET REVENGE

"4½ stars! Top Pick! Intense and thrilling...Filled with twists and turns and a heaping dose of adrenaline, Zanetti takes readers on a ride they won't soon forget!"

—*RT Book Reviews*

"Kudos to Ms. Zanetti on another fine Sins Brothers installment, definitely a series to watch!" —GraveTells.com

TOTAL
SURRENDER

Also by Rebecca Zanetti

TOTAL SURRENDER

|||||||||||||||||||||||||||||||||||||||||||||||||||||||||||||||

REBECCA ZANETTI

FOREVER

NEW YORK   BOSTON

Forever
Hachette Book Group
1290 Avenue of the Americas
New York, NY 10104

www.HachetteBookGroup.com

Printed in the United States of America

First Edition: March 2015
10 9 8 7 6 5 4 3 2 1

OPM

Forever is an imprint of Grand Central Publishing.
The Forever name and logo are trademarks of Hachette Book Group, Inc.

The Hachette Speakers Bureau provides a wide range of authors for speaking events. To find out more, go to www.hachettespeakersbureau.com or call (866) 376-6591.

The publisher is not responsible for websites (or their content) that are not owned by the publisher.

This book is dedicated to my grandparents:
Dale and Helen Cornell, Jim and Naomi English,
Herb and Ruth Zanetti, and Harry and Janet Voltolini.

ACKNOWLEDGMENTS

It's with both excitement and sadness that I finish up this fourth book in the Dean brothers' lives. This series found a wonderful home with Grand Central Publishing/Forever, and I'm grateful for the opportunity to work with so many wonderful, talented, and hardworking people.

A special thank-you to my editor, Michele Bidelspach, who has the rare talent to see how much deeper a book can go, and who works tirelessly to make sure the book gets there. She's insightful, kind, and brilliant...and I'm truly thankful for the opportunity to work with her.

Thanks also to Jodi Rosoff, Marissa Sangiacomo, Megha Parekh, and Jamie Snider from Grand Central/Forever for the hard work, dedication, and attention to detail. Thanks also to Diane Luger and Elizabeth Turner for the spectacular covers, and to Joan Matthews for the excellent copyedits.

A big thank-you to my agent, Caitlin Blasdell, who understands world building better than anybody I've ever met, and who also protects me, even from myself. She's the voice of reason in a wild industry, and I definitely owe whatever angel sat on my shoulder when I signed with Caitlin. Thanks also to Liza Dawson and the Dawson gang for the hard work.

Finally, thank you to Big Tone for the support, humor, and good times. Whoever said a marriage can get boring has never met you. I love you. Also, thanks to Gabe and Karlina for the fun and for being such great kids. I love you both!

PROLOGUE

Southern Tennessee Hills
Twenty Years Ago

JORY SET DOWN the screwdriver and shoved the computer guts off his legs. The feel of the wires against his small hands sparked all sorts of creativity, and he knew he could make the processor run faster. Way faster. "I don't want to train. Can't I finish putting this back together?"

"No." Nate, his older brother, crossed skinny arms at the door. Well, skinny for now. At about eleven years old, Nate was starting to get bigger, like their oldest brother, Matt, and would soon be all muscley, too.

Jory sighed and pushed to stand. Wires and electrical components dropped all around him. He'd never be big like his brothers. Even now, at seven years old or so, he was the shortest kid in the compound. "Training is a waste of time for me."

Nate's eyes blazed all sorts of gray fire in a bruised face. "Bullshit. You're going to train like a demon until you finally grow and we don't have to worry about the commander sending you away."

Jory swallowed. What if he didn't ever grow? Fear shook through his hands, so he slid them into his back pockets. He had to be tough like his older brothers. He needed to be a soldier and not a computer guy. "I think the commander's gonna send me away."

"Matt won't let him," Nate said, scratching a scab on his elbow.

The door pushed open, and Shane clomped his combat boots inside. Although Shane was probably only a year older than Jory, he stood almost as tall as Nate, with identical gray eyes. All four brothers had the same gray eyes, so maybe they'd all somehow grow big like Matt. Hopefully.

Nate glanced down at Shane's hands before hustling across the barracks to nab a towel. "You're bleeding."

Shane swallowed and held out bloody hands for the worn cotton that might've been white at some time. "I can't practice knife fighting any more today with all the skin wearing off my palms."

"Too bad." Mattie stalked into the room, bruises on his face, a Glock in one big hand. He'd probably been at the shooting range. His black hair had been buzzed short, showing welts down his neck from hand-to-hand yesterday. "You're going back out to practice for at least another hour. Tonight, when you're least expecting it, I'm coming at you. You had better defend yourself."

Jory swallowed and leaned back against the concrete-block wall. His hands shook harder in his pockets. Matt was his big brother, and he loved him, but sometimes Matt got scary. When he got all determined to train them.

Shane winced. "I don't think so—"

"Shane." Matt didn't raise his voice or move from his spot in the doorway. "Train."

Shane scuffed his boots and eyed Nate, his shoulders straightening when Nate nodded. "Yes, sir," Shane said quietly.

Jory gave him a sympathetic smile. Nate always backed up Matt, but Mattie seemed to need that, so it was okay.

Tension spiraled through the room. Jory cleared his throat. Sometimes, even though they were tough soldiers, so much emotion clogged the room he couldn't breathe. Matt was fierce in his obsession to keep his brothers alive, while Nate was constant in his worry for everyone's safety. And Shane. If Shane wasn't exhausted, Shane was pissed. So much anger in him sometimes.

Emotion hurt, and Jory shoved it down deep and did what he did best. It was his job to get rid of the hard looks on his brothers' faces. "Tomorrow is my birthday."

Shane grinned, while Matt and Nate exchanged glances.

Nate tilted his head. "We don't know when we were born, Jory."

"I know." Jory pointed to the computer he'd torn apart. "But I did some research earlier, and I found our birthdates."

Matt frowned. "You found records?"

"No. Astrology," Jory said, facing his brothers.

A grin split Nate's face, and Shane snorted.

Oh yeah. He got them to smile. Jory rocked back on his heels. "Mattie is a Scorpio, Nate a Capricorn, and Shane an Aquarius." Sure, he was probably wrong, but this was fun. Plus, he really had done some research, and the signs fit his brothers.

"And you?" Matt asked softly.

"I was born on August eighth. Eight-eight." Jory smiled. "I'm a Leo."

Shane coughed. "Why do you get to be the lion?"

Jory sobered. "Because even the smallest lion can have a big roar."

Understanding filled Matt's eyes as his chin dropped. "You're going to grow, little brother. Your feet are huge."

Yeah, and he usually tripped over them. "Maybe. But until then, I want to have a birthday party."

Nate blanched. "We have training all day tomorrow."

Yep, they sure did. Jory had memorized the schedule weeks ago, which was easy because his brain took pictures of everything he saw. But he forced a frown. "Shoot. Well, you could just give me a present."

Shane bit back a smile. "Nice. What do you want?"

Heat slid down Jory's throat to land in his stomach. So far, he hadn't been able to get his brothers to agree to what he wanted. "Since it's my eight-eight birthday, my golden birthday, it's important. Reaaally important."

Nate sighed and eyed the clock ticking on the wall. "What do you want, Jory?"

"A last name," he whispered.

Matt blew out air. "I told you we'd pick a name when we got out of here."

"Come on, Mattie." Jory yanked his hands from his pockets. "You're probably twelve or so…don't you want a last name we can all share?" He looked down at his feet, and his eyes stung. His brothers never cried, and neither would he. "Just in case the commander sends me away, I want us all to have the same name. Just so I know what it is so I can find you guys." His hands shook again, but this time he didn't care. Plus, if he died, he wanted the right name on the grave marker. He didn't even care if he got a cross or not, like the soldiers did in the cemetery outside of the nation's capital. He'd seen pictures once.

"Jesus," Matt muttered. "Listen to me, damn it. The commander is not going to send you anywhere. I promise."

Jory looked up, and Matt's face wavered through tears he wasn't strong enough to get rid of. Matt was the strongest boy Jory had ever met, Nate was the best fighter, and Shane was brilliant. But they were just kids, and the commander was a grown-up. "I know, Mattie. But I really want a last name."

Shane bit his lip. "I do, too."

Silence ticked around the room.

Nate lifted his shooting shoulder. "Um, I kinda do, too."

Matt looked at each one of them in turn, his eyes darkening. Finally, his shoulders relaxed, which usually meant he'd made a decision. "Fine. Does anybody have an idea for a last name?"

"Asskickers?" Shane asked, hope in his voice.

Nate laughed. "We need something untraceable once we escape. Something that's us but is a lot of other people, too."

Jory nodded. "I got an idea last week when we snuck into the secondary command center and watched those old movies via satellite."

Matt rolled his eyes, a real smile finally lifting his lips. "I'm not going to be Mathew Casablanca. Period."

Nate grinned, his body visually relaxing as Matt joked with them again. "Um, no."

"I meant that movie, *Rebel Without a Cause*," Jory said, holding his breath.

"Rebel?" Nate asked.

"Stark—after Jim Stark?" Matt rubbed his chin. "I think that might be too rare."

Jory shook his head. "Dean. After James Dean. He was kinda lost like us, and I think he would've liked to be in our family. The Dean family." Jory held still, trying not to hope too hard.

His brothers all remained quiet for several heartbeats.

Finally, Nate nodded. "I like it."

"Shane Dean," Shane murmured. "Yeah. It's good."

Jory sucked in air and focused on his oldest brother.

Matt studied him for a moment and then slowly smiled. "The *Dean* family it is."

CHAPTER
1

Utah
Current Day

IN A COLD and dismal cell, surrounded by concrete blocks, Jory Dean counted out push-ups, his brain shutting down pain receptors in his body. Sweat dripped onto the cement floor, and steam coated the bulletproof glass wall.

Yet he pressed on, aligning himself for maximum effect, strengthening each muscle in turn. His mind would save him, but he'd need speed and strength first.

For months, fighting insanity in the small quarters, he'd forced himself to behave like a good prisoner. But when he was sure he was strong enough, he ruthlessly pushed himself, knowing he'd need to be in top condition to get free.

He turned inward to listen to his heart rate and lung capacity. For the briefest of time, as he'd escaped a two-year coma, his blood had pumped slower than normal. But now, after three months of intense training in the freezing cell, he was back to normal.

The second his captors gave him an opening, he'd create the opportunity.

To flee this hell and finish what *they'd* started.

His body had taken more time than his brain to repair, and the senses that once had been merely superior now thrummed with additional power. Something was about to happen, and he was ready.

High heels clicked several hallways away, and he kept punishing his biceps until the sound neared the outside door. The click was off to a slight degree, as if the woman wearing them was limping.

Interesting.

He stretched to his feet and grabbed a ripped towel to wipe off his face, knowing full well who stood on the other side.

Heartbeats had signatures, as did breathing rates and bodily scents. He knew the woman's scent well.

Dr. Madison clicked inside the room, wearing her customary white lab coat over skirt and dangerously high heels. At around fifty years old, she appeared much younger. She'd piled her dark hair up on top of her head and had applied perfectly layered makeup that failed to mask a brutal black eye that extended to her temple.

Jory blinked, studying the pattern of the bruise. It was nonsymmetrical, not spread out enough to be from a fist, and looked a day old. A car crash?

Where had she been? Companionship, even hers, was better than being left by himself. Except for the techs who dropped off his food and picked up his tray, he'd been alone with his thoughts, and inside his head wasn't a pretty place to be.

He hadn't seen her in nearly three months. Should he give a shit about that? She was the closest thing he'd had to a mother, and even now, as an intellectual exercise, he couldn't help but wonder. Did he care? If not, what did that make him? He hoped to hell he hadn't become the monster they'd trained him to be, but if so? Yeah. They'd meet that beast soon enough.

Life, like computer codes, held symmetry. They'd created him in a test tube to be a heartless soldier concerned with one thing only—the mission.

It was unfortunate for them that *his* mission, the one that mattered, would most likely mean their deaths. "What happened to your face and leg?" he asked softly, so unaccustomed to his own voice that his breathing paused for one beat.

She fingered the bruise and looked up more than a foot to his face, her forehead furrowing. "Your brother blew up our DC facility, and I was caught underground in an airplane hangar."

Brother. The one word cut through protective layers of muscle to pierce his heart. He kept his expression stoic and forced his vitals to remain steady. "Which brother?" he asked, lowering his voice to keep it from trembling, even while his mind kicked into gear. He hadn't felt or heard an explosion, so he must be somewhere far away from DC. Add in the air chill, and he figured somewhere in the Midwest.

"Nathan." She pursed her lips in a tight, white line, studying Jory carefully. As usual. "He took my daughter with him."

Jory jolted internally and yet remained preternaturally still, his gut lurching. Nate was still alive. Confirmation—finally—that at least one of his brothers had lived through the last two years. Deep down, where humanity still hovered, Jory fought against the hope washing over him. Now wasn't the time for emotion.

He eyed Madison. Why was she sharing information? The woman always had a reason, and for now, he'd play along. "Good for Nate." Jory's big brother had never gotten over Audrey Madison, so it wasn't exactly shocking that he'd returned for her. "Was she willing to go with him?" He wouldn't put it past Nate to toss Audrey over a shoulder while bombs detonated.

Madison sniffed. "I believe so, but maybe the pregnancy has messed with her intellect."

Jory stilled. Only supreme control kept his heart from thumping against his ribcage. He lifted one eyebrow and pierced the doctor with a hard stare. "Audrey is pregnant?"

"Yes. With Nate's baby." Madison reached for a computer tablet from her pocket, avoiding his gaze. She'd started averting her eyes the second he'd learned to infuse power into his stare. "Congratulations, it appears the Gray family can procreate." She smiled, revealing sharp teeth, having control back into place.

Warmth burst through Jory, and he allowed himself a rare moment to ban the ever-present chill. Nate was going to be a father? Unbelievable. He'd make a great father...if he lived beyond the coming week. Jory wanted to smile but refused to give the doctor the satisfaction of reading his emotions.

Her focus dropped to his groin. "I wonder if we could—"

Jory fought the urge to cover his balls and stepped closer to the partition. "Not a chance in hell." He spoke low and kept eye contact as he gave her the absolute truth. She'd been the one woman as a constant in his life from the beginning, even tending his hurts after he'd trained as a kid. But not with motherly love. Instead she had stitched him up a time or two while taking copious notes at how fast he healed.

Still he'd rather not have to snap her neck. Yet.

She clucked her tongue. "It's hard to imagine you were the good-natured brother."

"Getting plugged in the chest several times and ending up in a coma for two years tends to piss a guy off." He kept her gaze and stretched his torso, trying not to go crazy in the small cell.

Dr. Madison licked her lips and eyed his scarred chest. "Your workouts and diet regimen have returned you to excellent shape in such a short time. I did a marvelous job with your genetics."

He rubbed his chin. "Yeah. You really did." Of course, the woman had no clue about his enhanced abilities or how successful she'd been in creating something new.

God only knew what she'd combined with soldier DNA to create him, and even now, he didn't want to know the particulars. He was Jory Dean, he had three brothers, and that was enough family history for him.

Her gaze traveled to the tattoo above his heart. "Freedom." She shook her head.

His hand moved on its own volition to rub his inked skin. The week they'd escaped, he and his brothers had created the matching design before finding the perfect artist to tattoo them. Now that he'd been recaptured, the design mocked him.

He swallowed and forced his body to relax when all he wanted to do was punch through unpunchable glass. When she looked at him like he was steak on a plate, he wanted to puke. So he turned and yanked a ratty T-shirt over his head. "Were Matt and Shane with Nate when he blew up DC?" The more information he could get about all of his brothers, the easier it'd be to plan now that he was strong enough.

Time was up, and he needed to strike.

Madison just looked at him.

With a sigh, he gave up the pretense. "Please tell me if they're still alive." Yeah, he could play her game if it earned him information.

"You know you've always been the easiest of your brothers to read," she said.

"I know." That's what she thought. Madison was tough

to play, but he'd figured out years ago how to manipulate her. False vulnerability and full truth worked because she liked to see reactions. So he reacted outwardly while his brain raced internally. For now, he'd allow her to believe she was smarter than he was, but at this point, she wasn't even close.

"I wonder if your weakness is from being the youngest, or if you inherited such traits from your maternal egg donor?" Madison tapped her chin.

"I don't know." Jory shrugged, changing tactics to keep her off balance and camouflage how much he needed an answer about his brothers. "Who was my maternal egg donor?"

She sighed. "Who cares? We paid for eggs from extraordinary genetic pools, and those women never wanted the ensuing children."

Jory kept his face blank, not even feeling the words that should cut deep. Who the hell cared about what came before? The Dean brothers shared a paternal donor, and their identical gray eyes served as a genetic marker. They'd given up long ago of finding any information on maternal donors—they didn't have mothers and never would. "I care little about genetics," he said.

"Yet it's so interesting how similar you boys are but how differently you handle the same situation," she mused.

"How would my brothers handle you?" he asked.

She smiled. "Shane would try to charm me for the answer, while Nathan would harass me like a rottweiler fighting for a bone. Matt? Well, Matt would play mind games and twist me up until I gave the information."

"I'm aware of my brothers' talents." Jory preferred hard drives to humans, which made Madison's brain easy to mine. The woman was almost a computer, completely lacking in emotion. Long ago, he'd given up his soul, so begging didn't mean much to him, even if he had meant it. "Please tell me."

She typed something in on her tablet. "As far as I know, Mathew and Shane are alive. They didn't help Nathan on the ground in DC, but I have no doubt they assisted in planting explosives."

Electricity sparked down Jory's torso, and his shoulders straightened. *Alive.* His brothers were all alive. Now he had a short time to keep it that way. "Thank you," he murmured.

She glanced up, and her eyes slowly focused. "There's more."

Man, she loved to see him beg, didn't she? "Oh?" Jory had given her all the satisfaction she'd get this morning. Either she'd give him the rest of the details, or she wouldn't.

"Yes." She frowned, irritation sparking through her blue eyes. "Shane went back for that woman he'd used on a mission once, and Matt kidnapped one of our doctors who'd betrayed us. They've committed themselves to women."

Now Jory did smile. "Bullshit." Whatever game she played, she could roll the dice by herself. He could see Nate rescuing Audrey since they'd gotten together so long ago, but no way would Shane or Matt drag a woman into the shitstorm of their lives. "Nice try, Madison."

She nodded, her forehead smoothing. "I don't understand, either. Soon we'll have them back home, and I can figure them out."

Oh, hell no. His brothers were never getting caught again, and Jory needed freedom to deactivate the kill chips near their spines implanted almost five years ago. He eyed the outside door. So close and yet so damn far. "Why do you want us here? I just don't get it."

"The commander and the organization are being attacked, and your skills and training are needed." Her voice remained level, but fire lit her eyes. "From several sides. The U.S. government is looking at our financials, there are competing firms out there getting stronger, and an organized fundamentalist group wants the commander shut down."

"Good. Then leave us the hell alone." He'd love to light the entire organization on fire, and he would. The second he got out of the cage and saved his brothers.

"That will never happen. Our base inland will be much more appropriate to contain you and yours, and it is a good place to retrain you. You'll be transferred within a few days." Madison glanced back down at her tablet.

His head lifted. If he allowed the transfer to a more secured facility, he'd never get free, so it was time to make a move. "I'm tired of gym shorts and T-shirts, and these tennis shoes are a size too small." He rested broad hands on his hips and glared around the dismal cell. One cot sat in a corner, and a bare-bones bathroom took residence around a partial wall. "Get me out of here."

"Why?" She arched one fine eyebrow. "That kill chip by your C4 vertebra will detonate in one week and you'll die. Your best chance of survival is staying here."

His eyelids slowly rose, so he flattened his hands on the bulletproof glass and leaned in. "The chip you screwed up? Yeah. I'm not expecting a rescue there." The bastard scientists had implanted kill chips near the Dean brothers' spines, and if the correct code wasn't entered in the right computer program in a week, the chips would activate and sever their spines. Unfortunately, the code changed every thirty seconds, so getting a lock on it from a distance had been all but impossible.

Of course, no damn code worked for Jory. "We both know I'm fucked."

"I do wish you'd watch your language. As a child, you were so well mannered." Dr. Madison typed something into her tablet. "I didn't make a mistake on the chips. When you got yourself shot, a bullet ricocheted off the chip, and it's damaged. It's shocking the device didn't explode then and there." She pursed her lips as if pondering what to have for dinner. "Just shocking."

"Who shot me?"

Madison lifted a slim shoulder. "You have the highest IQ ever recorded, young man. Those memories are in that impressive brain, and you need to access them."

Jory rubbed his eyes. Having no memory of a devastating event was normal, damn it. He might never remember who'd shot him.

But he remembered blowing his cover at the scientific facility where he had been gathering information about the commander's organization. He'd scanned the wrong computer system and had set off alarms, resulting in a flash grenade and drugs pumped into his system.

Damn rookie move because he'd been in a hurry and so close to finding the program to deactivate the kill chips. He'd deserved to get shot for his carelessness.

For now, he was a fucking monkey in a cage, and he had to get out of there before his *impressive* brain melted. So he tried reason. "Madison? I have one week to live. For once, have a heart and let me live out my last days." It was the closest he'd come to asking the brilliant scientist for anything after she'd started hitting on him when he'd reached puberty. She had a record for playing with cadets, and he'd kept his distance, as had his brothers, he was sure.

"I didn't raise you to be a quitter. Don't worry. I have a plan," she said.

As usual, he'd have to work against her. He shoved a hand through his hair, which had begun to curl at his nape. "What's the plan?" If he was going to figure out a way to save his brothers, he had to get out of there.

"For one thing, I'd like to schedule you for another MRI. Your brain is functioning…abnormally." She stared at his forehead as if she could see into his gray matter, her lip curling. "I'm having a PET scan set up for later today, also."

Fuck, shit, and damn it all to hell. He couldn't let her discover his special abilities, nor those of his brothers. They'd succeeded for years in hiding the very skills that had kept them alive. But ever since the coma, something new percolated in his mind. Something he apparently couldn't hide now. "You've been doing scans for months. Nothing is different."

"The scans from last week are different." She tapped a red fingernail against her lips.

Yeah. His best guess was that new paths had been forged in his brain during the coma, and a weird tingling in his lobe had begun the previous week. Maybe it was his special abilities increasing in power, or maybe it was something new. Either way, he had to mask the truth.

Two heartbeats echoed from outside the room, so he tilted his head to hear better while trying to appear bored. Dr. Madison had no clue about his heightened senses or his extra abilities, and he needed to keep it that way.

A soldier entered first, followed by a woman in her midtwenties, who slid out from behind him.

Jory's breath caught in his throat. *Exquisite.* For once, that word could be applied accurately. She stood to about five foot six in black boots wearing a matching leather jacket. Light mocha-colored skin, curly black hair, and eyes greener than the most private parts of Ireland.

She took one look at him and stepped back.

He moved forward and flashed a smile that made her eyes widen. If he had to scare her to make her leave, he'd do it. Anybody seeing him in captivity would be killed by the commander after serving their purpose. So he forced sexual tension to filter through the room.

How he could do it, he wasn't sure. Maybe pheromones and bodily heat waves, and the ability came easier now than it had before the coma. It was a hell of an advantage to use sometimes, and he ignored Madison's quick intake of breath when he employed it.

"Is she for me?" he asked, forcing his gaze to run over the newcomer's body and surprising himself when he hardened in response. God. He'd been on a mission and then in a coma for two years before spending time in captivity recuperating. When was the last time he'd gotten laid? Way too long ago.

He'd always liked women, although he'd never gotten close to one. Not really. They were either part of a mission or worked as doctors in the facility, and those certainly couldn't be trusted.

This one was petite with delicate bone structure and clear, intelligent eyes. Whatever her purpose, she sure as hell didn't belong in the dismal place. Hopefully she'd turn on her heel and get out since he'd leered at her.

Instead she lifted one eyebrow. Her face flushed. "So that's him."

Well, damn. Another angel with the heart of a demon. A pang landed squarely in Jory's chest. Beauty should never be evil. "Yeah, that's me," he murmured, dropping the sensual attack. "Who are you?"

She opened her mouth and shut it as Dr. Madison shook her head. "It doesn't matter who she is," Madison muttered. Grasping the woman's arm, Madison led her over to a computer console. "Get to work, and remember the rules."

The woman jerked free and stepped away from Madison. She eyed Madison like an opponent in a boxing ring—with wariness and determination.

Jory frowned, and his instincts started to hum. Was the woman a prisoner, like him? Maybe he could gain them both freedom, with her help. She was *outside* of the cage, now wasn't she? He smiled.

Dr. Madison glanced back toward Jory, her gaze narrowing.

"Leave her alone to work, and I won't have you tranquilized again." With that, she allowed the soldier to escort her from the room, and the door nicked shut behind her.

The woman sat at the console and turned toward him. "Piper. My name is Piper." She eyed the partition. Her voice was smooth and sexy...feminine. She guarded her expression well. "They didn't give me your name."

Yeah. They wouldn't have thought to give his name. "Jory." He really liked the way her tight jeans hugged her curves, and he appreciated the intelligence sizzling in those spectacular eyes. She'd have to be smart to help him escape. "Why are you here, Piper?"

She exhaled slowly and stretched out her fingers. "I'm here to save you, Jory."

CHAPTER
2

PIPER KEPT TYPING in code, her fingers flying over the keyboard. She couldn't spend another day failing at the task, if for no other reason than succeeding would piss off Dr. Madison. The snotty doctor gloated each and every day the solution remained outside of Piper's reach, her dislike evident in every condescending sniff.

The rudeness was personal and not from any sense of betrayal or righteous anger. If the doctor had been pissed Piper hacked into the organization's server a couple of years ago, accidentally earning her a job, then Piper could understand her behavior. But that wasn't it.

Not even close.

And now? Now Piper had been assigned the most important task in the entire organization—saving the prisoner's life. Why he mattered, she hadn't been told.

But everything seemed to be riding on her ability with computers.

Once a hacker, always a hacker—but now she had the chance to do something good with her skills. Something honorable that would cement her position with the organization because of her abilities and not connections.

Saving the man in the cell's life would make her very, very useful. Plus, the mere idea of a kill chip implanted near the man's spine was sneaky, and the notion of using a computer program to murder offended her.

So she put her head down and worked hard. Although the myriad of soldiers outside the doorway, armed to the gills, sped up her heart rate and slowed down her typing. Too many guns suddenly surrounded her.

She bit her lip and tried to ignore the itch between her shoulder blades. She'd worked for hours, her mind spinning. After trying unsuccessfully to engage her in conversation, Jory had gone quiet.

But he'd been watching her the entire time. His gaze almost felt physical, and a tension, a layered change in the atmosphere around them, seemed to come from the man in the cell. She'd read about charisma, and she understood tension, as well as instinct. Hers told her the guy had been watching her.

She just *knew* it.

Or maybe her imagination had gone amuck in the military-like facility, and he'd stretched out to sleep on the narrow cot, forgetting all about her. Was he watching or wasn't he? Unanswered questions pricked her like needles. So finally giving up, she turned to face him.

Nope. He remained sitting, his gaze thoughtful on her. "I

thought you'd never turn my way." Through the Plexiglas, his voice emerged deep and softened.

"I have work to do." She brushed hair off her forehead and tried not to squirm. Years ago she'd read a book featuring a hero with the face of a fallen angel, and she had rolled her eyes, while imagining a light-skinned, blue-eyed cherub having curly golden hair that *so* was not sexy.

Now, facing masculine, sculpted perfection...she understood. Angels held ideal beauty, while a fallen one would probably appear dark and deadly, like the man facing her. Gods had chiseled Jory's face into hard lines and sharp angles. The nearly brutal contours were arranged with full lips, dark brows, and a firm jaw. An unusual gray colored his eyes into the deepest of storm clouds, and a small scar cut into his left eyebrow, hinting at danger and strength.

Any woman would be attracted to him and find him compelling. Alone, in the utilitarian cell, his beauty alone would tempt any romantic to try and save him.

Bad guy or not.

He overwhelmed the cot, his hands and feet beyond large. Most guys his size looked like overgrown puppies, but the thought of comparing the warrior to a scampering animal was laughable at best.

"You're wasting your time with trying to engage the chip," he said. "I strongly suggest you give up now and get out of here."

Charismatic and too handsome, without question. A sense of sexual danger all but cascaded off him, and she had the oddest sense he knew it. Maybe even controlled it— which did nothing but intrigue her more.

She shook her head. The military place full of secrets was messing with her imagination, and the romanticism she had to tamp down. Her stash of romances would remain untouched for a while, and after the job had been successfully completed, she'd reward herself with a weekend of binging on alpha males and surreal adventures.

For now, she'd get the job done.

He watched her face as if fascinated by an engaging television show. Could he read her so easily? As if responding to her unasked question, he smiled. Even teeth, a flash of white in a devastating face.

Her breath sped up, and flutters beat through her abdomen. Her brain tried to shut down any response, while her body flared alive. A flush spread like wildfire up from her chest and over her face with such a force her skin flamed.

How was he doing that?

Her head snapped up. While her body seemed to be on the blink, her mind remained clear, but now incredibly intrigued. "I can figure out how to wirelessly reach your chip," she said, quietly pleased when her voice remained steady.

"No, you can't. While I appreciate the Hail Mary pass, you can't reconnect to the chip. It's damaged. Off-line. Unreachable. Trust me." His earnest expression would probably gain him admittance to heaven if he asked nicely.

Considering that her taste in men truly sucked until just recently, it figured she'd be attracted to him. But really, who wouldn't be? The guy was every movie hero, romance novel antihero, and sexy villain she'd ever seen all trumbled into one seriously hot package.

But he was full of shit, and he'd just made his first mistake. No way—*no way* had he given up on life so easily. Nobody worked at staying in such amazing physical shape to just roll over and die. Well, unless he had another reason to stay fit. "Trust you? Seriously?"

He cocked his head to the side and lifted one eyebrow. "Sure. Why not?"

She could take the mocking, and she could handle the

tension he seemed to shoot her way. But treating her as a dumb girl and trying to charm her into *trust*? Hell to the no.

She rushed from her chair and toward the cell. So stupid to let her temper free. Darn Irish blood. "Gee, I don't know. Maybe because you're a traitor?" Damn it. She couldn't let him get under her skin, but anybody who'd turn against their own country should be shot. Not saved. And somebody that freakin' amazingly hot had so many advantages in life it was even worse he'd chosen the wrong path. "Here I am trying to fix the chip planted in your back."

He stood slowly and deliberately, his dark gaze keeping hers, his expression inscrutable. "Who do you think planted the chip?"

She swallowed and fought the urge to step back. Damn, he was big. Instead, she lifted her chin, a necessity if she wanted to meet his gaze directly. "That's what happens when you double-cross Russians."

A low rumble of a laugh barked out of him. "Russians? Seriously? Fucking Russians." Dark amusement filtered through his tone and glittered in those amazing eyes. "You're not as smart as you look, green eyes."

She was a fucking genius, actually. Even though most of the world believed Russia was contained, her limited experience at the NSA during her internship proved otherwise. "While I appreciate your attempts to get into my head, I should get back to work to save your life. You know, in time for the court martial."

His smile revealed even white teeth. No dimples. Shouldn't a fallen angel have a dimple or two? "There's no way to fix the chip, as it was damaged physically by a bullet. No router problem, no way to repair the connection. Setting to WAP personal won't work and neither will setting to mixed network mode." He shrugged massive shoulders.

Interesting. She stilled and studied him closer, if that were possible. Intelligence filled his eyes, which she'd overlooked because of his hulking size...and his incredible looks. "So you know a little bit about computers, do you?" If he was as knowledgeable as he seemed, he could've sold all sorts of state secrets to their enemies.

"A bit. Don't waste time using stumblers or sniffers. The last techs they sent wasted too much time trying." He sighed. "Then they tried a wireless honey pot. Idiots."

She shook her head. He seemed to have the world at his feet, just from brains, brawns, and beauty. "Why?" she asked, her voice croaking.

Furrows dug into his forehead, and he stepped closer to the glass. "Why what?"

Although impossible, she could swear she felt heat from his body through the partition. "Why would you do such a thing? Betray your own people?" Sure, she'd made mistakes—big ones. But disloyalty wasn't one of them.

His gaze softened. "I have never betrayed my own people. Ever."

The words had to be a lie, but truth echoed in the low tones. She sighed. "So *your people* aren't the citizens of your own country."

One massive shoulder lifted. "I'd never turn against this country, but no. My *people* share my blood." He paused and rubbed his scruffy chin. "Well, and the women they might love—I'd never betray them, either." His smile returned at the last.

For some reason, the statement both intrigued and irritated her. "So your people are only men."

"*More* than men and never *only*." He didn't appear to move, but suddenly seemed taller. Bigger. More formidable. "Is there anybody you'd die for?"

"Yes." Absolutely and without question.

His lids half lowered. "How about kill for?"

She blinked. "Y-Yes." The order of his question as well as the flash of sorrow in his dark eyes bespoke of hidden hurts and unplumbed deaths. "Who are you?" she whispered.

"I like that about you. A lot."

Her chest warmed, and warning clanged inside her brain. "Like what?"

"The way you blurt out what's in your head without thinking. You've done it twice already." His full upper lip quirked. "While you're definitely on guard, your natural state is unguarded. Very appealing."

Oh, he did not get to read her so easily. "Maybe I'm working you."

Now his eyes darkened, swirling with something...male. "Baby, you could work me any day."

Laughter rolled out of her, quick and unexpected.

His eyebrows lifted.

She forced her lips out of a smile. "That come-on voice you use, trying to be suggestive. It's such baloney."

He rubbed his bottom lip, studying her. Deep. Before he'd seemed merely curious, now it felt like he dug deep and mined her brain. Maybe deeper. She wanted to step away, to get back to work, but the guy was like a refuge in the middle of chaos. Even trapped, a sense of calmness surrounded him.

When was the last time she'd been calm?

"Jory? Is that your real name?" For some reason, knowing his real name mattered. Why, Piper would figure out later.

"Yes. Always has been." Jory flattened his platter-sized palm against the glass. A wicked and faded white scar marred his life line. "Is Piper your name?"

Her head jerked back. "Yes. Always has been." An urge to press her palm against his, even to just marvel at the difference in size, propelled her back a step. "If you tell me who implanted the chip, maybe I could figure out where it came from and study the design so I can somehow reconnect wire-lessly with it. So the damn thing doesn't go active, slice your spine, and kill you."

No physical reaction whatsoever from the hard-ass prisoner.

"If I told you, they'd kill you." He kept his palm in place, the scar a deadly reminder of who he was and what he might do. "Get out now, Piper."

A chill skittered down her spine. "Nobody will kill me. We're both protected here."

He sighed.

She shook her head. Yeah, she wanted to save him, and not just to cement her place in the organization. To be truly useful and needed. Maybe there was a good reason he'd betrayed the people she now trusted? She shook her head. There was no good reason. "You're just too good-looking. Bad guys shouldn't look like you."

His cheek creased. "I'm not a good guy, I admit. But in this world, in the place you're standing in right now? I'm not even close to the baddest. Unfortunately."

Fanatics believed wholeheartedly in their cause and in the rightness of their crimes. She knew better than to trust him, and she was too smart to be manipulated. "I can see you believe your statement."

A line formed between his eyebrows. "What exactly did Dr. Madison tell you about me?"

Piper paused. There didn't seem to be a good reason to withhold information. "She told me you were an American asset, one trained in assassinations, who turned against our country and sold secret information to the highest bidders and then ended up working with the Russians. Apparently your new friends didn't trust you, so they implanted a kill chip next to your spine, and a bullet impacted the device, rendering it off-line."

Jory quirked his upper lip. "Great story."

She studied him. What if the story was untrue? Dr. Madison was a stone-cold bitch and probably had no problem lying. Especially since she couldn't stand Piper. "Want to counter?"

"No."

An odd regret weighed down her shoulders. "So it's true."

"No." He shook his head. "The less you know about me, the safer you'll remain."

What a bunch of baloney. "If you cared about my safety, you wouldn't have sold my country's secrets to our enemies," she shot back.

He shook his head. "You're really a patriot, now aren't you?"

She lifted her chin. "Yes." Although her reasons for working at the compound were definitely personal and not professional, she loved her country and couldn't understand how anybody could betray their homeland. "I studied computers and coding through college and graduate school just to be able to work here."

"So you're here voluntarily." Whatever openness had been in his gaze moments ago snapped closed—hard and fast, like a bank vault door.

She bit the inside of her lip. "Yes. I trained at the NSA, and that made me appealing for this organization." Of course, she'd already been in contact with the organization when she'd earned the NSA internship, but since the NSA didn't know that fact, neither should the prisoner. Now saving Jory was her assignment.

"Does the NSA know about this job?" A low thread of something dark wove through his words.

She blinked and told him the first lie of the day. "Yes."

His chin lifted. "Ah. Interesting."

She crossed her arms. "What is interesting?"

"You're a terrible liar, Piper. I like that." His eyes warmed.

She kept silent, not wanting to compound the lie. What was wrong with her? Every time the guy said he liked something about her, flutters heated her abdomen. He was the *bad guy*.

Now she worked in a covert military organization, and she needed to learn to lie better. When she'd moved to Utah, she'd known of the job's secrecy. Sometimes duty required sacrifice, she'd been told. Something whispered inside her head that the man in the cell had seen plenty of sacrifice. "I'm not lying," she muttered.

He lowered his chin. "You seem like a smart woman, so I have to ask you, does lying to the NSA seem like a good idea? Does an organization, one that professes to be part of the U.S. military, lie to the NSA?"

The back of her nape tickled. Sometimes, the NSA didn't want to know everything, which was why it hired out organizations such as the one she now worked for. That much, she'd figured out on her own without the covert training she was currently undergoing. "Nobody is lying to the NSA," she said evenly.

He snorted.

She cleared her throat. Time to get back to the job at hand. That's what he was, and what he had to remain. Merely a job. Her time of rescuing stray pets had ended, and she had to stop his attempts to dig into her head. "So far I haven't been able to reconfigure the code algorithm or to gain a connection between the computer and the chip. The code changes every thirty seconds, so you need the connection to make it work and to pause it. Help me to save you." Maybe he didn't want to be saved.

"You really want to help?" he asked, his gaze intent.

"Yes." She had to prove her usefulness in order to stay, and more than anything, she needed to stay. Plus, now she wanted to save the man in the cage. The Russians didn't get to decide when and how he died. The American courts would.

"Then give me the codes and the computer," he said.

They'd warned her he'd try to work her, and she'd scoffed. Now she saw the reason for the concern. Nobody should be that charming. "How exactly am I supposed to get you the computer?" she asked.

"Help me get out of here." He dropped his hand. "You're good, I admit it. But I'm better, and if I had the chance at the computer, I could fix this."

He was lying. She shook her head. "If you could save yourself, they would've given you the chance. You want the computer to contact your allies. The commander warned me."

That easily, that quickly, Jory turned from an amenable charmer into something…impenetrable. Cold swept the gray warmth from his eyes, and his jaw firmed into a shape harder than granite.

The mask slipped to reveal the killer deep inside.

For the first time, she had no problem imagining him as the bad guy. "I knew you were in there somewhere," she murmured.

His chin lifted, and his nostrils flared. "You have no idea who's in here, green eyes. No idea at all."

"Was it the mention of your allies that did it?" Her knees trembled with the raw need to escape danger, even though he was contained. The hair sprang up on the back of her neck, and her fight or flight instinct bellowed for her to flee. Would a mere cell wall keep a man like him trapped? Somehow, she didn't think so.

"No allies. Just how well do you know the commander?" Jory asked, his lip twisting.

Piper shrugged again and swallowed over a lump in her throat. "Pretty well. Considering he's my father."

CHAPTER
3

PIPER STRETCHED HER neck while her heels clicked on the hard tile in rapid succession. She shouldn't have told Jory about her father, but as usual, her mouth moved faster than her brain. Considering the neurons in her brain fired quicker than the speed of light, her mouth was a freakin' miracle.

The brief file she'd studied about Jory showed his proficiency with making connections with people—especially women. Charming them and gaining trust. He'd tried with her, and damn, she'd seen the appeal.

But she had a brain, and she wasn't some dumb girl to be manipulated. She had to prove that to herself as well as to her father.

Her strengths lay in her mind and computer skills, and she wouldn't allow any feminine, romantic silliness to get in the way. Not this time.

A swipe of her key card opened a heavy metal door into another secured area in the compound. While gorgeous mountains surrounded them, she'd been spending too much time surrounded by concrete blocks and alarm systems. Yet the computer facilities, the hardware and software, the sheer connection of the place filled her with warmth and pleasure.

These were better than the systems at the compound two hours into the flatlands, but those were being upgraded. She bit her lip. Right now she had the perfect setup and didn't want to move two hours from town. Why couldn't they just stay there like they had the last two months?

If she saved Jory, maybe she'd be allowed to work in the satellite office and stay put, which would also keep her mother happy. Her mom was still pissed she'd taken the job. Finally, Piper reached a closed office door at the end of the lonely hallway. She knocked.

"Enter."

The powerful voice straightened her shoulders and lifted her chin. She opened the door and stepped inside, instantly assailed by the scent of gunpowder. Her hands shook, but she forced herself to stride inside and stand by a sprawling wooden desk. "Commander."

Dressed in a black soldier's uniform, his unfathomable eyes serious, he nodded toward one of two metal chairs. "Sit."

She obeyed, crossing her legs and keeping her shoulders back to match his ramrod straight posture. Being nervous was just silly, but her hands sweat, anyway. Taking a deep breath, she braced herself. "I haven't been able to fix the connection to the prisoner's chip yet."

"We only have a week until the chip engages." The commander sat back, his sharp gray buzz cut gleaming in the harsh fluorescent lights. "I thought you were the best."

Actually, after talking to Jory, she might be second best. "The bullet's impact damaged the chip. I plan to write a new program tonight that may bypass the safeguards put into place earlier, which will hopefully reengage the chip. Hopefully awaken it, if you will." Her stomach swirled with the need to please him.

His eyebrows drew down. "Is there any chance the chip is completely dead and not just off-line?"

"It's possible, but I certainly wouldn't count on it." The chips had been expertly designed to withstand external pressure, but nothing could remain damage-free from a direct impact from a bullet.

"Then I suggest you remember the clock winding down."

She swallowed. "I've only been close enough to the prisoner to try a wireless connection for a day." Before that, she'd spent her time rewriting the program, trying to find a different program, or trying to destroy the program, as per her instructions. Letting her get so close to the prisoner with a computer and a wireless connection was their last shot at saving him.

"Humph." Disappointment rode the grunt hard. "A couple of years ago, when you decided to hack into my system and then taught yourself the chip program and how to manipulate it, I figured you'd be dedicated to solving my problem." A light that looked suspiciously like pride glittered in his dark eyes.

She shook her head. "I hacked into your servers trying to find my father, you, after an old college roommate of my mom sent her a box of stuff she'd never retrieved from their storage unit. Finding the chip program had been a coincidence." She'd found the picture of her father and had instantly begun investigating the mysterious commander. Of course, the second she'd discovered the intricate program, she'd set to figuring it out.

And had gotten caught.

She'd never forget the military soldiers showing up to arrest her and toss her in a cell. The lawyer she'd met had urged her to make a deal for ten years in a federal prison.

Then her father, the one she'd never met, had stepped in and saved her ass.

She owed him, but Jory's questions about the NSA swirled around her head. "How come you didn't want me to tell anybody at the NSA that I went to work for you?"

The commander shrugged. "You earned your internship with them on your own, and you should be proud of that. Then you went back to school and graduated before earning this job. Right now, is there any reason to let the NSA know you're working here?"

She wiped her hands off again. Was there any reason? "I guess not."

He leaned forward. "We provide vital assistance to the United States government, and some of our work is off the books, as is necessary when defending a country and way of life. I have little care if you let the NSA know you're working here, but I don't see the reason."

It wasn't like she'd really made any friends there between the work, her schooling, her part-time job, and her mother. And it seemed like the commander didn't really care if she contacted the NSA, so obviously he wasn't hiding anything. "I understand," she said.

"Good."

If he needed her, she could stay and actually get to know him better, and he seemed impressed with her talents. Every time he'd given her a glimpse into himself, she'd found herself intrigued and wanting to know more. For years, she'd dreamed of her heroic father, and when she'd tracked him down, she'd been thrilled. "I'll fix the chip." God, she shouldn't make that promise. What if she couldn't keep it?

"I hope so," he said, no expression on his hard face and the light disappearing from his eyes.

Piper swallowed, her gaze sliding to take in the large office and myriad of antique guns, all killing machines, decorating the walls. Nothing but the desk and two chairs sat in the room, leaving the overall effect as masculine and stark. Just like her father. Would he have been the same—so distant—if she'd known him as a child? "I could also use another pair of hands tomorrow using the second computer in the room. Any ideas?"

The commander nodded. "Yes. I'll have an aide sent to

you as soon as I can have it arranged, as I assume the new program will be written by then?"

"Yes." Even if she had to stay up all night, she'd figure out a way to reach the chip. "I appreciate the chance to work here and try."

He focused on her, no expression in those midnight black eyes. "You proved yourself in your grades and the internship work with Homeland Security. However, if you're unable to succeed, our genetic bond won't matter when it comes to working here."

"I understand." Her stomach lurched. She couldn't fail now that she was so close to getting to know him finally. The idea of having her parent think of her as a failure, especially in her chosen field, tightened her stomach until it hurt— especially since her taking the job had pissed off her mother so much. This had to work out somehow.

His gaze gentled. "Even if you can't write the code, you're welcome to stay in Utah. I find I like having you here."

Her throat clogged, and she blinked. He liked having her there? It was the nicest thing she'd ever heard from him, and all her silly, childhood dreams came crashing back. She smiled, barely keeping her lips from trembling. "I'll figure out how to bypass the computer safeguards. It's our only chance."

"Good." He clasped large hands together on the desk. "After such a rough start with computers, it'd make me proud to see you succeed here."

Proud? "Okay." She owed him her freedom, without question. "I know where I'd be right now had you not interceded." She paused and met his gaze directly. "You saved me."

The commander lifted one dark silver eyebrow. "I would've become involved in your life before you ended up in trouble, had I known you existed."

She interlaced her fingers to keep from wringing her hands. "My mother said you lived a very dangerous life, and she wanted to keep me safe from it." From the numerous armed soldiers in every passageway, her mother hadn't exaggerated. Although keeping a child from her father didn't set well with Piper, either. "I'm sorry we hadn't met earlier." Attending the father-daughter dance at her high school with her softball coach had left an empty place in her belly for a week.

Then at her lowest point, her father had swooped in and saved her.

"I'm glad I realized who you were when you hacked into my system," he said softly. He eyed his watch. "You're my daughter, and I couldn't very well let you go to prison for hacking, now could I? Once I discovered your aptitude, I saw a future for us together, and I need the help." He glanced at his computer and back to her.

Piper breathed out. He needed her. Now all she had to do was figure out the program, save Jory, and get her mother to relax. "You do understand that I was trying to find you and not just hack into your system, right?"

"I do." He smiled—a very rare sight. "Of course, once in my system..."

She winced. "I know. Curiosity is the bane of all hackers."

"Keep in mind what it does to cats." He lifted an eyebrow. A chill swept down her back. "I know."

He cleared his throat. "Has your mother come to terms with your working for me?"

Piper bit her lip, her stomach hurting. "Not really. While I was growing up, she said you were a super-spy for the government who could never contact us." The dreams Piper had spun of her hero of a father showing up to be in her life, to take care of her flighty mother, had never quite died. She looked around the secured room. "Which was actually the truth." So why did the truth hurt so badly? "I just wish she would've let you decide whether or not to be in our lives."

He tapped long-tapered fingers on his immaculate desk. "Well, you can't blame her too much. I do live a dangerous life, and her job was to protect you. She did so admirably."

True, but now it was time to let Piper make her own decisions. At her lowest point, sitting in a jail with reality smashing her in the face, her father had swept in and rescued her. The government had dismissed the hacking charges, and from that day forward, she'd wanted to please him. To make him proud, even though her mother had argued vehemently against any relationship. "I feel like we have an opportunity to get to know each other now."

He eyed her. "I thought that's what we were doing."

Most men failed at the emotional aspects of relationships, a fact she'd learned the hard way with boyfriends and a disastrous engagement that ended with her fiancé sleeping with not one, but two, of her bridesmaids. At the same time.

Finally, she was in the same place as the commander, and this might be her only chance to get to know him in person. To prove she was worthy and that he could trust her. Her mom rolled her eyes at the thought, saying Piper's romantic notion of a father didn't mesh with the reality. But the man didn't seem to have anybody, and she could be there for him. "I don't even know why you became a soldier." It seemed to define him. Hell. It was him.

He rubbed his strong jaw. "My father was a soldier."

She stilled and then took a deep breath. Carefully, like a scientist approaching a grizzly, she spoke slowly. Finally, some answers. She had a grandfather. "Is he still alive?"

"No. Died when I was eight." No expression crossed the commander's face. "The official reason was something about Agent Orange and cancer, but in truth? He wasn't strong enough. If he'd been stronger, he would've beat the poison dropped by our enemies. Soldiers need to be invincible."

She swallowed. Nobody was invincible, and how odd to demand it. "What about your mother?"

He shrugged a massive shoulder. "She died giving birth—also not strong enough. But she was a woman, so—"

Piper sat up and tilted her head to the side. Her paternal grandmother had died so young and without knowing her child, and something ached in Piper's chest. But he couldn't be saying—"So?"

He shook his head. "Nothing. Is that enough information for you?"

"No." For once, she held her ground. Did he think women were weak? Her eyebrows drew down, while stubborn will welled up. "Women can be just as strong as men."

His face smoothed into a smile. "Perhaps, but women shouldn't be soldiers."

Her breath caught. "Sure they should."

"No." He shook his head. "War is for men."

She sighed. Ah ha. So he didn't understand women at all. Interesting. That was probably a debate for another day, and she would get through to him. He never asked about her, but maybe that was because he didn't know how to communicate with anybody not in the military. "Without parents, who raised you?" She tried to squint and see the lost little boy he must've been, but only the larger than life leader took form.

"My uncle. Great soldier." The commander nearly grinned. "Taught me to shoot with an expert's aim." He rubbed his right shoulder. "Made sure I learned not to miss."

Heat uncoiled down Piper's throat into her stomach, her instincts flaring. "How?" she whispered.

"Any way he needed to. Once I missed two targets in a row, and he broke my arm." The commander tapped his keyboard and studied his computer screen. "I have a meeting, Piper."

Her hands shook while she forced herself to stand. Nausea filled her stomach. God. The poor little boy who'd grown into such a hard man. Her heart hurt for him. "Your uncle didn't have the right to harm you."

The commander's eyebrows drew down, and he pursed his lips. "He trained me, not hurt me. Soldiers need training."

Wow. Okay. Serious minefield there. Even so, for the first time, she could see beyond the soldier's image. Had her father never experienced love? Maybe she could help him. She cleared her throat. "I wondered if you'd like to come over for dinner sometime soon." She'd been issuing the invitation for months, hoping they could form a relationship outside the concrete walls, but he'd always refused.

He paused. "Your mother wouldn't mind?"

Hell, yes. Her mother was sketchier than a raccoon stealing dog food whenever the topic of the commander came up. But even though it was silly, the child in Piper wanted her family in one place just for once. Perhaps they could find some sort of peace. "My mother would be happy to see you."

The commander chuckled. "I'm sure. Well, I wouldn't mind checking in on her. I'm free tomorrow night."

Piper's head jerked back. Goose bumps rose along her neck. "Ah, okay. Great. I'll make something nice."

The commander nodded. "Very well. What did you think of Jory?"

She kept her face blank. "He's a traitor, and he betrayed you. What is there to think?"

Approval lifted the commander's upper lip. She warmed instantly. When in his presence, she couldn't think of him as her father. He'd always been the commander. Maybe she could transition into calling him by his first name, Franklin.

He nodded. "So true. Jory didn't try to convince you he was the victim here?"

A quick smile tickled Piper's mouth. "No. That guy is no victim." She leaned forward. "Although he did hint that Russians hadn't planted the chip and that you're the enemy."

"I'm not *his* enemy." The commander exhaled, a flash of emotion lightening his eyes. "I see the greatness in that boy, and I wish to help him."

Piper stared. What was that emotion? She couldn't read him. "How long have you known the prisoner?"

"A long time." The commander pushed back from his desk and stood. "I've put a tremendous amount of training and energy into him, and he will live to work for me again. Whether he wants to or not."

Piper stood, and a chill slithered down her back. "I'm sorry he betrayed you."

Hard black eyes stared back at her. "He'll be sorry as well. For now, go write my new program."

Piper drove through the quaint neighborhood, passing actual white picket fences, the mountains rising with jagged peaks all around her. She loved Utah. Loved the slow pace, the brutal mountains, the distinct seasons. Well, so far she'd only felt the bite of fall, but white already dusted the mountaintops, so winter would arrive soon.

She pulled the SUV into the garage of a two-story yellow house, right next to a compact and weathered two-door car. Older than dirt. She had to buy her mother a new car. With a sigh, she tramped up the steps and into the kitchen, instantly smiling as the aromatic scent of lasagna filled her senses.

Her mother bustled around the granite counter, her black hair piled high on her head, reading glasses perched on her slim nose. "Perfect timing, snooks."

Piper dropped her laptop bag onto a chair and washed her hands before sliding onto a seat at the round oak table. "This smells so good."

A wet nose instantly pressed against her leg, and she smiled down at the German shepherd, yellow Lab, and who knows what else mix of dog. "Hi, Riley."

He wagged his bushy tail and barked out a welcome. She'd taken him from the pound upon moving into the house, and he'd quickly become a dedicated watchdog. Well, he watched the television, the birds outside, and Piper's shoes.

Her mom poured two glasses of Shiraz and sat. She'd donned a bright pink jogging outfit along with lime green tennis shoes. "I have so much time on my hands, I need to find something to do before we both end up on that show featuring six-hundred-pound people." She sipped the red wine and pursed her lips. "Maybe I should go back to work."

Piper sliced the lasagna and placed pieces on the plates. Then she took a bite and hummed as the flavors exploded on her tongue. She shook her head. "You sold the yogurt shops when we moved, saying it was time to retire. You worked your butt off for years with your businesses." So many hours, so many customers, just to feed and clothe her kid. "Although—"

"Don't say it." Her mom raised a hand. "I don't want to hear one more time that our life could've been easier if I'd stayed with the commander." She lifted her gaze and met Piper's directly. "I thought we were past that."

"We are," Piper said softly, noting her mother's hands shaking. "I just don't understand."

Her mom shook her head. "He's a dangerous, bad man, and I was attracted to the sense of bad boy. Never go for a bad boy, Piper." She sighed. "Our affair was short, I saw how dangerous he really was, and I got the hell out with you."

"I know." Piper took another bite. "He's not that bad, Mom."

"Yes, he is." Her mom took another drink of wine, her gaze averted. "Even though I was just a lowly receptionist, I discovered something bad was going on there at his facility in Tennessee, and the second I found out I was pregnant, I took off. He didn't come looking."

No, but he hadn't known about Piper, now had he? "What was the something bad?"

"I don't know. But there were so many guns and so many secrets. And Franklin, although he believed he was doing good work for the government, he had his own agenda and probably still does." Her mom reached for her fork, still not meeting Piper's eyes. "I told you we shouldn't have come here."

Piper eyed her mother. "Yet you came with me. Why?"

"Oh, I wasn't letting you go into the lion's den on your own. He's a fanatic, and he'll sacrifice anybody for his agenda." Rachel shook her head. "I can't believe you actually tracked him down from an old picture I'd left in storage with *commander* scrawled across the back."

Piper smiled. "I'm a hell of a hacker." And did Rachel just keep the picture to share someday, or was there hope there? Maybe her parents just needed to be in the same room to work things out. Her mother perhaps objected too much? "I haven't gotten to know him yet, but I want to."

Rachel shook her head. "We all make mistakes, but he's not the type to learn from them."

Piper frowned, her mind spinning. "What aren't you telling me?"

Rachel glanced down at her full plate. "This just wasn't supposed to happen—you weren't supposed to go work for him. Ever."

"He got me out of prison," Piper said.

Rachel sighed. "Did he?"

Piper shook her head. "Yes."

Rachel took a deep swallow of wine. "Then that's enough talking about it. But the second you learn how dangerous he is, we're out of here. We can start a new chain of yogurt shops somewhere else."

Piper nodded. "Fine." Leaving Boston hadn't been that difficult for either of them. "The house is owned by the company, and we have no rent. I make tons of money, so why don't you relax? Or go back to school and study?" She peered closer at her mother. "If you could study anything, what would it be?"

Her mom lifted a slim shoulder and finally met her gaze again. At almost fifty years old, Rachel Devlin looked thirty, tops. Smooth mocha skin just a shade darker than Piper's, bright green eyes, and generous laugh lines showed a woman who smiled often. Well, until they'd moved to Utah. "I guess I could take a photography class." Her eyes sparkled. "Unless you're planning to get married and give me a grandchild, in which case I'd be a nanny."

Piper grinned. "Don't hold your breath on that one. I've only been dating Brian for three months." She'd taken the job with the commander at that time, and they'd moved to town.

Her mom's eyes clouded. "I was just kidding."

Piper sipped her drink. She'd started dating Brian the first weekend they'd arrived in town, and while he had a serious side, he was quite sweet. Definitely focused, which she liked. "Why don't you like Brian?"

Her mom sipped more wine. "I like Brian just fine. But he's so..."

"Safe?"

"Rigid. Boring. Focused." Rachel picked at her dinner. "Life is supposed to be fun, and romance should be crazy."

Piper shook her head. "Crazy romance didn't work so well for you, considering you ended up as a single mom. Working your butt off with one yogurt shop that turned into ten—you worked so hard."

Rachel kicked her under the table and paled slightly. "Enough."

Piper frowned. "Fine. Do you think you could find some happiness with us in Utah?"

"I'll certainly try." Rachel dumped Parmesan cheese on her plate, her gaze averted.

Piper chewed slowly and swallowed. "Are you sure everything is okay? You get sketchy every time I talk about my— the commander." Was there still a sort of tension there? The good kind? How crazy would it be if her parents actually ended up together? The commander was more than able to take good care of Rachel, and the idea seemed rather romantic, really.

"Everything is fine." Her mother still didn't meet her gaze. "Right."

Rachel pursed her lips together. "He gave me you. For that, I'll always owe him."

Warmth bloomed through Piper. "You're one of a kind, Mom."

"Let's talk about something else." Rachel cleared her throat just as a rap echoed on the back sliding glass door.

Piper jumped up. "I wondered if Earl would smell dinner." Sharing a grin with her mother, she pushed aside curtains and tugged open the door. "Hi, Earl."

Their neighbor stood on the back porch, his sixty-year-old frame braced against the wild wind, several mason jars filled with canned fruit in his worn hands. "I brought you peaches."

"Thank you." Piper moved aside. Why didn't the guy just ask her mother out and stop pussyfooting around about it? The guy was in excellent shape, retired, and seemed to love golf and canning foods. As a widower, he could probably get a date with any single woman in the small suburb outside Salt Lake City. Yet he continued to court Rachel like a friendly neighbor. "Would you like to join us for lasagna?" Piper asked.

He pushed his glasses up a straight nose, brown eyes twinkling. "Why, I'd love to." Putting the peaches on the counter, he turned and frowned. "I received an e-mail from my nephew after you fixed my bank account information. He said you might have goofed up his account?"

Piper bit back an unkind remark about his nephew, the one and only relative the poor guy could claim. "Nope. I just changed your passwords so he couldn't take any more money from you." She smiled as she lied. Once she'd seen how much money the jerk had taken, she'd sent him a nice little computer virus to melt his hard drive.

Earl shrugged wide shoulders. "That's what I figured. He must not understand much about computers, either."

"They are confusing." She was not letting her kind neighbor be taken advantage of again by his drug-sniffing shit of a nephew. So she smiled and patted Earl's arm. "Have a seat, and Mom will dish you up." She cast her mother a look to be nice and not get her feathers ruffled. The sweet neighbor obviously made her nervous.

Earl cleared his throat. "I want to double-check your front right tire before the first snowfall, Piper."

She paused. "Huh?"

"It looks low." He winked at Rachel. "Maybe you can assist me."

Rachel sputtered and turned a lovely shade of pink. Piper hid her smile but nodded, warmth flushing through her. What a nice man. "Thanks, Earl."

The doorbell pealed.

Piper sighed and hustled to yank open the door. "Brian." She smiled up at his smoothly shaven face. "Did we have plans?" It wasn't normal for him to just show up.

"No." He pushed an errant curl off her forehead. "But

you didn't call when you returned home from work, and you always call."

Oh. She'd completely forgotten, but she was happy to see him. "I'm sorry."

He shrugged, strong shoulders moving beneath his expertly cut suit. "I was in the neighborhood showing a house, so I thought to drop by." His blond hair waved back from his cut features, giving him the look of a wayward surfer wearing a suit. Although with his sparkling blue eyes, he looked sexy in the slate gray. "Also, I sold the brick rancher up on the hill and thought we could celebrate with a quick dessert down at Possums."

She blinked. A surprise date? Now that sounded like fun. Then she frowned, remembering the code she needed to write. "I have to work tonight." Regret tasted bitter on her tongue.

Brian frowned. "You don't have time for cheesecake?"

She shuffled her feet. So far, she'd disappointed every male in her life in one day. "I really shouldn't."

He reached for her arm, his fingers warm and firm. Reassuring. "You really should." A quick grin counteracted the demanding tone. "We've talked about you wanting to give more in a relationship, and I'm trying to help break down those walls you've built to protect your heart, which I'd very much like to see." He grinned, all good humor and charm.

She kind of liked her walls, but they had discussed her being more open with him, and she was seriously tired of failing at relationships. "I know, but I need to work."

"Just one hour." He leaned in close, and his mellow aftershave scent of salty ocean surrounded her. She breathed deep.

One hour probably wouldn't put her that far behind, and she liked the spontaneity. Plus, Earl would love to be left alone with Rachel for a little while, and maybe her mother would relax and have some fun. She was certainly due. If the woman wasn't going to rehash the past with the commander, maybe she could find some sweet romance with Earl. "Well, one hour. Then I have to get back to work."

Brian's gaze unclouded. "Perfect. Grab a sweater—it's getting cold."

She nodded and ran inside to kiss her mother on the cheek before fetching a dark green cardigan. She'd celebrate with Brian and then work on the program the rest of the night. Really, who needed sleep?

CHAPTER
4

JORY FLIPPED ONTO his stomach on the small cot, sweat coating his body, his heart racing. Somewhere, deep in his mind, he knew he was dreaming.

Even so, he couldn't stop the parade of images ricocheting off imaginary walls. Training as a kid—his first kill—the second he'd escaped. Memories upon memories.

Then, suddenly, the dream mellowed. Slid right into a parody of reality with him in the cage, his brain humming, death inching closer to his spine.

He stood from the cot and faced the empty vestibule. The commander and Dr. Madison morphed through the outside walls to hover beyond his cell, their images wavering in and out like ghouls. The commander drew a Glock and pointed it at Jory's chest.

Interesting. Yet he crouched to defend himself, somehow, because he couldn't die yet. Not before he'd accomplished the one thing he'd been created for: not until he'd saved his brothers. If he had a destiny, it was one he'd choose, and saving them would be his final act.

A whisper sounded behind him, and he half turned to find Piper standing barefooted in a pale pink teddy. What the hell?

Her green eyes sparkled in her pretty face, giving her the look of pure innocence.

He pivoted to defend her, only to find the outside of the cell empty.

"The monsters are gone," Piper said softly, her hand caressing down his arm.

He turned to stare down at her. "Are you one of the monsters?" His voice echoed hollowly in the dream cage. While he could snap her neck within a second, she posed no real threat and had nowhere to hide a weapon in the nearly see-through material.

She shrugged a slim shoulder, and a tiny strap slid down her arm. The material dipped in the front, revealing one breast. "I come from him, so I'm at least half monster."

Heat sparked Jory's balls, and his gaze focused on her taut, surprisingly pink, nipple. Against her darker skin, the peak all but begged for his mouth. "We're all part monster. Whose side are you on?" He needed her to choose him. Why, he didn't know. Just that it was imperative.

"I don't know." She sounded lost, even sad. "They'll find out about your gifts—about what you can do. They'll find out about your brothers."

"No." The word exploded from Jory, and he picked her up, shoving her against the far wall. Her legs wrapped around his hips, and before he knew it, his mouth was on her nipple. He sucked hard and then bit before leaning back. "You don't know about my gifts."

"Oh, but I do." A sexy flush engulfed her smooth skin, and an otherworldly glimmer lightened her emerald eyes.

"No." He ripped off the filmy lingerie, leaving her nude. Smooth and toned, so perfect his chest hurt. "You're different, Piper. You have to be."

"Show me," she whispered.

He didn't understand her, and he didn't understand himself. But something, deep down, some part of him, recognized her. Kicking off his shorts, he thrust into her with one hard shove. She clenched around him, her nails biting into his chest.

All of a sudden, he could feel. Emotion, the real kind, the stuff that mattered. Somehow, it was inside him, and he couldn't shove it down deep any longer.

Wild as a lost stallion, he pounded into her, nothing but the sensation of her core gripping him mattering. Hot and tight, she clenched around him, her head thrown back in pleasure.

A bullet whizzed by his head.

Without altering his rhythm, he dropped them to the hard floor and plunged harder. More shots fired over his head, and he didn't care. The electricity shooting down his spine to fill his cock consumed every thought, every action.

He came with a roar, sitting up in the bed.

His breath panted out, and he scraped both hands down

his face. It all had felt so real. Did the dream mean something? Was his subconscious just fucking with him? Sighing, he fell back and stared up at the ceiling for several moments as he controlled his body until his heart beat normally.

He stood and quickly cleaned up before pacing his cell.

One day in Piper's presence, and he wanted her naked beneath him.

The commander's *daughter*.

At first, Jory had wanted to laugh at the absurdity. Then he'd looked. Really looked at her bone structure, the indefinable elements shifting beneath her skin that only he could see. His ability to map terrain, to see patterns, to detect nuances guaranteed she told the truth. While she hadn't inherited the commander's size, the very shape of her eyes, the angle of her chin, and even the symmetry of her cheekbones showed her lineage. She truly was the commander's child.

Jory's shoulders rolled, unsettled, even after he'd cleaned up. So the commander had his own kid, not that Jory had ever wanted the bastard as a father. Matt had raised Jory with Nate's help, giving both him and Shane the closest thing to a childhood as possible in the hellhole of a compound they called home. Not once had he forgotten what his brothers had done, had sacrificed, for him to grow. To live long enough to save them.

The impossibility of Piper struck Jory anew. How had he never known? There had never been a hint. Did the commander actually care for her? Jory had begun to forge a connection with Piper the day before, using her patriotism to question her lying to the NSA. If she believed in the government, she had to wonder why the commander remained outside of it.

The first wedge between them had been almost too easy to plant.

But although he'd be successful, a part of Jory wanted to warn her to run. Hard and fast...away from this place.

How odd that the commander actually had a girl. Lucky Piper. If she'd been a boy, the commander surely would've forced her into training. Interesting the misogynist hadn't tried even though she was female, considering his ego.

Just who was Piper? The commander had been the only father figure Matt and Nate had had growing up, and yet he'd never acted as a father. Only a leader. Had the commander treated his daughter better? If so, perhaps he even cared about her.

The commander had never been Jory's father figure—not even once. Jory's loyalty, his allegiance, had been with his brothers from the first time he'd stood in the same room with both his brothers and the commander.

Sometimes a kid just knew. And when that kid had extra abilities, he accepted that knowledge.

Yet maybe the bastard did care about his only child. Which was something Jory could use.

As if conjured, Piper pushed open the door, a latte cup in her hand.

Even across the room, the fragrant scent of vanilla and cinnamon flared his nostrils, and it took three seconds to wonder which part was woman and which was latte. The day before, he hadn't noticed her scent, but Madison had already contaminated the room with roses and too-expensive perfume.

"What kind of drink?" he asked, stepping closer to the glass.

"Vanilla," Piper answered. "Why?"

Because now he could track her scent, anywhere in the world, just like the animal they'd created him to be. "No reason." His gaze raked her peach-colored sweater and tight jeans before focusing on her delicate face. Even though it had just been a dream, he could still see her naked, and he could still feel an echo of real emotion. Today she'd pulled her hair into a ponytail and seemed younger. More fragile. Dark circles marred the skin beneath her eyes, giving her the look of a damsel in distress.

He fleetingly wished he were the type of guy who could save her, but he quickly banished the thought. It was far too late for him to play the hero, especially since he planned to use her. And looks were deceiving. The woman might appear fragile, but she was obviously intelligent and knew whom she was working for. That put them on opposing sides.

Plus, he'd been given enough in this life with his brothers sacrificing so much, and it was his turn to give back to them. "You up late?" he asked.

"All night." She set down the cup and booted up the computer. "Rewriting a program to save your butt. You're welcome."

Actually, his butt was unsavable, but she wouldn't listen to him. So it was time to get down to business and figure her out, regardless of the cameras recording their every move. "Did the commander raise you?" he asked, wondering how he'd never caught a glimpse of her through the years.

"No." She turned to the side and typed quickly.

"Why not?" Jory asked, although her denial made sense.

She shrugged, her shoulders hunching forward. "I don't think we need to share our lives, Jory."

No, but he needed to get into her head and now. Plus, although he hated to admit it, he wanted to know more about her. "Come on, Piper. I'm stuck in a freakin' cell all by myself, and if somebody doesn't talk to me, I swear my head is going to explode." Far more truth lived in the words than he'd like to admit. "Please."

The final word had her turning to face him. "You put yourself in the cage."

Had he? From birth, every location had been a cage of some sort as the commander and Dr. Madison turned him into a killing machine. If he disobeyed orders, one of his brothers would be killed.

His neck ached, and he gingerly flexed his shoulders. Even that small movement caught the breath in his chest, considering his kill chip could detonate at any time. The damn thing was broken, and any second his back might explode.

But escaping had been fucking worth the risk. The Dean boys had followed the commander's orders until nearly five years ago when they found a way to escape. They'd blown a facility in Tennessee to hell and gotten loose. Unfortunately, the kill chips had already been implanted, and if the right code wasn't input into the right program in less than one week, the chips would detonate and kill them.

Death hung heavily around his shoulders. He had to gain Piper's trust to get free and save his brothers. "You're smart enough not to believe everything you're told—especially by Dr. Madison." Yet if Jory told Piper the full truth, she'd be a liability to the commander.

Unless he actually gave a shit about his real daughter.

Piper sipped her coffee. "Dr. Madison?"

Jory smiled and mined deeper. "Yeah. It was obvious she dislikes you, right?"

Piper frowned and then shrugged. "So?"

"So? The woman has been in love with your father forever. You're in the way, baby." The sooner Jory could infect the little command post with insecurity and distrust, the better.

"What are you, a muscle-bound Dr. Phil?" Piper rolled her eyes. Her cell phone rang a funky tune, and she retrieved it from her pocket. "Hello?" Her lips tightened. "I know. Yes, I understand, but—" She tapped her tennis shoe on the tile as she listened. With a glance at Jory, she turned and hunched over the phone.

Too bad she didn't know about his super-senses. He could hear her in the next room, if he wanted.

"I know." Her voice softened. "I guess. I'm sorry, too. Okay. Talk to you later." She hung up, her gaze meeting Jory's. Pink splashed across her cheeks.

Jory grinned. "Fight with the boyfriend?"

She blinked. "How—"

He shrugged. "My training goes beyond firing guns, sweetheart. What did he do?"

Her brows drew down. "Nothing. We just had a little misunderstanding last night."

He didn't like the kick in the gut at the thought of Piper with some guy. Why the hell did he even care? Man, he was off his game. "I thought you wrote code all night," Jory said.

Piper rolled expressive eyes. "I had a nice dessert and then went home to work all night."

"What was the misunderstanding?" Jory asked softly.

"None of your damn business." Her shoulders hunched.

"Tell me anyway." The direct approach seemed to work best with her, so Jory went with that.

She glanced at him through her lashes, thoughts flashing across her face. "Nope. Now stop bugging me." She turned back to the computer.

Jory nodded and sat down, having learned early on that his size intimidated people. Piper was more likely to confide in him if he appeared innocuous. "When did you move here?" he asked.

"About three months ago," she said absently, her fingers flying over a keyboard.

Interesting. "So you must've met the boyfriend at that time?" Now, that wasn't suspicious in any way, was it? God.

"I could have you tranqed, I think," she said, still not looking at him.

He lifted an eyebrow. In profile, he could still read her. "Piper, maybe you should cooperate with me."

"Why?" she snapped.

Ah. He was getting to her. "Because in the very near future, I'm gonna be out of this cage, and you're gonna need help. Work with me now, and I'll help you." So long as it didn't interfere with his main mission.

She snorted and turned toward him, although her gaze held an awareness he appreciated. "There's no way you're getting out, buddy. Sorry." She bit her lip, expressions chasing across her face while she apparently debated with herself. "Why do you think I'll need help?"

He stood and approached the wall again. "This is a dangerous place, and you're playing a deadly game. The second you're not useful, you're a liability." The words rang true, and he kept his gaze level, but he wondered. Would the commander protect his flesh-and-blood daughter? Perhaps. Although Jory didn't allow one ounce of doubt to show.

"Fuck you."

"I just wanted to have a nice conversation," he said calmly.

"Bullshit. You wanted to get into my head for an advantage. Sorry, pal. No chance." Her green eyes sparked all sorts of glimmers and shards. Truly beautiful.

Jory smiled and set his pheromones to work raising her blood pressure. "Oh, sweetheart. I'm already in your head."

"Oh yeah?" She blinked and narrowed her focus. "You're full of it."

He'd known she'd pick up the challenge. "Wanna bet?"

"No." She lowered her chin. "I'm trying to save your life here, and you're trying to distract me. What the hell is wrong with you?"

"You can't save me." He exhaled slowly, wanting nothing more than to punch through the glass. He had to get free. "Unless you help me get out of here."

"Not gonna happen." She started to turn back to the screen.

Fine. He'd get her attention one way or the other. "I'm assuming you met the boyfriend upon arriving in town?"

She snorted and shifted in her seat.

"Let's see. What would a convenient but realistic meeting be? Is he a banker?"

"You're an idiot." She shook her head and brushed back her hair with trembling hands.

Not a banker. "Car salesman?"

She sighed and kept typing.

"Realtor?"

"No." Her chin rose.

Ah. He was a realtor. "Don't you think it's a very nice coincidence that you met your charming boyfriend the second you came to town?" The guy probably could fight like a true killer, and Piper had no clue.

"No, and your attempts to make me doubt my job here are ridiculous." She straightened her sweater.

He let off on the sensual attack, just a little, pleased he'd thrown her with his accurate guess. "I'm thinking he's a realtor, which would lead to him being organized, ambitious, stable, and even a little controlling."

Her back stiffened just enough to let him know she was trying not to react.

Yeah. He'd nailed that one. "You like being controlled, baby?" He allowed his voice to rumble down to a masculine tone while sending sexual tension her way.

A pretty pink wandered up her neck, and she glared at her phone. "I'm having you tranquilized just so you shut the hell up."

Apparently he'd hit a nerve. The picture began to form. While Jory didn't know much about her relationship with the commander, he did know the commander, who had always been present at the military compound, so he couldn't have spent much time with his daughter. "So you like someone else taking charge," Jory said, easily spotting her need to please.

"No."

He let his upper lip quirk. Little girl raised without a father falling for a control freak? Yeah, that was a new one. Not. "So you like this take charge guy, but apparently you got in a fight last night. I'm thinking he went too far and turned into a jerk, huh?" Damn, this was too easy.

She turned toward him and eyed the phone next to her, but didn't pick it up to call for help. Little sweetheart didn't want to have him shot full of poison, now did she? With a shrug, she reached for her coffee cup and took a deep drink. Her pink tongue darted out to lick her cup.

Jory's balls drew tight and he grimaced. She had no clue what she'd just done to him. "So, ah"—he shifted on the cot to adjust a sudden rigid hard-on—"you do know that this asshole you're dating is wrong for you, right?"

She shook her head. "This is my last warning."

Jory opened his senses, truly reading her and ignoring the damn warning. "You need a good guy, one who knows the difference between right and wrong. One who is spontaneous, protective, and would kill or die for you."

"Oh, do I?" she muttered.

Yeah. How would she take a bit more truth? He watched her carefully. "While you're obviously independent and very smart, you do like to be told what to do, Piper. Possibly only in bed, but I'd bet the idea of an overprotective mate would make you feel safe. Whole and complete."

She paled, her chin lowering, sparks flashing in those gorgeous eyes.

He kept her gaze. "The prick you're dating isn't just over-protective, or you wouldn't have gotten pissed at him last night. My bet is that he's condescending, and that doesn't work for you."

She swallowed. "Have you made up enough stories about me?"

"No. Your ideal guy would have to be absolute in his beliefs, and he'd have to end up on the right side of the line, every time. You're a true believer, baby, and God help anybody who crosses the line."

She set down the cup. "Are you describing yourself?"

"No. I lost the line a long time ago." Had there even been a line? If the woman had an idea of what he'd done, who he'd had to become to survive, she'd run screaming from the room. "Although I think you should consider the timing with this prick. When you work for a covert operation, don't trust anybody."

She shifted on her chair. "Including you?"

"Definitely including me." He'd use her to get to safety and rescue his brothers, whether he wanted to or not.

"I don't trust you." She spoke the words quietly, while he could hear her heartbeat speed up with what had to be anger. "And while I appreciate your attention to my love life, maybe you should be more concerned with your own. As in, you're never going to have one...ever again. Might want to get used to solitude, asshole."

Fuckin' direct hit. Jory's temper, already frayed by the close confinement, sprang free, surprising him so much he didn't have a chance to reign it in. "I'm just trying to help you out, feisty. Don't trust the commander. Blood or not."

Her eyes hardened to green chips of ice. "You don't know him."

"The bastard raised me, so I think I know him pretty well." The words popped out before Jory could stop them, his laconic temper flashing in a rare moment. What the hell was going on with him? "Although I wouldn't let him know I said that. How safe do you really think you are here?" He had to get his emotions under control, but even at the thought, the walls seemed to close in.

Who the hell was Piper?

She rose and hitched toward the cell wall. Her hands slapped together, and her boots stomped on the rough concrete. Red spiraled through the pink still under her smooth skin, and air hissed out of her mouth. "He raised you? My father raised you." Her voice rose at the last.

"Not really." Jory sighed. He was fucking losing it in the cell. The guy who *never* lost control suddenly couldn't hold on to it with both hands. Damn it, he really shouldn't have told her that, and while she remained unaware, he could hear the hum of cameras busily recording. "The commander and Dr. Madison were constantly there, training us and studying us. I have brothers, and my brothers definitely raised me. The best they could, anyway."

Piper frowned. "What in the world are you talking about?"

She didn't know her father at all. "We should forget this entire conversation. Trust me." Man, he'd screwed up this time.

"Too late. Spill it, Jory." She put her hands on fit hips. "Now."

"No." He stood, easily towering over her even through the glass. Although he appreciated her fight to stay in place and not move back. The woman had grit, now didn't she?

"Then I'll ask my father." Her lips stumbled over the last word.

She wasn't accustomed to referring to him as such, now was she? Interesting. Jory shook his head. "That would be an incredibly bad idea. The less you know about me, the safer you are. Hell. The less you know about the commander, the better. He's not who you think."

"I know him better than you do." A childhood hurt echoed in her fierce tone, and something in Jory's gut ached.

"I'm sorry." The words came out naturally and before he could think.

"For what?" Her gaze didn't soften one iota.

For giving her the truth. For not giving her the full truth. For the pain she'd endure one day when she really got to know the commander, because even if he did have feelings for his daughter, he'd hurt her. For planning to use her to escape, which Jory would. She wouldn't be the first mark he'd manipulated for a mission, although the idea of hurting her settled unease in his gut. He didn't want to be a guy who'd hurt a woman, even one from the enemy's camp, but he'd do what he had to do. He'd warned her not to trust anybody. "For everything, Piper."

"I don't like you very much right now," she muttered.

"That makes two of us." The subtext between them pounded pain in his temples. They were on the same wavelength, whether they'd wanted to be or not, and he had to jump off. "I do, however, like you." He tried to pour charm into the words.

She lifted her head to meet his gaze. "Do you think that matters to me?"

"Yes."

Fire shot through her eyes at the direct hit. The truth sometimes pierced deep. She shook her head. "I don't give one fig if you like me or not, traitor."

"Liar," he murmured, instinct pushing him to goad her. "You're a smart woman, Piper, and you've already figured out something isn't right here." Maybe she had, or maybe she hadn't. Either way, he'd planted the seed, disliking himself more and more with each deliberate move. Taking a chance on the commander's ego keeping her alive, even if she screwed up, was a shitty thing for Jory to do.

Yet his brothers came first.

She opened her mouth to say something, probably something scathing, when the door slid open and the commander strode inside. In his late fifties, his black hair had gone to gray, showcasing his black eyes. Not dark, not deep...just black. Tightly coiled and still in fighting shape, his very presence added a tension to the atmosphere that reached through the solid wall and rose the hackles down Jory's back.

Jory's lungs compressed, so he loosened his stance into a relaxed pose, hiding the fact that every instinct he owned just sprang to life. He had the oddest urge to tell Piper to run. Instead, he raised an eyebrow. "I was just having a nice talk with your daughter."

The commander eyed Piper. "I'm not paying you to talk." His deep baritone echoed around the sterile computer room.

She flushed and headed back to sit at her computer. Jory stiffened. There was no need to be such an asshole or to punish her for taking a moment to talk to Jory. Or rather, yell at Jory. "Funny I never knew you had a daughter."

The commander clasped his hands at his back, his gaze raking Jory. "You've recovered well and quickly. I made you strong."

Piper's shoulders stiffened while she typed away on a keyboard. Definitely listening.

Jory frowned. What was the bastard's game? The less his daughter knew about Jory and his brothers, the safer she'd be. "We probably shouldn't talk." The bastard obviously trusted the pretty hacker, now didn't he?

The commander glanced over his shoulder and back, amusement lightening his eyes. "She's my daughter and could hack any system here. I don't give a shit if she knows I trained you."

But not created, raised, beat, or nearly killed. Fine. Jory could live with that. "She doesn't look like you."

"She has my mother's eyes."

Across the room, Piper jumped slightly.

The commander, his back to Piper, smiled at Jory. The smile that had once made Jory quake as a kid in combat boots.

Now, he didn't show any reaction. "What do you want?" Jory asked.

"Just wanted to check in and see if my brilliant daughter has saved your ass yet." The smile didn't fade.

Piper's shoulders went back at the word *brilliant*. The woman had no clue what a complete prick her father was, and no idea that he'd fuck with her mind just to mess with Jory. So he focused on the commander and tried to forget Piper was in the room. "Do you believe in God?"

"No." Irritation curled the commander's lip. "Why?"

"Just wondering if you ever considered what happens next. You created us, you trained us, and basically you're trying to enslave us. Don't you think there will be repercussions?"

"Of course not. You're property. How can there be repercussions?"

The words shouldn't surprise him. Not once while Jory was growing up did the commander show any affection or concern. Jory's entire sense of self came from his brothers and their unity as a family. "You can't beat us." The second he said the words, he believed them. "I won't let you."

"You won't let me?" The commander chuckled and glanced over his shoulder at Piper. "My hacker will save you, and then you'll pay for your disloyalty. In ways you can't even imagine right now." Anticipatory threat rode the words.

Piper's head jerked.

The sweet woman might not understand the subtext behind the threat, but she sure as hell felt it, didn't she?

That easily, that quickly, seeing the man screw with his daughter freed Jory. All of a sudden, he realized he had to look down to meet the commander's gaze. Several inches, actually.

The commander clucked his tongue. "Where's Matt? It's time we met back up."

Jory shook his head. "You're never gonna find Matt, that I promise you." For some reason, the commander had had a hard-on for Matt for years. Probably because he'd never been able to break the oldest Dean brother. "Matt is better than you are, stronger than you'll ever be, and you know it."

Sparks flew through the commander's eyes, and he leaned forward. "I'm going to rip the skin from his body while you watch. Inch by inch, I'll make him bleed until he begs to die," he whispered, his voice fierce.

Jory's chin lowered while his shoulders went back. "No. No, you are not." Any fear he'd lived with, any displaced loyalty he'd tried to find for the commander, disappeared. Deep down, in a place neither the commander nor Madison had found in their tests, training, or probing, he'd still held hope that they'd do the right thing and save his brothers. For history's sake, if nothing else. Now, he kept his voice low. "You'd really rather see us dead than out free."

The commander closed the distance until the tips of his boots touched the glass wall. "I created you, and I own you." His voice lowered and probably didn't carry across the room to Piper.

Jory's jaw clenched. As a kid, he'd been afraid of that look and would've instinctively stepped back. Now he moved forward until his battered shoes also touched the wall. "You don't own any of us."

Awareness flashed in the commander's eyes.

Yeah. Life had just shifted. Jory glanced around, shoving all emotion down hard before focusing back on the monster who'd haunted his dreams for too long. "I may not survive the implant, but my brothers will live and live *free*." He leaned in as close as he could without touching the glass and looked *down*. "And know this, you fucking prick. Before I die, *I* will be the one to put you into the ground."

CHAPTER
5

PIPER'S MIND SPUN with calculation and computer codes, the sense of failure weighing her down. The last thing she had time for was dinner, but it could be important to solving her conundrum, if she played her cards right. Something told her the commander knew more about Jory's problem than he'd admitted, and she needed the full story to continue her work. *If* she could get the commander alone for a few moments.

Aromatic scents of garlic, cheese, and spices filled the warm kitchen as Piper uncorked a bottle of Silver Oak Cabernet. Maybe inviting her father to dinner had been a mistake, although Brian should arrive any minute, and he definitely knew how to relax a group of people. Being a realtor made him good with folks, which was something she admired since she'd rather be alone on a computer than in a group. She tried to force a smile to calm down her mother before the commander showed up.

Rachel fluttered around, her face pale, her hands shaking

as she straightened the placemats for the tenth time. "This isn't a good idea," she muttered.

Piper sighed and finished tossing the salad. "Why not?"

"Because that man isn't one to trust." Rachel pushed unruly hair away from her forehead, revealing a line of blue paint along her hand she'd failed to wash off. She'd taken up the hobby of painting like she did everything else—completely. "You don't know Franklin."

Piper's shoulders went back. "That's what I'm trying to remedy. Seriously. What's one dinner?"

"You don't understand," Rachel whispered, way too pale.

Piper paused. "Don't understand what?" She strode around the table to reach for her mother's hand. "Did he hurt you?" God, had he forced her?

"No." Rachel rubbed her chin. "He didn't hurt or force me. We got drunk, I took him home, and you know the rest."

Piper studied the circles under her mother's pretty eyes. "Are you scared of him?"

Rachel straightened a napkin, her gaze on the table. "Of course not. I barely know the man."

Okay, the guy could be definitely intimidating. Plus, her mom had to feel odd about them having a child together and not really knowing each other. Nobody liked to admit they got knocked up by a one-night stand, but it happened all the time. Piper hugged her mom. "Just because I want to know him better doesn't mean I had a bad childhood or any regrets."

Rachel snorted and hugged her back. "Well, duh."

Plus, Piper had to figure out the truth about Jory. She'd spent many hours that day typing outside his cell, and he'd talked while she'd pretended to ignore him. The man understood computers as well as she did. And he'd hinted more than once that she didn't know what was going on.

In fact, she'd already determined it was time to mine the

servers a little deeper and discover more about him. If nothing else, she might find a clue for how to deactivate the chip. Hell. How to reach the chip.

But she'd been warned about his charm and his intelligence, and the warnings rang true. While she didn't trust Dr. Madison as far as she could throw the bitch, she did believe her father, who'd never lied to her. Even so, she wanted to dig a little deeper just out of curiosity, if nothing else. The hacker inside her demanded answers.

A knocking pattern pinged on the back door. Piper and her mother both straightened.

"Um," Piper said.

Rachel hustled toward the glass slider and pushed it open. "Earl. What a lovely surprise."

Piper jerked back her head. Lovely?

"Please come in. We're having company for dinner, and you're more than welcome." Rachel tucked an arm through Earl's and all but dragged him into the kitchen. "Piper, set another plate, would you?"

Earl flushed a charming crimson. As usual, he wore dark jeans and a nice golf shirt. "My computer is acting up again, and I was hoping Piper would take a look." He glanced around the cozy kitchen. "I wouldn't want to intrude." He tugged on his collar.

"You're not." Piper reached for another plate. Maybe having Earl there would diffuse any awkwardness. "I'll check your computer later tonight." The doorbell pealed, and she handed the plate over to her mother. Her heart sped up, and her hands grew moist. Taking a deep breath, she hurried to open the door. "Brian."

He smiled and handed her a bouquet of fall flowers. Charming and perfect.

Too perfect? Jory's words about not trusting anybody echoed in her mind.

Brian had dressed in khakis and a button-down shirt that matched his sparkling blue eyes. His blond hair was tousled from the wind, and his smile wide as he took in her forest green dress.

She grinned, her abdomen warming. "Thank you. Come on in." Humming, she hurried into the kitchen to find a vase to place the flowers in the center of the table.

She liked flowers, right? Yep. Safe and secure, that was for her. Not sexy and deadly. Not at all. Her odd physical reaction to Jory could be discounted as stress, plain and simple.

A sharp rap on the door had her pausing. Okay. Good. This was good. Forcing a smile for Brian, she once again headed into the living room to open the door for her father. She blinked. He stood in black slacks and a button-down shirt, freshly shaved. Good Lord. She'd never seen him out of his black uniform. The sense of danger still clung to him, but in regular clothes, he seemed even handsomer. No wonder her mother had been charmed.

Piper opened the door wider. "Come in, ah, Commander."

He strode inside, his gaze taking in the entire living room.

She looked at the gleaming wood tables and freshly plumped pillows. For hours, after returning home, she'd worked her butt off to clean the house.

He nodded. "You should probably call me Franklin outside of the facility." Then he stalked toward the kitchen, his back straight, his body visibly on alert.

Franklin. Well, that was a start. Her chest rose, and she took several deep breaths. Then she followed him into the kitchen, where Brian had clearly taken over for Rachel and was ushering people into seats. Earl hovered protectively near Rachel and held out her chair, while the commander— make that Franklin—studied Brian, his dark eyes inscrutable as he quite naturally sat at the head of the table. Earl sat at the foot like a vibrating cocker spaniel facing a bored Doberman.

Nerves jangled along Piper's arms as she delivered the food to the table. "Everyone dig in." Forcing a smile, she took a seat next to her mother, not missing Rachel's sigh of relief when she partially blocked the commander's gaze.

Piper shook off unease. Her mother's nerves were sending out panic signals strong enough to slicken Piper's hands with sweat. Why was Rachel so out of sorts? If she were frightened of the commander, she would've said so, right? Maybe the dinner had been a bad idea.

Brian winked at Piper from across the table, and her shoulders relaxed. He then dished salad and handed the bowl to the commander. "So. Piper says you own some type of security firm?"

Piper nodded and reached for the lasagna. While she'd hated lying to Brian, and her own mother for that matter, she understood national security. Not being able to discuss her work with either her mom or her boyfriend had made for more than one uncomfortable conversation. "The company monitors alarm systems," Piper lied smoothly.

Rachel snorted next to her and reached for the nearest wine bottle.

The commander lifted an eyebrow. "You're a realtor?" He said the last word as if asking if Brian handed out fliers on a street corner.

"Yes," Brian said calmly, amusement darkening his eyes.

"And you're dating my daughter." The commander leaned to the side to view Rachel. "I don't believe I was consulted regarding this."

Rachel poured herself a healthy glass of red wine. "It's a little late for you to be consulted, don't you think?" She took a gulp . . . and then another.

Piper blinked. "Ah, I'm all grown up."

The commander kept his gaze on Rachel. "I believe we had a nice talk a while back, and that I'd be kept apprised." His voice remained low and level, but a tenor hinted there that Piper couldn't quite discern. When had her parents had a talk?

Rachel shrugged and downed the glass, not looking his way. "So consider yourself apprised."

"Appraised," Brian said automatically and then flushed.

Oh, the dinner might've been a bad idea. Piper shot him a desperate look for help.

His lips pursed, and his gaze hardened. He appeared neither amused nor exactly willing to lend her a hand. "So, Franklin. I take it you don't like realtors."

Piper's hand brushed Rachel's as they both reached for the bottle of wine. At this point, she might as well open a couple more.

The dinner continued with Brian irritated, Earl bristling, and Franklin arrogantly unamused. At Piper's third glass of wine, the night took on a Cabernet mellow glow, and she finally relaxed.

They all sucked.

Finally, by some miracle, the dinner ended. Franklin politely thanked Rachel for the hospitality as he moved to go. Rachel may have snarled from a very happy place.

Piper scrambled up and pressed a hand to her forehead. The room swam as if it, too, had too much to drink. "Let me show you out." Stubbing her toe on a chair leg, she bit back a wince and hurried after her father.

He opened the door and gestured her outside into a chilly fall night, where he'd left an innocuous-looking SUV. For some reason, Piper had expected a Hummer. She grinned. "That was fun."

"A realtor?" the commander asked, looking down. Way down.

She shrugged. "It's a little late for fatherly concern, don't you think?"

One eyebrow darted up. "No. However, he seems all right."

Piper tilted her head. "Really?"

"Yes. Good posture, admirable eye contact, reasonably in control of himself." The commander lifted a shoulder. "Not everybody can be soldiers."

Geez. Had Franklin just given fatherly approval for Brian? If so, why did that make her uneasy? "Um, thanks."

"You're welcome."

Piper shuffled her feet and turned toward the frozen porch swing. "Ah, care to sit?"

"No." Franklin settled his stance. "Why?"

She rubbed her hands together for warmth. "I was hoping you'd tell me more about Jory. About his mission and about his past." How well did they know each other?

"Why?"

She cleared her throat. "So I could have a more complete picture. Did you really raise him?" A tiny part of her, one she didn't like, reared its green little head at the thought.

"No. We recruited Jory when he'd turned eighteen." Franklin clasped his hands behind his back. "I guess he might consider that his childhood, considering his earlier childhood consisted of him being a delinquent thief."

Piper frowned. "If he was a thief, why did you recruit him?"

"Because he was a master at it. Brilliant, charming, and ambitious. I thought if I could harness that talent, I could make an excellent soldier." Franklin sighed. "But once a criminal, always a criminal, I guess. Apparently I didn't make much of an impression."

Piper patted his arm. "I assume not many soldiers betray their country for the Russians. Nobody could've seen that one coming."

"Perhaps." Franklin ran a hand across his buzz-cut hair.

She bit her lip. "Jory mentioned he had brothers."

"Figuratively. The recruits often band together as brothers." Franklin winced. "Jory betrayed them, too."

What would make a man do something like that? Jory didn't seem like he'd betray somebody he'd cared about. What had her father and Jory been whispering about, and why couldn't she listen in? "I'm sorry," Piper murmured.

"Me, too. Good night." Franklin stiffened his shoulders, turned on his heel, and headed for the SUV, not looking back.

His feelings almost seemed hurt by Jory's defection, which signaled an emotional connection. What in the world was really going on? The air cooled her heated cheeks, although her head still swam as she hitched back inside to find Brian stretched out on the couch, the TV remote control in his hand.

"Your father is rather intense," he muttered.

"Yes." She peered into the empty kitchen. "Where—"

"Earl and your mom headed over to his place to fetch more wine." Brian tossed the control onto a pillow, his gaze serious. His gaze hardened, and his jaw firmed. "I'm afraid your mother is a lush. The amount of wine you consumed isn't exactly admirable, either." His tone could only be described as nasal.

Piper shook her head. "Excuse me?"

Brian stood, towering over her. "You drank too much," he said flatly.

Why the hell were all the men in her life so damn tall? She looked up at his face, her cheeks heating. "Watch your tone, jackass."

He grabbed her arm and yanked her toward him. His lips thinned into a tight line. "I'd watch your mouth."

Pain lanced up her elbow, and she jerked away. Who the hell did he think he was? "It's time for you to leave."

He stood to his full height. "I agree. Call me tomorrow when you sober up."

"No." Life was too damn short to deal with assholes, and the relaxed, almost relieved sensation sliding through her veins reassured her that she didn't want him. In fact, she should thank him for giving her an excuse to end it. "We're done. Don't call me again."

He sighed. "We'll discuss it when you're sober. Tomorrow." Smooth as any alley cat, he skirted the table.

She set her feet. "Look at my face, Brian. We're over. Don't call me, don't drop by, and please move on."

With a pretty impressive roll of his eyes, he let himself out.

Piper glanced around the now empty room. Well, that was a night of grand fuck-upery. She'd just lost another boy-friend and hadn't improved her work situation at all. While she'd discovered more about Jory, the information wasn't anything helpful. More than ever, she wanted to get the job of saving him done so she could get on with her work. The man didn't deserve saving.

The clock ticked quickly above the mantle, and the night turned to the next day. As of the moment, Jory had exactly five days to live.

Jory bit back a chuckle, sitting on his bed, his elbows on his knees. He'd finished a breakfast of runny eggs before Piper had finally arrived, being even more prickly than the day before. Whatever she'd learned about him had pissed her off apparently. "Stop ignoring me," he muttered.

"Ignore me back." Piper firmed her face, her gaze on the computer screen, and her profile to him. Her too gorgeous, smooth-skinned, beautiful profile.

"I don't know what you think you've learned about me, but listen to your instincts." Jory lost his smile. "Don't trust the commander, Piper."

She lifted her chin. "I trust him a hell of a lot more than I trust you." Her face clouded, and she rubbed her arm.

Jory narrowed his focus to the light purple bruise near her elbow. "What happened to your arm?" he asked, his voice going soft.

She blinked and stopped rubbing. "Nothing."

"Piper." This time he allowed the thread of command to echo in his tone. For the past two days, he'd studied her, and she responded to the tenor. Whether she wanted to or not.

She swallowed and turned back to the computer. "We should concentrate on saving your life."

Yeah, that was important. But the idea of somebody putting that mark on her pretty skin propelled him to his feet, and he didn't stop to wonder why. "I asked you a question."

She shivered. "Mind your own business."

"I'll hound you until you tell me."

Her shoulders hunched, and she kept her back to him. "Why do you care?"

Her question hinted at vulnerability, but he pressed on. Things were heating up, and the clock ticking down the deaths of his brothers echoed in his head. Perhaps it was time for honesty. "I don't know why, but I do care. The idea of somebody hurting you will keep me up at night. So tell me."

She turned around, emotion sparking in those expressive eyes. "None. Of. Your. Fucking. Business."

Fire rushed down Jory's spine, and his jaw clenched. "Did the commander bruise you?"

"Of course not," she scoffed.

"The boyfriend, then?" Oh, he'd find and kill the sonuvabitch the second he got free. Well, the second after he deactivated the chips and saved his brothers. Then he'd take out the guy who'd hurt the hacker.

Piper's lips trembled in a sardonic smile. "I can take care

of myself." She tilted her head to the cage. "Better than you, actually."

His growl tasted like frustration, because damn, the woman had a point. With a sigh, he dropped back to his chair. "What's your plan today?"

She glanced at a delicate wristwatch. "Supposedly I'm getting some help soon with working on this code. We need to hurry up and save your butt." Her fingers began dancing across the keys.

The woman was a joy to watch. Even from the side. His fingers itched with the urge to touch her, to see if her skin was as soft as it had been in his dream. Yet all he could do was watch and wonder. So he let her work for about an hour, contemplating how her boyfriend should die.

Footsteps echoed outside the room, the door opened, and a young teenager loped inside.

Heat filled Jory's breath, and his lungs constricted.

Piper turned toward the kid. "Um, hello?"

"I'm Chance, and the commander sent me to help you with the computer?" The kid strode to the second computer, all sinewy, trained, smooth muscle, not sparing Jory a glance. He moved with the grace of an animal, the symmetry familiar. Way too familiar.

Piper rubbed her nose. "How old are you?" Doubt filled her voice.

"Old enough, lady." He pulled out a chair and sat, his shoulders appearing relaxed. The low tenor tickled Jory's memory.

Jory stepped back and dropped to the cot, his mind swirling. Buzz cut, fighting shape, deliberate movements. Even the contour of the boy's head seemed familiar. "Turn around, kid," he croaked out.

The kid stiffened. "Screw you, buddy."

Jory's feet slapped the ground as he leaped up. "Turn

around. Now." This time authority rang in his voice, strong and sure.

The kid whipped around and jumped up, clearing the room to reach the glass. "What do you want, prisoner?"

Jory's mouth worked, but no sound emerged. His breath whooshed out as if somebody had kicked him in the balls. So he stayed silent, trying to remain upright, as he looked into the kid's eyes.

The kid's gray, very familiar, Dean brother eyes.

CHAPTER
6

PIPER TYPED AWAY on the keyboard, frowning as Chance's fingers danced faster than hers. The boy hadn't looked at her once and seemed more interested in the numbers flashing across his screen. "You're very good," she said.

"Yep." He kept typing, creating a new code with fresh commands to bypass the old safeguards put into place. While he concentrated on reactivating the connection between Jory's chip and the old computer program, Piper worked on her new program to see if she could forge a new wireless pathway to the chip. Plan A and Plan B both in motion.

"You're an intern here?" she asked.

He shrugged.

Jory hadn't said a word since the brief but odd interaction between them at the cell wall. Piper glanced to the side to see him lying on the cot as if asleep, every hard line of his body relaxed. She'd bet her last penny the man wasn't really asleep.

When Chance stepped up to the cell, no expression had crossed Jory's face. But something had happened. What, she truly didn't know.

The door opened, and Franklin stepped inside, smoothly crossing the room to stand outside the cell.

Jory unfolded from the cot and stood on the other side. A moment passed when the two men stared at each other, neither moving, neither saying a word. Jory's face remained hard and closed, and even his gray eyes remained veiled.

What type of silent communication were they having? Piper abandoned typing to watch what appeared to be two deadly predators sizing each other up. They seemed to be communicating in a silent mode of threat only they could decipher.

Franklin slid open the divider for lunch trays and took out a gun. Jory's head lifted, and he kept the commander's gaze. With nary a twitch, the commander calmly fired three darts into Jory's stomach. Jory doubled over, shuddered, and dropped to his knees.

Piper leaped to her feet. Heat roared through her ears, and her lungs compressed. "Wh-What?"

Jory's gaze flicked to her, and then his eyes shut. Almost in slow motion, he pitched face first onto the concrete. He landed with a loud thud.

Franklin whistled and typed in numbers on a keypad near the door. The cell door slid open.

Three orderlies rushed inside and dragged Jory onto a stretcher. One groaned as they carried him from the room.

Piper shook her head, her lungs seizing. "Why?"

Her father shrugged and strode for the door. "We need to conduct some tests, and we don't require him to be conscious for these." Without another word, he exited the room.

Piper swallowed and swiveled to face Chance, who'd continued to work through the entire action. "How are you still typing?"

He shrugged, his fingers tapping, his gaze on the screen. "Have work to do."

She blinked and slowly sat down, her knees shaking. The entire scene had been violent, and yet Chance didn't seem remotely affected. Her fingers trembled, and she stretched her hands out to the keyboard.

Enough of the secrets. She was a hacker, damn it.

Angling slightly away from Chance, she opened another window and began to tap. Layers upon layers of security hampered her, but she doggedly pursued information. Finally, she found the right section of the servers.

Within thirty minutes, she'd written a weak program, created a buffer overflow, and gained administrator privileges. This was much smoother than the brute force attack she'd employed previously in order to learn the computer program dealing with the kill chips.

Then she found the file.

Jory. Interesting. No last name listed. She pulled up documents listing his recruitment, training, and assignments. A photograph of Jory at eighteen showed him as already seasoned and hard, his eyes blank and his jaw appearing to be made of rock. Had he ever been happy?

The next few documents showed proof, with pictures, of his dealings with the Russians. Shit. She even recognized one of the Russian soldiers meeting with Jory from her time at the NSA. Definitely a bad guy.

Exhaling slowly, she closed the screens. Her father had told the truth.

A chill swept down her spine, while her cheeks heated. She shouldn't have doubted him, especially for a prisoner in a cage. And now she'd hacked into a very secure area. What would her father do if he discovered her infiltration this time? This time, her motivation wasn't to help him. It was to find the truth about Jory.

Chance stopped typing and stretched his neck. "You done hacking?"

Her head jerked up. "What?"

"Don't worry, lady. I don't really give a shit." He still didn't look at her.

She shook her head. "How old are you, anyway?"

"Old enough." His voice was already low, so maybe early teens?

"Are you an intern here?" she pressed, her instincts humming again. Who was this kid?

"Yep. Just on loan for a few days earning some high school credit." He popped his knuckles. "Back to work?"

Movement sounded beyond the door, and the three orderlies carried in a still-unconscious Jory to drop onto his cot. The second they'd locked the door to the cell, all three men breathed out heavily.

Piper glanced at the silent soldier in the cell and then at Chance's profile. What exactly was going on in this place?

Jory kept silent in the cell while Piper and Chance typed away on keyboards. He'd awakened nearly ten minutes ago, instantly sitting up to watch. For now, he wouldn't worry about whatever his PET scan and MRI had shown. Hopefully his brain had looked normal.

Did Chance have extra abilities, too? The kid had dark brown hair like Shane and Nate, Matt's square jaw, and Jory's mouth. Shit.

Just how many brothers did Jory have out there? This would fucking kill Matt. The idea of another one of them being held captive and trained to kill was almost too much to carry. The Dean brothers had only escaped five years ago, so where had this kid been?

Jory couldn't ask the questions with Piper in the room, but he'd damn well get answers.

While the kid typed away, he'd looked over his shoulder several times, curiosity in those gray eyes. Apparently he knew better than to question Jory in front of Piper.

Good.

Piper ignored Jory completely, her shoulders stiff, tension all but cascading from her. The woman seemed to be getting angrier and angrier every time she was in Jory's vicinity. He sighed. Whatever was going on, he'd have to handle it. The clock was ticking down not only on Madison discovering his extra abilities, but with his chip about to explode, he had to get to his brothers.

Finally, Piper excused herself to head to the ladies' room. She'd barely cleared the door when the kid stretched to his feet and approached the cell. He kept his face stoic, hard, but his eyes burned bright.

"Who are you?" Chance asked.

Jory flicked his gaze to the camera in the corner. The meet-up was deliberate, and surely Madison was scribbling in a notebook right now. "Jory."

"You look familiar."

"Yeah." Would telling the kid the truth put him in danger? Or rather, more danger than he lived with daily? Jory stood and approached the glass. The wave of protectiveness nearly floored him. "How many kids are here?"

Chance shuffled his feet, his lip curling. "Why?"

"Because I'd like to know how many brothers I have that I didn't know about," Jory said slowly. Forget the cameras. This was a brother, and he never lied to a brother.

Chance blinked. "I'm not your brother, asshole."

Jory grinned. The kid had balls. "Right. Because gray eyes are normal. I was created by the commander and Dr. Madison, trained as a soldier, and I'm not the only one."

Chance's shoulders went back, and his Adam's apple bobbled. "What do you mean?"

"I have three older brothers." Jory cleared his throat. And now one younger brother. At least. "That is, you and I have three older brothers. Same sperm donor."

Chance glanced at the closed door and back. "This is a setup."

"Yep." Smart kid. "But not by me."

The kid's hands clenched into fists, and he glared up at the hidden camera. So much anger rolled off him, Jory's gut heated. "Chance?" Jory asked.

In a clearly Matt Dean *Fuck You* head bob, Chance began to speak, defiance in every nuance. "Our sperm donor's name was Bruce Wilcox, he supported the program and voluntarily gave up sperm, and then he died on a mission."

The blood roared between Jory's ears, and he stepped closer to the glass. "You found him?"

"Yeah. I hacked the records." Chance shrugged, rawness in his eyes. "I can hack."

Something had hurt the kid and bad. Jory's throat closed with the need to help. The brutal need to break out of the cage and clasp the kid made Jory's hands shake. "Any records of our mothers?"

Chance exhaled, his already broad chest moving with the effort. "Just the program directives of buying top-grade genetic material and then hiring surrogates. Some grad students, some single moms, some whores. All records of who and when have been destroyed."

The records had been in Utah? That made an odd sense. The kid knew more about Jory's history than he did. Pride lifted his chin. "You're smart, kid. Now how many gray-eyed brothers are running around with you?"

Chance blinked, silent for several moments. Jory let him work out the thought on whether to reveal information or not, impressed when not one emotion crossed the kid's face. Well trained, now wasn't he?

Finally, Chance scratched his chin, a veil dropping over his gaze. "Two brothers younger than me."

Jory blinked. "There are three of you?" God. There were three more brothers. "Three brothers."

"We're not your brothers, so don't get any ideas. You're on your own." Chance still refused to look at him.

Jory eyed the kid. What was he hiding?

High heels clicked down the hall, and Jory stiffened along with Chance, their movements an exact mirror. The door swept open, and Dr. Madison clipped inside, four soldiers behind her.

She smiled sparkling white teeth. "What a nice reunion."

Chance shifted to the side, keeping her in sight. Everything in Jory stilled with the need to protect this newfound brother, and his body settled into fighting mode. "More experiments, Madison?"

"Yes." A gleeful gleam filled her blue eyes. "Same but different."

"Meaning?" Jory tilted his head to the side.

She shrugged. "Chance, get back to work. Jory, your brain showed some interesting activities on your tests earlier, and now it's time for a physical."

"No." The last thing he wanted was more poking or prodding. Although getting out of the cell held certain appeal.

"Yes. We need you awake this time." Madison jerked her head at the soldiers, who immediately fanned out and drew weapons. Madison then drew a small pistol from her lab coat and pointed the barrel at Chance.

Jory growled.

To the kid's credit, he didn't flinch, although his muscles tightened in anticipation of a fight.

"Fine." Jory backed away from the glass, and Madison turned the gun on him.

A soldier punched in numbers on the pad next to the door, and it slid open.

Jory gauged the men's stances and their weapons. He could get two of them quickly, but he'd have to kill the other two, and who knew if Madison would shoot him or not. He debated his options, his decision made the second Piper walked back into the room. Too much danger for somebody untrained.

Her eyes widened, and she faltered. "Wh—"

"Please get back to work. We're running out of time," Madison said, her cheerful voice contrasting with the gun in her hand.

Piper swallowed and glanced from Jory to Chance and back.

Jory tried to make his smile reassuring. "I would appreciate it if you found a way to deactivate the chip near my spine." There wasn't a chance, but he needed her focused and out of the way. So he allowed one soldier to shackle his wrists and ankles, shuffling out of the room, an ache pounding in his gut as he left his brother behind.

Again.

The walk through hallways took over two minutes. They reached a medical lab, and he hitched inside to jump on a table. "How could you?" he asked Madison.

She blinked, glancing up from a computer tablet. "Excuse me?"

"More creations?" he asked, fire bubbling up his throat.

"Yes." She squinted. "Four boys, an experiment to see if they'd bond like your family did. We wanted to see if the four behaved like you four boys did."

Jory stiffened. "Which is why you made Chance the oldest? To see if he'd behave as Matt did."

"Yes." Madison slid to the side as a pretty nurse entered the room. "He has. Treats those younger boys just as protectively as Matt did you."

Jory swallowed. "You said four boys, and Chance told me there were three of them. Why?"

Madison clicked her tongue. "We lost one months ago on a mission."

A rock slammed into Jory's gut. "How old was he?"

"Eleven." Madison sighed. "He showed such potential. What a pity."

Fire burned Jory's ears, and his hands clenched with the need to wrap around her slim neck. "You fucking bitch."

The door burst open, and heavy combat boots clomped inside. "Watch your mouth, boy," the commander muttered.

Jory lifted his head to meet the black-eyed gaze. "So you finally got one of us killed. Nice job, dickhead." With his hands shackled at his back, and his feet all but tied together, he'd need leverage to tackle the commander while keeping Madison from shooting him. So he shifted slightly on the table.

Madison smoothly shoved a needle into his leg and depressed the plunger.

Instant warmth filled his thigh, and his vision swayed. Damn it.

The commander widened his stance. "Soldiers die all the time, and it's a miracle you've never lost a brother. Hell, I can't figure out why you're still alive. As a kid, you were pathetic."

He was still alive because his brothers had made sure he survived. Without question, without his brothers, he never would've made it through early training before he grew. Now, he was a stone-cold killer who'd do what he had to do—even use Piper against the commander. He wavered on the table, trying to remain conscious. "You'll pay for getting that kid killed."

The commander glanced at his wristwatch. "Take blood and do a full mock-up, and then toss him into the training field. Let's see how fast he heals now."

Jory's head lolled. "Why don't you join me?" he slurred.

"I might." The commander clasped his hands at his back. "I haven't beaten you in a while, although I did have a good time with Nathan in DC."

Jory forced a grin. "You mean before he escaped with Audrey and blew the place up?"

The commander frowned. "He'll pay for his disloyalty, I promise you."

"Right." Jory sucked in air and tried to focus his vision while Madison drew blood. "Your daughter has no clue what a bastard you are."

Pain flashed in Madison's eyes, to be quickly veiled. Jory cleared his throat. He'd forgotten how much the batty scientist loved the evil commander. "Did you know the commander had a kid?" Jory asked.

She turned to tap info into her tablet. "Your vision should be graying."

Yeah, it was. He faced the commander again. "One-night stand?"

"Yes. She was a receptionist at the Tennessee compound. She was good in bed." The commander leaned to read over Madison's shoulder. "My first instinct was to force her to get rid of it."

"You didn't, though?" Jory concentrated on the blood pumping through his veins and tried to speed up the action. He needed to move the drugs quickly to absorb them.

"No." The commander sighed. "Ego, I'm afraid. I'd hoped for a boy to raise here, but alas, it was a girl. So I just left them alone."

Jory shook his head, his heart cracking for the poor girl. "Yet she's here now."

"Turns out she knows something about computers." The commander turned and smiled. "Good genes."

Was that fatherly pride or just ego? Jory couldn't concentrate. Pain flared along his leg again, and he glanced down to see another needle.

Madison sniffed. "We can't have you trying to escape again, now can we?"

His eyes fluttered shut as he sank into unconsciousness, his last thought of a little black-haired girl with sad green eyes, wondering why her father didn't visit.

CHAPTER
7

PIPER STRETCHED HER neck, pleased when the code finally uploaded. Chance had long ago left to do something else in the compound, and she missed his company. While he wouldn't talk about his life, the kid had been knowledgeable about everything from history to current politics, and she'd enjoyed bantering with him.

But he'd kept his face averted most of the time they'd talked, completely avoiding making eye contact. Maybe he was just shy. Really shy.

Why was such a young person at the compound? If it was some sort of internship, why wouldn't he talk about it? Nothing seemed to be adding up, and her mind worked overtime to make sense of the entire situation.

The door burst open, and two soldiers dragged in a nearly unconscious Jory. His feet thumped on the ground, and his head lolled on his neck.

Piper jumped up and gaped at Jory's face. A cut above one eye trickled blood, while a purple bruise swelled along his jaw. Mottled bruises and lumps showed on his neck, and torn flesh marred his knuckles. "What happened?" she breathed.

One soldier eyed the other and typed in the code. "The guy is a fucking machine. Did you see him take out Anders? And Jonese?"

The other guy nodded, heaving Jory inside with a harsh grunt. "Guy ain't human. No way, no how."

Jory lurched forward to land on the cot. Blood dripped across the entire cell.

The door closed, and both soldiers heaved sighs. The first rubbed his neck. "If the commander hadn't darted him, this guy would've taken us all out."

The second soldier nodded and patted the glass. "Thank goodness for cells." They hurried from the room as if something predatory chased them.

Piper swallowed and slowly approached the cell. "Jory?"

He groaned.

"How badly are you hurt?" She squinted to see better. Maybe the soldiers were supposed to take him to the infirmary.

He rolled over and fell onto the floor, his eyes closed. Blood sprayed across the cell to land on the far wall.

Oh God. She pressed her hand on the glass. "Jory?"

His eyes opened, dark gray and in pain. Then his mouth worked, but no sound emerged.

"Take a deep breath. How badly are you hurt?" she asked, turning to eye the door. She should find help.

He huffed out a breath, and his eyes rolled back in his head. That quickly, his entire body convulsed, his head hitting the metal end of the cot. More blood spurted.

The world tilted. Dizziness swung her head around. Her stomach lurched. "Jory?" she breathed. He was going to kill himself. If he hit the metal any harder, he could nail himself in the temple. God, he might even puncture the kill chip, thus deploying the blades. His body continued to convulse, his large frame slamming the concrete.

Going on instinct, she rushed to the keypad and punched in the code the last soldier had used, her eidetic memory easily keeping track of the numbers. The door breezed open, and she rushed inside, dropping to her knees. Putting a hand to his heaving chest, she glanced frantically around for something to put in his mouth to prevent him from biting off his tongue.

His hand wrapped around her wrist.

She tried to shrug him off. "I'm trying to help you," she said as gently as she could.

"I know." Faster than a whip, he jumped up, taking her with him.

Her brain fuzzed. "What—"

An iron band of an arm wrapped around her waist, turned her, and lifted her against his chest. "I'm sorry," he murmured against her ear, his warm breath brushing tender flesh. More than a foot off the ground, her back against his chest, her butt against his groin, realization slapped her hard in the face.

"Let me go." She struggled against him, her nails scraping his arm.

"No." He tightened his hold until she couldn't breathe. "Don't fight me, Piper. You won't win."

Her lungs screamed. Tears filled her eyes, and she stopped moving. Slowly, his hold relaxed marginally, just enough to allow her air. "Don't do this," she whispered.

A shout echoed down the hall just as an alarm blared through the facility. Jory rushed them out of the cell and through the computer room, kicking open the door and carrying her easily. Way too easily.

Soldiers ran from the northern end of the hall, their boots clomping.

Jory turned the other way, grabbing her key card and swiping a pad without missing a beat. The door closed behind them, and he pivoted, kicking the pad square in the middle. Wires popped out, and sparks flew. Then he calmly proceeded down the hall again and through another doorway.

Chance barreled around a corner.

Jory paused. "Chance! Come with us."

Chance faltered, his gaze going from Jory to Piper. "No. Can't leave them."

"Damn it, Chance," Jory hissed. "Come with me now, and we'll come back for them. You have my word."

Chance's eyes veiled. He shook his head. "No." He disappeared around the corner again, and running footsteps echoed.

"Fuck." Jory closed the door and kicked off the faceplate. "I can't figure out what that kid is hiding." Scrutinizing the circuitry, he frowned. "If he's working with the commander, I wouldn't hold it against him." Still holding her tight and seeming not to notice her struggles, he yanked open a desk drawer. "Hmm."

"Who can't Chance leave?" Piper muttered.

Jory ignored her, scrambling through the contents.

"Jory—" She gasped when he grabbed two paper clips and a piece of gum, shaking out the gum and keeping the foil. "You're kidding me," she muttered, wanting to keep fighting but suddenly curious.

He unbent a clip against his jean-clad leg and shoved it into the keypad with his free hand. A twist of the foil around the other clip, and he shoved that in, too. Then he pushed them together.

A spark flew, and metal singed. The locks engaged again—this time permanently.

Piper's mouth dropped open. "You're freakin' MacGyver."

"Best television show ever." Jory turned and continued down his path, squiring them through two more doorways—with her card.

Damn it. She needed to fight. Panic heated down Piper's throat. She jerked her elbow back and into his ribs. Hard.

He didn't even flinch, his even footsteps more frightening than if he'd started running.

"Let me go." She pulled to the side and tried to nail him in the throat with her elbow.

He ducked and held her closer. "Where are we?" he muttered, shoving open one last door to the outside parking lot.

Bellows echoed behind them, and glass shattered. Good. The soldiers were at least through one door and would be there soon. She screamed, long and loud.

"Damn it." Jory pivoted and easily tossed her over his shoulder, loping into a jog. Seconds later, he shoved her inside a battered Ford truck just as soldiers poured from the building, guns out and already firing. "Shit." Jory ducked and yanked the door shut, ripping wires out and rubbing them together.

A bullet shattered the back window.

Piper cried out and ducked, scrambling for the passenger-side door. Jory jerked her arm and tugged her flat, her head in his lap. "Stay down. They have fire orders, and it won't matter if they hit you." His voice remained flat and calm.

Why the hell wasn't he freaking out? Soldiers were shooting at them. Even if he was a trained assassin, surely he could feel fear, or at least have some sort of a physical reaction. The side window blew open, and glass rained down. Jory curled over her body, protecting her from jagged shards, just as the engine engaged. His thigh tensed, and suddenly the truck jumped forward. He grimaced while propelling the truck out of the lot.

"Where are we?" he asked, his hands turning the wheel as more bullets ripped into metal around them.

"Outside of Salt Lake City," she whispered, biting her lip to keep from screaming as glass cut into her side.

He snorted. "No kidding. Perfect timing, too."

It was about rush hour. "We'll get caught in traffic. Please, Jory, turn yourself back in. They won't stop coming for you." God, she had to get out of the truck. Who the hell was this man? Even now, he maneuvered the truck quickly, expertly turning the wheel, not even breathing heavy. "How are you so calm?"

"Training." He jerked the wheel, and the truck careened sideways, pressing her cheek into his groin. She tried to move. "Not yet." One heavy hand landed gently on her nape, holding her in place. "They're in pursuit, and they'll fire." He leaned to the side and glanced out the window as they drove wildly.

After what seemed like an hour, but was really probably only half that, Jory grabbed an old shirt from the floor and wiped off all the blood. Soon, the sounds of honking horns and engines filtered through the air. They were in the city. Finally, Jory spoke again. "How far is the main compound?"

She snapped her lips closed. If he thought she'd help him, he was crazy.

The hand on her neck flexed in warning. "How far?" he repeated.

"Bite me."

A wisp ripped through the air, and metal impacted the truck with a fierce screech. "Shit." Jory slammed the brakes, his hand keeping her head from smashing the steering wheel. "Missiles. Get out." Grabbing her under the armpits, he leaped from the vehicle just as it exploded.

CHAPTER
8

HEAT SMOLDERED ALONG Jory's face as he kept hold of Piper and hustled through the gathering crowd, the burning truck behind them. The bastards hadn't cared if they'd killed her. She stumbled along next to him, her face slack with shock.

He probably had less than a minute before she freaked out completely. The missile had been too close, and he hoped to shit nobody had been hurt by the blast.

She felt fragile under his arm, and her scent surrounded them. His mind measured steps and precision, while his body tuned into *woman*.

All woman.

Without missing a stride, he filtered through the sounds. Running feet, com-links, guns cocking. Two soldiers left behind to watch the police and run interference if necessary. Six more soldiers fanning out. They moved with confidence, no doubt sure they could overcome one escaped prisoner and a captive.

The soldiers had no clue who he was or what he could do. For that matter, neither did the commander.

Jory shoved through the crowd, holding Piper tight. She brought out something in him, something *new*. Powerful and intense. He'd have to figure out what later.

Up ahead, he caught sight of an entrance to the mall. Good. Crowds, corners, and cover. Tightening his hold on the trembling woman, he all but carried her across the sidewalk and around a wide fountain, calculating the most likely route through the mall to a parking area.

Sirens trilled in the distance, and he ducked them into a mall. His grip on Piper's arm both contained her and kept her upright. One glance at the kiosk, and he memorized the layout. Keeping his head down, he put her on the escalator in front of him, guarding her back just in case.

They'd have to go through him to get to her, and they wouldn't come close. His focus narrowed, and his chin lowered. Like the creation they'd spawned, he allowed instinct and intellect to take over.

To protect. To defend. Ingrained in his DNA and then his training, the power of a warrior surged through him.

Soldiers poured into the main entrance. A quick ride up, and he ushered her toward the southern exit, where he glanced around.

A sharp breeze cut into his face.

Piper lifted her head, her eyes focusing. She stilled and jerked against his hold.

A young mother with two toddlers hustled toward the entrance, their heads ducked to avoid the wind. Piper sucked in air.

If she screamed, they were screwed.

Jory pivoted and put her against the wall, covering her mouth with his before she could let out a sound.

Warmth and woman. An electric shock flared his entire nervous system alive. Soft and sweet, she breathed in as he pressed against her. He'd meant to subdue her, to throw her off balance, but shock ricocheted through him.

Need compelled him. He shot both hands into her hair, tilting her head so he could go deeper. So fucking deep he could get lost.

The second he tasted her, all cinnamon and woman, hunger slaked him. Devastating in its intensity, a demand he couldn't deny. Her smooth, velvety lips softened under his, and for once, he lost himself.

Strands of her silky hair caressed his hands as he held her jaw, nearly lifting her up to meet his mouth. There was nothing but getting...*more.*

She stilled against him, her mouth parting. He swept his tongue against hers, taking in a primitive claim too powerful to deny.

Her gasp mingled with his low groan. She pressed harder against him, her mouth curving under his, and he forgot... everything. Who he was, where they were, the fire and danger. Only the woman against him, warm and willing, sweet and sexy, filled his mind.

He clasped her tight, forgetting any gentleness. Any seduction, any mission. Only this woman and this moment mattered. Letting go of himself, he allowed the creature inside, the one so rarely let loose, to take over. To push deep, to demand more. To take.

And give everything.

His mouth overtook hers, memorizing every groove, every small nuance. His free hand gripped her butt, hauling her up against his steel-hard erection. Heat from her core nearly dropped him to his knees. Pain and sparking pleasure flared along his skin, and he deepened the kiss, tightening his hold.

He needed to get inside her. *Now.*

A siren trilled on the lower street, and he jerked his head free.

Danger.

She blinked, her eyes the green of a rain-filled meadow. Desire burned there, hot and bright. Somehow sweet.

Possessiveness gripped him with a chokehold. One kiss. One kiss and she'd changed him. He had to get her out of the parking lot before guns fired again.

That quickly, realization crossed her face. Then shock, as she tried to take a step back. Her hands rose and shoved against his chest.

Denial gripped him to be quickly quashed with cold, hard training. So he grabbed her wrists and hauled her closer, his face lowering to hers. He wiped away any expression and shoved down all emotion. "Those men don't care who they shoot. They're scrambling and might kill you—or innocent bystanders." He spoke low, commanding.

She blinked, her mouth opening but no sound coming out.

"If you fight me, they'll find us, and they might shoot. Collateral damage doesn't mean a thing to them."

She shook her head and looked around.

He pulled her closer and lowered his voice to pure, no-bullshit command. "We're getting in that four-door Jeep, and we're leaving here quietly. Your only choice is alert or unconscious? Decide now." He let conviction ring in his tone. If he believed he could knock her out, then she'd believe it, too.

No fucking way could he knock her out. Scaring her held little appeal, but he didn't have a choice if they were to both live through the night.

She quickly nodded. Gulping air, she relaxed her body as two teenagers giggled while walking by.

He knew full well she agreed to keep bystanders safe and not because the kiss had changed anything for her. She had no reason to trust him, and she'd never really know him. Why that pierced his chest with the cleanness of a sharpened dagger, he'd figure out later. For now, they had to run.

Piper clenched her knees together and bit back a scream as Jory careened the vehicle around a post and darted into traffic. She'd thought the safest course of action was to leave the bystanders unaware behind them, but what if Jory crashed into a car? "Slow down," she hissed. Horns blared behind them.

"Put on your seat belt." He dodged around a minivan and took a ninety-degree-angle turn down an alley. His hands rested loosely on the steering wheel, while his shoulders remained down and relaxed.

As they fled for their lives. The guy couldn't be human. Yet he sure kissed like a man. Her lips still tingled, and desire lay barely controlled in her abdomen.

He'd kidnapped her, and yet...damn he could kiss. What in the hell had she been thinking? Her entire body had flared alive, while her brain had just shut down.

While his hold had been tight, dominant—there was no question she'd kissed him back.

Her father's enemy. A man who'd betrayed his country and his soldier brothers.

What was wrong with her?

Even now, minutes later hurtling through traffic, her body hummed in full alertness next to his. Completely in tune with every movement he made.

But something was seriously off with him. He was too fast, too in control, way too damn smart. His MacGyver move with the keypad had been incredible—and his reflexes unbelievable. No military training, no matter how intense, was that complete.

She clutched the dash, and the car whipped around a taxi. The cabbie hit his horn, the sound yanking her out of her head.

"Just let me out." She scrambled for the door handle, throwing her shoulder into the window. No way was she dying in the old SUV.

"No." Not even glancing her way, he reached out and yanked her into his hard body while executing a perfect turn into one-way traffic. Warmth and the scent of male washed over her. "Hold still."

Her nipples pebbled. God. She punched him in the ribs, trying to scoot her butt back across the seat.

"Piper." A calm warning.

He swerved, and a woman walking a gaggle of dogs jumped back, screaming, her face contorting. A Pomeranian leaped onto the back of a Great Dane, and the Dane shot in front of a moving bicycler, his teeth baring. The guy on the bike flew over the handlebars and landed on an apple green Volkswagen Bug. He flipped off Jory.

They were going to die. Piper gulped in air. Sparks flickered up her back, and her ears rang. Energy rushed through her, and she pummeled Jory's side, her vision fuzzing. Garbled words flew from her mouth, and she didn't even try to stop the tirade.

If he didn't slow down, they'd die. She screamed high and loud. Black spots danced in front of her vision.

Jory sighed, his hand sliding down her arm and around her torso to clasp her wrists in a hard hug. In a movement so smooth it didn't seem real, he lifted a knee into her leg, pulled up, and effectively twisted her onto her back. Her head hit his iron-hard thigh, and he jerked her head toward his door, his hand flattening hers to her chest, immobilizing her.

She blinked up at the steering wheel. Her mouth opened and closed. The worn leather cooled her back. How had he done that? No way would she let him control her in such a way.

She twisted her head, trying to get purchase to bite, while kicking the passenger-side door with ineffectual thumps. Damn tennis shoes.

"Mellow out before I accidentally hit somebody," Jory muttered.

The man held her too tightly for her to gain leverage. Panting, she settled, staring up at his cut jaw. This close, lines of tension cut into the sides of his mouth, leading down to rigid muscles along his corded neck. So he was affected. Thank God. She was starting to wonder if the commander had created some sort of rabid half-robot soldiers.

"Jory, you can't outrun them." Her voice shook, but she spoke softly, trying to reach the man that had to be inside this guy. The man who'd kissed her with enough passion to burn them both where they stood. "They'll have air support soon."

He nodded and turned the wheel again. "In about an hour. Plenty of time."

Unfortunately true. "I'm just slowing you down. Let me go."

His gaze lifted to the rearview mirror. "You don't get it, do you? Those men were shooting at you, too."

She shook her head, static electricity popping her hair against his shorts. "No, they weren't. They were trying to take out the vehicle, and you know it. My father wouldn't hurt me."

"The commander is a monster who'd hurt anybody and everybody to get what he wants."

Her breath heated and her chest tightened. "What is it he wants?" Yeah, she really wanted to know.

"Right now? Me." Jory's jaw relaxed. "Once we get to safety, I promise I'll let you go."

Sure he would. Right after he turned her over to the Russians. Or whoever he had yet to contact. A scream tried to rise from her gut, and she shook her shoulders to hold it in. "Vodka isn't my thing. Just let me go."

He chuckled. "I'm not aligned with the Russians, and you have nothing to worry about."

"I've seen your file." If she could just get him to relax his hold, she could grab the wheel.

"What file?" He frowned and jerked the wheel to the left. A horn honked.

She blinked up at him, her back tensing. "Your entire military file, starting when you joined the organization. Even the proof of your betrayal with pictures."

He snorted. "Sounds like a nice plant. How hard did you have to hack?"

Damn hard, actually. Yet his calmness in the face of her proof gave her pause. "So you're denying perfect proof?"

"Is any proof perfect?" He ducked his head to stare up at the quiet sky.

She tried to move her hands without any luck. "You're saying somebody actually went to the trouble to plant that file and make it nearly impossible to find just in case I started to investigate you?"

"Sure." He glanced down at her. "Could Chance plant a file like that?"

Well, yeah. So could she. "No." When those gray eyes narrowed on her, she fought the urge to squirm, considering where her head currently lay.

"Right." Jory lifted his head back to the window.

"Where are we going?" Her jaw ached from her muscles tightening. She wasn't strong enough to break his hold, damn it.

"I need to reach, my, ah, group."

She bent her knees to relieve the pressure in her lower back. "Who's your group?" More important, what would they do to her? A chill slithered down her spine.

"They're good men, and I'll contact them as soon as we're out of the city and hidden from the air support." He cocked his head to stare up at the sky again. "What I need from you is agreement and obedience. Temporarily, of course."

Her head snapped back. She may have to kill him. "I'm neither agreeable nor obedient. Sorry, pal."

His lip quirked. "I figured."

The sounds of the city slowly dissipated. Piper bit back a scream. "Did you lose them?"

"Yes." He turned the wheel again, drove around a worn-out gas station, and cut the engine. "Any chance you'll cooperate with me?"

"Of course," she said as sweetly as she could, fury banishing the fear. Finally.

"Humph." With masculine grace, he opened his door, pulled her out, and tossed her over his shoulder. Her ribs impacted solid muscle, and the breath whooshed from her lungs.

Ow. She blinked and took a second to get her bearings. Drawing in cool air, she opened her mouth to bellow for help...and the world spun. She ended up coughing as Jory yanked open the driver-side door of a rickety old Chevy and dropped her on the seat. A spring poked her in the ass. Fire lancing her blood, she punched him as hard as she could in the thigh.

He leaned over, calmly tore free the driver's seat belt, and wound the strong strap around her wrists, knees, and ankles. She squirmed, kicked, and tried to hit him. Where did he get such strength? The man was unreal.

Her gaze darted around only to see overgrown grass and abandoned tires. A cricket chirped in the distance. With a hiss, she tried to throw a shoulder at him.

His hand cupped her chin and turned her to face him. "Is anything too tight?"

Her head jerked. "Are you fucking kidding me?" she yelled, even her breath heating. "Too tight?"

He frowned, and his hold firmed on her chin. "Answer me."

That was it. She freakin' lost her mind. "Fuck you, Jory. You fucking asshole of a cold-blooded soldier traitor son of a bitch." The words started to flow together so rapidly she lost track of verbs. "You are all robot—not even fucking human. You don't feel a thing, you sociopathic dickhead."

He lifted one eyebrow, and something glimmered in his odd eyes.

Oh, hell no. Rage scalded her throat. "You are not fucking amused right now!"

He pressed his lips together. His thumb swept across her jaw. "Nope. And you're wrong."

A tremble wound through her. The gentleness from the dangerous soldier threatened to short-circuit her brain. Her heart clenched. "About what?" Her tone quieted, and her shoulders hunched in what actually felt like defeat.

"I feel way too much with you." Ducking his head, he swept his lips across hers.

She blinked, stunned. Sweet warmth caressed her mouth and blazed through her, landing in her abdomen and spreading. She swayed.

Humming, he released her to gently push her over on the seat. Quick motions had him leaning across her.

Her lungs compressed, and she pushed back against the seat.

"I won't hurt you." He secured the passenger seat belt around her. No threats, no anger, no freakin' emotion at all from him. She blinked, fighting the effects of his kiss and her struggle. She'd fought him with everything she had, and he hadn't even broken a sweat. Who the hell was this guy?

She tried to rub her mouth, and her hands remained bound. Anger torpedoed through her again. He ripped free wires and ignited the engine, and she glared with every ounce of mental strength she owned, picturing his head imploding. Or exploding. She didn't give a shit which way his head blew.

He had no right to be so calm, and definitely no right to control her body with something as simple as a quick kiss. No right at all. Left with no other alternative, she screamed.

He clapped a hand over her mouth, no emotion on his fallen-angel face. When she stopped, panting in breath, he exhaled and pointed to a bunch of filthy rags on the floor. "That's all I have to gag you with. It's your choice."

Bile rose from her stomach. Dirt, oil, and who knows what else covered the rags. She'd die if he shoved one in her mouth. She searched his face, his expression, for any reassurance that he wouldn't follow through on the threat.

Nothing. No doubt, no give glimmered in his eyes or softened his hard jawline.

Finally, she nodded, and he slowly removed his hand. She hunched her shoulders, her stomach sinking that he'd consider gagging her. Oh, this was so not over, but she didn't have much of a choice. Helplessness should make her feel vulnerable, but instead, fury boiled through her veins. "I'm so going to kill you," she muttered.

He jerked his head. "Can't say I blame you." Then a grin split his face. "I'd much rather die looking at you than the commander or Madison. If we get to that point, feel free."

She blinked. Her heart thumped. "How can you be so blasé about death?"

He chuckled, the sound lacking any warmth while he drove over potholes to the quiet road. "Baby, I've lived with death since my birth. Believe me, if I didn't have a promise to fulfill, I'd probably be ready." His grin disappeared, regret coloring his tone. "Sometimes the fight just ends, you know?"

"Then stop fighting," she said softly. What demons lived in the guy's head?

He drew in air. "After this job, I'm done fighting."

She tried to loosen her hands, but the seat belt didn't give. "What promise?"

"Huh?" He kept his gaze on the two-lane highway.

"You said you have a promise to fulfill. What promise?" Maybe she could get him to relate to her and let her go. That worked with serial killers, right?

"Oh." He settled back onto the worn seat, his gaze flicking over her. Finally, he shrugged. "To save my brothers since they did nothing but save my life since day one. I owe them, and I promised myself that I'd take care of them even if I don't make it. I owe them."

Brothers? The commander had mentioned soldiers that he related to as brothers. Was that what he meant? Didn't he betray them? "I don't understand." What about the Russians?

"I know." Thunder cracked overhead, and black clouds raced across the wide expanse of sky. A raindrop splattered against the glass. "I figured the less you knew, the safer you'd be. But the commander will assume I've told you everything, even if I haven't, so it's up to you. Do you want the truth, or do you want to go back to him and hope he believes you don't know anything?" Jory's odd gray gaze raked her. "Maybe you won't be in danger since you share a genetic link."

Why did he sound so doubtful? "I don't understand why you'd kidnap me." Unless he planned to use her against her father.

He leaned back into the leather seat. "To start with, I took you because you're going to write down what you remember from the new computer program you just created. Now I have you because the assholes chasing us consider you collateral damage and will kill you." His voice remained calm and almost thoughtful. No stress, no remorse, no worry.

She tried to calm her racing heart. "So?"

"So?" He glanced down, gray eyes intense. "I'm not allowing you to get killed just because I'm being hunted. I have a plan, and after you tell me what I need to know, I will make sure you get home safely."

Oh, she'd get free on her own, and she had no reason to trust him. For now, she needed to keep him talking until she found the right moment to escape. "Fine. Tell me the truth as you see it." Perhaps Jory was just delusional. He had been shot several times, and who knew what kind of damage that could do to a guy's head? Of course, considering he'd turned her body into a bundle of needy nerves, her head was screwed up, too. "Please."

"I'm an experiment created by the commander and Dr. Madison to be a killing machine."

Oh God. Her vision tunneled. "Like a robot?"

He coughed out air. "No. Well, not exactly. I think we're all human." Doubt lowered his consonants. "At least, I hope so."

"You said 'we.'"

"My brothers. We were raised together as an experiment, and we got loose five years ago. With the kill chips in our spines." His knuckles whitened on the torn steering wheel. "Chips implanted by your father and Madison."

Piper shook her head, the mere idea drying the spit in her mouth. "No. That's impossible." She'd been warned how charming and manipulative Jory could be before she'd stepped foot inside the computer room. "You're lying."

"Am I?" He kept his gaze straightforward. "Believe what you want, Piper. But something tells me you're more than a pretty face and a big heart. You have a huge brain or you wouldn't have been able to create that computer program so quickly. So use your brain. Figure out the truth."

A rock slammed into her gut. Too many questions assailed her, and the answers only lined up with logic she didn't like. At all. So she turned to watch the trees fly by as the storm gathered in force. "Where are we going?"

Lightning flashed across the sky, angry and violent. Jory swerved to avoid a downed tree limb. "How do you feel about camping?"

CHAPTER
9

JORY LED THE way through swaying pine trees, his mind
fighting training, his boots leaving large imprints in the
moist soil. While he could remain outwardly calm, emotions crashed through him in an unreal succession. Could the
coma have unleashed emotion he had always banished? Or
had it been Piper? The woman was...unique.

He didn't need to turn to be completely tuned into her.
Breathing, heart rate, scent. What the hell was happening
to him?

But even now, Matt's voice rang in his ear.

Think. Don't feel.

The smart move was to head into the forest where the
commander's air support couldn't find him. The forces
would search all around but concentrate more on the city,
thinking Jory would reach out for help.

So he had to find safety before reaching out.

Behind him, Piper mumbled incoherent words as she followed him through the dark forest. Every once in a while, he
caught a *bastard*, a *shit-tard*, and once she may have threatened to yank his balls out through his ears. That one was his
favorite so far.

He'd disabled the car after driving as far as possible into
the forest and then carried her a few miles until she wouldn't
know how to get out. At that point, being a smart woman,
she'd chosen to follow him.

While probably planning his death.

He liked that about her. Spunk and intelligence went

nicely with her rounded ass and gorgeous face. Too bad she hated him now.

Or maybe that was good. She was the commander's daughter.

But damn, she intrigued him.

And when he'd finally gotten her talking about the program she'd created during their long car ride, she'd impressed the hell out of him. Brilliant, really. His brain was already adding to her program, and by the time he was in front of a computer, he'd have it altered enough to save his brothers.

Which meant he could now let her go. They were probably still enemies, and he'd promised her freedom.

So why did the thought of releasing her make his gut hurt like he'd been punched?

The river rushed wildly next to the barely there path, surprisingly full from the many rains of the past several weeks. Coming off the Wasatch Mountain Range, it appeared crisp and cold as hell.

He pivoted to put Piper in his peripheral vision. The woman kept glancing at the rushing river. "Planning to toss me in?" he asked.

Her head jerked. "Of course not." Pink rose to cover her high cheekbones.

"Liar." Why did they have to be enemies? Or did they? The commander would just hurt her, so maybe that should put them on the same side? Jory's unreal desire for her went beyond the physical.

Just who the heck was this woman?

Why did it matter?

The scent of wet pine permeated the air, while the roll of thunder in the distance promised a hell of a storm heading in. They had to find shelter before rain began again, and from a cursory glance at the map, he figured cabins would soon line the riverbanks.

Abandoned cabins this late in the season.

From there, he could plan. It was doubtful a seasonal cabin would hold a cell phone, but he'd get his hands on one somehow.

The scent of smoke wandered through the pines.

Good. Late-season campers. For now, he had to get Piper to safety before the storm broke. She struggled on behind him, having suddenly gone quiet. So he paused and reached for her arm. "You all right?"

"Peachy." She shrugged him off, glancing into the rapidly darkening pines. "You have a plan here?"

"Of course." Although she probably wouldn't like it. A slight narrowing of the brush caught his attention, and he led her through a myriad of cottonwoods to a quaint cabin all boarded up.

Lightning zagged above, and Piper jumped.

"For now, let's get inside." He threw a shoulder into the door, and the rugged wood opened with barely a protest.

She stomped up the stairs and followed him inside. "No super-spy MacGyver moves, huh?"

The woman actually sounded disappointed by that, and Jory's chest swelled. It was rare for somebody to appreciate his geek side. "With an old door, the direct approach works best."

Her lips tipped in a quick grin she quickly quashed.

He sighed to view their new digs. A mattress took up one corner, while a small kitchenette lined one wall. The doorway took up a third wall, and a carved fireplace the final wall. No frills. Yet a sense of intimacy filtered through the tidy space, speeding up his breath.

She swallowed. "You're kidding me."

"City girl." He immediately went for the wood and paper near the fireplace, no doubt kept in place for lost hikers. The scent of wood competed with the fresh scent of woman.

Man, she went right to his head. He had to let go of images of Piper naked and get to the business at hand. The woman was way too appealing, and the fact that she might want him dead should cool his libido. Although it didn't. Seconds later, he had a fire going. The river rushed mercilessly outside, striving to reach the ocean so far away.

Piper hovered by the door, her body language saying it all. Thunder cracked like angry gods.

"There's nowhere to go, green eyes." He gestured toward the faded floral couch. "Take a seat and warm up."

A myriad of expressions crossed her face, each easy to read, and each more fascinating than the last. "No."

He barked out a laugh, unable to help himself. For sure he thought she'd go with either a heartfelt *fuck you* or another argument to let her go. Pure defiance looked good on her, even with the near exhaustion darkening those amazing eyes. But the lingering glimmer of fear there caught him up short.

"I know dozens of ways to kill somebody, Piper. If I wanted you dead, it'd be a done deal already. Please don't be afraid." Yeah, the words probably failed to reassure her, but he'd never been smooth with people. Computers made so much more sense.

Her lashes lifted, and her gaze sharpened. "I'm not afraid."

So brave, or rather, trying to be so brave. "Good. And I really am sor—"

Her eyes flashed. "Don't you even fucking *think* of saying you're sorry. You're not sorry. You're guilty as hell of kidnapping, and you do not get to say you're sorry."

He nodded. "You're right. I'm sor—"

"Stop." She held up a hand, fury dancing red across her cheeks. "I will drown you if you try again."

Fair enough. He could give her that. No more apologies. "Fine. Then how about a plan?"

She lifted one eyebrow in an oddly endearing way. Most people looked dangerous or focused with the one eyebrow lifted. Not Piper. Damn cute. Way too damn cute. "What's your plan?"

He licked his lips. "First, you get warm." Moving slowly so as not to alarm her, he drew her toward the sofa. "Please."

"No politeness." Her voice held snap, while her shoulders held fatigue. "Don't even think it."

"I won't," he said gently, his body relaxing when she sat nearer the fire. The world had chilled outside, and he wouldn't allow her to become ill. She seemed tough, but her skin was soft and her bone structure delicate. Then he crouched, placing both hands above her knees, startled again by the fragility of her bones. Touching her felt right, and the clamoring always alive in his chest quieted. "I'm going to find a phone and call my brothers. Then we'll figure out a way to get you home—if you want to go back home."

Her forehead wrinkled when she focused on him. "Of course I want to go home. Why wouldn't I?"

Damn, her naïveté hit him square in the solar plexus, aiming hard for the bundle of nerves that could decapitate him. Or was it naïveté? Being in the commander's vicinity meant strategies and lies, so maybe she'd just been in the dark for too long. The commander had gone so far as to plant false files about Jory. Part of him wanted to explain reality to her, while the other part thought it'd be best for her to retain a sense of wonder with her father.

He'd never had a father.

Sure, he'd Matt and Nate, but even then, they'd been brothers. They all probably had different egg donors, but it didn't feel that way. They were brothers, bound to the soul.

He liked it that way.

Even so, what about Piper? She had a real, living, flesh-and-blood father. But he was fucking evil.

Although, would he be evil with Piper? Jory knew his brothers could be brutal killers, and yet they loved and trusted each other completely. Maybe Piper had a chance to see, to experience, a different side of the commander. Although what Jory had already seen didn't look good.

Deep down, where hope still managed to keep a tendril hold, he hoped for Piper. He didn't want to tell her the full truth, but he might need her cooperation. "Didn't you wonder why the commander wasn't really in your life?"

She shook her head, her chin lifting. "He didn't know about me until I turned seventeen."

Jory blinked. Shit. Should he tell her the truth? The commander was lying to her, and it wasn't right. "He knew about you, sweetheart. He told me when he discovered he was having a girl, he decided not to get involved."

Twin splotches of red spun into Piper's face. "You're lying."

"I'm not." Should he have? Although he was suddenly experiencing emotions, he didn't know which ones to trust. Currently, he just needed her safe. "Piper, just think about it. For now, I have to go find a phone in one of the nearby cabins." He'd seen smoke, so somebody was out camping. "Can I trust you to stay here?"

She held her hands out to the fire, her shoulders shivering, dismissing him. "I don't have anywhere else to go."

The mournfulness in the statement hit him square in the gut, but he knew better than to apologize. "I'll be back as soon as possible, and then we'll figure out a way for you to get home."

She kept her gaze averted, her focus on the fire. "Fine."

He sighed. Yeah, he'd left her with nowhere to go, and that sucked. But at least he was keeping her safe. Temporarily. "I'll be back shortly."

Even so, he paused at the doorway to take one last look at her. Just to make a memory in case the night went to hell, which was more than possible. In profile, she looked like perfection. Angled face, small features, strong jaw. She held her hands out to the fire, and shadows danced across her freely. She didn't look his way—pure stubbornness.

He loved that spunk.

Closing the door, he took a deep breath to view the raging storm. Even while standing under the small eave, rain and hail smashed into his clothing, turning him instantly wet. He banished the sense of cold as he'd been trained, this mission being nothing compared to one in the Ukraine years ago. He'd nearly frozen off his ears there while trying to find a hidden computer control room.

He'd found the room and disabled the computers.

Even now, he could feel the cold, though.

Ducking his head, he dodged into the melee, brushing pine needles out of his hair. He wove through trees, sticking close to the river. The scent of smoke tickled his senses, and he followed the smell.

He found a cabin sending beacons of light out wide windows. Rustic but well built, the porch held a myriad of fishing equipment. Inside, boisterous laughter echoed. Tuning in his senses, the ones way beyond normal, Jory discerned three heartbeats, a mixture of rum, beer, and Jack Daniels, as well as the scent of two dogs.

Man camp.

One of the heartbeats skipped every once in a while. The guy should get that checked.

They'd have a cell phone or two, so there were a couple of options. Jory could ask for help or just take the phone with force, but remaining unseen was a better choice. Plus, he really didn't want to beat up a few older guys just having a vacation. So he'd be back when they'd passed out.

From the smell of booze, it'd be a couple of hours.

He spotted two coolers off the side of the worn porch and

slowly eased open the first one. Eureka. Cold cuts, cheese, and crackers. He could at least get some food into Piper while they waited for a chance to steal the phone.

Yeah, he was self-aware enough to know that he wanted to spend more time with her, and he knew this was his only chance. So he took it.

Grabbing the food and a couple of sodas, he fought through the storm to reach their borrowed cabin.

Ten yards away, he knew she wasn't there. The cabin lay too quiet in the storm. No breathing, no heartbeat, no sense of life.

Holy fucking damn it.

He ran inside and tossed the food on the table. The woman was supposed to be a genius, and she'd gone out in the storm? A rare heat wound down his throat, and his fingers clenched. What if something happened to her?

Drawing deep, he centered himself in a crazy universe and opened his senses—the ones he never used. The ones he was afraid made him less than human, and more something else.

God knows what the scientists had done to him.

Her scent caught on the breeze, and like a bloodhound, he turned and tracked.

The wind fought him, throwing rain, hail, and even rocks at his face. Like an animal, he stayed low, weaving through trees and shrubs. A branch slashed across his jaw, and he paused. The trail split into two directions. One looked like it widened into almost a road, while the other narrowed into tall grass toward the river.

The obvious choice was the road.

So he turned toward the river. Piper was anything but obvious.

Mud coated his legs and tried to capture his feet in the cheap boots, but he plunged ahead. The rain chilled and dug deep, and he needed to reach Piper before she froze. She had to be struggling by now.

Movement up ahead narrowed his focus.

Damn woman.

She jogged alongside the swollen river, her head down, water beating her small body.

Admiration filtered through him to compete with the fury.

As she stumbled, anger won.

"Goddamn it, Piper," he yelled, rushing toward her. If she wasn't careful, the woman would drown.

She whirled around, her eyes wide. "How the hell?"

Now that would take much too long to explain. So he reached her in several strides, his fury rising.

Her red nose and watery eyes showed her struggle, as did the shivers wracking her tight little body. Mud covered her to her knees, and the rain had plastered her clothing to her.

Her very fit, very nicely curved body.

She held out both hands to ward him off. "Get the hell away from me." Her voice barely carried through the storm, and the wind seemed almost gleeful at whipping the sound into nothingness.

He stepped into her and looked down. "Where exactly did you think you were going?" His voice had no problem beating the wind.

She pressed her hands to her hips. "I was following the river down."

Yeah, good plan. A river always led somewhere. She eyed him and then sighed.

A gust of wind hit them, and Piper stumbled.

Jory grabbed her to keep her from going over the bank, and she reacted instantly, shoving him and screaming.

He let go, hands up. God. He'd only wanted to—

The ground gave away, and suddenly he was falling. Shit.

He tucked his arms close while drawing up his legs, prepared to impact hard.

He hit a rock, and pain lanced through his hip. The river caught him, swinging him around. Instant cold shot up his legs. He levered up onto his chest and kicked against the water, trying to get out of the current, his fingers digging into loose rocks lining the bank.

"Jory!" Piper dropped onto her stomach at the remaining edge of land, looking down at him with wide eyes. She reached for him, scattering small rocks and chunks of mud down the embankment.

He waved her off. "Get back."

"No." Her face contorting, she grunted while trying to reach for him.

Contrary woman. She'd thought about tossing his ass in the river, and now she was risking herself to save him? Damn but she was a true sweetheart, and she deserved a hell of a lot better than she was getting from anybody. He grabbed the nearest rock while the river fought to drag him into the rushing current. "Get the hell back," he yelled.

Her eyes widened, and she yanked her arm up.

Too late.

The entire bank erupted, sliding toward the river with a roar of sound. Mud and weeds sprayed in every direction. Lightning crackled above with glee.

Piper yelped, her arms windmilling, her legs kicking as the mudslide carried her down toward the river.

He ducked his head as the entire rolling disaster roared by him.

With a thickening splash, the mass hit the rushing water.

CHAPTER
10

JORY REACHED FOR her, but Piper flew over his head to crash in the center of the river. Her loud yelp echoed as the river tried to sweep her way.

Damn it. He released his hold on the bank and shoved himself into the current, his arms stretched out to prevent his head from hitting rocks. The smell of dirt and pine filled his nose. Up ahead, the river bounced Piper along, careening her into a bunch of branches.

Her face paled to an alarming pallor, and she scrambled to grab hold of safety. The water smashed her into a bumbling log, and she bent backward, going under.

Jory growled and kicked against a rock, propelling himself closer to her.

She came up sputtering, her hair matted against her face, her arms flailing.

The roar of the angry river destroyed any forest quietness. Jory reached her and grasped her biceps, tugging her into his body to keep her from the rocks. She fit into him so easily—so damn small. The river increased in pace, barreling over a rush of rapids. A rock smashed into his thigh, and he bit back a grimace.

Piper clung to him, her face buried in his neck. He wrapped an arm around her, keeping her close, while trying to prevent them from hitting any of the jagged edges. Panic unfolded inside him, and he banished all emotion. One sharp stone scraped across his hand, and red colored the foam around them. Pain flared a second later.

Piper tried to turn and fight the water, and he tightened his hold. "Go limp, baby. Just once. Trust me," he murmured, his mouth nearly touching her ear. He couldn't fight both the woman and the river.

She stiffened and then slowly relaxed against him.

He let out a breath he hadn't realized he'd been holding. On some level, she trusted him.

Determination filtered along his spine and through his muscles. He wouldn't allow the river to win.

A rock cut into his shoulder, spreading agony. Pain quickly became irrelevant, and his attention focused razor-sharp to protecting Piper. He kept her head above water, kicking off the bottom, trying to find a way out of the rapids. The river attacked them, sweeping them along, and a branch nailed him in the cheek. Pivoting around, he grappled for purchase, his hand sliding along the wood. Slivers pierced his skin.

With a growl, he wrapped his hand around the wood. The other end of the thick branch remained entrenched in mud and attached to the bank. Wood cracked, and he propelled closer to muddy land, dragging Piper while the water fought him. She'd wrapped her arms around his torso, and her thighs clasped his.

When the woman decided to trust, she did it completely, now didn't she? A totally inappropriate thought of her wrapped around him in another way flashed through his brain.

He shook his wet hair and inched toward the shore. Keeping Piper upstream, water pooled against her back, shoving her even closer into him.

She manacled herself to him, her back stiffening.

"We're almost there," he whispered, hitching them toward the bank. With a grunt, he swung her around and tossed her to safety.

She landed on her hands and knees in the mud. Water sprayed, and she began to crawl toward the bank. Thank God.

Jory's shoulders relaxed even as the river fought him. Rain splattered down, reducing visibility to a gray haze. He hauled himself along the branch while the river battled him with debris and roaring water. The shore was so close. Suddenly, the branch broke with a shattering crash.

He tumbled back, hitting his head on something sharp. Flashes of light sparked behind his eyes, and pain ripped through his brain. Nausea slammed hard into his gut.

On his back, he lifted his head, trying to stay free of the water as it pummeled him. His boots dug into the rocky shore, while the river tried to break him free.

"Jory!" Piper yelled. She turned in the mud and shoved herself toward him, hands outstretched. Cold fingers dug into his muddy sock, and she grunted while trying to pull him away from the river, her knees sliding in the mud.

His head went under, and water splashed up his nose. Shaking his head, trying to focus, he lifted up, coughing. What in the world was going on? He opened his eyes.

Piper had scrambled up his body, one hand clutching his chest while the other held on to the remaining portion of the branch, anchoring her somewhat to shore. She pulled at him, her neck stretching with the effort. "Come on."

Now she was trying to save him? The river beat against his face, and his temper finally roared. Enough of this crap. He sat up, yanked his legs free, and then stood.

The water rushed against his legs, trying to knock him over.

Lowering his chin, he clamped what was left of the branch with one hand, grasped Piper by the arm with his free hand, and dragged them both out of the water through reeds to the bank. They both staggered as if on a three-week bender. The river bellowed, sounding angry to lose them. Sucking in air, he continued on and up the bank until reaching a shelter of swaying pine trees.

He glanced down and faced Piper. "Are you hurt?"

She shook her head and wiped water off her face. Her clothes were plastered to her body, and she shivered. Even her lips had turned blue.

He took a quick inventory of his injuries. Headache, cuts and bruises, and maybe a sprained knee. Nothing he had to feel right now.

So he glanced around and calculated the distance to the cabin. Not bad. The river had turned suddenly, so much of their downstream jaunt had been perpendicular to the cabin. "Stay on my six." Turning, he began jogging through the brush, ignoring all pain.

For once, she didn't argue. And she kept up well enough that his body began to relax. While his head ached and his hip pounded, Piper seemed to be moving smoothly, thus showing no injuries.

Good. He'd never forgive himself if something happened to the spunky computer guru on his watch.

Kidnapping somebody did carry responsibility, after all. The thought made him grin.

Thunder continued to bellow, and lightning lit the sky once in a while, reminding him they weren't out of danger yet. The smell of wild nature, pine, and mud filled his senses. A tree shrieked in the distance, no doubt being uprooted. What a storm.

Finally, they reached their temporary oasis.

Jory headed inside first for a cursory glance to make sure nothing had been disturbed. Piper straggled in behind him, weariness in every movement.

He quickly stoked the fire and then turned to survey her. "Are you sure you're all right?" he asked quietly.

Sparks returned to her eyes, brighter than the ones he'd just created. "All right?" Both hands went to her wet hips. "Besides being kidnapped and plunged into an icy river? Yeah. I'm freakin' great."

He knew better than to apologize. "Thanks for trying to save me."

Pretty color rose into her face, and he watched, fascinated. She swallowed. "I couldn't just let you drown."

"You're a sweetheart, Piper." Damn but those were true words. His chest warmed, and he studied every inch of her, wanting to take the moment with him, the taste of her kiss still lingering on his lips. A part of her would always be with him, that much he knew. Her shivering was beginning to concern him, however. "Time to take off your clothes, darlin'."

Piper stilled. Her head tilted to the side, and total awareness wandered down her freezing spine. "Huh?"

He smiled. Slow, dangerous, and way too gentle. "Clothes. Wet. Discard."

Smart-ass. She shook her head. "I'm not taking off my clothes." Her instant sneeze may have negated the power from her voice.

He glanced around and reached for a threadbare quilt from the sofa. "You can put this on, but you're taking off the wet clothes. I'm not allowing you to catch pneumonia and die when you're my responsibility."

"I'm not your responsibility." The words popped automatically to her mouth, which went dry as she took a good look at him. The wet shirt molded way too defined muscles in his torso, and even displayed the impossibly hard ridges of his abdomen. Tight jeans encased powerful thighs. His thick hair was slicked back, leaving the stark contours of his handsome face on full display. The purplish lump above his right eyebrow only served to make him appear even more dangerous.

Sexy as hell.

And the bad guy. Definitely the bad guy.

Except he didn't seem like a bad guy, and while he'd been using his body to shield her from rocks in the river, he hadn't felt like a bad guy. He kind of felt like a badass hero.

He cocked his head to the side. "What in the world is going through your head?"

"I'm not getting naked." Although seeing him naked held certain appeal. From an artistic standpoint, of course.

"You are." His jaw may have been made from rock. "We both know I could have your clothes off you in seconds, so I'm giving you a chance to control the situation here."

Warmth spread through her abdomen. Oh, she didn't think he'd meant the words as innuendo, but her body didn't care. Naked. With that amazing specimen of a male. She'd seen his strength and his stamina. Suddenly, her face burned.

His gaze gentled. "What are you thinking?"

"Nothing." She reached out and grabbed the blanket. What in the hell was wrong with her mind all of a sudden? Make that her hormones. "Turn around."

He snorted. "I've seen naked women before."

Oh, she could just guess. "Turn the hell around."

With a suffering male sigh, he turned around. And shoved down his wet jeans.

She gulped. Wow. Great ass. Tight, hard, and perfectly masculine. Apparently he had no trouble getting naked in front of her.

But why would he? The man was perfection. She bit back a moan as he shrugged out of his briefs.

Take off the shirt. Take off the shirt. Take off—

Good Lord. He took off the shirt. Hard muscles rippled as he yanked the wet cotton over his head to toss next to the fire. Scars of different sizes punctuated his impressive back. Round scars, long scars...probably knives and guns.

She swallowed. Something sad, something so damn feminine in her wanted to kiss his hurts. To smooth the pain away. No matter the mistakes he'd made, somebody had harmed him badly. More than once. "You said my father raised you with brothers, and he said he recruited you at eighteen and gave you soldiers as brothers—who you betrayed."

His back stiffened. "I've never betrayed my brothers."

It sounded so much like Jory was telling the truth. "I don't know who to believe."

"I know, baby." He sighed and stretched. "I'm sorry."

So was she, and even the thought of doubting the father she'd always wanted to know flushed her with shame. But Jory didn't seem to be the cold-blooded killer her father had described. She had to get some answers. "How long you been a soldier?"

Jory turned around, eyebrows raised. "My entire life."

It probably felt that way. Three scars from what appeared to be bullets marred his chest but somehow had missed the intricate tattoo right above his heart. "Pretty. What does it mean?" she asked.

"Freedom," he said, his voice a low rumble.

Heat flared again to her face as she tried to keep eye contact. She would not look lower than his chest. Or abs. "Not shy, are you."

"Nope." His grin turned charming into something lethal. "Your turn."

She was a grown-ass woman. A computer genius, and she'd certainly seen a nude man before. Yet her hands shook, and her eyes actually stung with the need to look lower.

Do. Not. Look. Lower.

Holy fucking shit. She looked lower. The guy was built. Really, really, really built.

As if sensing her perusal, his cock perked up.

Oh God.

Her gaze flew to his face. Humor lit his odd gray eyes, and he barked out a chuckle. A totally comfortable, making fun of himself, male chuckle.

Her heart thumped—and warmed. "You have *got* to put something on."

"I'd love to put something on," he murmured, his voice lowering to hoarse and hot. Those eyes darkened to the color of the storm clouds outside, lit within from heat. A whole lot of heat.

A shiver wandered down her spine, and her thighs softened. She ignored her traitorous body and rolled her eyes. An impish part of her would love to take him by surprise and agree, but he'd no doubt meet her halfway, and then she'd be in a pickle. So she went for defensive, unable to keep her lips from twitching. "Knock it off."

"I can't seem to help it." Good humor creased his cheek. Yet he sighed and turned to rummage through a cupboard near the fireplace. Seconds later, he'd wrapped a worn flowered blanket around his hips.

He should've looked ridiculous, yet the feminine cover-up just enhanced his wildness.

And something wild lived in Jory. There was no question.

A part of her, one that she'd tried to tame with logic and computer science, perked up. Temptation to meet his wildness with her own warmed her core and softened her thighs.

His gaze grew predatory, as if he sensed the battle waging inside her.

Her heart beat hard enough to speed up her breath. The storm raged outside, while the fire crackled inside. She swallowed, trying to control herself. Enough of this silliness. "Turn around."

He turned around, once again revealing his warrior's back.

The man embodied danger, and she had to keep that foremost in her mind. Most serial killers were sexy and charming, too.

He snorted.

Shit. She'd said that out loud. Her fingers cramped when she shoved off her wet clothes, hurriedly wrapping the rough blanket around her. Why did he make her feel like a bumbling innocent? "Um. Okay. I'm not a virgin for Pete's sakes." She mumbled the last.

He laughed again as he turned to face her.

She frowned. "You heard that?" How in the world? She'd mumbled so quietly she couldn't even hear her voice, and yet he'd somehow heard her? Supersonic hearing wasn't possible, was it?

"Yes. I'm not a virgin, either. Was that an invitation, by any chance?" Boyish hopefulness curved his lips.

Hell. There wasn't anything boyish about the man standing strong and sure, the fire lighting him from behind. "No." Her nipples hardened in pure denial to her words. "Not a chance."

His gaze penetrated her, and a long shiver wound down her spine. His gaze darkened. Yeah. He'd seen the shiver. Damn it.

"Are you sure?" he rumbled.

Her voice trembled. "Yes."

"Okay." He reached for her discarded clothing to lay out near the fire.

His acquiescence sounded temporary somehow.

As she shoved away sexual desire, the cold took over. She tried to bite her lip to prevent her teeth from chattering. Tremors shook her shoulders, but her feet remained planted. To get nearer to the fire, she needed to get closer to Jory, and the safest spot for her right now was on the other side of the sofa.

Finished with his task, he turned to survey her, more heat in his gaze than from the fire. "You're still cold."

She shook her head. "Keep your clichéd ass on that side of the sofa."

He smiled and reached over the back of the couch.

She couldn't help her smirk. No way could he get the leverage to lift her. Nobody was that strong.

So when he wrapped strong hands around her arms, she didn't struggle. Then he lifted her. She yelped as she all but flew over the back of the couch to impact his corded chest.

So much heat enfolded her, she forgot all about the cold. Her breath caught, and her body began to hum.

Turning, he dropped onto the sofa with her cradled in his arms.

She gaped. "That's not normal strength."

"You don't weigh *that* much." He settled her more comfortably on his lap.

"Hey." She wanted to punch him, but so much warmth came from his fit body that she had to fight the urge to snuggle right in. Or turn and straddle him. Her mouth actually watered with the need to run her lips across his unbelievable neck. Strong cords tempted every taste bud she had.

The fire heated her other side, catching her between two infernos. With the storm outside, the fire's glow inside added a surreal intimacy to the moment. If she forgot herself, if she let go of suspiciousness and reality, she could jump right into the heat.

He snuggled her closer, and her eyelids dropped to half-mast. Maybe she'd been more chilled than she'd feared, because she was completely losing control.

"Just relax, Piper. You're safe." His breath brushed her hair, and her body went on full alert. Full, sexy, sitting on a hard male alert.

Her lips almost touched his bronze skin. "This is unbelievable."

"I like it."

She breathed out. "I'm sure. Don't tell me. You imagined us in a romantic cabin with a storm outside—both of us nude and warming up. You're kidding me, right?"

"That's not how I imagined us." His lips barely grazed her forehead. The husky tenor of his voice caressed her, zinged right through her, and landed hard between her legs. Right where she wanted him to be.

She knew better. Yep. She totally knew better, but she asked anyway. "How did you imagine us?" Then she held her breath. God, she truly was a moron.

"Under the stars, you on your hands and knees, me taking you from behind."

Her nervous system sparked alive, while her chest hitched. The image smashed into her brain, vividly alive and vibrant. Desire flushed through her to heat her sex. "I, ah, didn't expect you to be graphic."

"Sometimes honesty is graphic." He shifted, the powerful muscles in his chest moving against her back.

"This can't happen, Jory." Sitting in his arms, warmed by the fire, it was difficult to keep a grasp on reality.

"I know."

His easy acceptance spiked down her spine. "You kidnapped me, and you're my father's enemy." Yet confusion swirled through her brain. Not her body, though. Her body was all in right now, hungering for the man holding her so tight. "I'm sorry." Why did she apologize? Maybe because reality sucked, and she wished for a fantasy. With Jory. She so had to change the subject, and she had to uncover the truth. Any truth, because too much wasn't adding up. "You said you have brothers. Are you the oldest?"

He shook his head. "Nope. I'm the youngest of four."

She blinked. "If that were true, I'd be surprised. You're so in control of everything."

His laugh rumbled through her. "Then you should meet my oldest brother, Mattie. Talk about in control."

She played with a loose string on the blanket still covering her. "You also said that my . . . the commander . . . raised you?"

"Yes. They created us and raised us as an experiment—as soldiers. My first kill happened when I was thirteen. A drug overlord in a jungle that doesn't even exist any longer."

Her chest hurt with the idea of his childhood—real or imagined. He sounded like he was telling the truth, but he was trained, right? Though how could she be this attracted to him otherwise? "Is that true?" she whispered.

"Yes."

He sounded so truthful, but how could that be? "I don't understand. The military doesn't just create people."

"I don't think the commander has exactly worked within the military guidelines his whole life. He really is the one who had the chips implanted near our spines." Jory let out a low groan when Piper wriggled to get her balance on his hard groin.

She stilled. "Um. Sorry." How could he be telling the truth? "If they created you, why were you in a cell?" Even half turned on by the impossibly hard body surrounding her, she felt nausea spiraling through her stomach. Could it be true?

Jory brushed his lips across her forehead in a gesture far more comforting than she'd ever received from her father. "We escaped five years ago. Blew up the Tennessee compound and got loose—even went to Disneyland for a week."

Her mind spun. "I can't take all of this in. It doesn't make sense."

Jory's large hand cupped her head and pressed her into his neck. "Try to get some sleep. I'll head over and secure a cell phone from the fishing cabin in a couple of hours when the men there pass out."

She lifted her head to face him. "I'm not sure whether or not to believe you."

"I know." He smoothed the hair from her face. "I don't blame you."

Then why did she feel so damn guilty? Her gaze dropped to his lips. Full and sensual, she already knew the kind of electricity they could generate.

"Piper?" he asked.

Damn. She leaned forward, pressing her mouth to his. Just for saving her from the river, just for being somebody she wished she could know better. Just to quench the fire crackling in her nerves.

He inhaled, going still.

Possessed by something unreal, she flattened her hand over his chest and molded her lips to his.

With a sound of torment, his mouth moved, and he took over. Completely. Cupping her head, he held her in place, going deep. His tongue played with hers, while his body enfolded her.

She kissed him back, fire lighting down her spine. So much need.

The kiss went on forever until she was writhing on his lap, needing more than anything to get closer. So much closer.

Finally, he broke the kiss, levering back to study her.

They both breathed heavily, and lust had turned his eyes a dangerous midnight-filled smoke. His cock pulsed full and hard right beneath her buttocks.

He licked his lips.

She groaned.

Then he shook his head. "This can't happen."

"I know." Her voice came out breathy. More than anything, her body wanted this to happen. Her mind knew better. "I'm sorry."

His grin was slow. "Don't be. This just became one of my

favorite memories." At the sweet sentiment, he once again tucked her into his neck. "Go to sleep, Piper."

She sighed into his heated skin and tried to relax. While her body's need didn't surprise her, the ache in her heart surely did. There was a lot more to Jory than she'd expected, and the fact that she wouldn't be able to peel his layers hurt somewhere deep inside.

Not only had he kidnapped her, but she wasn't sure whether or not to believe him. She wanted to, but honestly? Soldiers created in test tubes? Unbelievable. Even so, she kissed him on the jugular—a good-bye and sadness for what could never be.

He responded by tightening his hold and dropping his chin atop her head. "I know," he whispered. "I know."

CHAPTER
11

J ORY KEPT HIS back to the cabin door, waiting. The rain continued to pummel the earth, while thunder bellowed and lightning struck like an angry child. As storms went, it was a master.

He'd tossed on wet clothes, run through the woods, and had easily confiscated a cell phone from the snoring fisherman to text a coded message to his brothers around dawn. Yet another day closer to the chips exploding—four days left on earth for him. More than anything, he'd wanted to call his family, to hear a familiar voice, but he knew better. The coded text would bring his brothers to him as soon as possible.

Man, he hoped they were all alive and well. Dr. Madison had lied to him before, and he wouldn't be surprised if she'd lied again about their being alive. But in his heart, wouldn't he know if something had happened to one of his brothers? Something deep in him, past his gut, would hurt. Bad.

Piper slept inside, sprawled on the couch, her slumber punctuated by restless movements. He'd waited until she'd fallen asleep before heading out for the cell phone. Yeah, he'd thought about tying her up to ensure she didn't run again, but he just couldn't bind her.

She'd trusted him completely in the river, and then she'd tried to save his life. In his book, that meant he worked with her instead of against her. If she wanted to run, he wouldn't stop her.

Plus, the woman had been *out*.

Now, he waited. For nearly two hours, he'd been on high alert... waiting. For any sign, any sound, any damn vibration in the air around him.

He could see vibrations. Always could.

But the storm was fucking with his perception, causing his shoulders to tighten harder than rock. And even after running through the storm for the cell phone, his dick remained at full attention. Having Piper on his lap had nearly killed him, and letting her fall asleep, so warm and naked, had taken every ounce of control he possessed.

She'd been vulnerable, and he might have been able to seduce her. But while he hadn't had a mama to teach him right from wrong, he knew the difference.

Piper should be protected at all costs. Even from him. Shit. Especially from him.

A vibration of a different frequency caught his attention.

The door opened inward behind him, and only his sure stance kept him from landing on his butt. "Go back inside,

Piper." He tried to keep his voice low and controlled while staring into the storm. Something was coming.

"No." She slid to his side, her knuckles white on the blanket wrapped around her. Tentatively, she reached out to touch his arm. "Why are you standing outside?"

The pretty woman liked physical contact, and her touch was gentle. He shut his eyes to just feel. He'd been with women before, and he'd actually liked a couple of them. But this one had a softness to her, a natural way of touching that spoke to his heart. It was all Piper, and he wished he could know more of her. Know all of her.

"Jory?" she asked, still caressing his arm. She probably didn't even know she did it, and that made the moment all the sweeter. "Come back inside. The storm is getting worse."

She was a temptation, but he could hear a helicopter coming from a distance. Fast and flying low. The air shifted around him just enough that his eyelids flipped open. "Go back inside, beautiful." Somebody was coming—either the commander or Jory's brothers.

If the commander had intercepted the message, the bastard needed to believe Piper had been taken against her will. So she had to get inside and look like a prisoner.

If Jory's brothers were coming, he wanted a chance to explain who she was before they started making plans.

More important, he wanted a moment alone with them.

"I'm staying," she breathed.

A light flickered through the clouds. He settled his stance, gauging the forest for secured areas. Were his brothers coming, or would he need to run for cover?

If the commander had somehow intercepted his message, then he'd bring four soldiers on the copter, fully armed. Jory would need to incapacitate one soldier in order to confiscate a weapon. He'd need only one gun against the four soldiers.

The commander had no clue as to his true killing abilities, and neither did the other soldiers.

If the commander had sent only one helicopter, he'd drastically fucked up.

Jory turned and set Piper inside, shutting the door before she could blink, much less protest. Then he crossed to the side of the cabin and crouched, ready to attack the first man to hit the ground.

He welcomed the sense of battle into his movements. For years, as a cadet, he'd spent time waiting. Always looking out windows. He banished all memories of being a frightened kid in the facility waiting for his brothers to return from war.

There was no fear, and his reality was war.

Helicopter blades whipped through the early morning. An unfamiliar Blackhawk dropped onto the ground, slowly going quiet.

He prepared himself to spring. His muscles tensed, vibrating with the urge to run and rip off the door of the helicopter.

The pilot's door opened, and a figure stepped into the storm.

Emotion hit him like a bat to the gut. "Mattie," he croaked. Then he was running. Hard and fast across uneven ground, through the pelting rain, straight for his oldest brother.

They impacted with the sound of muscle hitting muscle. Matt caught him in a hug that was hard, fierce, and definitely home.

Tears and rain ran down his face, and he truly didn't give a shit.

He leaned back and took a shuddering breath. "Matt."

Matt nodded, emotion swirling in his eyes. Fierce and strong, he'd gotten even bigger in the last two years, danger all but cascading off him like steam. "You okay?"

So much more than the mere words lived in the question. "Yeah." Jory's shoulders settled. "I'm good. You?"

"I am now." Matt grabbed his arms and looked deep.

Jory nodded. The only thing Matt had ever asked of him was to stay alive, and he'd done it. "Yeah. I'm really okay now."

Matt nodded, his chest visibly settling. "We left you all alone. I broke my promise."

Ah. Their mantra from childhood. *Never alone.* "No, you didn't. You trained me to survive, and I did. You made sure I was never alone, and here I am. Definitely not alone."

Something eased in Matt's eyes. Something haunted now cleared.

A side door slammed open. Rough hands whipped him away from Matt, and Nate had him tight, holding on. He laughed and clapped him on the shoulder. "It's you. It's really you," Nate said on an exhale, joy in the sound.

Jory smiled as he could actually feel tension drain from Nate. The middle brother had split his time between ensuring Matt stayed sane and trying to keep the younger brothers safe. Having a brother lost somewhere would've tortured him. "I'm fine, Nate. I missed you."

"Missed you more, brother," Nate croaked. He smiled at Matt, relief curving his lips.

"My turn." Shane Dean yanked him close, hitting his back hard enough to bruise. "God. I knew you were alive. I *knew* it."

As the youngest brothers, Jory and Shane had shared everything. He'd worried about Shane, who was often angry. Jory nodded and stepped back. "You okay?"

Shane wiped his eyes. "Yeah. Now." He shook his head, his muscles visibly vibrating. "So many times everything got dark, and I thought we'd lost you. So fucking painful."

Jory's eyes filled again, and he hugged Shane one more time. "It's all good. We're together."

Shane leaned back and chuckled right into the rain. "Good? It's a fucking miracle. Thank God."

Jory took them in. To see them. Three men, tough as steel, standing in the rain and welcoming him home. Identical gray eyes, rock-solid bodies, and pure emotion cutting lines in their faces.

"I'm sorry," he said. He'd hurt them by disappearing, even though he hadn't had a choice.

"Shut up." Shane punched his arm as if he couldn't help touching again. He'd kept his brown hair shaggy to his collar as a *fuck you* to their military upbringing, and he had to shove it out of his face in the wind. "Are you all right?"

"Yes. Was shot, was in a coma, and am now here." He could barely speak in complete sentences. They were alive...and together. Finally.

Matt nodded. "We know. Saw the tapes. Do you know who shot you?"

"No." It didn't surprise Jory that his brothers had chased down what had happened to him. "Any ideas?"

"A woman is all we know," Matt growled.

Jory bit back a wince. The only woman in his life was Dr. Madison, the closest thing he had to a mother. Even though she didn't consider him human, the thought that she'd really try to kill him spiraled nausea into his stomach. "Madison shot me?"

"Maybe. Maybe not." Matt ran a hand through his black hair, his gaze roaming over Jory's shoulder. "Speaking of women, who is that? I can hear her heart beating hard enough she sounds like she's about to have a coronary."

Jory swallowed over the lump in his throat as he turned to view Piper. She stood on the porch, her green eyes wide, her hands clutching the blanket like a lifeline. "That's a long story."

"Then I suggest you tell it," Matt said, keeping his gaze on Piper.

Jory grinned, joy all but whipping into him. Two years

apart, and Matt slid right back into giving orders. "Fine, but she decides her next move. I won't have you kidnapping her if she wants to go back."

Nate frowned, his rugged jaw square and stubborn. "Back where?"

Man, this was going to be tough.

A vibration cut through the air. Low and...heavy. An attack helicopter armed with missiles. Jory stilled and glanced up. "Did you bring reinforcements?"

"No." Matt reached for a gun in his waistband and shoved a Glock into Jory's hand. "Do you sense somebody?"

While his brothers all had enhanced senses and gifts, he was the only one to detect vibrations and changes in cosmic patterns. "Yes." The air moved as if an attack helicopter flew low.

He turned to view Piper. Heat washed down his torso, and blood rushed through his head, echoing in his ears. If they sent in missiles, she'd die. "I'll get the girl. Load up."

Piper tried to tuck the blanket more securely into her breasts, keeping them covered. Chills swept up her bare feet against the rough planks. So Jory had gotten dressed and called for help? The reunion with his brothers—and there was no question they were brothers—had spiked tears in her eyes and pummeled her abdomen with emotion.

So he had been telling the truth.

The men were huge and cut muscular hard. Dangerous men, without question. Yet a sweetness lived in the moment as they'd reconnected. Family. Definitely family. One that wasn't afraid to let tears show.

The reunion nearly broke her heart. How long had they been apart?

Why had her father lied about Jory's family? More important, what else had her father lied about? A hollowness echoed through her abdomen.

Four pairs of identical gunmetal gray eyes focused on her, yanking her out of her thoughts. An absolute pinning focus. Her knees trembled. She couldn't move.

She gulped air. Who the hell were they? Really?

Running seemed like a good idea, yet totally absurd. Her mind clicked scenarios and reality into statistical analysis. Shoeless and wearing a blanket, she wouldn't make it three yards—and she'd probably lose the blanket.

So she lifted her chin and met Jory's gaze directly. He'd been careful with her, and he'd saved her from drowning. If she had an ally in the gray-eyed group, he'd be it.

He glanced up, said something to the others, and then all hell broke loose.

A weird pattering sound filled the morning, while men dropped from the skies on ropes. Jory raced across the distance in a zigzag pattern. She held out a hand to stop him, her mind fuzzing.

He reached her, yanked her up, and smacked her in a chest hard enough to knock the wind out of her. Without missing a stride, he turned in one smooth motion before she could utter a word. She grabbed on to his shirt for balance and screamed. He ducked his head over her to zigzag back toward the helicopter. Mud popped up next to them, and she gasped. Her mind swirled.

They were being shot at.

Jory's brothers' helicopter whirred into action, and his family leaned out, all shooting at the men in black who'd dropped from the sky.

One of the brothers jerked back, growled, and kept fighting.

How badly was he shot?

Jory bent low over her, protecting her. Panic heated up her lungs, all reality faded, and she started to struggle.

She had to get out of there. Away from the shooting and blood.

They reached the helicopter, and her fists pounded into his chest. A man shouted as he ran around the cabin, and she turned to stare.

Her father. She gasped. He faltered and stopped firing, his black eyes blazing. "Your brother gave you up, Matt. Brought you right to me." His voice rose like power over the fight and through the rain.

Jory faltered. "Asshole."

"Let me go." Piper shoved at Jory's chin, squirming to keep him from throwing her in the copter. She didn't know him—not really. Where were they going? What about her mother? Piper couldn't just leave.

"Let Piper go. Now." The commander braced his legs as if unafraid of any bullet.

"No." Jory used his body as a shield around her, and she tried not to find comfort in his protection. This was over the top.

The commander slid dark glasses off his eyes, his gaze sliding to the front of the craft. "Matthew. So good to see you again. Come home, boy."

Jory's black-haired brother leaned out the pilot's window, his gun out. "I have a new home, asshole. Leave us alone, or I'll take you out." He ducked back as bullets pinged into the side of the copter. "Everyone load up," he ordered, returning fire.

He sounded a lot like Jory, in control and threatening.

The commander ducked to the side of the cabin and out of the open.

Jory bent low, holding her against the metal as his brothers fired around them, providing cover. "One chance to come with us. I won't force you."

She shook her head, surprised to find him blurry through tears. Those eyes. She'd never forget those eyes. "I can't leave my mom."

Jory's jaw tightened. He faltered, and an odd vulnerability glowed in his eyes to be quickly snuffed out. "I never had a mom, but if I had one, I wouldn't leave her." He brushed a kiss across Piper's forehead as the firefight waged on around them. "Okay. Then fight me, and make it look good."

What the hell did he think she'd been doing? But her mind swirled that he thought her father needed to see her fight. That her father wouldn't trust her otherwise. Opening her mouth, she screamed and punched with every ounce of fear consuming her.

Jory's grip faltered. "More," he hissed. She kicked and screamed and fought, honestly with everything she had.

"Sorry about this, Pipe." Dropping her, Jory grabbed his eye as if she'd punched him, and yet held on to the blanket. "Run."

She screeched. The blanket shredded away as he jumped into the helicopter. It rose into the air, the men firing all around. Fury heating her ears, she turned and ran full bore for her father by the cabin door. Buck-assed naked.

The gunfire increased, and the soldiers ignored her barefoot dash through mud and weeds to reach the door.

Somehow, she knew Jory wouldn't let her get shot. She leaped into the cabin and whirled around to see him watching her, his gun covering her. He'd made sure she got safely inside.

She panted out air, and her chest hitched. The oddest part of her wanted to change her mind and go with him.

Then, with a quick nod, he pointed his weapon toward the forest as the helicopter continued to rise. Even as the storm pummeled him, he fired toward the forest, his gaze remaining on her. She watched him until he disappeared into the clouds, her body trembling with a shocking sense of loss.

Heart pounding, she leaped inside and went straight for her clothes at the fire. Jerking them on with shaking fingers, she ducked against the sofa until the firing stopped. She slowly lifted her head.

Silence.

Drawing in air, she crept toward the door and glanced outside. The commander was speaking into a radio. "They're up and out of here. If you can't bring them down peacefully, blow them out of the air. I want proof of life...or proof of death."

Piper opened the door, her eyes wide. "No," she whispered.

His black eyes narrowed. "You need to be debriefed."

CHAPTER
12

JORY FINISHED TYING a bandage around Matt's upper arm. "Went right through," he said, patting tape into place. The smell of mildew and old cigarettes filtered around and made him need to sneeze.

Yet being with his brothers, finally, felt like home. "I didn't bring the commander to you." They had to believe him. No matter what, he'd never give up his brothers.

"We know." Matt kept his gray gaze on him while sitting on a ragtag orange bedspread in a hotel in the middle of nowhere. Nate and Shane nodded.

"Duh," Shane muttered and slapped his back in a show of support.

Jory threw him a glare in an attempt to hide the relief coursing through him. His brothers believed in him. How could he forget that, even for a moment?

No expression softened Matt's hard face, but emotion shone hard and bright in his eyes. "I'm sorry, Jor."

Jory blinked. "Getting caught was my fault, Mattie. Not yours." For as long as Jory could remember, Matt had taken responsibility for them all. Not knowing where Jory had been for two years would've torn him apart. "I'm sorry."

Shane tossed him a beer while Nate smoothly slid needle and thread through Shane's forearm to seal a hole. "Enough apologies. We're here, we're alive, and we just crashed a helicopter into a Utah forest." He grinned. "Let the commander go through that wreckage."

Nate snorted.

Jory rubbed his aching neck, almost too full to speak. God, he'd missed them. "That was quite the plan you had." They'd landed the copter and immediately jumped into an SUV hidden in the trees before blowing the Blackhawk to pieces while the other helicopters chased their asses in the clouds. "How did you put it together so quickly?"

Nate took a long swallow of beer. "We called in a couple of favors. It worked."

Jory opened his beer and studied his brothers. Being away from them, not sure if they lived, had been like a fist continually gripping his heart. Now, finally, he could breathe.

His brothers were all about six-five, and he had an inch on them. One he'd gloated over so long ago. In the last two years, his brothers had hardened even more, which he wouldn't have thought possible. But new lines fanned out from Matt's eyes. Laugh lines. Shane seemed relaxed...for Shane. He sat easily, leaning against an ugly yellow chair, his face more angular than Matt's but his eyes just as fierce. And Nate. The worried brother, the furious protector...calmness surrounded him. Even on high alert, he owned focus.

"What the hell did I miss?" Jory asked before tipping back his head and letting the cool brew slide down.

Shane shrugged. "I recaptured my wife."

Jory grinned. He'd never met Josie, but he'd seen pictures.

The woman looked like Tinker Bell with an attitude. "Was she willing?"

"Eventually," Shane said.

Good. That was good. Jory nodded. Shane had been miserable when he'd left Josie, and seeing him happy was the best thing that could've happened for Jory. No more anger for his big brother.

Nate smiled. "I hunted Audrey down, and now she's pregnant."

Jory nodded and scrutinized his brother. Nate seemed... happy. "Yeah, I heard. Congrats to you both." Sweet Audrey was somehow Dr. Madison's daughter, and they couldn't be more different.

He'd missed a lot, and he wished he could've been there to help his brothers. But the idea that they'd actually found happiness, that they'd move on once he died, settled an ache in his chest. This was good.

He turned toward Matt, wondering what Matt thought of having women in the family.

Matt finished his beer. "I fell in love with one of the commander's doctors, and now she's ready to take the chips out of our spines the second we force them off-line."

Jory stilled. He stopped his beer halfway to his mouth while studying his oldest brother. No tell. Then he looked toward Nate and then Shane. No amusement. "You're kidding."

"Nope." Matt reached for another beer.

Nate shifted a knife against his calf. "Laney Lou is a sweetheart. You'll like her, Jory."

Jory scratched his chin. Nate was the most cynical person ever born, so if he liked the woman, she must be amazing. Still. One of the commander's doctors? "Congrats?"

"Thanks." Matt tossed him another beer. "You'll meet her when we get picked up tonight."

Now he really wanted to meet the woman who'd captured Matt's heart. But first, they had another mission to take. Jory took a deep breath. "We can't leave."

Nate leaned forward, his elbows on his knees. "We have the computer program, and now that your brain is back with us, you can figure out how to deactivate the chips."

Jory nodded, his chest all but bursting. Even though they had the program, they didn't have the frequency or the codes. The damn fucking codes that somehow changed easily in the right program. "That's exactly what I'll do."

He'd watched Piper on the computer, but too much needed to come together in the time frame they had left. There just wasn't enough time left. He'd tell them about his chip after he rendered theirs useless, which was already a nearly impossible task. Just trying to remove a chip might detonate the damn thing, even with the right codes put into the right program. "But first, we have an extraction."

Matt frowned. "The woman? You released her."

Jory nearly groaned as the image of Piper running nude toward the cabin zipped through his brain. The woman had an amazing ass. Full and ripe...just his type. Then he took a drink as reality smacked him. A deep breath. His gut swirled at the thought of Chance and the other two boys still under the commander's thumb. At the boy who'd been lost.

Matt leaned forward. "Spit it out."

"There are more kids," Jory said, his voice going hoarse.

Tension slammed through the room. Matt went stone still, Shane leaped to his feet, and Nate put his back to the door.

"You sure?" Matt's voice dropped to the dark tone of death.

"Yes." Jory shoved a rough hand through his now dry hair. "Met one named Chance. Gray eyes—definitely one of us. Saw his bone structure and caught his scent."

Nate exhaled slowly, through his nose. "How many?"

"Three, counting Chance. Now." Jory tried to force emotion into a box. "We have three more brothers."

"Three *now*?" Nate asked softly.

Jory nodded, rage nearly boiling his blood. "There were four. Lost one a month ago in the field—he was eleven."

The sound Matt made could only be termed a tenor of pain.

"Fuck." Shane threw his bottle across the room to smash into the bathroom wall. "Fucking fucktard of a bastard fucktard dickhead commander. I'll take his balls and make him eat them before I rip off his fucking head."

Ah. There was that anger.

Matt paled and glanced down at his hands, failure curling his lip.

Nate, always the balancing act to Matt's guilt, kept his gaze on Matt, his back ramrod straight. "We didn't know, and now we do."

Matt rubbed his chest.

"Mattie?" Jory set down his beer, his voice softening. "There was no way for us to know. The kid—he reminded me of you. Badass attitude and total dedication to the other two kids."

Matt's head lifted, his eyes going dark. "He lost a brother. God." Agony exhaled with his breath. "Is he all right?"

"No." Jory gave the truth. "He's fucking tortured, and he's worried about the other two. He's definitely hiding something, and he may be working wholeheartedly with the commander, or he may be getting ready to make a move for freedom. I'm not sure."

"Either path will get them killed," Nate murmured.

Matt stood. He exhaled slowly, his shoulders going back. "No. Nate, cancel our pickup. Shane, clean up the fucking beer bottle. And Jory? Sit the hell down and tell us everything about the organization, the two locations, and the woman."

Better get this out of the way now. Jory cleared his throat. "She's the commander's daughter."

Shane stopped in picking up a piece of glass to glance up and over his shoulder. His eyes widened. "Have you lost your ever-lovin' mind?" He straightened.

"No." Although he had been shot in the chest and lay in a coma for two years. "I don't think so."

Nate ground a fist into one eye. "You're sure?"

"Yep. They both acknowledged the paternity, and I can see the resemblance beneath the skin." Jory reached down for a shard of glass and straightened up.

"And we let her get away, why?" Matt stood, nearly nose to nose with Jory.

Jory held his ground. "She's innocent. Last time I checked, we didn't hurt innocents."

"The commander's daughter is not innocent," Matt ground out, his eyebrows drawing down hard.

Jory kept his voice mild and his body relaxed. He let the truth in. Piper was innocent, and she wouldn't be harmed. "With that reasoning, Nate's Audrey is bad because Dr. Madison, her mother, is a psychopathic, sadistic bitch?"

Matt's nostrils flared. Tension spiraled through the oxygen again, setting the hair on the back of Jory's neck alive. Finally, Matt breathed out. "That's a good point."

"Sometimes I have one." Jory tossed the glass into a mangled bucket serving as a garbage can perched in the corner.

Matt nodded and clapped him hard across the shoulder. "I'm sorry."

"We're fine." Jory grinned. "I missed you."

Matt huffed out breath. "I haven't slept more than an hour at a time since we lost track of you. Thanks for staying alive."

Jory nodded. "I promised, didn't I?"

Matt's eyes darkened. "Yeah. Yeah, you did. Thanks."

But he couldn't stay alive for much longer, and that just

sucked. He'd worry about telling them after they were safe, but he couldn't tell them a lie because they'd all scent it. If they didn't ask the right question, it wouldn't be a problem. For now, they had to strategize. "I think Piper might help us. Since I let her go and she saw the commander in action. She's smart enough to know he's lying to her."

Nate frowned. "Wait a minute. How did the commander find you today?"

Jory froze. "I don't know."

"The woman?" Shane growled.

"No, and her name is Piper." Jory clicked through events in his head and then glanced down at his body. Where the hell was his brain, anyway? "Shit."

Matt reached for the hem of Jory's T-shirt and yanked it over his head. "Strip."

What had he been thinking? He shucked out of his clothes and stood in the middle of the room, arms out, legs spread, as his brothers poked and prodded every inch.

"Got it," Shane muttered, shoving at a scar covering one of the newest bullet holes in his sternum. "Knife."

Nate handed him a knife and leaned in, his head next to Shane's.

Pain lanced through Jory's chest, and he caught a breath as Shane yanked out a tracker device to smash on the floor. The commander had tagged him like a dog at the vet's. While Jory could sense devices in other people if he really concentrated, he couldn't sense or feel anything within his own skin.

Unfortunate but ironic, really.

Shane grimaced. "Sorry, Jor."

"It's fine," Jory muttered, knowing full well Shane had gone as easy as he could. "Doesn't hurt a bit."

"Tough guy." Matt leaned around and poured beer onto Jory's wound. "This might hurt."

Jory coughed and breathed out to keep from biting Matt's

head off. They had to disinfect the wound. "We need to run, now," Jory muttered, reaching for his jeans.

Matt nodded and tossed him the shirt. "Wait. You sure you're okay?"

Jory nodded. "Yes—stop worrying." Although it felt damn good to be around family again. People who cared. "We need to move and now."

Matt rubbed his chin. "Our best bet is to take the commander's daughter and bargain for exchange."

"No." Jory drew the cotton over his head. "The commander wants us more than her." Yeah, it was the truth, and it sucked. But the green-eyed hacker had a soft heart, and no way would she allow three kids to remain in danger, once she comprehended the danger. "I have another idea. I think she'll help the boys get free. She'll help us."

Nate shook his head. "We can't get to her. The commander will have guards on her."

Jory finally smiled. "That's all right because we'll use his own surveillance against him. I have an idea."

Piper stepped gingerly around the damaged hydrangea, a glass of Chardonnay in her hand. Her third of the night. Her mind swirled with intrigue and doubt, and she wished she could get ahold of Jory just to ask some questions.

A bush scratched her leg. If she didn't know better, she'd believe Earl was sabotaging his own computer in order to get some alone time with Piper's mom. Well, at least somebody was getting romanced. Brian had called several times, and she'd ignored him. She'd meant it when she'd said they were over.

Her mind remained steadfast on one gray-eyed badass soldier who'd protected her from rocks and bullets before letting her go free.

While being buck-assed naked.

Even so, while she'd tried to pepper the commander with questions about Jory, he'd shut her down fast. They'd ridden in different rigs back to the facility, and he'd set a meeting with her for the next morning. A chill skittered down her spine at the thought. Just who was he?

Enough with questions and with uncertainty. The wine wasn't doing anything to answer anything, but it did leave her nice and mellow. Calm. Shoving open Earl's back door, Piper wandered inside and to the computer desk tucked into an alcove off the kitchen.

A soft meow filtered up before a fur ball the size of an overgrown watermelon rubbed against her boot. "Hi, Payton Manning," she said, reaching down to pet the tabby. He licked her fingers and rubbed some more. Earl had rescued the cat from under his car at the mall a year or so ago, according to Earl.

She began to type in Earl's password when she stilled, her instincts on full alert. Silence. Heavy silence surrounded her.

Her fingers encircled a sharp letter opener, and she slowly turned around.

A lamp glowed on, and Jory sat on the side of a leather sofa, overwhelming the straight lines. "Piper."

Something inside her shimmied. Danced, heated, and uncoiled. "Jory."

His gaze flicked to the letter opener. "Drop the weapon, sweetheart."

How had he found her so easily? "No." She turned around more fully to face him. Her heart rate sped up, and her breathing increased—and not from danger. The man permeated every space, taking over, filling it.

He smiled.

She frowned. "What's pleasing you?"

"You." His gaze dropped to the chest she was desperately trying to calm. "You try so hard to be something you're not, and the real you always shines through." Satisfaction tilted his lip. "I like that about you."

His voice. Jesus. Gravelly, hot, and masculine, wrapping around her with hoarse warmth. Her chest grew heavy.

She shivered. "Look who's talking."

"What do you mean?"

"You're all scary and big, kicking down doors and kid-napping women." She focused absolutely on him. "Yet the only time I've seen you really happy, really engaged, is when you were MacGyvering that keypad back at the facility." In her experience, geeks didn't look like Jory, but geek he was. "Computer nerd."

The smile widened, making him look like a predator who'd trapped prey and now wanted to play awhile before taking a bite. Nobody should be that good-looking. Damn fallen angel face—all sharp angles and hard lines. Set with a deadly intelligence. As if drawn, her gaze dropped to his full lips. Talented lips. She knew firsthand.

A low groan rumbled up from his chest. "The way you look at me."

This was madness. She sucked in air, her body alive. So damn alive. "Why are you here?"

"Your place is being watched. Heat signature devices as well as listening devices."

She glanced toward the sliding glass door. "You're lying."

"Nope. They're on you and will remain so. Just in case you know too much or if I try to contact you." He shrugged. "I warned you about them."

"You're crazy." Although so far, he had given her the exact truth, as evidenced by his brothers hugging him in the rain. She shook her head to dispel the memory and concen-trate on the matter at hand.

What exactly could the soldiers spying on her see? "With a heat image, they can't, like, you know, see everything?" Holy crap. The things she'd done in the shower earlier...imagining Jory there touching her. Teasing her. Taking her.

Amusement creased his cheek. "Pretty much everything. Why? What have you been doing?"

"Clumsy yoga." Heat rose in her face, which hopefully the soft light lost. Anybody deserved a good fantasy life and a great shower experience. That didn't make her bad, although the jury was still out on Jory. Was he a good guy or as bad as the commander claimed? In her fantasies, he was freakin' awesome. Here in reality? Overwhelming and dangerous with a side of sexy. Make that a whole shit load of sexy. She had tried so hard to curb her penchant for jumping feet first into the fire, and yet here she stood, dancing with flames again.

Her hands fluttered out, tingling with the need to touch. "I'm getting confused."

"I lured you here."

She lifted her chin. Her heart beat faster, and her lungs compressed. So her brain focused. "You messed with Earl's computer?"

"Yes."

"Damn it, Jory. It's taken me forever to get him to work with a computer, and now you've scared him off." Good. If they could just keep talking normally, her body would relax.

Jory's cheek creased. "I'm sorry."

She stood, the letter opener cool in her palm. "And you made me run *naked* through soldiers and bullets."

Jory winced. "I know, and believe me, I would've liked to have seen you from the other side. But I have to tell you, darlin'. You have a great ass."

Heat flushed into her face and a completely unladylike snarl curled her lip.

He waited, all male patience. "I'm not going to ask again about the weapon."

She glanced down at her hand and then back up at him,

fire all but burning her from inside. Too much. Want, need, fear, uncertainty...way too much all around. So she let her glorious temper loose. "Fuck you, Jory."

She had the briefest of seconds to appreciate the quick smile he flashed before she found herself flat on her back on the Persian rug, hands over her head, her body covered by an impossibly hard man. His knees nudged hers apart, and he settled against her.

Only a vicious bite from her own teeth to her own lip kept her eyes from rolling back in her head. This was so much better than her shower fantasy. Her lids half-closed as she studied his hard gaze. How could gray be warm? It should be a cold color. This close, heat spiraled through the gray like fire in a storm.

"Your move, green eyes."

Oh yeah? Her mind blanked. "Jory."

His gaze softened while his powerful body pressed her to the floor. Masculine knowledge lifted his lip. Arrogance and something indefinably Jory. Pure male.

Challenge rose up so quickly in her she stiffened. He wanted to play? Yeah. So did she. She wriggled her butt, allowing his groin closer to hers. Hard. Definitely hard.

With a smile that even felt dangerous, she levered up and captured his lower lip between hers. Someday she might wonder what in the hell possessed her to push a guy like Jory, but not right now. Now? She wanted to feel, and she wanted to take his control. She'd fucking earned it. So she swept her tongue between his lips.

A low, rumbling growl vibrated against her mouth—a sound of warning. The echo shot right down to where his cock pulsed between her legs.

Too bad she liked playing with fire. Heated her right up. So she nipped. Hard.

He levered back, slowly and in perfect control. "What

was that?" His voice whispered along her skin, winding down to heat her clit.

She shivered. "My move. Remember?"

He licked his lips with a soft hum. "That wasn't a move."

"No?" Why in the hell was she still pushing him? "So show me a move."

If her dare had taken him by surprise, he didn't show it.

"Gladly." His hold tightened around her wrists, keeping her in place. Not hurting, but definitely tethering. He was stronger than she, by a lot, and he seemed happy to let her know it. His gaze dropped to her lips, and his groin pressed her cleft. Hot and rigid, he slid against her. Her thighs trembled, and she ached deep inside. She gasped.

He nuzzled her neck and pressed harder against her core. He bucked his hips, pressing unerringly against her clit, and lava shot through her body. Her thighs widened naturally, and her body trembled with a need so great it couldn't be real.

She tried to breathe, wondering why she'd thought he'd kiss her instead of playing her body like a musical master. "Always do the unexpected, don't you?" she gasped, fighting every urge to rub against him.

"Yes." He lowered his chest to hers, and her nipples peaked into diamond-hard points. "I like the feel of you. Tight and needy. Fighting so damn hard."

"You don't know me," she bit out, her body crying for relief.

He leaned in, his breath hot on her ear. "Spread your legs wider, Piper." A slight Southern twang lifted his consonants.

Her legs moved before she could think, and she arched up into pure masculine perfection. Vulnerability caught her breath as her body took over. She was way out of her element, without question. "Stop playing games."

He licked her earlobe before tracing her jaw with his mouth, sure and warm. "Don't have time for games." He lifted up, his lips right above hers.

Her mouth tingled, needy and desperate. More than any-thing, she wanted his on hers. "Kiss me, Jory."

His head lowered a bit more, leaving barely a breath between them. "My way only."

"Okay." Any way would work. She closed her eyes.

"Open." He waited until she opened her eyes to focus on him. Then his mouth covered hers.

She'd expected hot and deep. Had prepared for it, pre-pared herself to handle him with delight. Instead, he moved softly, at his leisure, enjoyment on his hum. He licked the corners of her mouth, tracing her lips with his.

"So sweet," he murmured. "So soft."

She fought to stay sane and in control. Yet he continued to caress her, his mouth on fire as he wandered across her cheek, down to her jaw, and up again to her earlobe, where he nipped.

Not enough. Not nearly enough. She ground against him, and he clamped a hand on her hip, holding her still.

Then he continued to play. So gently, so intently.

Sparklers spiraled around in her mind, and her vision clouded. "Jory," she breathed. She couldn't control him, and she didn't really want to. Making the realization, her body softened under his. To just *feel*.

"There it is," he whispered. Then his mouth covered hers again, this time with force. He rocked her back into the rug, his mouth moving, his tongue tasting her. Moving where he wanted, *how* he wanted. He definitely took, but oh. How he gave. Hard and deep and fierce . . . so much in a kiss.

She could barely breathe, wasn't sure she cared, when he lifted his head. "Wow." For a deadly badass computer geek, Jory could really kiss.

"Yeah," he said softly, his eyes glittering.

There was a demand in the way he touched her, in the way he kissed. One she should run the hell away from, if she had any sense of self-preservation. The sexy soldier wanted everything she had to give, and she knew better. She had yet to meet a man she could trust, and the soldier on the run was a seriously bad bet.

"Why did you come here tonight?" she asked, trying to focus.

His nostrils flared. "To talk." He pressed down against her.

Electrical sparks shot through her erogenous zones, catching her breath. She was so damn close. A tingling started deep in her abdomen, and her clit started to pound. "We're not talking." If she moved against him just right, if she just found the right friction, she might actually orgasm. That quickly and that easily. Her eyes widened, and she held very still. She couldn't let go like that. Couldn't let him know how close he'd brought her so easily.

His eyes darkened. Too late. He'd caught her, and he knew. Somehow, he knew.

His slight smile cascaded shivers along her skin. "Now I'm here for another reason." That Southern twang increased in force.

"What?" she gasped.

"One taste, Piper. Before I die, one taste of you. I'm not going to heaven, but maybe I could have a taste before I go."

CHAPTER
13

JORY KEPT THE advantage, grinding his cock into her softness. Piper's eyes, clouded with need, widened.

Yeah, she wanted him. And even though he was a class-A

asshole, he wanted one good memory with her to take to his grave. There wasn't a way to save him, and he figured they both knew it.

For now, he wanted one taste.

He smoothed his hands down her arms, encircling them, not feeling any ridges. Good. On to her shoulders, while she watched him with that wide-eyed stare as she tried to control her body.

So amazingly sweet.

Regret gripped him. He wouldn't be on earth much longer, and he wouldn't see her through the pain to come. The commander would hurt her, and she'd have to be strong enough to walk away. "I wish we had more time," he said softly.

She blinked. "I'll figure out the chips." Then she gasped. "You only have three days—we don't have time for this."

"There's time for this." If he had to go, he needed to take something good with him. Then she shifted against him, heat from her core tempting his dick, and he forgot all about the chips. Instead, he ran his hands along her shoulders and down her chest, unbuttoning and removing her blouse.

A strangled groan rippled up his throat.

Fucking beautiful. She hadn't worn a bra, and her nipples were a light pink against her mocha skin, pert and ready to play. Never one to deny himself, he lowered his head and flicked one.

Her hands dug into his hair and clenched. Erotic pain lanced along his scalp, so he hovered over the other breast, letting his breath heat her. He licked and sucked, moving his way down her torso. Abdomen muscles undulated under his mouth, and he took careful pains to touch her everywhere, to feel for anything out of place, even as he enjoyed himself.

She had on a tiny skirt that he smoothly flipped out of his

way. Her strangled moan flooded him with pleasure as he snapped the sides of her panties. Then he tasted her.

Holy heaven on a stick. She tasted like cinnamon, spice, and all fucking woman. At the contact, the beast at his core, the one he shoved down at every opportunity, roared. Barely keeping a hold on himself, Jory took a deep breath and looked up at her flushed face.

"Say you want this," he said.

She blinked and nodded, amusement filtering through the lust in her eyes. "Oh. I want this. Right or wrong."

Who the hell cared about right or wrong? He kissed her clit, appeased when her entire body shuddered. "Then it's my way. Remember?"

She bit her lip, desire and uncertainty crossing her face. "Okay?"

"Hands back up, Piper."

The hold tightened on his hair. "Or what?"

His girl wanted to play, did she? With an easy motion, he flipped her onto her stomach and smacked her ass. Hard.

"Hey—" she protested, her hands now flat on the rug. "You are way too strong."

He rubbed the imprint of his hand, quite liking it there. A quick survey of her legs and back revealed a scar just under her right shoulder blade. He reached up and fingered the puckered skin, feeling the small tag beneath the skin. Drawing in a breath, he tuned into the frequency to memorize the pattern. She probably didn't even know it was there. "What happened?"

She shook her head. "Um. Oh yeah. A chair at work had a loose spring, and the damn thing cut me. Had to have stitches."

His head dropped, and his shoulders slumped. Well, he'd found the tracker. For now, they'd leave it there. If he had any more time for regrets, his heart would break at the thought that the commander had tagged her, the lying bastard. For now, Jory could steal a few seconds of heaven.

Taking the moment, he wanted to bring pleasure to the one woman who'd dug under his skin to see the real him. When she'd talked about his MacGyver moves, she'd seen the true geek beneath the soldier's training. More than anything, he wished he could be that guy. For her.

They didn't have much time. Her being in Earl's house was part of her normal routine, so the soldiers would think he hadn't considered their surveillance, even though he knew full well they were listening. The commander would think he had fooled Jory. He wouldn't try to capture Jory now, not when there was a chance to get all four brothers.

The soldiers were probably on surveillance only. No doubt they were recording all sound, but right now, he didn't give a shit. Time was short, and the woman was sweet. So he flipped her back over and sucked her clit into his mouth.

She arched against him, sighing.

He looked up at her. Glorious. Tousled hair, needy eyes, so much softness a guy could get lost. Forever. Instead, he wanted to push her over. To see her in the throes, completely lost to him. "Hands up."

Expressions crossed her pretty face as she considered her options, each one more revealing that the last. The woman should never play poker. Finally, with a snort that *almost* sounded like submission, she slid her hands back up over her head.

He rewarded her by slipping one finger inside her, and then a second. Twisting and turning, brushing a bundle of nerves that made her thighs tremble. With a sigh, he lowered his face and licked her clit, going to town with just enough pressure to drive her crazy. Forcing her up, waiting until sweat slicked her body and she mumbled incoherent pleas, he waited until one of the pleas included his name.

Then he nipped.

She went off like an AGM-65 Maverick missile, all explosion and fury. Crying out his name, she arched her back off the rug, waves wracking her body.

He gripped her hips to hold her in place, and continued playing until she settled back down with a soft sigh. Still, he tasted.

She shuddered and smoothed the hair back from his head. "No more." The sound came out like a whimper, and he smiled. One more kiss, and he levered up. God, she was fucking perfect. "Thank you, Piper." There weren't any words to explain what her trust meant, nor how much he wished things could be different. But he'd taken enough time for himself and now had to get back to saving his brothers. Setting her clothes back in place while she lay limply, he picked her up and dropped to the couch, warm woman in his arms.

A warm, snuggly woman. She cuddled her face into his neck, one hand rubbing his chest as she wiggled on his raging hard-on. "What about you?" she whispered.

His heart thumped. Hard and just for her. "I love that you just asked that." The woman cared with everything she had, and the bittersweet moment attacked his heart. "But we don't have time."

She lifted up, her eyes luminous in the soft light. "What do you need, Jory?"

He reached over his head to flip on the radio to a mellow country station. Loud enough anybody listening in wouldn't hear the gist of his words. "Help. I need your help, sweetheart. Please," he whispered.

"How?" she asked.

"Chance, the kid from the facility? He's one of my three brothers held captive in the facility by your father." Jory gripped her chin, turning her to face him. His jaw hardened, and he tried to remain gentle. "Time to make a choice, sweetheart. Please. Choose me."

In the middle of the inland facility, near a massive mountain range, Chance cleaned the weapon, his hands steady, his senses tuned to the surroundings. Outside the barracks in the inner Utah compound, construction noises continued throughout the day. The beeps of backing up equipment, the yells of men, the sounds of more buildings being built.

Apparently the commander was consolidating his base in Utah.

Too bad. A beach in Hawaii would've been a lot more fun.

A chill hung in the cement barracks this time of year, and Chance drew the cold into his body. Accepting was easier than fighting it.

Four cots scattered throughout the hollow room, and the fourth bed would forever haunt him. The gun lay heavy and sure in his hand, and if he didn't have two brothers to save, he'd use it. Right now and directly to his temple. Life was just too fucking damn hard.

Instead, he glanced at Kyle, his younger brother, sitting on a bunk and sharpening a Sharkman blade while humming an old AC/DC tune. "How did blade training go?" Chance asked.

Kyle lifted his gaze, and dark circles lined under his eyes. The kid hadn't slept through an entire night since Greg had died. "Fine. The commander's off his game, though."

"I know." Chance engaged the safety on the Walther 9mm pistol. "I think the guy in the cage escaped, and the commander is freaking."

"Jory?" Kyle asked, his shoulder hunching.

"Yeah. Why?" Chance eyed the bruises down Kyle's slender arms. The kid was about ten years old and needed to grow. Fast. They also had to spend more time with knife practice after grappling training the next day.

Kyle shrugged. "You should've gone with him when he escaped. You know that."

"I'd never leave you." Chance shook his head. Besides, he didn't know shit about Jory, now did he?

Kyle slid the knife into a sheath and scooted to sit on the army cot with his back to the wall. "Me and Wade were talking."

Chance lifted an eyebrow. Wade was probably a year younger than Kyle and rarely spoke after Greg's death. "That had to be a short conversation."

Kyle didn't remotely crack a smile. "Yeah. It was."

Chance tilted his head to the side, narrowing his gaze on his brother. "So? What did you two talk about?"

Kyle's shoulders went back, and his eyes darkened to emerald, making him look much older than ten. "You go on more missions than we do. If you get the chance, we want you to escape and have a life. To be free."

"No." Chance forced command into his voice. He'd give anything to have escaped with Jory but not without his brothers. If there was a way to freedom, he'd find it with them. That much he knew.

"Yes." Kyle plucked at a string on the rough wool blanket. "Maybe that Jory will come back for you? He saw you, and he knows you. Right?"

"Probably not." Chance hated to erase the hope from Kyle's face, but they had to be honest with each other. "If he actually made a full escape, then he's long gone from here. He has to be."

Wade jogged inside, his boots leaving mud tracks. "The commander is pissed, and we've gone on high alert."

Chance stood. "From the prisoner escaping?" It was easier using designations instead of Jory's name. He couldn't get attached, because no way would the soldier come back for a few straggly kids.

"That and something else." Wade dropped onto his cot,

his blond hair standing up in freshly cropped spikes. His blue eyes opened wide. "Some other threat that really pissed him off." He wiped mud off his cheek. "You said that Jory guy was huge and scary?"

That's not exactly what Chance had said. "I said he was bigger than the commander and didn't seem frightened at all." Chance's chest puffed out. "He stood up to him, and the commander kind of seemed worried. Even Dr. Madison stepped away from Jory's cage." Yeah. That was pride in Chance's voice, and he needed to knock that shit off. "Not that it matters."

Wade's lip twisted. "Maybe Jory will come back and take out the commander. Help us get the hell out of here."

Kyle nodded. "You two need to get free. You do."

Chance frowned. "What about you?"

Kyle's chin lowered. "I'm not leaving Greg."

The figurative punch to the gut nearly doubled Chance over. "He's not here anymore. Only his body is buried on the other side of the training field." Beyond a barbed wire fence, and beyond their reach—there to remind them what happened if they failed. But they'd seen the casket, and he'd seen Greg's body. The kid was dead and hopefully in a better place. Hell. Any place was better. "If we find a way out, you're coming. Period."

Kyle slowly focused. "It sounds like you have a plan."

Not yet, but he was working on it. "We're on our own, and we need to come up with an escape." Because his instincts were on full alert, and something bad was about to go down. He'd never understood his special abilities, the ones that had saved his life more than once, but he trusted them. "The only strategy I can think of is to invite to dinner the folks who want us dead."

If he didn't get his brothers out soon, they'd all join Greg in the ground.

CHAPTER
14

Piper wrapped her cardigan closer around her body and adjusted the computer chair again. She just couldn't get comfortable. Since Jory had escaped his cell, she and her computer system had been moved to an office just down from the commander's, and all day he'd been behind closed doors.

Something was going on.

Trying to grab a thought was like trying to harness a firebug right now. Jory had pretty much blown her mind, first by going down on her, and next by asking for her help. Claiming that Chance, the kid from last week, was his brother. Created in a test tube and forced to train as a soldier to kill.

By Piper's father.

The day she had worked with Chance, the kid had kept his gaze on the computer, and she hadn't really looked at his facial features too closely. Damn, she wished she would've looked.

How was any of this possible? Better yet...how was it not?

The door slid open, and Chance loped inside. "We have less than three days to fix the computer program," he said, sliding onto the adjacent chair.

Piper stiffened. "Look at me."

The kid turned, one eyebrow raised.

Heat slammed into her gut. Gray eyes. Seriously gray eyes, black lashes, hard fallen-angel features. God. It was so obvious. "You're his brother."

Chance blinked. "Who?"

Her head lifted. "You know who."

"You're crazy, lady." Chance turned back to the computer, quickly engaging the correct program.

"Are there two more kids here?" she whispered.

Chance glanced up at a vent in the ceiling and then turned his head toward her while continuing to type. "Yep."

"His brothers, too?" She could barely breathe. How was this even possible?

Chance nodded, his gaze again sliding up and over. "Yep." His shoulders stiffened.

"He's coming for you, you know." She wanted to touch the kid, to reassure him, but instinct held her back.

Chance swiveled to face her completely, the keyboard forgotten. "If he's that fucking stupid, he's going to get us all killed." Familiar fire burned in the kid's gray eyes. "God. It's a fucking trap, lady. He'd better be smarter than you are."

He was, actually. Piper blinked. "Did you plant the file about him so I could hack it?"

"No." Chance went back to typing. "No more questions."

Was he lying? The sense of urgency surrounding the kid transferred to Piper, and she focused on the computer program. If she didn't find a way to reach Jory's chip, he'd be dead in days. Her stomach clenched.

She tentatively reached out and cupped Chance's shoulder gently.

He stiffened.

"I promise, this will all be okay," she whispered.

A shudder wound through his body.

"You can trust me, Chance. Tell me what's going on."

He glanced at her, brows furrowing. "You can't be for real."

She released him. "I am. Trust me." The phone buzzed at her elbow, and she glanced at the alarm she'd set on her smartphone. Then she swallowed. Okay. She could do this.

Standing, she smoothed down her navy blue pencil skirt. She'd paired it with knee-high brown boots, which for some reason made her feel tougher than normal. Her white blouse was rather plain, but she'd donned silver jewelry to dress it up. To further add sophistication, she'd tamed her curly hair up and away from her face. However, after working all morning, some tendrils had escaped.

"I'll be right back," she murmured.

Chance sighed and leaned back. "Don't tip your hand. You don't know it, but we're all expendable. Even you." His voice softened at the end.

A chill swept beneath her skin, and she shivered. "I can handle it."

Chance grunted, turning back to his screen.

Straightening her shoulders, she stood and left the room, traveling at a swift clip to reach her father's office. A business-like rap on the door earned her an "Enter."

She swallowed and wiped her expression clear before opening the door and walking inside. "Our meeting is set for now."

The commander remained at his desk, a pile of papers in front of him, a slight scruff covering his jaw. "Sit."

She took a seat and crossed her legs. Her heartbeat ripped into a roar. "I'm closer to figuring out a way around Jory's damaged chip, but I need Chance to stick around and help me out."

The commander lifted one still dark eyebrow. "Oh?"

"Yes." She tried to relax into the hard chair and breathe normally. A part of her wanted to blurt out every question she had about Jory and Chance, but her father knew more about subterfuge than she'd ever learn. If she tipped her hand, she'd never be able to help Chance. How did she somehow end up in a Bond movie? "Chance is quite knowledge-able." Was she too obvious?

"I see." The commander clasped his hands together. "I trust you are recovered from your kidnapping ordeal?"

She searched for concern in his eyes, in his expression. Nothing. No emotion. Hurt cut through the fear. The hacker inside her propelled her full on to seek answers. "Do you care?"

He sat back, his mouth opening slightly. "You're my daughter, and I asked, didn't I?"

She shook her head. Adrenaline pumped through her veins, striking her nerves into an alert fight or flee state. "That doesn't mean you care."

He eyed his computer. "I don't have time for word games. What did Jory tell you?"

Before or after he'd brought her to a mind-blowing orgasm? "Why?" She lifted her chin.

The commander sighed. "Insolence? That man got to you." He steepled his fingers beneath his chin. "I don't think you understand the training he has had."

"Oh, he's a hell of a soldier." What she didn't understand was her own father. Did he care, even a little?

"No. I mean, ah, other training. In seduction, in sex, in manipulating a mark to gain information or cooperation."

Piper coughed. "You trained him in sex?"

"Yes. The best experts in the world have trained him. Not just in technique, but how to get beneath layers and earn trust." The commander tapped a couple of keys on his keyboard. "That boy seduced the mistress of a high-ranking Chechnya military leader and gleaned secrets you couldn't imagine when he was just eighteen. He's very good at his job."

She blinked. A rock settled into her stomach, and her body ached. Either Jory had used her, or her father was lying to her. Or, more likely, both. "I haven't slept with Jory, for goodness' sakes."

"I'm aware of that fact." The commander rustled papers. "We had surveillance pointed at Earl Frank's house as well as yours last night."

A strangled cough choked her, and heat rushed up her torso to burn her face. "Excuse me?"

He cleared his throat. "I have your encounter recorded, if you'd like to hear it."

How loud had she been? She dropped her face into her hands. "I don't believe this." Then fire burned through the embarrassment, and she lifted up. "How could you?"

"I felt Jory might contact you again, and surveillance is necessary for your safety. You don't realize how dangerous he can be."

Oh, she had a clue. Had Jory anticipated the surveillance? If so, he'd known everything they'd done had been recorded. He'd known the commander would hear and thus understand Piper's doubt. Her lungs compressed and tears tried to prick her eyes. She blinked them back. "Erase the recording."

The commander punched in a couple of buttons. "Done."

"Really?" she breathed. Oh, she could play the game to get some answers, and she wasn't leaving until she knew exactly what was going on. "Thank you."

He pinned her with a look. "I don't want that recording out there any more than you do."

"Okay." She frowned. "If you knew what was happening, why didn't you recapture Jory?"

The commander didn't blink. "The time wasn't right, but don't worry, we're watching Jory closely and will retake him soon. For now, there's more danger focusing on us than just Jory."

She sat straighter, her instincts humming. "I thought something was going on."

"We were hacked." Irritation curled his lip. "They were

looking for specific personnel records, I'm afraid. Including yours."

"Who?" How much danger swirled around? Finally, some answers. Maybe she should send her mother on a cruise or something.

He shook his head. "I don't know. We're trying to trace back the hack, but no luck."

"I could."

"Perhaps." He shrugged. "But I need you on the chip issue with Jory. It's more important right now."

"Okay." She'd rather save Jory's ass, anyway. But had he used her the previous night? Set her up in front of her father? One issue at a time, and she'd get to them all before leaving the office. "How much danger are we in from the people looking for personnel lists? If I'm in danger, is my mother?"

"No, and let's drop this issue. I will take care of them. I'm more disturbed at present that you didn't tell me the lies Jory told you before he, ah . . ."

"It was after the *he, ah,*" Piper snapped. She wiped her eyes. "This is all too much. Secrets, people shooting, soldiers . . . I'm a computer analyst."

"I warned you of the secrecy of our mission before you took the job." He sighed. "I think we'll have to move you and your mother inland to the larger compound. The construction is coming along nicely, and soon we'll have a lot more space and better computer facilities."

Piper stood. "Absolutely not. My mother is happy where she is, and we're not moving." She clasped her hands together. "Did you, or did you not, create soldiers in test tubes, raise them, and make them kill?"

"Of course not."

"So Jory and that Chance kid are not brothers you created?" If the commander was listening last night, he knew exactly what Jory had revealed.

The commander scoffed. "What is this, a science fiction movie? Military organizations do not bear and raise children. Jory is trying to manipulate you to get what he wants."

"What is it he wants?" she asked, her breath heating.

"To return to our enemies with more information about our military bases throughout the world." The commander nodded at her vacated chair and waited until she'd reseated herself. "Jory did work for me, and he stole military records to sell to the Russians, who inserted that damn chip near his spine and sent him back here. He was discovered and fought his way out, killing three of my men. They returned fire. Naturally."

The bullet holes along his chest, one of which went through and damaged his chip. "So you captured him."

"Yes, and I'm trying to save him. So he can stand trial." The commander gestured wide, toward the maps, flags, medals, and weapons lining the walls. "This means something to me—I don't just kill people. Justice matters."

Piper rubbed her arms. "Then why is Jory still in town and not halfway across the world by now?" Yeah, they'd had a wild night, but she didn't figure he'd expose himself to prison and probably death just to make out with her. "I don't understand."

"There are more records, and I'm sure he has to return with them or be killed." The commander shrugged. "He's trying to use you to get to the computer records."

In truth, it had felt like she was using him. The guy had left with a raging hard-on. Time to show her hand. "I can see the resemblance between Jory and Chance, and I know those men who picked Jory up are his brothers. They look exactly alike."

Her father leaned back and steepled his hands beneath his chin.

She swallowed, a rock slamming into her gut. "You lied to me."

He studied her for moments and then finally sighed. "Yes. I would've committed treason by revealing classified information otherwise." He shook his head. "I'm sorry."

"Who are they?" she croaked, the blood rushing through her veins.

A light glimmered in his eyes. Regret? "It's a program instituted by the United States government, hence the top security and threat of treason. We were hired to create the brothers, and we raised them. Then they turned on us."

She gasped. Would the government really sanction such an action? "So it's true?"

"That part of it is true."

Betrayal cut a hard path down to her heart. She narrowed her focus. The commander had no problem acting outside the scope of his government contract. How could she find out if the government really instituted the program? "You forced them to kill? Jory and his brothers?"

"We're a military organization, and we created weapons." The commander leaned toward her, his gaze intense. "Never forget, that's exactly what they are. No emotion, no conscience, no regrets. That's why we have to get them back here."

God, no. "I won't help you capture and use them again."

"You don't have to." His chin lowered. "But if they don't come back, we can't deactivate the chips, and they die very soon. In addition, if you don't reconnect Jory's chip, he dies. Painfully."

Tears filled her eyes. "I don't know you."

"No. But I'm not the bad guy here. For now, focus." He leaned back. "Unless you think you can help them without my resources?"

She slowly shook her head. "No." The computers and program at the facility surpassed most systems across the globe.

"Piper."

She looked up and at her father, confusion and pain plucking at her thoughts. "Yes?"

"I know we haven't been close, but I am your father. You can trust me. I had to lie to you, and while you probably don't accept our methods here, they're necessary to keep the country safe. We've done a lot of good." He kept her gaze evenly, his dark eyes intent. "Learn to trust me. Please."

She swallowed and nodded, once again standing up. How was she going to get Chance and the younger boys to freedom? She wouldn't let them be used as killers. "I understand."

"Good. I, ah, enjoyed dinner the other night and hope we can do it again."

She faked a smile. "I'd like that." Maybe there was a chance with her father, away from work, but she doubted it. She didn't know him, and what she discovered didn't feel very good.

He sighed. "Even though you're angry with me, please think clearly. Jory isn't a good man, and part of that is my fault. We trained him to manipulate and kill. He's been manipulating you—probably because you're my daughter."

"Has he?" She shook her head.

"Yes. Like I said, sexual manipulation is one of his strongest skills."

She turned toward the door, her chest aching. "I have to get back to work." What was the truth? Could everybody be using her? She paused at the doorway as if just curious. "Why didn't you retake Jory last night instead of recording us together?"

Silence. Then another sigh behind her. "Because I want his brothers as well, and if he's out, he'll lead me right to them."

No response was necessary for that statement, so she didn't give one. She exited the room, her brain spinning. The short walk didn't help, and soon she stared at her keyboard, not sure where to begin, especially since Chance was gone. Where the hell had he gone? She had more questions for him.

Well, she was a hacker. Maybe she could get into the military files and find the information she needed. Was she brave—or stupid—enough to hack into the U.S. military servers to see if there really was a program? It was the only way to see if her father worked alone or not.

High heels clopped down the hallway, and Dr. Madison entered the room. "The commander asked me to bring you this." She set a computer disk on the desk.

Piper glanced at the innocuous silver disk, her blood boiling for a good fight. "What is it?"

"Knowledge." Dr. Madison's blue eyes narrowed behind glasses, and she shoved black hair out of her face. As usual, she wore a lab coat, her tablet sticking out of a pocket. She had to be in her fifties, but the woman looked younger. Ageless, really. "I'm sure it'll help you in deciding whom to trust." Latent sarcasm tipped the words.

What a complete bitch. Piper leaned back in her chair. "You don't like me, do you, Dr. Madison?"

"I don't find a real use for you." Dr. Madison leaned against the door frame. "Franklin and his sentimentality have truly shocked me, to be honest."

Right. Because he was such an emotional guy. But... maybe the snotty doctor could help in that regard. If Piper didn't get some real answers, she was going to go crazy. "You've known my father a long time. Right?" Yeah. She purposefully called him that.

The doctor's perfectly symmetrical nostrils flared. "Yes, and we've been close that entire time."

Anybody with half a brain could tell they'd been lovers. Probably long-term lovers. "He doesn't seem that emotional."

"He's brilliant." Dr. Madison sniffed.

"I'd just like to be able to see beyond the mask, you know?" Piper mused.

Dr. Madison licked her pink lips, her gaze narrowing. "You silly girl. What you see is what is there. The man doesn't have a mask."

Irritation clawed down Piper's back. "Nobody is that hard and emotionless."

The doctor glanced at her phone. "Keep telling yourself that." She turned on a four-inch heel and clicked away.

What a freaking witch. Piper eyed the silent disk. Somehow, she just knew this wasn't going to be good. But she slipped the disk into her optical drive and slowly opened it.

A word document, a bunch of pictures, and a video lined up. She leaned forward. Interesting. A couple of keystrokes, and the word document opened. Jory's picture sat in the left top corner. His black hair was shaped in a buzz cut, and his eyes lacked the warmth she'd seen in them. He looked younger—maybe the photo had been taken six years or so ago. Mission parameters were set forth next to the picture. The soldier was to make contact with Mara Jorge, a Las Vegas showgirl with ties to a local mobster. Seriously? This wasn't even the Chechnya file.

Her skin heating, Piper opened the pictures into a slide show to see different shots of Jory with a stacked blonde. A blonde with gorgeous blue eyes, perfect bone structure, and a dancer's body. Slim and sinewed. As he squired her everywhere from a park to a museum to a show, Jory wore Armani. Even with the short hair, he looked amazing—strong and virile in the expensive suit.

He and the woman seemed close, and his hand often rested at the small of her back or on her arm. His smile seemed to be for her only.

A surprising pang pierced Piper's heart. Was she that easy to fool?

When the slide show ended, she took a deep breath. All right. In for a penny...

The video opened up to show a plush hotel suite with a sparkling view of the Vegas strip. The woman wore a long red gown, and Jory wore a black suit, an amber-colored drink in his hand.

"You're beautiful, Mara," he murmured, his gaze hot. "Lose the dress."

The woman laughed, her voice low and throaty. Slowly, as if drawing out the moment, she slid the dress to the floor, leaving her nude. Perfectly in shape, nicely muscled, dancer nude. "If he had any idea you're here, he'd kill us both."

Jory set his drink down and tugged free his tie. "I'll protect you."

Mara chuckled. "You sound so sure, for a stockbroker."

Jory grinned, not revealing anything in his handsome face. "You're special and worth killing for. Don't ever forget it." His clothes joined hers on the floor.

If Piper hadn't known better, if she hadn't seen the documents about the mission, she would've believed he was entranced. Willing and falling in love. Something in her solar plexus ached. Even so, she couldn't help but marvel at his amazing physique. Hard, muscled, so damn tough—lacking the three new scars or new tattoo across his chest.

She should turn off the video.

Yet she watched the couple fall to the bearskin rug. Watched as Jory took the woman, soft and gentle. Treating her as something precious.

Three fucking times.

Finally, the blonde fell asleep in front of the fire.

Jory stood and stretched, no expression on his brutal face. But something burned in those eyes. Lava and regret? He covered the woman with a sofa blanket and tugged his pants back on. Glancing around, he stalked to a laptop sitting near

the window and punched in keys, seeming unconcerned for
the woman sleeping on the rug.

After several more moments, he shut down the computer.
Must've stolen whatever information he needed.

The video was a little grainy, but soon Jory looked up
at the camera, and now, years later, Piper drew back. She
shook her head. This was from the past.

Jory nodded.

The screen went black.

Blood rushing through veins in her head roared sound
through Piper's ears. Her taste in men truly, truly, truly
sucked. Not only was her father a world-class liar, but Jory
was a master manipulator.

She clenched her teeth, and her stomach burned. How
screwed up was she? A part of her, deep down, searched for
a way to make Jory the hero. Proof that the DVD had been
doctored. But it hadn't. She could tell. Her father and Jory
were two of a kind, and they both lied and manipulated people. Even worse, Jory had probably learned his skills at the
commander's knee. She didn't mean a thing to either of
them.

She was alone again.

CHAPTER
15

PIPER FINISHED OUT her workday in a trance, cursing her
own stupidity. How in the hell could she have been so
wrong? Even now, she tried to find a rational explanation

for what she'd seen. Besides Jory's ability to go the distance three times. With a mental shake, she shoved the image of his hard ass out of her mind.

The guy was a professional liar, and she'd been had. Worse yet, she'd been used. Kind of. Could a guy use you if he didn't orgasm? Of course, that certainly had gained her trust.

Apparently he'd learned more from the commander than she had.

As she exited the building to the parking lot, her phone rang. She glanced down and sighed at seeing Brian's smiling face cover the screen. Why wouldn't he give up?

At this point, she'd believe any explanation. Maybe Brian, Jory, and the commander were in it together like some weird spy movie. But Brian needed to get lost and maybe get some anger management therapy or something. Either way, he wasn't her problem.

At the moment, she was heading home to check on her mother, eat dinner, and then come back to work. The time clicked quicker and quicker, and she only had a short time to figure out the damaged kill chip.

She reached her car, and the earth shattered.

Warmth rushed over her. She ducked and cried out. A rush of heat slammed into her, nearly burning her skin. Fear poured through her veins.

Turning almost in slow motion, she caught fire billowing from the building. Her keys dropped. Several car alarms began to blare. Her knees shaking, she took a step toward the door, only to have another explosion knock her onto her butt. Pain ricocheted up her spine, and the concrete chilled her skin. She scrambled up, her breath panting.

A man shouted from the other end of the lot. "There she is."

She turned, the air wheezing from her panicked lungs. Three men, all running—two with guns. Shit. Pointed toward her.

All instinct, she turned and ran through cars, trying to reach the main street. The quiet street in an industrial part of town. Warehouses and storage units lined the road, and in the chilly air, nobody lounged about. Running bootsteps came closer.

How many people had been hurt in the blast?

With a sob, she shrugged out of her long coat to allow more freedom. Her boots weren't the best for running, but at least the heel was short. Her brain shrieked a message to run, so she did. Ducking her head against the wind, she pumped her hands and feet as hard as her cold breath would allow. If she could just reach the corner, she could turn onto a much busier thoroughfare.

Fear propelled her, and adrenaline increased her speed.

From the corner of her eye, she caught movement on the other side of the street.

Solid arms grabbed her at the waist, and she flew forward in a tackle. Her knees hit first, followed by her hands. Instant pain. Even so, she couldn't stop her face from smacking the frosty concrete and turned to the side so only one cheek took the impact. Pain exploded through her head, and she moaned, shocked into stilling.

"I've got her." Thick fingers banded around her upper arms and yanked her to stand. The world spun around, and she tried to settle her stance. Bile rose in her throat. She gulped it down, blinking to focus as the hands whipped her around.

The guy who'd tackled her wore a tight T-shirt over tattoos. Many tattoos. A scar crossed over his many-times broken nose, and calculation filtered through his brown eyes. "You run again, and I'll knock you out." A slight accent colored his words, but she couldn't quite place it. He shoved his gun into his waistband. The hand on her arm tightened until she could almost feel bruises forming, so she nodded.

The other guy jogged across the street. "Nice tackle." This one had nearly white hair, green eyes, and pocked skin. A tat along his forearm matched the one on crooked nose's neck. PROTECT.

Now that wasn't creepy in the slightest.

A small Toyota lurched to a stop, and Crooked Nose opened the back door. She couldn't get in there. Pivoting on one aching heel, she kicked him square in the gut. Her foot landed, and she turned to flee.

Fingers clawed her hair and yanked her back. Raw agony ripped along her scalp, popping down her back. The other guy moved fast. She yelled, her arms swinging, until he cracked his knuckles across her already pounding cheek. Stars flashed behind her eyes, and she coughed out a sob.

Using her hair for leverage, he threw her into the car. Her forehead smacked into the far door, and pain filled her cheek. She scrambled to sit. He sat next to her, manacling a hand around her arm while Crooked Nose jumped into the front seat next to a stocky man with a black goatee. The PROTECT tattoo wound down the side of his neck and disappeared into his shirt.

"Go," the guy next to her ordered.

The driver torpedoed the car away from the curb and toward the main road.

Piper struggled, trying to reach for the door handle. They were crazy if they thought she wouldn't fight. Wherever they wanted to take her wasn't good, so she needed to get out. Now.

A huge SUV barreled out of the nearest alley, headed straight for the passenger side of their vehicle. She gasped in shock at Jory at the wheel, leaning forward, his gaze intent. He held a phone to one ear, obviously bellowing out orders to somebody.

"Shit," her driver screamed, yanking the car up onto

the sidewalk. Sparks flew as they scraped against a chain-link fence. Swearing, he turned the wheel onto a wide alley between two metal industrial buildings. Jory drove up next to them, slamming into garbage cans and sending them spiraling away.

Piper slapped her hands on the back of the seat, trying not to pummel into it. "Who the hell are you people?" she yelled.

The guy next to her slid down his window and pushed the barrel of his gun out. "We're God's right hand, bitch. Soldiers directed to take down your father and finish his unholy quest." He fired, and bullet holes sprayed the front of Jory's silver SUV.

How in the hell had they found her connection to the commander? It couldn't have been in the files that were just hacked, could it? Had to be.

Taking a deep breath, Piper shoved the guy into his door, and his face smacked the window frame with a satisfying thunk. He bellowed and threw an elbow back into her shoulder.

Hurt swelled. She cried out and fell back, already swinging her legs up to kick.

He growled and half turned to swat at her, his weapon still out the window.

Jory creased into the right front side of the vehicle with a terrifying thud, shoving it across the road and onto the opposite curb. Piper screamed and rocked into her door. Glass shattered, and she ducked her head to avoid getting cut. The passenger-side door was ripped away, and the guy next to her disappeared. She blinked and scrambled over glass shards for the gaping doorway, seeing Jory twist the guy's neck with a loud pop. The guy dropped, his eyes blank.

The driver gripped her hair and yanked her over the front seat. Pain assaulted her scalp. She fought, kicking and screaming, yet landed hard on the console between the two seats just as Jory tore Crooked Nose from the front seat. Grunting and the impact of flesh hitting flesh echoed followed by pained gasps.

The guy holding her shoved her out the passenger-side door while keeping a tight hold on her hair. Once outside, he yanked her up to his chest, a knife instantly pricking her jugular.

She sucked in a breath and stilled. Fear compressed her lungs.

Sirens trilled in the distance, and smoke billowed up over the surrounding buildings, which blocked her view of the bombed facility.

Her ears rang. The guy behind her panted, his chest hitting her back with each exhale. The grip across her waist bruised, and the knife at her throat hurt.

In front of her, Jory kicked Crooked Nose's gun into the air, where it flew yards away. Nose attacked with a series of punches and kicks—well choreographed. His training evident, he danced easily on his shoes, nailing Jory in the jaw with a solid punch.

Jory changed in front of her eyes. Not anything obvious, but the person she'd met left him, leaving cold gray behind. His jaw hardened, while his shoulders relaxed, his hands dangling by his sides. It was as if humanity had disappeared, leaving a stone-hard killer in its place.

Her breath disappeared, and her eyes widened. The guy holding her trembled.

Crooked Nose punched out, and Jory caught his fist in one hand. No expression marred his fallen-angel face. He twisted.

The loud crack of a bone breaking rent the musty alley. The man shrieked, pain in every syllable.

"Mother of God," the man holding her muttered.

Jory followed up by a smooth glide into the man to turn

him, a thigh kick knocking the guy to one knee. He went for the neck next.

"No," Piper whispered, jagged ice ripping down her throat. Horror should be hot, not cold. Yet she shivered.

Jory pulled up and swiveled his torso, and Crooked Nose's eyes widened right before his neck snapped. He pitched forward, facedown in the asphalt, his head bouncing and his legs kicking up before landing hard and silent. Death clouded the air.

The knife dug into Piper's throat, bringing her back to reality. She could probably reach down and grab the guy's nut sack, but what if he shoved the blade in her throat? She'd bleed out too fast to get help. Even as her mind tried to save her life, she couldn't help but cringe when Jory took three steps toward them.

"Let her go," Jory said, his voice guttural and barely human.

Was it even him in there? She swallowed and tried to focus. Maybe he was some kind of crazy robot. Would he kill her, too?

The guy holding her tried to back away, taking her with him. "Stop there, or I'll slice her neck." The knife dug in deeper, and warmth spread down her neck.

Jory's nostrils flared like a wolf's catching a scent. Then he leaped. One hand slid past her throat for the guy's neck, and the other wrapped around the hand holding the knife.

CRACK.

The guy shrieked and dropped the knife. Jory had broken his hand. How was that even possible?

He pushed her to the side, shoved into the man, lifted him up, and flipped him over his shoulder, somehow holding his head in place. Something loud snapped, and the body went limp. Jory dropped him like a sack of garbage.

He'd just killed three men with his bare hands—easily. Piper backed up, her hands out to ward him off. "Uh."

He stalked toward her, his chin down. So big, so deadly.

She glanced frantically at the ends of the alley. The sirens increased in pitch, no doubt getting closer. But would they see her in the back of the alley? What if they didn't arrive in time? Her knees bunched to flee.

"Don't run." His force remained the same.

She trembled and focused solely on him. "Okay." No way could she outrun him. Was there any way to reason with him? Was he even in there any longer? "Thank you for saving me," she breathed, searching for any sense of humanity or kindness.

He nodded and reached her to spin her around to face the mangled Toyota. Her hands slapped the chilled and crumbled metal. "This is going to hurt," he said in a full Southern accent as he yanked her shirt down over her elbows. Fabric tore, and cold air whipped across her bare skin.

He unsnapped her brassier clasp.

She cried out softly, too softly. But fear seized her lungs, and breathing became near impossible. "Please, Jory—"

The silver glint of a knife blade caught her eye and trapped the rest of her words in her throat. Her knees wobbled, and she almost went down. Then fire raged through her. She might not be able to beat him, but she sure as hell was going to fight until the last second. She kicked back, nailing him in the shin, and then tried to spin around.

He set the wicked knife down. His hands covered hers on the car, and his big body caged her in place. Warmth heated her bare skin from his body, frightening her anew at how close he was. "Please let me go," she whispered, tears blurring her vision.

He leaned over her, enfolding her completely. So much bigger and stronger than anybody she'd ever met. His lips hovered close to her ear. "I'm sorry I scared you. There's a tracker inserted beneath your left shoulder blade, and I have to remove it before we move. Hold still, and I'll be quick."

She bit back a sob. The man was crazier than crazy. "Please, don't."

His big hands pushed hers together, and he flattened them under one of his. His groin pressed hard against her lower back, his legs against her ass, holding her in place. He retrieved the knife. "Hold still, Piper," he murmured.

Nothing could've prevented the whimper that rolled up from her gut.

He stiffened. "I'm sorry." Then the knife cut into her flesh.

Pain flared. She bit her lip to keep from crying out, but tears rolled down her face. He prodded with the knife, and nerves fired along every nerve ending in her back. She whimpered again. "There's nothing in me, Jory. Please stop." She'd beg if it meant survival.

He grunted. Something let loose in her shoulder blade. He stepped back and gently turned her around.

She sniffed and wiped her eyes. In his hand sat a tiny cylinder, silver and covered with blood. "What the hell?"

"Tracker." He dropped it to the ground and smashed the device under his heel.

She blinked and shook her head. How was it possible? But she'd seen the device. Hell—she'd felt him pull it from her body. Realization tried to dawn, and bile rose in her throat. "I don't understand." Her teeth chattered, and she began to shake uncontrollably. She'd cut that shoulder on a chair, and Dr. Madison had stitched her up.

Fucking two-faced bitch. Did her father know? Piper pressed a hand to her roiling stomach. Yeah. He had to have known.

They'd tagged her like a dog. Tears filled her eyes again.

Jory frowned and drew her shirt back up, handing her the ripped ends to cover her breasts. "Get in the SUV, Piper."

A Jeep careened around the far end of the alley, speeding straight for them. Shock kept Piper in place. The car screeched to a stop, and two hulking men jumped out. Gray-eyed men.

"You—your brothers." Piper shook her head, trying to clear the dizziness.

Jory swept her up and strode toward his damaged SUV to set her in the passenger seat. "Scoot over." Then he turned back around.

The black-haired brother frowned, surveying the scene. "I told you we needed one of them alive."

Jory shrugged. "No choice. Take care of the bodies and the car. I need to get Piper patched up, and then I'll call." He pushed her to the passenger side and slammed the door, which only partially closed due to the damage.

Piper gulped and peered out the window. Identical frowns marred the rugged faces of the guys outside, and the brown-haired one muttered something that made Jory grin.

At the smile, a buzz of relief spread through Piper's abdomen. "Should we leave them?"

"Yes." Jory ignited the engine. "Matt and Shane can handle the bodies. For now, we need to get somewhere and talk."

She hunched down, her shoulder hurting, her head aching, and her heart fucking breaking.

CHAPTER
16

J ORY OUTWARDLY KEPT his gaze on the road while in reality he watched the woman huddled against the door of the vehicle. Her smooth skin had paled, and her hands trembled in her lap.

He'd scared the ever living shit out of her.

His hands tightened on the wheel, and his shoulders hunched forward. Yeah. He'd give his left nut to be able to shield her from his true self, but it was too late now.

She'd seen him in action. Hell. She'd seen him kill.

"I'm sorry I scared you, Piper." Why was he apologizing to her? There was no going back now.

She blinked and wiggled her back against the door frame. "How could he have inserted a tagging device in my shoulder?" The bewildered tone of her voice hit Jory somewhere deep in his gut.

Jory sighed, wanting to lie to her. To tell her that maybe the commander had tagged her to keep her safe. "They don't trust anybody, and every person is merely a pawn. Even you."

Her eyes narrowed to a deep jade, the usual emerald sparks subdued. "Who were those men you killed?"

He shrugged, eyeing another back street. The noticeable damage in the SUV made them conspicuous, and they had to get away from the public. "I don't know."

She frowned. "Yet you were conveniently in place to smash your car into theirs right after they kidnapped me?"

Now she got suspicious? "No. I was in place to seek you out after work." Yeah, he'd planned to get her help in freeing Chance, and he might've thought about kidnapping her again to do it. But he hadn't considered removing her tracking device until the opportunity arose and he had to get her out of there. "What did those men say to you?" None of this was making any sense.

She sighed. "Just a bunch of nonsense about bringing my father to his knees and ending his unholy quest."

Jory started and glanced at her while turning onto a narrow back road. "They knew the commander was your father?"

"Yes." She shook her head. "I don't know how they knew.

There was a hack into the system the other day, but that information can't be in the files, right?"

Who the hell knew? "Maybe. So they said they wanted to take the commander down? Unholy quest? Exact words?"

"Yes." She pursed her lips. "All three had PROTECT tattooed somewhere on their bodies."

Unease tingled through his gut. "What does that mean?"

"How the hell should I know?"

His burner phone buzzed, and he lifted it to his ear. "Yeah."

"We're in a bigger clusterfuck than we feared," Nate said without preamble.

Weren't they always? "I figured. What's going on?"

"The men who tried to take the woman—"

"Piper. Her name is Piper." Jory took a hard left onto a main road, hoping the window tint hid their faces enough from any cameras.

Nate growled. "Fine. The men who tried to take *Piper* are part of a crazy group against any genetic manipulation. They've been after the commander for years." He sighed. "We thought we'd taken them out in DC, but it looks like there are more people in the group than we knew."

That's all Jory freakin' needed. "How dangerous are they?"

"They're insane. Apparently they know about your girl and her paternity."

"Shit." Jory didn't bother to argue the designation of her as *his girl*. As of the moment, she was his responsibility, and that was just fine with him. "Did Matt take care of the bodies?"

"Yes."

"How bad is the facility?" He couldn't miss Piper's sudden focus on him, and he couldn't blame her for wanting to know about her father, regardless of his betrayal in tagging her without her knowledge. "Any casualties?"

"Yes. Two deaths and several injured—none the commander or Dr. Madison. Right now they're no doubt trying to deal with the publicity of the bombing, so you have a little time before they come looking for Piper."

"If we're lucky, the commander will think the PROTECT group took out her tracker."

"When have we ever been lucky?" With the last shot, Nate hung up.

Good damn point. He glanced toward the pale woman. "It looks like your father survived the bombing."

She shuddered and suddenly focused on the rough foliage outside. "Where are we going?"

He could hear her heart speed up, and frankly, he couldn't blame her for being frightened of him, even though he'd lose a limb before he allowed anything to harm her. "Somewhere safe. I'm taking you there to talk, and when we're finished, I promise I'll take you home."

A myriad of expressions crossed her face as she weighed her options, finally resulting in a quick nod and a resigned sigh.

While he appreciated her agreement, he didn't want her giving up or losing that spirit. "I need your help, Piper."

She coughed out a slightly hysterical chuckle. "You're kidding, right?" Crossing her arms across her chest, she pressed her feet to the dashboard and focused outside at the residential subdivisions blurring by.

"I'm not kidding. How's your shoulder?" They needed to get a bandage on it as soon as they arrived.

"Fine."

Damn, she was cute when pouting. Well, if she felt comfortable enough to put out her lip and ignore him, then maybe the fear had dissipated. "I don't want you to be afraid of me." Why the hell had he said that? He couldn't control his damn mouth around the woman, his too-logical mind just scrambled like a hard drive on the fritz.

He drove between brick pillars. One proudly held an oval neon sign proclaiming SUNRISE RETIREMENT COMMUNITY.

Piper lifted an eyebrow and cut him a look. "Seriously?"

"Yes." His gaze caught on her bruised cheekbone, and fury rose inside him. He should've used more pain when killing the PROTECT idiots. "Is your face okay?"

"Fine."

Stubborn, contrary, brave woman. Her courage touched him deep, and he wanted to cuddle her close. A guy without emotion suddenly finding some.

He wound around several tame duplexes until reaching a tidy rancher painted an innocuous peach. Once he'd pressed the garage door button and driven inside, he finally breathed out. Good.

Shoving open the mangled car door took more effort than he'd expected, but he put his shoulder into it, and the damaged metal dropped to the concrete and bounced twice. He jumped out of the gaping hole and tapped the button attached to the wall. The garage door slowly shut.

Silence pounded around the sparse room, and peace descended.

Sure, any peace remained temporary. But still, he took several deep breaths and let his body relax.

Piper had remained in the vehicle, staring out the gaping hole in the driver side with a *what the fuck is going on, you crazy bastard* expression.

On her, the look was adorable.

Man, he had it bad. The kiss the other day had left her taste on his tongue, and even now, he wanted more. Something whispered in the back of his head that her taste belonged just there.

"Get out of the car, Piper."

Glancing warily around the innocuous garage, she scooted across the seat and gingerly stepped out, trying to hold her ripped shirt together.

Even so, tempting glimpses of a pink bra and full breasts rolled an untimely need to his groin. His nostrils flared like a wolf catching a scent, and his instincts started to hum.

He covered her hand with his, leading her into the kitchen, scanning the room for any threats before allowing her in. Then he tuned into his senses, the ones he shouldn't have, and listened as well as smelled the entire house. Nobody had been there.

The scents of woman and cinnamon tempted him, and his mouth watered.

Piper shook free and wandered toward the cream-colored refrigerator, which showed pictures of several elderly ladies playing bridge, cricket, and even golf. A postcard to "Aunt Edna" hung next to the pictures.

"Ah, where's Aunt Edna?" Piper asked quietly.

Jory stilled. Shit. She didn't think he'd off an old lady just to gain a safe house, did she? "Aunt Edna won a cruise for four the other day, and her nephew Jack came to take care of her place."

Piper turned around, her lashes fluttering open. "Hi, Jack."

"Hi." He took in her pinched lips and her hitched movements. "Take off your shirt, baby."

Piper knew exactly why he wanted her shirt off, and based on the pounding ache in her shoulder blade and the warm stickiness down her back, she needed a bandage.

She also knew he expected her to argue.

He eyed her, eyes veiled, sexual tension filtering around him. The man could overtake any environment, filling it with...him. The kitchen walls closed in, cocooning them in intimacy. His eyes burned into her in a move that even felt physical.

So she shrugged out of her shirt and let her still unhooked bra slide to the ground.

His eyes glinted, and his mouth slacked open.

Keeping a triumphant grin off her face, she turned around and placed her hands on the bright yellow Formica table. Yep, playing with fire once again. But the guy had been in perfect control since the second he'd rammed the kidnapper's vehicle, and the woman in her wanted to take some of that away.

Instant warmth heated her from behind. Man, he moved fast...and silently. Then he dug in drawers until finding a clean dishcloth and opened the cupboard beneath the sink to draw out a first-aid kit.

"Take a deep breath, sweetheart."

The low voice warmed something deep in her abdomen. "So, ah, how did you know the tracker was in my back?"

He pulled in air. "Ah..."

Her eyelids shot up, and her shoulders went back as memories awakened her. "Wait a minute." When they were rolling around and kissing on Earl's rug...when Jory had made her come like a locomotive. "The other night. You were searching me for a tracker?" The anger spiraling through her remained welcome, but the hurt dropped hard into her blood.

"Believe me, darlin'. That wasn't my main focus." Wetting the rag, he gently wiped off her back. "Not bleeding too badly, which is good." Drying the skin, he then slid a bandage into place. "No stitches needed." His voice came out low. Intense.

Oh, the man was sex on a stick and arrogant enough to think he controlled the damn universe. He was about to learn better. Just who did he think he was?

She set her jaw. "Is that all?"

"Yes."

Not bothering to reclaim the ripped cotton shirt, she turned around, carefully keeping her face blank.

He inhaled sharply, that impressive chest moving with the breath. "What's your game, green eyes?"

"Game?" She lifted an eyebrow and tried to look innocent, even as the cool air peaked her nipples. Her fully exposed, rather achy, nipples.

Crimson spread across his masculine cheekbones.

Yeah, she was tempting him. Teasing him. Completely messing with him. He deserved it for throwing her so off balance.

His smile was slow and somehow dangerous. Then his face softened in a way she'd never seen before.

Her breath caught, and she belatedly wondered if she'd pushed too far. "Uh—"

Warm hands manacled her hips and lifted, setting her down on the table. He stepped into her, his muscled thighs forcing hers apart.

She gripped the table, trying to keep from falling back. Vulnerability flashed through her, followed by a blast of heat so rapid it stole her breath. "What are you doing?"

He leaned in, hands flexing. "Picking up your challenge." Smooth as silk, his lips brushed her cheek. "Didn't you think I would?"

"No." *Danger, red sign, clanging error message.* "I, ah, didn't."

"That was your first mistake." His voice rumbled so close to her ear, the tenor vibrated just under her skin. Oddly soft, and intriguingly gentle.

"Wh-What was my second?"

"I'm hoping you make that soon." Not giving her time to think, to react, he wandered his mouth down the side of her face, leaning her over to gain better access. With a low growl, he nipped at the area between her neck and shoulder. His mouth was hot, smooth. Devastatingly firm.

She shivered and bit back a moan. Her fingers curled into his chest.

He remembered. Just how to touch her. She was so out of her element.

"We need to talk," she breathed, trying to calm her rioting body. Two more seconds, and she wouldn't care about talking. She wouldn't care about anything but the pleasure she already knew he could create. "Please."

He levered back, keeping his hard groin against her needy one. "So talk."

"Um. This is a bad idea." How in the world was she even talking about this? Really. "I don't trust you." Yet did she? The man had taken on three armed kidnappers just to save her. That meant something.

"So trust me." He slid his hands under her arms and curled one hand behind her neck to fist her hair. "What will it take?"

How was she supposed to concentrate with him so close, smelling of male and aggression? Yeah. Aggression. And damn if it wasn't turning her on. "The truth."

"I've never lied to you." Those fingers tightened, one pressing on the pulse point beneath her ear.

Until this moment, she hadn't realized that was an erogenous zone. "So you're some super-soldier created by my father who escaped and is now back." She tried for sarcasm, but her voice emerged way too breathy.

"Yes." His thumbs ran along her jawline from front to back, and his eyes warmed as if marveling at the touch. "There's something here, Piper. I have less than three days to live, and I'm not playing anymore. You feel it, I feel it, and I'm fucking tired of pretending otherwise."

"I'm not pretending there isn't something here." She found lying a waste of time. "However, it might not be something good." And they didn't have time for it, since the clock was ticking to detonation. He'd be dead in days if she didn't figure out how to reach his chip.

"You and me? We'd be fantastic."

"Like you were with Mara from Vegas?"

His face turned to stone. Not froze, not stilled...just lost all expression. All humanity. Faster than possible, he pressed against her until she was flush against the counter.

She shivered, exposed and vulnerable. Controlled.

"They told you about Mara?" His touch lost the gentle teasing quality and turned intense, and he bent toward her, his body over hers.

"No." She tried unsuccessfully to yank from his grasp. "They showed me a recording. You're impressive, going all night like that." Sarcasm nearly burned her tongue as she spat it out, oddly jealous, and oddly hurt.

Then she lost her breath as he gripped her hips, lifted, and pressed her against the fridge. Not hard but not exactly gentle. Pictures rained down.

"What do they know about Mara?" he ground out, no mercy in those unholy eyes.

Her body jolted, and her head swam from being jerked upright so quickly. She blinked. "What do you care?" she coughed out. The guy had used the blonde for information as part of a mission.

"I care." He leaned in, easily holding her aloft, a new darkness chasing away the light in his eyes. "Please tell me about Mara. Now."

It hit her suddenly, and with the oddest force, that she didn't fear him. Call it instinct, call it stupidity, but any fear she'd had was gone. "Why?" she asked softly.

His head jerked back. "She's my friend. At least she used to be, and I can't let them get to her."

Right. "I can see how you'd use a friend like that."

"Damn it." He set her down gently. Then he bent and rummaged in a duffle bag before yanking out a laptop, setting it next to her, and quickly punching up a screen.

Piper tried to sidle to the door.

His arm snaked out and yanked her into him, her chest to his side. "Stay."

Stay? Oh, he didn't.

He typed quickly. Several seconds later, a cute blonde came on. "J?" she asked, her blue eyes wide.

Same woman, but she looked softer. More like the girl next door than an exotic dancer involved with a mobster. She wore a pink sweatshirt, minimal makeup, and had cut her thick hair into a cute bob.

Piper tried to draw back, and the iron band around her waist turned to solid steel.

Jory nodded. "Hey."

Mara pushed her face closer to the screen. "Oh my God. Where have you been? I've worried so much, then I was afraid you went undercover again, and then I got worried you'd been..."

"I'm fine but was undercover." He kept the screen angled so Piper could see Mara, but Mara couldn't see anything but Jory. "Are you all right? I had to check."

Mara smiled. "I'm totally great. Devon was just promoted at work, and Katie is taking ballet." She snorted. "Believe me, her affinity for dance isn't lost on me."

Jory chuckled, his shoulders visibly relaxing. "What about Jackson?"

Mara's eyes softened. "He just started preschool, and I bawled all day to have him gone, but he's the smartest kid in the class."

"I'm sure he is." Jory's voice softened. "You're safe? No signs of any problems?"

"No." Mara leaned even closer to the screen. "I'm safe, J. I promise. How about you?"

"Getting there." He pressed his fingers on the keys. "If you need anything, or if you feel any danger, you know how to contact me. My lines are back up."

She nodded. "I've missed you. Glad you're alive."

"Ditto." He clicked off. Then a huge sigh rolled through his impressive chest.

Sweet. Undeniably sweet. Piper curled her fingers over the table end. "I didn't say she was in danger. The commander just has the video of your time in Vegas—I didn't see anything besides you using Mara and taking information from a safe. No indication that she's in any danger."

He breathed out. "Thank you."

"No problem. Although now I'm more confused than ever." And a little jealous.

He nodded and stepped back, releasing her. "Mara was a job, and then she was a friend who wanted to get the hell out. So we played it up for the camera, I got the info, and then I found her a new life. Last I checked, two years ago basically, she was a real soccer mom in the suburbs married to a banker. Turns out she still is."

Was any of this true? "Why two years ago and not since?"

"That's when I got shot and ended up in a coma. Came out of it three months ago." Jory rubbed his chin and glanced down at her bare chest. The environment shifted again. Tension spiraled around, nipping and sucking. His gaze darkened. "Either put on a shirt or let's take this where we want it to go."

She swallowed. Her body warmed and thrummed. But her mind clicked into gear, and she backed away. "Shirt?"

With a low snarl of impatience, he yanked off his T-shirt and slammed the cotton over her head.

Warmth, spice, and man filled her senses.

Then muscle, hard male, and danger filled her view. "Your chest is freakin' unbelievable." As were his abs.

"Look who's talking," he said, a smile hovering on his full lips, his intensity not diminished a bit.

She eyed the sexy tattoo above his heart. "Freedom. It means everything, right?"

He glanced down and tapped the smooth lines. "All four of us got it when we escaped. You could say it's our family crest."

Sweet. Desperately sweet. She hugged herself and meandered over to sit in a chair. The adrenaline rush of the day was waning, and she needed some balance. More and more she was starting to believe him. Seeing Mara in the flesh, happy and serene, had certainly helped. "You mentioned my assisting you."

"Chance." Jory crossed the table and dropped into a matching chair. "He and two other boys are at the facility being trained by your father and threatened with death. I need you to get information about them to me so I can get them out. Get them freedom."

"I will." Chills wandered down her back. The back that had until recently held a foreign device without her consent. Her father had lied and basically tagged her like a dog.

Her heart spasmed, bombarded by harsh reality. She'd wanted to trust her father, and she'd wanted to know him. Much like she wanted to know Jory. Could either man be trusted, or were they cut from the same damaging cloth?

Her chest hurt, and she rubbed over her heart.

"The commander only knows cruelty and his own odd sense of destiny, and I'm sorry." Jory leaned both elbows on the table. "I don't want to, but I'll prove it."

"Okay." Her chin lifted.

He dragged a nondescript phone from his back pocket. "Call the commander and tell him you've been taken by PROTECT, and that they want Chance. See what he says."

She eyed the phone and considered the possibilities, her head pounding. "You want me to lie to my father?" It would be taking a side, an absolute one.

"Yes."

"I can't," she breathed, her gaze caught on the innocuous device.

Jory brushed his thumb across her lips, and she looked up. "I wouldn't ask if they weren't kids. They need help."

Tears filled her eyes. Again. "Won't he be able to track me?"

"You won't be on that long."

She swallowed, her gaze on the innocent-looking phone. Making the call, if she was caught, would forever end her relationship with her father. But he had lied to her, and he had inserted a tracking device into her flesh.

Jory slid a warm hand along her jaw. "This sucks, baby, and I know it. The commander is a sociopathic prick, I'm a stone-cold killer about to die, and neither of us is a good bet. But you have to choose a side, and since I'm dead in three days, you have to choose now. Whatever side you choose, I'll support."

She lifted her head to meet his gaze directly. "If I don't choose you?"

He studied her. "I'll make sure you get home, and I'll get those boys out myself. Nobody touches you—nobody hurts you. My word."

She believed him. Right or wrong, she believed him. "Jory."

"Choose me," he said softly, a strong man who could be so devastatingly gentle.

The words resonated through her, so much meaning encapsulated in them she couldn't breathe.

He waited patiently, his gaze intent.

She took a deep breath and exhaled slowly, her mind spinning through memories of the last week. In the end, in defiance of her impressive brain, she went with her gut, or maybe her heart, which was already full of him. "Fine." Drawing the phone to her ear, she quickly dialed. Somebody had to save those kids.

"Yes," the commander barked.

"It's Piper," she whispered.

Silence for a moment. "Where are you?"

"I don't know." Her voice shook, from the lying and the adjoining confusion. "Some PROTECT group has me, and they want Chance. Why would they want that sweet kid?"

"I don't know. How far away are you?" the commander asked.

"I'm not sure." She lowered her voice. "Is it true? Are you genetically enhancing soldiers?"

He scoffed. "I expect you to get free, and once you do, contact me immediately. Not the police, not your mother, me. It's life or death for our cause here, Piper."

What cause? "I understand. But you didn't answer me about your experiments." Jory nodded, and she frowned back at him.

He sighed loudly. "Obviously you're using their phone. Give it to one of the men who has you."

She blinked at Jory, and he held out his hand. Taking the phone, he pushed the SPEAKER button. "We'll kill her. You know it. Where are the newest abominations?" His voice emerged thick and with a Middle Eastern accent. If Piper hadn't been watching him, she never would've realized he was the one speaking.

"They're not abominations, and you'll never get to them." The commander growled low. "Release my analyst, or there's nowhere you can hide from me."

"Already hiding. Hand over your creations, or I'll kill your daughter. With great pain." Apology lingered in Jory's eyes, even as he kept up the flawless accent.

"My daughter understands my cause, and if need be, she'll die for it."

Piper shook her head, her eyes widening. She opened her mouth to protest, and only Jory's quick snap of his fingers kept her from speaking.

"Just how far off God's course have you fallen?" Jory asked, his voice serious while his eyes rolled.

"All the way. What I've created will be the ultimate soldiers—beyond anything created by the God you love so much," the commander said.

Piper's mouth fell open. Now it sounded like he was taking full responsibility. "Is your program sanctioned by the government, or have you gone rogue?" Her voice thickened with tears.

"Stop asking stupid questions," the commander ordered.

Fine. How about a more direct question? She sucked in air. "They cut a silver tracking device out of my shoulder. Want to explain?"

He hitched in a breath. "No. Now tell them to let you free, or I'll send my best men after you."

"Why don't you fucking come get me?" Her temper exploded, erasing the hurt.

He sighed. "You'll be safe soon. Don't worry about your mother, as I'll leave her a message that you're working late and won't be home tonight."

Yeah. That'd go over like an anvil to the head.

Piper's gut hurt. Tears pricked the backs of her eyes. The fantasy she'd harbored of her father wafted away like mist in a storm. He was a monster, and he didn't care about her. Plus, he'd created soldiers on his own. No way was the government involved in that program.

Jory winced and then continued. "You made your choice, old man. Your daughter dies." He ended the call.

Piper sat back, her mind spinning. "You're not going to kill me."

"No."

Was her mother safe? Piper jumped up and rushed for the door. She had to get home.

Jory was on her that quickly, his back to her front, his

hands caging her against the light-colored oak. Slowly, he turned her around. "I can't let you leave, either."

She shoved him back an inch. He pushed back, and being stronger, she ended up plastered against his hard frame, the door firm against her back. "You can't stop me."

His gaze morphed into something new. Not anger, not interest, not amusement. What was that?

Her breath caught. Determination. Hard, male, iron-clad determination.

He leaned down, his gaze right above her. "You made the choice, baby, and you chose me. Period."

CHAPTER
17

WARMTH CAGED HER, and Piper's knees wobbled. "You can't keep me here."

"We both know that's not true." Jory's lips hovered near her right ear, spiraling along her neck. "Just for the night, and I promise I won't touch you."

"Then?" She cleared her throat to sound in control.

"Then you're going to escape your PROTECT captors and head back to the compound. I'd appreciate it if you'd get me information on Chance and the other boys, but if you don't, I'll go another route. The commander believed you, so you're not in danger."

She kept perfectly still so as not to brush up against him. "How do you know?"

"I can hear a lie. Easily." Jory's lips enclosed the top of her ear.

Her knees wobbled, and her eyes closed. "Nobody can hear a lie."

"You trusted me, so I'm trusting you. Whatever the scientists did to me in those petri dishes gave me extra abilities. I can hear and see beyond normal, and I can detect wave patterns even in air."

She tried to focus with his heated breath against her neck. "That's impossible."

"I can also use pheromones to increase sexual tension." His lips wandered down her jugular.

"Right." She tipped her head back to allow him more room.

"Pay attention to your body," he whispered against her collarbone.

Heat flared through her, vibrating with intensity, shimmering from her breasts to her clit. Hunger edged into a craving that forced her to flatten her hands against his chest. Her heart thundered, and her lungs overheated.

Desire. Red hot and devastating.

She opened her eyes, her vision blurring and then clearing. "How?"

The warmth in the air caressing her skin slowly dissipated. "Don't know, just can." His gaze dropped to her lips.

Even though he'd halted the sensual attack, her body thrummed, primed and ready. She shook her head. "Don't use that on me again. Ever."

"Don't need to." He grinned. "And you know it."

True. Definitely true. "Why do you have a Southern accent sometimes?"

He stilled. "We were raised in Tennessee, and the accent gets loose every once in a while."

The tenor melted her panties. Easily. Her mind turned to the crazy plan. "I have to escape tonight and get back to the computers to save you." A large clock shaped like a bird ticked in the corner, each second a harsh reminder of the kill chip in Jory's spine.

"No. Not until tomorrow." He caressed down to nip her earlobe. "Too easy. And we need time to hide the bodies so they won't be found. Right now, you're safer here than if you returned home too quickly."

Her nipples scraped against his chest, and she whimpered. "What about my mother?"

"Matt is keeping an eye on her house, on her, and on her neighbor. He won't let anything happen to the people you love. I promise."

Pure truth echoed in the low tone. Piper shook her head, her body moving against his. Her nipples brushed his chest, even through the shirt he'd tossed over her head, and this time, he groaned. "You're the real deal, aren't you?" she asked, finally accepting the truth.

"I'm afraid so." Sadness and a lingering regret glimmered in his odd gray eyes.

Man. Weird as it felt, she'd give anything to comfort him. To give him some sense of hope. "I have to get back to the computer."

He shook his head. "No, you don't. My brothers have the program, and I can figure out the code to save them."

"What about you?" she breathed.

His fist unfolded through her hair, and he cupped the back of her neck. "We both know there's no way to reach my chip. It's damaged too much."

Tick. Tick. Tick. She shook her head. "I need to try."

"You can try starting tomorrow. Tonight? You have to stay here."

She couldn't fight him and get free. What if she couldn't figure out a way to connect wirelessly to the chip? "Please don't give up," she murmured.

He nodded. "You're on board?"

"Yes." And they had a night. So she threaded both hands through his silky hair and rose to her tiptoes before sliding her lips between his.

He breathed her in, his pectorals clenching. "What are you doing?"

"We have a night." She spoke against him, not moving back an inch.

He blinked. "I'm letting you go tomorrow no matter what."

She grinned, enjoying the firmness of his mouth against hers. "I'm not trying to seduce you to gain my freedom."

He levered back, a veil drawing down over his eyes. "Then what are you doing?" Warning and something darker, something deeply intriguing, echoed in his low tone. Something she wanted to explore.

"Living." She lifted her shoulders, stirring the scent of him in the cotton. "I've never been much for regrets or not jumping in. I believe you...all of it. And I want this night." She believed him in that her mother was safe. And maybe he was right and she wouldn't be able to deactivate his chip. The idea flared pain into her heart, and she shoved it away. Maybe this night was all they had. Trying to keep eye contact, she drew the shirt over her head.

He swallowed. "You saw me kill."

She nodded. "I did. Interesting, that. It was self-defense, but even so, I got the feeling it wasn't quite you. Not like when you MacGyvered the keypad back at the facility. That just seemed more...you."

His chin lifted, while his gaze warmed. Hell. It heated over. "You think you know me?"

"No." She kept a firm hold on his hair. "Something tells me I'd like to, however."

He remained in place this time. "I don't have long on this

earth, Piper, and the time I have is going to be spent saving my brothers from the kill chips near their spines."

Yeah. She got that. "You're free tonight."

His nostrils flared. "You sure?"

That warning voice in the back of her head screeched a *hell no.* "I'm sure." She'd never listened to that bitch, anyway.

He didn't ask again. Instead, his broad hands encircled her waist, and he traced her rib cage up and over to caress her breasts, his gaze following his movements.

Sparks zipped straight from his talented fingers to her clit. She gasped and leaned into his touch, so much need coursing through her she wondered at her own sanity.

Then, as he tweaked, as he twisted with just enough bite to weaken her knees, she forgot all about saneness.

Who wanted to be sane?

This? This she wanted. "Jory," she murmured, releasing his hair to run her hands over those amazing pecs, the badass tattoo, and down to trace each individually ripped ab. "You're nearly airbrushed."

He chuckled. "You confuse me."

"Then we're even." She slowly unbuckled his belt. "I'm attracted to you, and I know you're telling the truth. The other night was good, but..."

"Not enough." He reached for the button of her jeans. "I know."

And life was short—probably too damn short for him. Although neither one of them said it, the truth of that sad fact hung like a fine mist in the elderly lady's home.

Almost as if reading her mind, Jory glanced around. "You deserve better than this."

She kicked out of her jeans, trying to erase shyness at her plain pink panties. This, more than ever, was one of those times she needed to accept herself, to like herself. But a guy like Jory? Yeah. He'd probably been with perfection before.

He glanced down at her, a low hum emerging with his breath. "You're beautiful, Piper."

This was crazy. So damn freakin' crazy. But when he looked at her like that, when she considered the counting-down clock, when she allowed herself to acknowledge the danger she'd courted by trying to be in her father's world... she wanted crazy. "Just take me away, Jory. Just for one night."

His smile gentled, while his expression hardened into something so masculine he took her breath away. "That I can do, darlin'. I promise."

She gulped and tried to concentrate, even though his too-warm hands had cupped her breasts. "What about your brothers?"

His cheek creased. "I think I'll keep you for myself."

The possessive tone wandered right under her skin and to her heart. "You know what I meant."

"We have the night. I promise."

She swallowed and tried not to blush. "I want this."

He'd let her go. She knew, without any question, if she said no, he'd release her. This wasn't about rebelling against her asshole of a father, nor was it about wanting to trust Jory. This was about her and taking the moment. For fun, danger, and dancing too close to the fire. "I want this."

Then his mouth was on hers. No hesitation, no more talking, he went deep and hard, shoving her head back. His mouth was firm, his tongue demanding, all hesitation or question gone, leaving absolute possession in place.

His tongue thrust with hers, hard and sure, sending tingles through her entire body. Good. He was so damn good.

The world shifted. He swung her up and strode through the tidy home to sit on a bed, her thighs encasing his. One humungous hand pressed down on her head, pushing her entire body down on his full length. He controlled the kiss like he had everything else, with complete ease and a burst of passion.

All intelligence and masculinity rolled up into an explosive package.

The possibility of that explosion, of that detonation, had been hinted in him since the beginning.

She knew, without a doubt, that was the exact characteristic of his that attracted her. She wanted to detonate with him.

God help them both.

She kissed him back, her hands roving over his muscled arms and to his back, riding him even through his jeans.

Somehow he lifted her with one hand while still kissing her, and before she knew it, chilled air brushed across her bare ass. Then he set her down onto granite, smooth, lava-hot male hardness.

Her eyes flew open.

Even with his mouth working hers, those gray eyes met her gaze.

She stilled. He felt huge. Not huge in a make a guy feel good way, but freakin' real huge. She'd seen him the other day, but he hadn't been fully erect. She had to look.

Levering back, scooting back, she looked down. He was long and thick, verrrry thick. A dark vein wound around his penis, somehow looking both promising and menacing. "Wow," she breathed.

He threw back his head and laughed, his body gyrating against hers. "You make me happy, Piper."

She swallowed. "From the looks of things, you're about to make me happier."

The idea that this might be their only time flared pain into her, and tears filled her eyes.

He stilled. "Be here, baby. Just be here."

She nodded.

Wrapping an arm around her waist, he flipped them and

moved her up on the bed until she lay on her back, covered by the most amazing male specimen she'd ever imagined.

"I hope I can trust you," she breathed, batting back the tears.

He pressed a soft kiss on her nose, his pulsing shaft rubbing against her. "You can, although I'm not some easygoing accountant, sweetheart."

Yeah, she got that. He'd killed easily, and there wasn't much of a doubt that he'd done it before. But something sweet, something genuine, lived in Jory, and she wanted to know that side of him. While she still could. "Just be you. That's what I want."

His head jerked back, and an emotion she couldn't track flashed across his face. Before she could question him, he dropped his head to the nook of her neck and nuzzled. Then nipped.

His hands went to work, exploring her, a combination of rough hands and gentle touch. Of need, lust, and futility.

Kisses rained along her skin, under her jaw, over her collarbone, to take possession of both breasts. He nipped and sucked, harder than she would've thought, more than she could control. Could anticipate.

His talented fingers found her, and she arched into his hand, crying out. Too much and yet not enough. She caressed down his flanks, knowing he couldn't be quite human, marveling at the power barely leashed right beneath his skin. At the shift of muscle, the nearly animalistic perfection of his form, she believed he had been created on purpose.

Such perfection had to have a master crafter.

She gyrated against him, her mind blanking when he found that sizzling bundle of nerves inside her. "Now, Jory."

"Slow," he murmured against her breasts, his damp forehead slicking her skin.

"Later slow." She was incapable of full speech. "Now

fast. Please?" The tension built and created true pain, so her body rubbed against him as if reality no longer mattered. As if it ever had. "Please." She dug her nails into his fine butt.

He stiffened.

So she did it again.

"You like to play with fire," he groaned, his breath brushing her nipple.

"Now you figure that out?" She chuckled, but in the face of such tremendous need, the sound came out high-pitched and desperate. "Please."

One hand slipped under her ass, cupping her completely, and lifting. "Spread your legs wider," he groaned.

She complied, opening herself as much as possible, any doubts shot to hell by the raw need clawing into her.

He plunged into her with one brutal stroke, his balls slapping her butt.

She cried out, bombarded, taken over. Pain flared inside her followed by an unbelievable burn of erotic fire. It licked at her, tempted her, destroyed her. From her clit to so far inside her she hadn't realized her own depth, she felt him.

He levered up, his mouth enclosing hers, his tongue thrusting inside.

It was too late to slow him down, and she knew it. He withdrew and slammed back inside, somehow gaining strength. Her eyes fluttered shut, no longer able to see when feeling was all that mattered.

He took her over, and for the first time in her entire life, she let surrender happen. The pinnacle she needed to reach more than she needed to breathe was in his control, in his hands, and in that spectacular body. The power and the strength.

So she widened her thighs and clasped her feet at the small of his back, her arms winding under his arms to dig into his moving back muscles.

At the moment of her surrender, her submission, his grip tightened on her butt hard enough to bruise. Another sensation bombarding her with the rest.

With a low growl, barely sounding human, he threaded his free hand into her hair and twisted his wrist, holding her in place. Jerking her up enough to take her completely, to render her helpless.

A sensation she'd already succumbed to.

Then he started to thrust. Hard, full, hot...thick and so damn deep she truly forgot where he ended and she began.

For the briefest of seconds, they both belonged to him.

His hand slipped, his fingers dipping between her ass cheeks. She gasped, more feelings taking her over. Now, caught in the throes, she'd even give him that.

Everything she had, everything she was, everything she hoped to be somehow coalesced into this one moment and this one man.

And somehow...he knew it.

"Mine." He said the word against her lips, not a question, not an ounce of arrogance.

Pure truth.

She nodded, tears filling her eyes as her thighs tightened. Energy uncoiled inside her, a rushing spark of burning fire, slowly—way too slowly—unraveling. He pumped harder, his grip tightening, his groin brushing her clit.

She exploded, her body slamming up into his, her cry echoing throughout the universe. Shattered into a million pieces, she could feel each one return to the whole, bringing her back together.

Not the same. Definitely reassembled differently into a complete puzzle created by Jory.

He released her mouth to once again press his lips against her neck, his pumping increasing in force, his body tightening, as he came against her.

His heart beat a rapid tempo against her chest.

Slowly, he lifted his head.

Sweat littered his brow, and a lock of his black hair fell onto his forehead.

Surprise and a darker emotion swirled through those gray eyes. It took her a moment to regain her breath and catch the emotion.

Possession. Sure and absolute.

Then he smiled.

CHAPTER
18

JORY SAT IN the old lady floral chair, his elbows on his knees, his gaze on the woman sleeping in the antique bed. The small, fragile, now bruised woman.

Things had changed. Hell. One night with her, and he'd changed. The plan from the day before, the one where he'd send her into danger, no longer worked. The woman couldn't lie worth shit, and the aftermath of the night they'd just shared would be stamped all over her face for the commander to see. She couldn't get hurt any more than she'd already been damaged.

As a kid, Jory had known love. But this feeling? This feeling could only be had by a man for a woman—*the* woman—a combination of possessiveness, need, and protectiveness. He neither understood it, nor did he want to quash it.

He'd been way too rough on her the night before.

But he'd wanted her... wanted to claim her in a way he

couldn't quite understand. Wanted to mark her, to make sure she always remembered him.

When he fucked up, he liked to do a great job of it.

Shit.

She stirred and slowly sat up, gazing around the surroundings with wide green eyes. In the morning, sans the makeup, she looked about eighteen. Smooth skin, wide eyes, black curly hair.

Wild and innocent.

The perfect woman.

He cleared his throat. "I'm sorry if I was too rough."

She pulled the sheet up to her neck, meeting his gaze directly. "You were fantastic."

He studied her facial expressions and took note of her tone of voice. While Nate was a human lie detector, Jory could usually tell a falsehood. "Are you just being nice?"

She rolled her eyes and stretched her hands above her head. The sheet dropped to her waist.

He swallowed, his gaze dropping to pert, well-loved breasts...kissed a lovely pink. He'd left his mark there, and damn, if that didn't please him on some primitive level he wanted to deny. "Are you sure?"

"Stop fishing for compliments."

He wasn't. More than anything, he wanted to scoop her up and spend the day in bed together and soothe any aches he'd caused. But there was no time. "We have to plan your escape in a way that keeps you safe and doesn't give away my brothers."

She blinked, and then her bottom lip quirked. "You sweet talker you. Stop with the compliments."

Smart-ass. But at the thought, the tightness released his chest. "You're really all right?"

"Yes." Her smile remained slightly sleepy. "Aren't you?" Doubt crept into her tone.

"I'm wonderful. Last night was amazing." He could give her the truth there.

"Good." Her smile nearly blinded him, and he had to blink to keep concentration. "So . . . a good plan, huh?"

He shook his head. "Not yet." One quick stride, and he planted a knee on the bed. Reaching for her, he caressed her fragile jaw and wrapped his hand around her neck. "Good morning." Lowering his head, he took her mouth.

He moved against her softly until she sighed, and then he went deep. Her nails dug into his chest, and he growled, enjoying her little shiver. The woman was a keeper. At the thought, he drew away.

Her eyes were dreamy, her lips a pretty pink. She'd chosen him, and now he wanted to choose her. He couldn't let her go back into the facility and put herself in danger. If she went back, it had to be for the mere purpose of getting a message to Chance and nothing else. Then she needed to get out of town.

He took a deep breath. "You can either flee with your mom, or you can go back and tell the commander I kidnapped you and forced you to lie about this kidnapping. I can't ask you to lie for *me* and about the PROTECT group in case he figures out the full truth. I won't let you be in danger."

She rubbed her chin and once again drew the sheet up to cover herself. "Why would I tell him the truth? I thought we were going to say the PROTECT group kept me."

Jory shook his head. "You suck at lying, so you'll have to stick closer to the truth, which is that I have you. If you go in, it's for one day only to get a message to Chance on how we're getting him out. Then you get to safety." He frowned, fighting the urge to reach over and drag down the sheet, to prevent her from hiding any aspect of herself from him. To prevent any barriers. "What do you want to do?"

She smoothed the sheet over her drawn-up legs. "Want to

do? I already made my choice. I have no intention of playing both sides." She tilted her head to the side. "I choose you, Jory. I'm all in here with the original plan. Danger or not, I'll make good the lie."

He stood, the blood rushing through his veins in a definite fight or flight speed. All in? He just needed her to get word to Chance, not to become a super-spy for Jory or some double agent against the commander. The woman wasn't a good liar. "What are you saying?"

She bit her lip. "I believe you. With the tracker, your abilities, Chance, my not knowing the commander…and last night? I believe *you*. I'm in this now, and whatever I need to do to save you and your brothers…I'm in."

He backed away from the bed, his breath heating. Gratitude and warmth slammed him so hard in the gut he nearly buckled in two. She chose *him*. Just him, and she intended to put herself in danger for him. More than once. "No."

She chuckled. "Yes." Relief unwrinkled her brow. "I've known—instinctively about my father. Sure, I wanted him to be a good guy, to care about me, and maybe he does. But what's going on there is wrong."

Jory tilted his head. "You're thinking with your brain."

She snorted. "I usually do."

Funny. The thought of anything or anyone dampening her spirit blazed fire through him.

"I can help you get insider information." She hugged her knees, her voice nearly eager.

There was no safety for her on his side, no protection when all hell broke loose, and it surely would. He'd be dead in less than two days, and he couldn't leave her unprotected. "Absolutely not."

"Wow. Such a dictate. I'm doing it." Amusement and a feminine understanding curved her upper lip. "Take a breath, Jory, ah, dude. I'll protect you."

Dude? She'd protect him? Was she crazy? It was his job to protect her. And if she thought she could distance herself from him with a stupid nickname, she was in for a surprise. "Dean. Jory Dean."

Her smile split wide open. "You do have a last name."

"Yes. The commander doesn't know it." He frowned. "I don't think he knows it, anyway. I've been out of touch for a couple of years. Coma and all that."

"Because somebody shot you." She frowned. "Not the Russians."

"No. A woman, apparently." He sighed and ran a hand through his thick hair. A *trembling* hand. She'd rocked his world with choosing him. Over her own biological father—both a logical and an emotional choice. "My brothers saw a video, and it was a woman who shot me, but they couldn't see who."

"Dr. Madison?" Piper said quietly.

Jory shrugged. "Maybe."

Piper frowned. "That hurts you."

"No, it doesn't." The woman saw way too much beneath the surface, and he refused to dwell on that right now. Not on top of everything else.

"Yes, it does. Believe me, I understand parental failure." She paled.

Anger roared through him, and he twisted his head. "Okay, if she shot me, that bothers me a little. Not because I care about her or anything, but because that means the closest thing I ever had to a mother was just fine with killing me. There's something fucked up about that."

Piper plucked at a bed string. "I know. My own father tagged me like a dog. That sucks, but it doesn't change who I am or what I want. And right now I want to help Chance and save you."

Jory focused and then slowly forced his body to relax. "I want your help, but it'd kill me if something happened to you."

She nodded. "So we plan. I escape, get help, and lie and say the PROTECT people took me. Then I need to find a way to the inland facility to rescue Chance and his brothers as well as get the computer codes."

"No. Absolutely not." Jory finally lost his sense of wonder and returned to the problem at hand. The idea of her putting herself in any more danger ripped holes in his fucking gut. She'd given something of herself to him. He had to hold that tight for as long as he could. "You're in to give a message to Chance on when to be ready for *me* to rescue him, and then you get out. No spying, no working on computer codes. Just a message. This isn't up for debate."

"Good thing I'm not debating."

Oh yeah? There was another way to go here, and one that finally eased the pressure pounding through his temples.

He saw the second she realized what he was thinking, because she bolted straight up in the bed. "You are not keeping me here under wraps."

Maybe he should. "We both know I could make that happen." He kept his gaze direct and lowered his voice to the tone of command he'd learned long ago on missions.

She shook her head, thoughts scattering across her pretty face. "Okay. I won't try to get to the inland facility and will just get a message to Chance on whatever your plan is once you figure it out."

Ah, she was cute. So damn cute when she thought she was playing him. Jory smiled. "The city facility pretty much blew up yesterday. Where exactly did you think the commander will have Chance?"

A light pink stole across her smooth cheekbones. "I hadn't thought of that."

She was also cute when she lied. "Hadn't you?" Jory asked, reaching for a T-shirt to drag on.

"Not exactly," she groused. Holding the sheet in place,

she swung her legs from the bed and stood. "This is my decision."

He moved instinctively and without much thought, deftly jerking the sheet from her body.

She yelped, moved to cover herself, thought about the situation with a quick bite to the lip, and then stood to her full height, hands at her sides.

Damn, the woman was *something*. Jory shook his head. "You gave something of yourself to me last night, Piper, and you know it. I won't allow you to put yourself in danger, not even for me."

Somewhere during the sentence, her temper ignited, if the sparks flashing through her emerald eyes were any indication. He watched, fascinated, when her pupils narrowed to pinpricks.

"You don't get to *allow* anything with me, butthead."

Glorious. Fucking glorious. How he'd ended up, however briefly, with such an amazing woman, he'd never understand. Protecting and defending were what he did best, and he knew how to get results. For the first time, his heart, instead of his brain, pushed him to use his skills. He moved into her space, appreciating when she swallowed in reflex. "*Allow* was a poor word choice, as was *butthead*."

"*Butthead* was the perfect word choice." She slammed her hands on her hips and tilted her head way back to meet his gaze with a hard glare.

He'd known she was going to say that, and the thought filled him with gratitude. And determination. Even though they were currently engaged in a battle of wills, one he had to win to ensure her safety, he loved that he could guess her thoughts.

So he traced a line from her collarbone down to the undersides of her breasts.

Her breath caught, and her nostrils flared. Desire warmed

those sparking eyes. His body awakened instantly in response.

Then he pushed.

She squinted in a frown.

"That bruise?" He pressed again, not too hard, anger drawing through him that he'd harmed someone fragile— someone who trusted him. "That's from me."

Her head tilted farther, and her eyes narrowed. "So?"

So? He'd beat to death anybody else who dared to bruise her, and yet look what he'd done. He caressed down and around to the perfect fingerprints embedded in her ass. "These, too."

"So the heck what?" Her breath came out husky this time, and his cock flared to attention.

"I marked you." How could she not understand what he'd done?

She patted above his heart, right beneath his tattoo, none too gently. "I left a reminder, as well."

He nodded, having appreciated the scratches earlier while she slept. "Not the same."

"Why not?"

Challenge launched through him. Then he leaned down until they were almost nose to nose. "Because I'm a fucking killing machine, and you're a sweet little hacker who likes to flirt with danger. Baby, I am danger." He put every ounce of threat and menace into his voice.

So when she threw back her head and laughed, hard and deep, he frowned. Even her nicely jiggling breasts couldn't take his attention from that throaty chuckle.

"Seriously, Jory," she gasped out, wiping a tear from the corner of one eye.

He shook his head. "I've never met a woman who needed a taming more than you do." The words popped out, bemused and thoughtful.

Her eyes widened, and her back went ramrod straight. She coughed and then tried to back up, the bed at her knees halting her retreat.

Interesting. His mean voice didn't work, but his thoughtful one, quite serious to be honest, had made her think twice. Honesty did work with his woman.

His woman?

Yeah. He smiled. They may be short-lived, but while he lived, he had a woman. Piper.

She held both hands up and out to ward him off. "Now wait a minute here."

"Why?" He leaned over until his hands clutched the mattress on either side of her hips, forcing her to sit. "I feel like I finally have your attention."

She shook her head, a jerky movement. "There's no *taming* women, for goodness' sakes."

He nodded, his arms caging her. "I don't want to tame women, just you."

She eyed the door, his groin, and then his face, her thoughts a blueprint to her escape plan. "I'm not sure exactly what that means, but I don't think I like it."

"I wouldn't either, were I you," he said somberly, having way too much fun all of a sudden. God, she was wonderful to mess with. "So how about we come up with a plan we both think is safe?"

"That's fine"—she spoke slowly, carefully—"but part of the plan has to be protecting my mother and my going back to work. Even if your brothers have the computer program, I'm close to figuring out the coding sequence so you don't have to. Plus, if Chance is really held captive there, I have to get your plan to him. At least to let him know you're coming."

Oh, she was trying to work with him, and Jory could appreciate that. "If the commander gets you inland to the facility, there's a damn good chance he won't let you go." How could she not understand how dangerous the commander could be?

Piper rolled her eyes. "My mother will call the National Guard to come looking, so I'm not too worried."

"What if he takes your mother, too?"

She frowned. "I hadn't thought of that." Then she rubbed her chin. "I think maybe I should send my mother on a cruise or vacation somewhere until we get this figured out. Just like you did Edna."

Jory nodded. "That's not a bad plan, except unless you've been planning it, the commander will get suspicious. Like it or not, he'll see that move as you getting your mother to safety before all hell breaks loose, which would be an accurate interpretation."

Piper bit her lip. "What if she wins a vacation like Edna?"

"Still suspicious." Jory stepped back and sat down. "The only way to get your mother to safety is if you go with her. I'll keep the commander busy enough he won't come looking."

Piper picked at a loose string on the blanket. "No. Unfortunately, I'm in the best position to not only get word to Chance but to unravel the codes for the kill chips as well as open a line to yours. I'm it, Jory. Use me."

"I can't." His hands actually shook as he gave her the truth.

She tried to roll her eyes again but failed miserably. "Listen, it was just sex. Really. It was great sex but just bodily functions for us both. The fact that it's been so long for you has emotion clouding the issue."

Did she just say *just sex*? It was one of the best fucking nights of his entire life. His shoulders went back, and his vertebrae straightened. "Just sex?"

"Yes." Relief slackened the muscle along her jaw. "It's okay. No emotion, no promises. Stop making something out of last night that wasn't there."

He shook his head and focused on the scent of the lie. She was lying so he'd allow her into danger, and he could understand that. So he'd ignore the figurative kick to his balls and not shove her stubborn ass back on the bed and kiss her until she relented. The night meant something—to both of them. He could hear her heart even now, and he could see beneath her surface. "You're the worst liar I have ever met. Don't even think about playing poker with my brothers. Ever."

Her eyes widened and her eyelashes actually fluttered. "I'm not lying or trying to hurt your feelings. But you making more out of last night than was there is causing a problem in what was a perfectly good plan. I can take care of myself."

"Remember that taming?" he asked softly.

Flaming red climbed from her chest to her face. "Stop threatening me."

"Then stop lying to me." He could tell she was lying, and he appreciated her need to help him and his brothers. But either they worked together, or he'd have her cute butt locked down somewhere with her mother. "You have one chance here, Piper."

She studied him, her gaze probing deep. Finally, apparently believing him, she nodded. "Fine. We'll agree together, but I have to lie about who had me. If I admit I was with you, they'll know the truth. About us."

He studied her. That was a good point.

She smiled. "So let's work together. What's the plan?"

Smart girl.

The rumble of an opening garage door vibrated the floor. He stood and reached for her clothing on the antique settee. "Get dressed. My brothers are here. Together we'll figure out a way to keep you safe and possibly get the information to Chance." Before he sent her somewhere safe that the commander could never find.

Maybe Chance could somehow get the codes on his way out, because Jory doubted one day was enough for Piper to get the information, considering she'd probably spend most of it being debriefed.

Jory paused at the doorway. While he didn't particularly like this new side of himself, he had no choice but to be honest and embrace it. "But if you deviate from my plan in any way, Piper, you'll understand the meaning of the word *taming*."

Her snort as he left the room failed to reassure him. Shaking his head, he loped into the kitchen just as Nate entered from the garage.

Nate lifted an eyebrow and shut the door behind himself. "You had sex."

Damn it. The downside of having genetically enhanced brothers slapped Jory in the face. "Shut up."

"You shut up." Nate ran a hand through his tousled hair, his gaze thoughtful. "You okay?"

Jory grinned. "Fabulous."

Nate snorted. "If you say so. Will she work with us now?"

A rare temper tickled the base of Jory's neck. "That's not why I slept with her."

Nate scratched his chin, gray eyes darkening. He leaned back against the pristine bright yellow counter and crossed his feet. "Jesus. You're not falling for the commander's daughter, are you?"

"You fell for Dr. Madison's daughter." Two seconds in Nate's presence, and he was a five-year-old little brother again. "I like her."

"Okay." Nate shrugged, the innocuous movement failing to mask his sudden concern. "Will she help us?"

"Yes, but I don't want her in danger."

Nate shoved off the counter. "Right. No danger." He eyed his brother. "We can send her to the ranch right now if you want. Get her off the radar and to safety."

Jory's world settled. That quickly, with one statement, he remembered he was a Dean brother, and he'd never be alone. Now neither would Piper, and his brothers would protect her to their last breaths. "Never alone, Nate."

"Exactly." Nate watched him carefully. "If we need to get her out of here, we have to come up with another plan to get those boys."

Jory nodded, on alert. "She's everything to me, and I know it's been quick."

"So?"

Yeah. So? "If anything happens to me—"

"She's covered. I promise." Nate smiled. "She's pretty and brilliant. I'm happy for you."

Jory forced a smile, tempted to share the truth about his chip with his brother. But he needed Nate focused and not obsessed with saving him. "Thank you."

Nate nodded. "So current plan or new plan?"

Good question. "What is the current plan?"

Nate scrubbed a hand down his face. "We found a cabin about a mile away and took the bodies there. Nice job on the clean neck breaks, by the way. Left print and DNA evidence around the cabin before making sure the bodies will never be found. Now we need the woman to go there, escape, and call for help at a gas station about a mile away."

"Piper." Jory crossed his arms.

"Huh?"

"Her name is Piper." He spoke through clenched teeth. "Stop calling her *the woman*."

"Sorry. Piper. She's ours now, huh?" Nate glanced at his phone. "Okay. So this is your call, and I'll back you no matter what. Do you think *Piper* can jump out of a window, run a mile, and then lie her ass off to her father?"

CHAPTER
19

PIPER EYED THE rustic cabin in the middle of nowhere as Jory's brother pulled his SUV up next to Jory's. She and Jory had spent the drive discussing the plan, and even now, she shook her head. "This is kind of crazy."

"I know." Silence descended in the forest, and he rested his hands on the steering wheel. Moments later, a bird called, the sound oddly chipper. "You don't have to do this."

"If I don't do this, we won't be able to help Chance. I know you don't think I'll have time to work on the codes, but I do." Taking a deep breath, she turned toward him. "Have you told your brothers about your chip yet?"

"No." His jaw hardened. "I'd like to keep the information to myself as long as I can, or they'll spend their time trying to figure out my chip and not save their own asses."

"Okay." Although, she'd figure out his chip if it was the last thing she did. "There's not much they can do without the computer codes, anyway." Too bad the damn things changed every thirty seconds, or she could've just copied them down. "If Chance or I can't get the code algorithm out of the facility, what will we do?"

Jory shrugged. "We'll go in. There's Nate."

A sharp rap sounded on her window, and she jumped, turning.

Nate opened her door. "Are you ready?" His gaze remained shuttered and his face expressionless, but as he took her arm to assist her from the SUV, his hold was infinitely gentle.

"No." Her feet squished in the wet leaves.

He barked out a laugh. "Fair enough. You fight me as hard as you can, okay?"

"No." Jory stood on the other side of the SUV, his head easily clearing the rooftop. "I've got this." Slamming his door, he strode around the vehicle to reach for Piper.

Nate paused. "You sure? The scene and struggle have to look real."

"I'm sure." Jory turned Piper until her back pushed against his front and then he wrapped his arms around her. A quick kiss to the top of her head, and he tightened his hold. "Fight."

The kiss caught her off guard, and she kept her gaze averted from Nate. The idea that Jory wanted his hands, and his hands only, on her was sweet and took root. The whole situation would be so much easier if she didn't like him.

But she did. He was infinitely likable. And sexy as hell.

He lowered his head, and his breath brushed her ear. "Fight me, baby."

She shivered and tried to ignore the blast of heat to her abdomen. Taking a deep breath, she began to buck against him, patting him on the thighs.

He paused. "I need you to actually fight. I promise, you can't hurt me."

She sucked in air and nodded. Then she wriggled against him, shoving her butt into his legs and gently digging her elbows into his ribs.

He chuckled. Then a slap cascaded across her ass hard enough to stop her breathing.

She jerked her head around, her eyes widening. "What the hell?"

"Fight me." He held up his hand. "Or you get another."

Anger blasted through her. He wanted a fight? Oh, he'd get one. She punched him in the stomach, and pain shot up her arm. He nodded and began dragging her toward the cabin. She gave it all she had. Kicking, shrugging, throwing elbows, she made sure to leave evidence of a struggle as Jory dragged her along the path and to the front door. Her boots scraped the warped porch, and she kicked hard. Finally, Jory shoved open the door and pulled her through a gathering room and a kitchen to propel her into a bedroom.

A dingy queen-sized mattress took residence against the wood paneling, a crumpled pillow had been shoved against the wall, and a patched wool blanket had been folded at the edge. The precise crease along the blanket's edge seemed creepy in the dusty space. A one-clasp window was set in the center of the wall with the bed. No other belongings were in the room.

The area smelled stale and like old fish. Dead old fish.

She shook to gain her balance and stomped her boots to leave mud on the scuffed floor. Even though the fight had been pretend, her heart beat a rapid tempo against her rib cage, and her breath panted out. No matter how hard she'd fought him, Jory hadn't hurt her. Not even one little pinch. His strength in containing and somehow not harming her sent little tingles through her. She shoved her hair from her face. "You okay?"

He grinned. "Fine."

The guy wasn't even out of breath. Then he cleared his throat. "You need to use the bathroom, touch the sink, door-knob, everywhere. Leave your DNA and prints, because supposedly you stayed the night here."

A blush rose over her face at where she'd really spent the night. "Do you really think they'll sweep the cabin?"

"Yes."

She didn't even want to imagine how the Dean brothers had gotten the now deceased PROTECT men's DNA and prints all around the cabin. Instead, she eyed the narrow bathroom off the bedroom. "I don't need to go."

He grasped her elbow and drew her to the door. "No choice." He was in full soldier mode, and something about his confidence served to calm her enough to concentrate. Then he turned and caught a pair of black surgical gloves tossed at him by Nate, quickly yanking them on his hands.

Creepy. Way over the top creepy.

She backed into the tiny bathroom.

Jory reached for the doorknob. "Say the PROTECT kidnappers had succeeded in getting you somewhere like this. After they shut the door, what would you do?"

"Look for a weapon or an escape." Of course.

He nodded and walked from the room. "Do it, then." The door closed behind him.

Well, okay then. She scrambled around, looking for a weapon, under the bed and then toward the bathroom. While dusty, the small room seemed fairly clean. Olive green toilet, sink basin, and shower...and that's it. No vanity, towel bar, or drawers anywhere. She quickly shut the door and used the bathroom before washing her hands and hustling from the room.

The door opened again, and Jory stalked inside. "You need to lie on the bed."

Just the suggestion warmed her blood and unfurled tingles in her abdomen. Her heartbeat increased again. She cleared her throat.

His cheek creased, and she cocked her head. How in the world could he know what she was thinking about? "I am not getting in that bed."

"Just on it. As if you had to sleep." His eyebrows rose, waiting.

She had no doubt he'd toss her on the bed if she refused, so with a purely feminine huff, she gingerly sat on the bed.

"Down."

"Fuck you." The words shot out of her instantly.

He eyed the dirty mattress. "Well, if you say so." Two long strides brought him knee to knee with her.

A strong hand in the middle of her chest pushed her over, and she fought a grimace as her back hit the bed. "If I get germs from this..." she muttered.

He stood back and surveyed her, his eyes glinting. "Roll around a little. Like you slept there."

She glared. The man had to stop ordering her around. She kicked the folded blanket off and rolled around, curling into a ball. "Enough?"

For answer, he pulled her up, and she smashed into a chest harder than stone. She sputtered and looked up.

Firm lips covered hers. Warm and seeking, he took her away from the dingy room—away from reality. His tongue slid against the roof of her mouth, eliciting a sigh from somewhere deep in her core. She leaned into him, kissing him back, her fingers curling into his T-shirt.

Only the snap of a padlock clicking into place jerked her back into the room.

Panting, she broke the kiss to see Jory's brother tugging on a rusty lock he'd just attached to the window. She hadn't even heard him come into the room.

"Are you two about done?" Nate asked, his tone dry.

Jory exhaled, amusement dancing across his face.

Piper patted his very hard, oh-so-nice chest and forced a sarcastic smile. "We are now. Unless you want to leave? I was just getting revved up."

Nate's face split in a smile, and his gray eyes warmed. "I love a good smart-ass. Excellent."

"I don't like this." Jory gently moved her to the side and kicked the metal bed frame. The entire room shook. He kicked again, bent, and pulled on a rusty nail. "Piper? Grab this and twist it out."

He thought of everything. She knelt and grasped the head

of the nail, pulling and turning. The rough metal scratched her finger pad.

"Don't cut yourself." Jory bent closer to watch.

She nearly fell back when the nail let loose, and he caught her, helping her up. "This isn't a good plan," he muttered.

Nate tapped the lock with his gloved hand. "Your woman—your call. If you don't want to go with this plan, we won't. But decide now."

Piper's head jerked back. "Whoa there, Sparky. I'm nobody's woman." Yeah. That didn't come out quite like she'd hoped.

Nate Dean turned his full attention on her for the first time, and she fought the urge to step back, not expecting the intensity. The seriousness—hell, the deadliness—suddenly emanating from him proved he was every bit the dangerous predator she'd witnessed lurking in Jory.

"Did you sleep with my brother last night?" Nate asked silkily.

Fire bloomed through her face. "None of your damn business," she ground out.

Nate shrugged. "Even so? That means he decides. If he says you're locked down, away from danger, then you are. *Sparky.*" Warmth, amusement, and an odd gentleness coated his words and glimmered in his eyes.

Even so, that man was a lost cause, so she turned on the one she knew better. A whole hell of a lot better. "You don't believe that nonsense, do you?" Gingerly holding the nail, she pressed her hands to her hips, expecting a nice dismissal of Nate's ass-backward attitude.

What she got was one word and twice the deadly intensity.

"Yes." Jory kept her gaze, waiting. Always waiting, so damn patiently.

"Well, that's, well—" She sputtered. "You're both assholes."

"Yep." Nate sauntered through the room. "You're not the

first one to make that remark. Josie, Shane's wife, held a gun on me once."

Jory blinked. "She did?"

"Yep." Nate grinned. "Come to think of it, Laney, Matt's woman, held a Glock on me once, too." He chuckled. "Good thing Piper doesn't have a gun."

Piper sputtered, looking from Nate to Jory and back. "You guys aren't bonding over this Neanderthal code, are you?"

Nate's gaze warmed as he looked at his brother. "Nope. We bonded decades ago, as solid as can be. Right, Jory?"

"Right." Jory grinned back. "I wish I could've seen them hold a gun on you."

"Good times, and we'll make more in the future." Nate headed for the door. "I'll be outside to make sure she doesn't hurt herself when she falls. Unless the plan has changed?" He paused without looking back.

Jory studied her, no expression on his face. "Do you want to go through with this plan, and if so, will you follow orders?"

She stepped into him, knowing the move to be one of intimidation, although with their size difference, she only succeeded in cranking her neck to keep his gaze. "I am going through with this plan because it's the only way to save your ass as well as rescue those poor kids. Get on board, now."

"Nate?" Jory called out, not moving an inch. "The plan is off."

Damn it. "Fine. I'll follow orders." She shuffled her feet, left with absolutely no alternative. God, she hated making such a promise. It was a somewhat military plan, right? Orders kind of made sense.

"Good." Jory took the rusty nail from her fingers and stalked to jam it into the lock, which gave easily. He stepped back. "Jump out, and be careful when you land. I'll meet you in front." Without another word, he turned on his heel and strode from the room and out of the cabin.

She had the oddest feeling he had to leave before she tried to shimmy out of the window. The glass swung up easily, and she held it open with her head. Slivers pierced her palms when she pressed on the edge and heaved herself up to plant one knee. Then gravity took over.

Her yelp as she pitched forward echoed in her head, and she landed in a bush that prickled. Scrambling, she rolled into the mud and shoved to her feet just as Jory rounded the corner.

"Damn it." He started toward her, and Nate grabbed his arm.

"She's okay. Don't disturb the area." Nate squinted, eyeing her. "You are okay, right?"

"Fine." She brushed off leaves and stretched her aching back.

Nate chuckled. "Tough. Our women are tough, thank God."

She warmed from the compliment and flushed at being included in the Dean brothers' women. Old-fashioned to the point of being silly, but she kind of understood. Lost boys raised by the military with no mother? They probably did have a slightly skewed sense of relationships and protectiveness. "Now what?" she asked quietly, wondering if she'd have a chance to teach Jory how to be modern.

Jory pointed toward the rough road. "Stick to the sides, hidden by trees, until you get to the main road. Feel free to touch trees, branches, and even tumble once or twice in your desperation to get free."

Man. Somehow she'd ended up in a spy movie. "And then?" The prickly bushes had scratched her arm, and she fought the urge to rub.

"Go left, hit the gas station, and call the commander. We'll keep eyes on you until you make the station. Go to work, and then I'll meet you at Earl's house afterward."

She caught her breath. "They know about Earl's house—they have surveillance there."

"I know."

She blinked. "You do?"

"Yes, but they don't know we know, so it's okay. We can feed them information this way. Trust me. This is old hat."

"But we, I mean we—"

His gaze softened. "I know, and that convinced them that we didn't know we were being watched."

Heat flared into her face. So Jory had known about the recording? That they could be heard? "You used me."

"No. Actually, I completely lost myself in the moment. I promise." He grasped her jaw and slid his finger along her lips. "Trust me, Piper."

She didn't have a choice at this point and already had enough to worry about. Plus, she'd lost herself in that moment, too. "Okay."

Jory took a deep breath, his massive chest moving. "Are you sure you want to do this?"

She took in his serious gaze and allowed for a moment to think. She had to do this. If she didn't, she was leaving three boys in hell, and she couldn't live with that. Plus, if anybody had a chance at finding the correct algorithm for the codes, it had to be her. "I'm sure. Trust me."

"I do." His eyes darkened, and the muscles visibly shuddered in his well-developed arms.

Plus, she'd damn well find a way to reach his chip so it would accept the codes. She'd just found him, and she wanted a future with him. "Don't worry," she breathed. She'd be the one to save the super-soldier, and she had to get to it.

He exhaled, tension filling the air around them. Harsh tension filled with worry and a hint of anger. Yet he trusted her enough to let her go. "Be careful . . . and good luck."

CHAPTER
20

H ER FATHER HADN'T come for her personally. For all he
knew, Piper had been kidnapped, possibly harmed,
and had escaped...and her father hadn't come personally.
He'd sent a contingent of soldiers to the gas station, who'd
promptly loaded her up and driven her to the center of Utah
and the heavily armed compound.

Yeah, Jory had been right. Inner compound, here she was—
and if she didn't convince the commander she was telling the
truth about her ordeal, she'd probably never leave. She took a
deep breath and slowly let out the air, counting to ten. Sweat
slicked her palms, and time slowed down.

Once arriving, she'd instantly been debriefed by two soldiers after being told her father was on an important confer-
ence call.

Now she waited alone in the commander's office, trying
to push down hurt. It wasn't as if he'd ever acted like a father.
Why would she expect concern now?

She clasped her hands together and wondered what it
would've been like to have had a father. One who cared. Her
stomach hurt, and tears clogged her throat. She'd managed
to call her mother to reassure her she was all right, and Earl
had been there comforting Rachel. Earl had even gotten on
the phone to hear Piper's voice himself.

Why couldn't Earl have been her father?

The hurt she could handle—the fear, maybe not. Pounding ached along her temples as the first adrenaline rush
faded. She swallowed over a lump in her throat and allowed

herself to wallow for just a moment. Okay, enough of this. She didn't have time for fear or regret if she wanted to survive, so she steeled her shoulders. Time to figure things out.

She had to get out of this meeting and back to the computer to figure out the algorithm that changed the codes, and to finish the new program that would hopefully bypass Jory's damaged chip. If she'd had any doubts about helping Jory and his brothers—and frankly, she hadn't—they'd be long gone now. She didn't give a hoot that they were trained killers and quite possibly not the good guys.

Her father sucked.

This office was much more plush than the city one that had been blown up. Well, if leather chairs, oiled weapons, and heavy walnut furniture could be considered plush. The scent of gunpowder and rich cigars permeated the furnishings. On his desk he had a computer and a stack of files. Peering closer, she studied a glass paperweight encapsulating a bullet casing. Weird.

High heels tapped down a hallway outside, and Dr. Madison swept in. White lab coat, red heels, a computer tablet in her hands. Her lipstick matched her shoes, and she'd pulled back her black hair. No gray. "I've been told you hurt your arm." All business, Madison brushed around the other leather chair and sat, leaning forward and grabbing Piper's left wrist.

"I fell in a bush." How dangerous was the rude woman? Piper studied her and played along, wrinkling her nose at the heavy floral perfume cascading around the brilliant doctor. "I'm fine."

Madison reached in her lab coat for a tube of ointment to hand over. "Use this. It'll take care of the burn."

"Okay." Piper extricated her arm and unwound the top of the tube. She had some size on the woman, but she'd bet her last penny Dr. Madison had been trained in hand-to-hand.

The woman moved with a grace that suddenly appeared deadly.

"Our men swept the cabin in which you were kept. The PROTECT men were no longer present." Madison sat back, sharp eyes narrowing.

Piper rubbed ointment on her arm and tried to appear casual. "I suppose they left when they discovered I'd jumped out the window?"

"I suppose." No emotion colored the doctor's monotone. "I read your report and have a couple of questions."

Fine hairs rose down Piper's back. She'd never been a good liar. "Go ahead."

"Did these men say anything to you?"

"They threw me in a car, drove to the middle of nowhere, and tossed me into a room in a cabin. The guy with the accent said something about the commander messing with God and genetics, and then we called the commander." Piper half turned to fully face the other woman. "Since you're so close to my dad and all, I'm sure you know all about that conversation."

Heavily blackened eyelashes stilled as Madison's concentration focused fully on Piper. "I wanted to get your perceptions as well."

Piper screwed the cap back into place, trying to keep her body relaxed while her heart thundered into action. "To be honest, they made me curious. Have you and my father genetically created soldiers? Raised them to kill?"

"Yes."

Yeah, Piper had figured the doctor knew all about the program. The woman had no conscience, did she? How could anybody raise little boys to kill? Piper hissed out air.

Madison chuckled. "The commander has always been driven, and combined with my genius, we've done remarkable things."

The woman sounded, almost, aroused. Bile rose in Piper's throat. "People aren't things." She slammed the ointment tube on the desk. Her father had lied to her—repeatedly. No way did the U.S. government sanction the creation of soldiers from birth. She barely knew him, but she'd held such amazing hopes and dreams, as they died, she hurt. "Did you ever think about the damage? The actual kids you created?"

"No." Madison sniffed. "They were never kids. From day one, they were creations with one purpose."

Piper tilted her head to the side. Her heart burned for those poor boys. For Jory. "Which was to kill?" she asked softly.

Madison's eyes sparkled. "No. To fulfill the commander's destiny. Their creation, their training, their very essence as soldiers are *his* destiny." She jerked her head. "Right or wrong."

"Do you see the wrong?"

Madison's lips thinned. "We were right, but our results went wrong. But we were on the brink of something brilliant before those boys escaped."

Thank God the Dean brothers had gotten free. "Wow." Piper breathed out. "You're all in, aren't you, lady? Drinking the fruit juice and falling right down."

Madison clucked her tongue. "Don't be snide. Someday, you'll understand love."

Piper shook her head. "Lady, that isn't love. Not even close."

Madison's pink tongue darted out. "Then what is it?" She frowned as if truly wanting an answer.

"Desperation. Obsession." Piper breathed and tried to quiet her now rioting mind. "Not love."

"More than love, then." Madison shrugged, and eyed Piper. "Love is pain, right? Clouds judgment until it's too late. Believe me, it's too late now unless we get those weapons back."

What the hell did that mean? "They're people, not weapons."

"If you really think that, they're working you. Perfectly," Madison all but purred.

Now that was a direct hit. Madison was probably one of the smartest people Piper had ever met, and yet she'd blinded herself with love to a sociopath. The commander was charming, that was true... and Piper could see the similarity between Madison's craving for the commander's love and Piper's earlier need for his approval. But while Piper was seeing the truth, Madison still seemed obsessed. "Did you know about me? That he had a daughter?" Piper asked.

For the first time, genuine emotion flashed across the scientist's face. She paled, and then red burst across her smooth skin. "No. Not until you showed up for work months ago."

The agony of the betrayal was almost palpable, and Madison's eyes flashed fire. Yet even that subterfuge hadn't turned Madison against the commander. Did love make every smart woman a fool? "Discovering that the man you'd devoted yourself to for decades had a child with another woman must've hurt you. I'm sorry," Piper murmured.

"No matter." Dr. Madison crossed shapely legs, her fine-boned hands shaking.

Piper fought the real urge to offer comfort to the damaged woman. "Maybe the commander isn't capable of emotion."

Amusement lifted Madison's lip. "Like a sociopath?"

"Perhaps." At this point, who the hell knew?

"He's a genius, not a sociopath. Let's discuss something else. What did you think about my Jory?" Madison's smile widened like a cat who'd found a bowl of cream.

Her Jory? Oh, hell no. Piper's head snapped up. "I didn't get to know him, but if he's one of your creations, the guy deserves freedom."

"Hmmm. Interesting."

The door opened, and the commander strode inside. "Is she damaged?"

Dr. Madison stood. "No. Just a scratch." She studied the commander and then crossed the room to the door. "I have work to do." The door closed nearly silently behind her.

Piper cleared her throat. Just how dangerous was her father to his own flesh and blood? Did the guy even have a heart? "You've hurt Dr. Madison."

The commander frowned and crossed to sit behind his desk. "Don't be ridiculous."

"Do you love her?" There wasn't a puzzle in the world Piper could resist, and the man was all sorts of pieces.

"No." He flicked dust off his desk. "Silly emotions get in the way." Then he typed several keys near his computer. "I read the report of your ordeal, and some of it doesn't track."

She stiffened. "What doesn't track?"

"I don't know yet. But I can assure you I have men tearing apart the cabin." He turned from the screen to focus on her again. "If there's anything you'd like to tell me, now is the time."

"I told the guys interviewing me everything." She clasped her hands together in her lap. "Who are the PROTECT people, anyway?"

The commander sighed. "They're a nuisance, nothing more and nothing less. A group dedicated to erasing the work I've done. They won't succeed, and you shouldn't worry about them. If you're not telling me the truth about your kidnapping, then I'm your concern right now."

Piper sighed, her heart aching for what she knew would never be. Every silly daydream she'd had of a father, of having somebody there as a grandpa for her kids someday, faded away. He'd raised Jory and had no more feeling for him than for a coffeepot. How much more could he have for a daughter he'd barely just met? Not much. But was he a danger to her? "I wish I knew you."

Taking a hard look at her, he reached under his desk and tapped. A door slowly slid open behind him, revealing a small room. "Very well. I guess it's time you did." Then he waited.

A shiver wound down her spine. The hair on the back of her neck stood up.

She instantly fought the dual urges to run away and investigate. Giving in, she slowly rose and walked around the desk to enter the room. Boxes of Cuban cigars lined one shelf. DVDs took precedence on another, while various antique weapons perched throughout. Several drawers were perfectly aligned beneath the shelves. An older, dinged laptop rested on a middle shelf.

A picture caught her eye, and her lungs compressed. Taken about twenty years previous, when Jory had to have been around five years old, he sat on a cement block next to another boy with gray eyes. The other boy was bigger and had thrown an arm around Jory. Two other boys, also with gray eyes, stood behind them. One with serious eyes, the other with angry ones. The angry kid looked like Nate.

"They look so young," Piper murmured. She picked up the picture and turned. Was there some sense of nostalgia in her father? "Why do you have this?"

His chair swiveled, and he faced her. "I made them. They're mine."

She shook her head. "They're people."

"No." He steepled his fingers beneath his chin. "They're creations. I still have the video of you and Jory at your neighbor's."

Yeah. Figured he hadn't erased it. She shrugged off a sense of the willies. "Why?"

"No reason, really. But I do doubt he just up and left you after the exchange on the floor."

True, that. He'd pretty much rocked her world in a retirement community instead. Her muscles tensed. "I haven't seen him since."

"Pity. What did you think of him?"

"Why?"

The commander smiled. "Just curious."

"I think if we had a relationship, and psycho avengers kidnapped me, he'd be there if I called for help." She eyed the man she'd never quite know.

"I think you're right," the commander murmured. "Where is he, Piper?"

She inhaled slowly. "I have no idea."

"Well, then. Please bring me the DVD dated two years ago with Jory's name under it."

She rolled her eyes, her feet itching to hurry from the room and keep on running. "I don't need to see another Jory sex tape. Thanks but no thanks."

"Now, Piper."

Fine. She'd go along until she could get home and then make a new plan for her life. She quickly found the DVD and hurried from the room, tossing it on the commander's desk. "You're wasting your time." Her legs shook to flee and never come back before she had to watch Jory with yet another woman, but she dropped back into her chair.

"This isn't a sex tape." The commander removed the disk from the plastic container and slipped it beneath his desk. Then he turned his monitor so she could see the screen. "This shows the day he was shot."

She sat up. If the commander was showing her this, then he had something to prove, and it probably wasn't going to be good for her. "I don't want to see this," she whispered.

"Too bad. It's time we understood each other better." He

frowned and concentrated on the keyboard, and a slide came up of Jory lying in circles of blood. Red covered his chest, and spray had arched up over his neck and jaw. His eyes were closed, and he appeared dead and gone.

The image slammed into Piper's stomach and cut straight to her heart with the heat of a sharpened blade. She swayed in her seat. "Please turn it off."

"Hmmm." The commander peered around at the screen. "Let's watch the video, which I took great pains to retrieve." He punched in a couple more keys, and the screen went blank before starting at the beginning.

Jory sat in a chair, his hair long, his chin down, anger turning those spectacular eyes gunmetal hard and gray. His hands had been tied behind his back. "I don't give a shit who you are—and there are no other creations like me." Power and promise rode his strong voice.

A man, broad and muscled, stepped into the screen. Bald and in fighting shape. "I'll torture you until you beg me to take their location from you."

Then Jory smiled. "You have no clue what you're talking about."

The man shook his head. "I'm willing to let you live if you give up the other locations of the creations. My group could use you."

"Screw you." Jory's eyelids dropped as if the entire situation bored him enough to sleep. "We done?"

Two years later, watching the video, Piper's shoulders relaxed. "Who's the man?"

"A leader of the PROTECT group," the commander said.

Piper's mouth dropped open, and she quickly shut it. "You've known about the group for two years? They actually found Jory?"

"Yes. Apparently Jory had gone undercover at a facility being watched by PROTECT—everybody trying to find me.

They took him because he was watching for me and didn't have a clue about them. Bastards." The commander tapped his chin.

Piper looked back at the frozen screen. "You lied. The Russians didn't shoot him."

"Of course they didn't." The commander tapped the screen. "Keep watching. I fetched this video after we rescued Jory—the shooter was also wired with a camera, but you don't need to see that one. This one will do better."

Well. Even though it sucked she had to watch her lover get shot, she knew he survived. Since he hadn't lied to her, she relaxed. "Let 'er rip."

"Just watch."

In the DVD, the PROTECT leader picked up a sharp blade.

Piper hissed out a breath. "I don't need to see torture."

On the screen, a commotion set up outside the torture room. A woman yelled something, and the door banged open. "I'm sorry," a female voice whispered, the sound distorted through the screen.

The PROTECT soldier pivoted on the screen and then dove to the ground. A gun fired three times, the bullets impacting Jory's chest and throwing him back onto the cement. Blood sprayed up and arced through the room.

Kicking up, the soldier grunted, and the gun flew across the screen. "You shot him!"

"Yes," the shooter snapped, turning and kicking the soldier in the head.

Watching the screen, Piper frowned. Why did the voice almost sound familiar?

Heels came into focus, and then a head bent down. "He's dead."

Piper gasped and bolted straight from her chair. The woman in the video turned, her face fully on display.

"Mom?" Piper gasped. Two years ago, her mother had shot Jory?

The screen went dark.

The commander slowly, deliberately turned the monitor back into place. "I'm sure it's an odd feeling knowing your mother shot your lover."

Piper fell back into her chair. Her lungs compressed. "I don't believe this."

"It's true. Your mother is actually a crack shot. Always has been."

The world screeched to a full stop. Piper's mind whirled. "Excuse me? A crack shot?" Piper pushed hair out of her face, her hand shaking. "My mom doesn't even own a gun." The woman ran yogurt shops, for hell's sake.

He cleared his throat, black eyes serious. "Well, she might not have told you everything."

"You think?" Piper snapped.

The commander straightened. "When our contacts in the PROTECT organization let us know that one of my soldiers had been taken, I had no clue it was Jory, so I thought to just end the problem. I needed to get somebody in there to shut the prisoner up before he spoke. Somebody unremarkable. Like a yogurt shop deliverer from a few towns over."

Piper shook her head. "What?"

The commander nodded. "Fortune shines on the bold. You were caught hacking, and all of a sudden, I found a way to solve both your problem and mine."

Wait a minute. Piper rapidly clicked facts into place. "Now that's quite a coincidence." Sarcasm coated her words.

He kept her gaze, not moving.

Oh, hell. "You set me up." She shook her head. "You fucking set me up." The box of stuff sent to her house had been deliberate. The one that had set her on the path to finding her real father.

His upper lip twitched. "Well...yes."

Piper's breath heated. "Okay. Let me see if I can figure this out without my head blowing off my shoulders."

"Cease with the dramatics, please." His voice remained cordial.

Asshat. "Jory was taken by the PROTECT group, and you discovered his location. So you set about learning everything you could about the PROTECT group and the area in which it worked."

"I knew one of my soldiers was a prisoner, but I didn't even consider it was one of the Gray brothers and just figured it was somebody expendable. Your mother's yogurt shops weren't close to the facility, but we sent several flyers about the business expanding and looking to move into the neighborhood to the receptionists of the building. Then we sent yogurt."

Piper frowned. How had all this happened under her nose? "But when you found my mother—wait. Wait a minute. I'm getting confused." It was all too much. She'd been living in a spy movie and hadn't even known it.

The commander sighed as if truly disappointed with her lack of understanding. "I did all the prep work with the flyers and contact, and your mother was easy to google, so anybody looking for her online would've found her. Once we had the road paved, you tried to hack into my server and ended up in trouble."

Piper's head slowly lifted. Heat flushed through her. "I wasn't arrested by the government, was I?" Son of a bitch. She'd been scared out of her mind.

"No. That was us." He shrugged. "We have facilities that appear like a jail."

The fucking liar. She'd been so easy to set up. The scenario was unbelievable, and her brain quickly caught up. Fire lashed through her. "When you pretended to arrest me—you blackmailed my mother."

The commander kept Piper's gaze. "Yes."

Oh God. "But she worked as a receptionist for you so long ago." Not a super-spy.

"True, but she was undergoing training to be an operative when she discovered our genetic experiments, and she had qualms. She became pregnant and ran." He shrugged as if the entire scenario wasn't ass-backward crazy.

Piper shook her head almost in slow motion. "You didn't follow her?"

He chuckled. "I found her within three days, Piper. But I let her be until I needed her again. This time to shoot one of my captured soldiers before he gave everything up about our organization."

So he had never given a crap about Piper or had wanted to reach out to meet her. She tried to slow her erratic heartbeat. "Why not just rescue Jory?"

The commander sighed. "We didn't know it was one of the Gray brothers until your mother reported back after the shooting. We'd wired her with a camera, of course. Our sources said the PROTECT group had one of our soldiers, but at that time, we were still regrouping after the Tennessee mess and working to save face with the government, so we didn't know it was a Gray brother."

Dean brother, asshole.

Piper frowned. "This was more than just you making my mom shoot an absent soldier."

The commander finally smiled. "There's the brain I'm hoping you have. You're right. This was about getting rid of the soldier, pulling you into my organization, and neutralizing your mother from stopping me. With the recording of her committing murder, of course."

Piper swallowed. "So you wanted me?"

"You have impressive computer skills—quite impressive. Your skills combined with one of my super-soldiers might create an unheard-of next generation." He nodded as if giving her approval.

She shoved back against the chair. "You wanted to *breed* me?" she yelled.

He nodded. "Yes."

Her head actually spasmed. "You're fucking crazy."

"Really, Piper."

She covered her face with her hands. "I don't believe this. I really don't." She lifted up and frowned. "Wait a minute. Jory didn't die."

"No." The commander blew out air. "The second I saw the video, we went on a mission to retrieve his body. At that point, we didn't care about the publicity. Of course, we found him alive, took him, and our surgeons went to work."

Piper gagged and swallowed quickly. "Why didn't you seek me out before—when I was young?"

"You were a girl." His voice remained dispassionate. "It wasn't until I discovered you were exceptional that I considered using you."

A figurative blade sliced into Piper's heart. What an asshole. And what a relief that she didn't have to worry about him any longer. They weren't on the same side. They never really had been. "So if I hadn't had an aptitude for computers?"

"Then I wouldn't have interceded." No emotion showed in his black eyes.

Piper blew out air, letting go of any hurt. Then she focused on the problem at hand. "My mother has lived with this for two years? This video?"

"Yes. If she tells you about me, or about our past, she goes to jail." The commander scratched his arm. "She might not know Jory survived."

So her mother might've been living with the thought she'd murdered a man? Piper stood. "I have to get to her."

"No. Work with me, or I'll turn the DVD over to the

authorities along with a body pretty much matching Jory.
Close enough. Your mother will go to prison."

"Bullshit." Piper turned and headed for the door.

"Try me, Piper."

She stopped. He was serious. Could she get her mother to
safety? Away from Utah?

"I'll have soldiers on her the second she tries to flee, and
she'll be in federal custody a moment later. Believe me, I have
excellent connections within the United States government."

A rock slammed into Piper's gut. The commander con-
tracted with the government for assignments and missions.
He probably did have decent connections. She slowly turned
around. Her hands shook, so she stuffed them in her pockets.
Time had moved from ticking to a full-out run, and she had
to get back to her computer. Maybe Jory could protect her
mother while Piper figured out how to save his life. "What
do you want?"

"Well, for starters, I want your help bringing in Jory."

"I don't know where—"

The commander lifted a large hand. "Stop lying. I have
cameras lining the street outside the old facility and saw
Jory rescue you. I'd like to say I'm disappointed in you, but
women always lie. Worthless bitches, all of you."

"Well. So much for the soft touch, Dad."

He cut her a hard look. "There's no need to try a soft
touch with you any longer. This is the truth, and this is reality. You will help me, and like I said, I saw Jory rescue you."

She blinked, and her shoulders slumped. All of the running through woods, the preparations, the use of the cabin.
"We didn't see cameras."

"Where is Jory?"

"I don't know. Once I'm home, I'm supposed to meet up
with him." How could she save her mother and Jory at the
same time?

"Have you met any of the brothers?"

"Yes—" She paused. Shouldn't he know that? Two of the brothers had shown up and taken the bodies. She gasped.

The commander nodded. "Yes. I lied. No cameras."

Stupid. God, she was so fucking stupid. "You didn't know Jory was around."

"No, and now I do."

Oh man, she'd just betrayed Jory. Just set him up along with his brothers. Her belly knotted, and she scrubbed both hands down her face. "What have I done?" she whispered.

"You've been quite helpful. So either do what I ask, or I send your mother to prison for the rest of her life. What's it to be?"

There wasn't much of a choice, now was there? "What do you want me to do?" Piper whispered, her chest lighting with pain.

CHAPTER
21

J ORY WAITED IN the darkened room, tuning out the tick, tick, tick of the mantle clock. Menthol scented the air along with lemon cleanser. Neighbor Earl must have an ache or pain somewhere.

He had already, rather predictably, scurried through the backyard to Piper's house right at dinnertime. Jory had immediately abandoned his hiding place in the back room. A monstrous orange cat eyed him from across the room and then turned, apparently bored.

Good. He wasn't used to animals, and he was pretty sure

the cat wouldn't like him. Animals had good instincts with other predators.

Now his abnormal senses allowed him to hear Piper's door shut across two yards, and he could make out her footsteps. Slow and plodding, while her heartbeat was elevated.

For the last night, he could do nothing but think about her. Her skin, her scent, her spectacular brain nearly haunted him. He didn't believe in fate, and he sure as hell didn't believe in love, but somehow the pretty computer hacker had dug right into his heart, maybe deeper, and found a home. One that warmed him while scaring the ever-living crap out of him.

What had he been thinking letting her go back into the lion's den? The commander didn't care about her, and if he thought she was betraying him, he'd harm her. Jory had been an ass for allowing her to help.

The sliding glass door opened, and she stepped inside. "Jory?" she whispered.

He flicked on the light.

Pale. The woman was too pale, and even from across the room, he could see the small vein along her neck pulsing. She was about two seconds away from an anxiety attack.

He frowned and stood, allowing adrenaline to flood his system. To narrow his already unreal focus. "Are you all right?" He reached her in two strides and found comfort with wrapping his hand around her arm. Touching her. Reassuring himself that she was safe.

"Yes." The smile she forced to her pretty face hurt to see. "I'm fine."

"Good." He leaned in and brushed her lips, keeping his expression clear when her mouth trembled against his. More than anything, he wanted to gather her close and reassure her that everything would be all right. He would make sure of it. Instead, he levered back and studied her. The air around her.

It morphed, waves cascading. He shouldn't be able to see such a thing, but there it was. In fact...different frequencies expanded in nearly invisible waves. Piper had been wired. Sight and sound. Probably the top button of her simple shirt.

She licked her lips and glanced around the room.

Ah. They were being watched from afar as well. Jory tuned in, but the narrow beams shot by the heat devices were hard to detect through walls unless he was closer to a window. No need to move, considering now he fully knew they were watching as well as listening.

Good thing the commander hadn't a clue about the Dean brothers' extra abilities. They'd faced death in hiding such a thing from him as they grew up, but the risk had been worth the payoff. Now they had an advantage over the bastard.

Tears gathered in Piper's eyes.

Fury threatened to choke him. She was the worst spy in the entire universe. He loved that about her. So he decided to help her out. "I've been worried about you going back to the commander. Did he believe your story about the PROTECT soldiers?"

She blanched. "Yes." Panic clearly bubbled up, and her eyes widened.

Shit. She was going to blow the entire thing. He grabbed her and kissed her. Hard.

She shook her head.

He leaned in, softened his assault, and took her under. With a soft groan, she grabbed his chest and nearly threw herself into him, kissing him back with a desperation he felt in his own bones. Heat slammed into his cock, and he ground against her softness. Yet he kept his chest from crushing hers, not wanting to harm the camera.

Giving her arms a little shake, *trust me*, he pulled away. "I promise this will all be okay, Piper."

She blinked, her eyes cloudy and her lips a pretty pink. Color returned to her skin over her fine cheekbones. "Jory, I—"

"No. I won't stop kissing you." He slid his foot over hers and tapped out Morse code. *Trust me.*

She frowned, confusion blanketing her features.

Okay. It was a long shot that she'd know Morse code. So he kept tapping just random taps and pressed down hard enough to still her. The camera couldn't see their feet, and he'd keep the taps silent.

She licked her lips and tried to free her foot.

So he stepped on it. "I missed you today, baby."

"Jory?" Her eyebrows drew down, and she tried to pull away.

He flattened her foot and kept tapping. "You feel me, baby? I missed you."

She cocked her head, still frowning. "I, ah feel you."

"Good." Even though she obviously didn't know Morse code, and why the hell not, by the way . . . she must've realized he was trying to tell her something.

Realization dawned in her emerald eyes. She half shook her head, her eyebrows drawing down.

He nodded. *Yeah. Not clueless here.*

She exhaled slowly, her eyes filling with hope and gratitude.

Relief blasted into him with the force of a wrecking ball. Having her afraid, hurting, had dug deep inside him with a surprising sharpness. Leaving her behind when he died would fucking suck, but his brothers would protect her. He knew it. "How was the main compound?" he asked.

She shrugged, the pinched look leaving her face. Her small hands caressed down his arms in a show of comfort.

Natural and so damn feminine. "Um, I didn't get very far inside. Just saw the main building and my father's office. He's not worried about the PROTECT soldiers."

"He should be. The guys I took out were well trained. In fact, I doubt any of the commander's other soldiers could've beaten them." Yeah. Making the dig while the bastard was surely listening felt good. "Not that it matters. The commander and his organization are down to one tiny little compound in Utah. Soon he'll have nothing." All right. Probably enough goading. He reached out and enclosed her hands, providing warmth. She was still chilled. "Did you get the algorithm for figuring out how the code is chosen and changes every thirty seconds?"

"No." She shook her head. "But I figured out how to get it."

"Really?" He forced a smile. She had to sound more relaxed, or the commander would know she couldn't lie. So he leaned in and took her lips again, hovering over them to talk, intrigue sweeping down his spine from her softness. "Awesome. When?"

"Tomorrow." She took a shaky breath, obviously repeating what she'd been told. "I'm back on computers tomorrow, and I think I can save the algorithm on a USB drive. Will you and, ah, Nate meet me tomorrow night? Right here?"

Did the commander really believe Jory would fall for this? Arrogant bastard. "Yes." Jory rubbed her arms and tried to look like a lovesick puppy as he levered back. "My other brothers are in town, too. Ready to get those chips deactivated." That would have the commander salivating.

Her head jerked back. "Oh. Okay. That's good."

"You're so special to me, Piper. Do you think we can really be together after all of this? If we somehow can reach my chip?" He poured on the charm and the lovesickness.

Her lips tightened, and she cut him a look. *Knock it off.* "I really do."

Good thing the camera only focused on him and not on her. He rubbed her arms. "I've never met anyone as much into computers as I am." Which was the absolute truth, actually.

Fire leaped into her eyes, although her mouth curved in a sad smile. "You are geekier than my normal type, to be honest."

His girl had a backbone, did she? Good. At least she wasn't sounding like a high schooler who'd memorized a speech for class. And the sadness, he understood but couldn't help. Time was too short. "Geekier?" Jory asked.

She shrugged. "Yes. I usually go for more physical guys. Tough guys, you know. But you're a sweetie, Jory."

Sweetie? Nobody on earth found him sweet. "No. You're the sweet one." He moved into her and caressed down to her butt to clench. Her "eep" of surprise flooded him with amusement. She should've thought twice before starting this game.

She struggled to retreat, and he kept her easily in place. "I should get going soon so they don't know I'm talking to you."

Nice try. All of a sudden, with death breathing down his neck, he was having fun. Real fun, and he didn't have much time left to play around, considering the commander would wait until tomorrow to capture all the brothers. The bittersweet moment cut him deep, so he ran with it. "The commander isn't smart enough to have surveillance here, so I'm sure we have time. How about we go for round two of last night?"

Her mouth dropped open. Pink flushed up her face. "But—"

He silenced her with another kiss. Hauling her up, he made them both forget they had listeners. She touched him deep inside, and he wanted to keep her there forever. Finally, when his jeans were about to burst, he released her. "That'll have to do, I guess. The second you get home with the USB, come over here. We can then go meet my brothers with the information."

She shook her head, her eyes cloudy with passion. Pretty pink lips pouted at him. "Have you told them that your chip was damaged?"

"Not yet." He leaned in and pressed a soft kiss to her forehead, his gut churning. "We'll tell them after we save them, and maybe we'll figure out a way to reach my chip. If we don't, I need to tell you how much you've already meant to me. Thank you, Piper." He gave the truth, not caring of the camera. She'd made a difference in his life in a very short amount of time, and no matter what happened, he wanted her to know that. To maybe remember him with a smile.

"Jory, I care about you." She rubbed her foot against his.

"I know." His chest filled.

The arrogance brought a genuine smile to her face. Finally. "Then I'll see you tomorrow night with the info. I can't wait to see your brothers."

He nodded and led her to the sliding glass door and watched her walk through the night to her house. The sight of her leaving him, of being too far away to protect, uncoiled heat inside his gut. He had to fight himself, his every instinct, to let her go. Shutting down all emotion, he ran outside, full bore for the back fence. He'd be followed, but he could lose a tail.

Then he had plans to make.

Morning came too damn early. Jory's chip would explode the next day. Did he even know at what time?

Piper rubbed her eyes and opened the front door dressed in jeans and a green sweater. She'd pulled her hair up and tried to hide the dark circles under her eyes with makeup, but at this point, she was finished trying to make an effort for her father. She'd spent the entire night on the

Internet looking for any sort of help with the algorithm program, and she'd even reached out to the few hackers she still knew.

Nothing. Failure weighed down her shoulders, compounded with raw fear. She couldn't lose Jory now.

After leaving Jory, she'd headed upstairs for her computer, leaving her mother and Earl to a peaceful night. Once in her room, she'd tossed the shirt with camera into her purse. There were men watching the house, so the commander would know she didn't leave. They didn't need to listen to her visit the bathroom or toss and work all night. She'd disconnected the tiny battery out of spite. Now they couldn't see or hear her.

Jory knew.

Somehow, he'd figured out about the camera. Thank God. Then he'd totally messed with her and suggested they make out again. While she'd still been reeling from that offer, he'd kissed her senseless, not caring who listened.

Now, Piper had to save her mother from federal prison. Somehow. She didn't have a lot of faith in the running and hiding plan, but if that's what they had to do, they would. After she saved Jory and those poor kids at the facility.

The creak of the porch swing caught her up short, and she whirled to see Brian slowly pushing back and forth. "What in the world?" she asked.

He held out a latte cup. "Peace offering."

"No thanks." What in the hell was he doing on her porch? Jory's warnings ran through her mind. Was this guy actually dangerous? No, she was seeing subterfuge everywhere.

Brian smiled and pushed a hand through his already tousled blond hair. "Can we talk? I'm sorry I was unkind."

She frowned. "Hell, no. We're not dating, and we're not friends. Sorry." She didn't have time for niceties or playing games. Life was unfortunately too damn short. "I seriously think you need anger management. Plus, I'm pretty infatuated with somebody else." Why not give him the truth?

Brian stood, towering over her. "I don't believe this." Irritation sparked his eyes, and his body stiffened.

She shrugged. At this point, a pissed-off realtor didn't scare her much. "No offense, but I have bigger problems than your disbelief. Bye." Turning to go, she halted when he grabbed her arm.

"You have no idea what you're doing." Tension cut hard into the sides of his mouth.

"I usually don't." She tried to wrench her arm free, but he held tight. Brian was much stronger than she would've thought, and she stilled. "However, I know a dickhead when I see one, and right now that's you. So we're over, you're done, and let's just move on."

He yanked her close. "That is not how this is going to happen. You do not break up with me."

"Okay." Her temper began to heat the skin down her back. "Then you break up with me. Either way, let's get this over with."

"Oh, hell no." Arrogance and something darker crossed his face.

The door opened, and her mother stalked outside, a frying pan in one hand. "Let her go, or I'll break your head."

Piper coughed out a laugh, even while her body went on alert. "Okay dokay here. Brian, let go."

He glared at Rachel. "Go back inside."

Earl shoved beyond Rachel, his hair mussed, the buttons on his shirt askew. His still impressive chest vibrated as he stepped onto the porch. "Let her go, or I'll break your hand, boy."

Piper's mouth hung open. "Mom?"

Rachel blushed a fluorescent pink. "Good-bye, Brian."

Brian slowly released her.

Keeping her gaze on her mother and avoiding the tousled Earl, Piper continued, "Brian, leave now. Please."

Muttering about crazy women and life, Brian stomped down the stairs and to his car.

Rachel slowly lowered the pan. "You okay?"

"Fine." Piper studied her mother with new eyes. The woman could be deadly when protecting her child. Deadly, period. "I love you, Mom." Soon they'd have a long talk about everything—especially the disgruntled half-nude neighbor hovering protectively close. When they had a chance to be alone.

Rachel smiled, a lingering sadness darkening her eyes. "Sometimes I lose my temper. But I love you, too."

Piper leaned in and kissed her mom's cheek, definitely intrigued by the layers she hadn't realized lived in her mother. "Everything is going to be all right. I promise." She then turned toward Earl. "Um."

He grinned. "You do know I served in the Marines for a stint or two, right?"

"No. No, I didn't." She looked at Earl and lifted both eyebrows.

"I'll protect you and your mom. Don't worry." He slid an arm around Rachel's shoulders.

Piper nodded slowly, her mind spinning. She glanced at her mom again and patted her arm. What courage it must've taken to try to run and hide from the commander. She smiled at her new hero. "I'll talk to you two later." Without waiting for a response, she turned and hurried into the driveway and her SUV. If she knew where the men were who watched her, she'd flip them off. But since she didn't, she ignited the engine and all but rammed out of the driveway, barely missing Brian's car on the road.

"Ooops," she muttered, her shoulders going back. For too

long she'd been out of the loop, and that had changed last night with a simple game of footsie with Jory. They were on to the commander, and they'd figure out this entire mess. Then she'd save Jory's life, because she just couldn't let him die.

He had to live.

The mere thought of his dying, just when she'd found him, forced tears to her eyes. She turned a corner and paused at a four-way-stop. Her back door suddenly jerked open, and Jory jumped inside.

She yelped. "What in the world?"

"I thought I'd hide back here and go with you today." Settling back in the seat, Jory just studied her. "Drive. Now."

She pulled into very mild traffic and shook her head. "There are checkpoints." Yanking out her badge, she flashed it in the rearview mirror. "I have a badge."

"So use it. I'll hide"—he turned and glanced into the back—"under the blanket and grocery bags."

She hadn't had time to clean her car, damn it. "Gee. What could possibly go wrong with that plan?"

He laughed, but the sound seemed forced.

She frowned. "What's wrong?"

"Wrong?" Jory leaned forward, and his tone was, well, scary.

She swallowed, her body going on full alert. "What's the problem?"

"Problem?"

She huffed out air, wondering if she should pull over. "Stop repeating everything I say."

"Don't fucking think of pulling over. You have a tail, and I had to jump in at the right intersection so they didn't see me." He hunched down in the seat.

Oh. She pressed the gas pedal down. "Want to tell me why you're swearing at me?"

"Gladly."

She braced herself, because his tone of voice seemed anything but *glad*. "Well?"

"You want to explain why a guy on your front porch was able to manhandle you earlier today?" Jory spoke through clenched teeth.

She stiffened against the harsh tone. "I was trying to get away without causing a scene. What should I have done?"

"When a guy grabbed you like that?"

Yep. Scary voice. Big time. "Yes."

"Fucking kicked him in the balls. You don't talk, you don't try to avoid a scene, and you sure as hell don't stand on your own front porch and take that crap." Jory's voice was all the more menacing for the softness to it.

She shivered. "I handled it."

Silence. Dead, pissed off, definitely masculine silence came from the backseat. She dared a look, and fire all but spit from his eyes. Good thing the guy couldn't jump over the seat because the tail would see him. She swallowed. "You're just pissed you couldn't take care of him."

She spoke without thinking, and from Jory's instant stiffness, she'd nailed that one on the possessive head. But he'd never admit the truth, would he?

"You're fucking exactly fucking right I'm pissed because I couldn't rip off his fucking head and throw it in the bushes while tearing off his fucking arms for hurting you." Jory's hand tangled in her hair as if he couldn't help but touch it. "I was a second from breaking cover when your mother showed up with a frying pan. Then the guy with the cat."

Okay. Jory's protectiveness should not be giving her twinges. She liked it. A lot. "Everything worked out all right. We just had one night, Jory. Let's not go caveman from it."

His eyebrow lifted. "You made the choice of the night, and now you'll accept what comes from it."

The night had touched her in ways she couldn't even explain, and her mind was full of him. Her heart was vulnerable to him, and that wouldn't do. Especially since he had a kill chip in his spine, and an overdeveloped sense of possession. "Excuse me?" She tried to sound in control.

"You felt that night as much as I did, and you made the choice to be there. You're a smart girl, Piper. Don't play dumb."

She jerked the wheel around a pothole, not surprised when he didn't move an inch. "I'm not playing dumb, but I can take care of myself." She was even turning into a bit of a spy, now wasn't she?

"That isn't how this is going to work, darlin'."

Was that a Southern twang again? She eyed him in the rearview mirror. "Then how exactly do you think it's going to work?"

"You're driving me in today, and you have today to get the codes. I'll get the layout of the facility, and then we're out of the place—with Chance and the other two kids. For good. You and your mother are going under, and I'll take care of the commander."

"That's not my plan."

"It is now. This is too dangerous, and the only reason I'm allowing you in today is because the commander thinks he's got you where he wants you. So you're safe today— especially since the chips are set to blow at midnight tomorrow. But that's all you get." The Southern accent came out in full force.

She glared in the mirror. Midnight tomorrow? God. "You don't get to decide for me."

"Baby, I already have."

CHAPTER
22

S HE COULDN'T BELIEVE that worked. Not in a million freakin' years. Jory had hidden in the back, and they'd made it all the way inside the compound, where she'd had to drive around all of the new constructions and a bunch of tractors. She'd been instantly escorted to a computer room, being told by Dr. Madison that she might as well continue her work until the end of the day, when they'd set the trap for the Gray brothers.

Madison had licked her lips when saying the words, pure anticipation lighting her dead eyes.

Creepy bitch.

But she didn't know them, did she? She certainly didn't know they had a real last name.

For now, Piper had work to do. So she logged in and quickly found the additions she'd written to the computer code that would save Jory's brothers. Her fingers flew over the keyboard as she added code, her mind spinning. If she tried to download it, an alert would be sent out. She had to figure out how to reach Jory's chip and somehow reset it, but without him near, she couldn't tell if her alterations did any good.

Sleet smashed against the window, and she shivered.

The door opened, and Chance strode inside. Finally. It was nearing the end of the day.

She stiffened. "Hi."

"Hi." He leaned back against the wall, a tall kid with dangerous eyes. Very familiar, Jory-like gray eyes. Today

Chance wore a black soldier's uniform with a gun strapped to his leg.

"What's with the gun?" Piper asked, her breath heating.

"I'm supposed to shoot you if you try to leave." No expression sat on Chance's young face.

Piper rubbed her chin. "That's unfortunate." The kid looked way too young to be so serious and carry a gun. "You shoot people a lot?"

He didn't answer. Yeah. That's what she'd thought.

The commander stepped inside. "You did well last night with Jory."

She flushed. "I didn't like setting him up."

The commander glanced at his smartphone. "No matter. Tonight, when you meet him, we'll move in and take all of the Gray brothers."

Dean brothers. Apparently the commander's intel wasn't as good as he thought. "Why do you want them back so badly?" she whispered.

"They're mine." Now he glanced over at Chance. "It looks like you'll get the opportunity to know your real brothers."

"I already know my brothers." Chance's chin rose, making him look more like Jory than ever.

A red warning flashed on Piper's computer. "What the heck?"

The commander drew closer. "What's going on?"

Adrenaline flooded her system, and she reached for the keyboard. Heat rushed through her veins. "Virus. We're being seriously hacked." If the hacker destroyed the computer program, she'd have no way to save Jory. Battle roared through her, and she typed faster. She couldn't lose Jory now.

"Who?" the commander hissed.

"No clue." Her fingers flew over the keyboard, trying to protect the program. More warnings flashed. "It's somebody within the system." It couldn't be Jory. Who was trying to infect the entire compound? Her stomach rolled. She quickly went internal and flipped off the wireless before reaching for wires and shutting down the entire tower. The screen went blank.

Tingles cascaded along her arms. "That'll help a little."

The whir of a helicopter emerged through the snowy rain pelting down. The commander frowned. "I don't have any-one scheduled to arrive today."

Piper glanced out at the drizzly day. Jory's brothers owned a helicopter. Were they coming? If so, why hadn't he given her some warning the way in today?

The commander jumped toward the window and peered out. "What the hell?"

The helicopter landed, and four men jumped out, guns out. They wore brown soldier uniforms with PROTECT stitched across the front. Piper didn't recognize any of them. The people who'd kidnapped Jory. She had to run. She stood and faltered when Chance reached for his weapon.

"Watch her," the commander ordered, turning for the doorway. He lifted his phone to his ear. "Those aren't my men. All hands, attack." Then he paused and listened, turn-ing toward Chance. "Why the hell isn't the alarm blaring?"

Chance shrugged, his brow furrowing. Then he glanced at the now silent computer. "The attack came from within. Maybe somebody gave them clearance to land?"

Outside, the PROTECT soldiers fanned out without any resistance.

"Damn it. On my six," he ordered Chance. "Stay here, or I'll have you shot," he said to Piper.

Gulping, she nodded, her gaze darting around. How could she get to safety?

"You are not leaving," came a cultured voice from the doorway.

Piper's head jerked to see a tall soldier in the doorway, his bald head gleaming, a big shiny pistol in his massive hand. God. It was the man from the video so long ago when Jory had been shot.

"Who the fuck are you?" the commander asked, mere curiosity in his tone.

The soldier pointed the gun at the computer. "I'm the one who's going to take down your organization. For good." He fired.

Piper yelped and tried to jump in front of the tower, but the bullet impacted the black casing. She backed away, her eyes widening on the threat. "What the hell?"

The soldier stepped inside, light blue eyes glinting eerily in the light. "I know all about you and your creations, which are abominations to our God."

Piper edged toward Chance. Fear hitched her movements, but she plowed on. "Maybe we should leave you two to talk about this."

"Put the gun down," the commander ordered. He reached for his sidearm and hesitated when the soldier shook his head. "Now."

A shadow crossed outside, and from the corner of her eye, Piper could see Jory beyond the window. He levered closer to the window, having donned one of the black soldier uniforms.

The commander snorted. "You're surrounded on every side by well-trained men, and if you don't put down the gun, I'm going to make sure you beg for death."

Fear hazed her vision, but Piper tried to slide toward the window. Urgency focused the moment into a narrow tunnel.

"Stay put." The new soldier settled his stance, the gun still pointed at the commander.

Faster than a thought, Chance drew his weapon and aimed at the soldier. "Drop the gun."

"I know all about you, you freak." The soldier focused on Chance. "I'll shoot you while my soldiers take out your brothers. Right now."

Chance's gaze hardened. Keeping his gun levered on the soldier, he edged toward the window.

"Your brothers should already be dead. We'll have to go after the other soldiers—with the intel my forces are gathering right now. But first…" The soldier changed his aim and fired at Chance.

"No!" Piper jumped in front of the boy. The bullet impacted her shoulder and icy pain ripped into her flesh. She cried out, thrown against Chance. He caught her, stumbling back against the wall. Blood bloomed across her chest.

Chance tucked her close. "Oh God. I'm so sorry. I'm so sorry," he murmured.

The commander didn't spare her a glance and drew his weapon. "You're dead, asshole."

"Everyone stop." Piper tried to stand straight, but her vision wavered. Her right side had gone numb, which was better than the pain. But she was about to fall, and she knew it. She had to get Chance out of there before the man shot him.

Men's shouts and gunfire peppered down the hallway. Finally. Somebody had figured out they were being attacked.

Chance gently moved her to the side. "I'll get you out of here, Piper." His voice trembled on the last.

The soldier sighed and fired three shots at the commander. He flew back into the cedar-blocked wall.

Piper screamed.

Glass shattered inward, thrown in every direction as Jory barreled inside.

Chance fired at the soldier, hitting him in the arm. The guy bellowed, turned, and ran from the room.

Jory leaped for Piper. "Where were you hit?"

"Her right shoulder," Chance said, scrambling for the demolished window. "This is my fault—I'm so sorry. Right now, I have to get my brothers. Those people want to kill them."

"Damn it." Jory yanked off his black soldier shirt and ripped a piece to tie around Piper's arm.

Agony flared alive in her bicep, and she gasped. Tears filled her eyes.

"Sorry." Jory grabbed Chance just as he was about to jump through the window. "Stay on my six." He leaned down and grabbed the commander's gun.

Bile rose in Piper's throat, and she swallowed rapidly. "Is he dead?"

Jory frowned and leaned down to rip open the commander's shirt. The bullets had impacted a bulletproof vest. "He's always worn one. Just knocked out cold." Almost absently, Jory rubbed his weapon. Then he turned and eyed her.

She swallowed again and tried to blink the dots from her vision. "If you need to kill him, I'll forgive you," she gasped, her heart hurting.

He lifted his chin. "He told us that if he dies, a signal goes to our chips and explodes. I can't kill him. Yet."

She nodded, sadly relieved. The firefight continued, and her body bunched to run. "Are we taking him?"

"No. We have no use for him. He won't break, and I don't want him to know anything about our lives." Jory dropped the unconscious man to the floor.

"My brothers," Chance said, his eyes determined. "We have to go."

Jory turned and nodded. "Where are they?"

Piper tried to bend her arm and press it against her stomach to ease some of the pain. She truly hadn't wanted to see her lover kill her father. No matter what a sociopath the man was.

Jory jumped out the window. "Help Piper."

"Wait." She hurried toward the computer and tried to lift the tower with one arm. Pain scalded through her other shoulder. "We need this."

Chance huffed out a breath and grabbed the tower before helping her to the window. "Out."

Bossy like his brother. Piper scooted over the sill and dropped to the wet ground. Jory steadied her, his hands strong and sure. Chance smoothly leaped out with the tower tucked under one already muscled arm. Gunfire punctuated the fighting within the facility. A man screamed in what sounded like agony.

Jory glanced around, his gaze landing on the empty helicopter. He turned and nodded at Chance. "Get her inside, and I'll find your brothers."

Piper eyed the helicopter, trembles cascading down her back. "You can fly?"

"Of course."

She shuddered, and nausea attacked her. They didn't have enough time. "I'll make it myself. You guys get the kids." The fighting continued inside the building, and she had a small window of time to make the helicopter. Wincing, she grabbed the tower. "Go."

Jory tugged her jean waistband and shoved the gun in. "The second you get to the copter, put the tower down and pull the gun."

She bit down a wince and tried to mimic Chance's determined look. "No problem." Ducking her head against the rain, trying to ignore the incredible pain in her arm, she ran toward the helicopter. God, she hoped Jory and Chance found those kids.

Jory scanned the area for threats, his blood calming with every step. Chance kept to his six, his weapon out.

"Where are they?" Jory asked, heading for what looked like barracks. Once he'd found a way inside the facility, he'd stolen the shirt and pants that made up the uniforms and then pretty much had free rein of the facility outside the secured areas. Putting on the uniform had pissed him off and made his head swim at the same time.

He'd sworn he'd never wear it again.

Chance moved up and ran past Jory. "Follow me." He skirted the building and jogged toward a field edged by trees. Stopping, he let out a low whistle. "We have a contingency plan in case anybody ever attacks. Hide in the trees, find each other, and get the fuck out of here."

Good plan. Jory's shoulders relaxed as two boys hustled out of the forest. Dressed in the uniform, wearing buzz cuts, weapons strapped to their legs, they reminded him of his childhood. Of his brothers. Something in his gut ached and bad.

They hustled up, eyes on him.

"Kyle and Wade, this is Jory." Chance turned and pointed his gun at Jory. "We're all going, and we have to run. Now."

Jory stilled. Ah. Kyle had green eyes, and Wade had blue. That's what Chance had been hiding. They weren't genetic links. He blinked, his skin tingling. His shoulders straightened with understanding. If they were raised in this place, regardless of genetic donor, they were his.

Wade stared at his brother. "Why you aiming, Chance?"

"He knows why," Chance said softly, sounding so much like Matt that Jory's gut hurt. Bad.

Jory turned toward the other boys. "I'm Jory, and I'm your brother, too. We have three other brothers, and they're waiting to get us out of here. You with me?"

Wade nodded, and Kyle lifted his chin.

Jory turned toward Chance, letting the boy see the truth in his eyes. He didn't give a shit about genetics. Brothers were brothers. "You with me, kid?"

Chance slowly lowered his gun. "You for real?" Chance asked.

Jory turned toward the kid, his chest burning. "All real. We're together, Chance. All of us. Brothers."

Chance's shoulders relaxed, and for the first time, actual hope glimmered in his too-worldly eyes. "Good."

"You guys go." Kyle shook his head. "I'm not leaving Greg."

Jory glanced at Chance. "Greg?"

Chance paled and jerked his head toward a field on the other side of a barbed wire fence. "Our brother. Buried over there."

A mini-explosion rocked the earth. "We have to go," Jory said.

Chance nodded. "We'll come back for him. I promise."

"No." Kyle shook his head. "Go, Chance. It's okay." He turned to head back to the forest.

Chance grabbed him from behind in a solid bear hug. "You're coming."

"No." Kyle began to kick and struggle, his voice going hoarse. "I'm not leaving him. I'm not."

Tears sliding down his face, Chance moved his brother into a chokehold. Kyle struggled, and then his eyelids fluttered shut.

Jory's heart hurt so bad he wanted to double over. Instead, he kept his voice calm. "Here. I'll take him."

"No. He's my brother." Chance flipped Kyle around and yanked him over his shoulder.

Jory nodded, his shoulders going back. "He's mine now, too." Now they had to get to Piper.

They zigged and zagged through the rain, reaching the helicopter just as soldiers poured out of the main building. Jory didn't know which group came out first, and frankly, he didn't care.

His steps slowed as the soldier who'd shot the commander dragged out a protesting Dr. Madison by the lab coat. The woman gave a good fight, struggling, even kicking with her pointy shoes. Within seconds, the soldier had tossed the woman into another helicopter.

Her eyes met his, and she screamed for help.

He paused, his memories flashing of his childhood and her presence. But the woman he loved was behind him, wounded and worried. He made the choice and turned to jump inside his helicopter. Piper had been shot, and he had to get the kids to safety, both trumping thoughts of saving the evil doctor.

He ignited the copter, his motions routine, although he hadn't flown in nearly four years. Piper sat next to him, while the boys remained in the back of the helicopter. Her pain resonated through the air, as did the coppery scent of her blood, and the animal deep inside him stretched awake, wanting to destroy whatever had hurt her.

Rising into the air, he yanked a burner phone from his pocket and dialed Matt.

"Status?" Matt barked.

"Shit-storm of epic proportions." Soldiers began firing up, and Jory took evasive maneuvers. "I'm landing outside of Base 2 in about twenty, and you need to evacuate and jump in for headquarters."

Silence came over the line. "You have the code algorithm?"

"Maybe." It depended on how badly the tower had been damaged. The hard drive for the computer was in the tower, and Piper had managed to secure it. Everything they needed was there . . . if the bullet hadn't destroyed it. "We have the best we're going to get."

"Copy that." Matt clicked off.

Jory turned and eyed Chance. "What did you mean that Piper getting shot was your fault?"

The kid paled, his Adam's apple bobbing, but he didn't look away. "I sent out a message telling the PROTECT people our location."

Jory's head jerked, and his body calmed in preparation for a fucking fight. "You did what?"

Chance shrugged. "I weakened our system to allow for a big hack, and then I planted files that gave our exact location so they'd attack." He leaned up and patted Piper's arm, tears filling his eyes. "I'm really sorry you got shot. Didn't think that would happen."

Piper smiled wanly and caught his hand. The poor kid had done what he'd needed to do to save his brothers. "It's okay, sweetie."

He blinked and then frowned. "I, um, I got you shot."

"Nope. The bastard who shot me...shot me. Not you." She sighed and released him. "It was a good plan, really."

Jory blinked. Gray shards of ice glittered in his eyes. "What?"

"Take two enemies, let them fight it out, and escape during the carnage." She smiled as if proud at Chance. "You're such a smart boy, and it worked. You're free, and I promise you'll stay safe. We're sticking together, Chance."

The kid wiped a tear off his cheek. "Okay." He sat back with his brothers and then quietly asked, "What is Base 2?"

"Piper's house." Jory glanced toward the bleeding woman, impressed by her amazing brain. She was right, and Chance's move had been brilliant, yet he had to shove down pure fury that wanted to consume him. Only his force of will kept his voice level. "We'll get your mother to safety."

Piper nodded, her head leaning against the chair and her eyes closing. "We probably should talk about my mother."

Lightning flashed, and Jory jerked the stick. "Now?"

"No." Piper sighed. "Soon though."

Jory frowned. What in the world did that mean?

CHAPTER
23

PIPER TRIED TO wipe some of the blood off her shirt, her mind fuzzing. She'd been shot. Now she rode through a sleeting rain in a helicopter, about to set down on the street in front of her house.

Life had gotten way too bizarre. Three young kids, trained as killers, sat quietly in the back. The unconscious one, Kyle, had awakened and promptly begun throwing punches until Chance ordered him to knock it off or be choked out again. Kyle had then chosen to stare silently into nothingness and ignore them all.

The smallest kid, Wade, seemed to huddle into himself as the other two boys fought.

Poor kid. She sighed.

Jory reached over and covered her hand with his. Warm, solid, and big, he provided safety in an entirely unsafe world. "Thank you for getting me out," she murmured. How in the hell was she going to tell him that her mother had shot him?

"Of course." The way he said the statement, with so much easy confidence, showed the trained soldier in full force. A thread of anger still wove through his words, however. Fury that she'd been harmed on his watch. He turned to the back. "We'll touch down, and you three cover the copter." He turned to Piper. "You have exactly two minutes from touch-down to back in the air to get whatever you want to take."

She nodded.

"How's the wound?" he asked, his jaw tightening. Concern and fury glowed in his eyes, and tension vibrated from him as it if had wings, turning him back into the too-scary, deadly soldier she'd first met.

"Good." Hurt like hell, actually. But the blood flow had seemed to stem, and she needed to calm him down. They had less than a day to fix the chips, and he had to focus.

"We'll get you patched up as soon as we can. Just keep pressure on it." He expertly maneuvered the helicopter through the storm and dropped down along Piper's and Earl's front lawns. "Go. Now."

Piper jumped out and ran for the house, shoving open the door while holding tight to her bleeding shoulder. "Mom?"

Rachel came out of the kitchen, wiping her hands on a towel. "What—" Her eyes widened, and she rushed forward. "You're bleeding."

Piper nodded and grabbed her arm. "I need you to listen. We have two minutes to take whatever we want and get out of here. Now."

Rachel shook her head. "I don't understand."

Earl hustled in from the kitchen. "What's going on?"

"We have to go." Piper gave her mom a little push toward the bedrooms.

The front door opened, and Jory hurried inside, followed by Nate.

Rachel froze like an animal being scoped. Her face paled so much, blue veins stood out in her forehead.

Piper took a deep breath. "Mom, this is Jory."

Rachel blinked, her mouth opening and closing. She swayed.

Piper shook her. Hard. "Later, Mom. Right now, the commander is after us, and we have to go." She dragged her mother down the hallway and pushed her toward her bedroom. Rachel stumbled but kept on going. Piper scurried into her bedroom and shoved her photo albums, laptop, and jewelry into bags. She nearly collided with her too pale mother in the hallway, who'd also grabbed a couple of bags.

Riley ran around their legs, barking wildly.

They all hurried toward the doorway and out onto the front porch.

Piper paused. Shock stilled her. "Brian?"

The realtor stood on the porch, next to Jory, fury in his gaze. "We need to talk, Piper. There's a fucking helicopter on your lawn."

Rain cut a harsh path down and over the helicopter. Piper nodded. "Yeah. I have to go. Bye."

"No." He moved to grab her arm, his eyes widening. "You're bleeding."

Jory shoved him into the vinyl siding and pressed a gun to his jugular. "I'm finding it interesting that you started dating Piper right when she arrived in town. Working for the commander, are you?"

Brian squawked and shook his head. "Nooo. Really. I just met the guy once at dinner."

Jory frowned. "Why don't we just fight it out now?"

Brian shook his head, and his eyes filled. "No fighting. Let's use our words."

Nate whistled from the damp lawn. "Hurry up, Jory. The clock is ticking. Fast."

Jory growled and leaned in. "You're working for the commander."

"No. Really." Brian coughed loudly.

Jory frowned and sniffed the air before turning toward Nate, who stood in the rain waiting. "Nate?"

"Truth." Nate grunted. "He's telling the truth."

Jory growled. "That's my read, too."

Piper glanced from one to the other.

Jory slowly removed the gun and released Brian. "Nate's a human lie detector."

Interesting. Piper brushed by Jory. "You're not working

for my father?" To be honest, since Jory had planted the thought that she shouldn't trust anybody, she had wondered.

"Of course not." Brian yanked down his disheveled shirt.

Piper nodded. "I guess sometimes an asshole is just an asshole." She turned toward Jory. "We need to run."

He lifted his shoulder and slammed his fist into Brian's jaw.

Brian's head crashed back against the siding, his eyes closed, and he slid to the ground.

Jory snorted. "I barely tapped him. Moron."

Piper grabbed his hand. "We need to go." He nodded and enfolded her in gentle strength. They sloshed across wet grass, and he helped first Piper and then her mother into the helicopter. Riley jumped in, and the boys all reached for the dog, wonder in their eyes.

Rachel started to speak, and Piper shook her head. "Later."

Earl splashed water as he ran from his house, a backpack over one arm and his cat in the other. "Payton Manning has to come, too."

Piper reached for the cat, her eyebrows lifting.

Rachel patted back wet hair. "I very well can't leave Earl. He knows too much."

The guy didn't know a damn thing. "Of course," Piper said, hiding her smile.

Jory jumped back into the pilot's seat while Nate took the passenger side.

"We'll meet our brothers at the base of the mountain and switch helicopters. Then we'll head to headquarters," Nate said.

Jory turned and met her gaze. "The chips will detonate at midnight."

Jory lowered the helicopter through the night sky, his shoulders finally relaxing once reaching Montana airspace.

Nate had spent serious time and money securing the property, and the control room under the main cabin was strong enough to withstand a direct missile blast.

The ride had been made in silence, but just having Nate next to him in the passenger seat had provided reassurance.

Dawn rose on his last time on earth. They'd picked up Matt and Shane earlier, and now he'd get the chance to save them like they'd saved him so many times through the years. But they had to hurry.

Plus, they'd make sure to protect Piper, which would allow him to die in peace. Sure, they'd be pissed he died, and he'd try his best to figure out his chip after taking theirs out, but chances weren't good.

Once a wireless link was broken, there wasn't much of a chance to repair it. Not really.

Considering he was the computer geek of all computer geeks, regardless of his ability to fight and kill, he understood the impossibility of the challenge before him. How ironic that the one thing he truly excelled at was computers, and one would soon kill him.

The idea of leaving Piper alone cut him deep, and he exhaled some of the pain.

But he'd save his brothers first, and that was a good death, if he had to die.

He set down with a silent thud, and switched off all electronics.

Nate jumped out and opened the back door while Jory stretched to his feet and loped around to help him.

Matt and Shane leaped out and assisted Piper, Rachel, Earl, and the three kids.

The front porch light on the ranch house flipped on, and the door banged open. A petite blonde ran out with a happy yip, raced across the lawn, and jumped full bore into Shane's outstretched arms. She peppered his face with kisses.

Riley the dog jumped around their feet, catching the excitement, barking.

Another woman walked out of the house, her brown eyes soft and concerned.

Next to him, Matt blew out a soft breath. Relief? He strode through the darkness and up to the porch, gathering the woman and dropping his head into her neck.

Jory rubbed his chin. Interesting. He'd never seen Matt in love before. Looked good on his brother.

A sixty-something rancher type in blue flannel and worn jeans assisted a really pale woman to the door. Jory squinted. Audrey Madison. He remembered the sweet girl from when she'd dated Nate years ago. Now, pale as hell, she was just as beautiful as he remembered.

Her eyes widened, she turned, and promptly threw up into the scraggly leaves of a hibernating geranium plant.

Nate sighed and walked her way. "Still having morning sickness, darlin'?"

Audrey nodded and waved him back, bent over the bush. He continued on and gathered her hair into one hand while rubbing her back with the other.

Wow. Nate in love turned him, actually, *nice*?

"Who's the rancher?" Jory asked Shane.

Shane smacked the blonde on the mouth in a quick kiss and then grinned. "Senator Nash."

Piper gasped. "I thought he died."

"He did." Keeping hold of his blonde, Shane made introductions and then introduced the three boys as new Dean brothers.

The entire group eyed the boys and then smiled.

Accepted. Jory watched the boys feel it and accept their new reality. With hope and a sense of wonder.

Seeming entirely comfortable remaining wrapped around Shane, Josie Dean waved at the kids and held out a hand for Jory. "I'm so glad you're not dead."

Yeah. He instantly loved his sister-in-law. "Me, too. I'm glad Shane found you again and was smart enough to keep you this time."

Josie grinned. "I had to hit him over the head a couple of times, but it's all worked out." Then she lost her smile. "I mean, if we can get rid of the chips."

"We can," Piper said, reaching for the mangled hard drive tower. "I need to get working, actually."

"After Laney patches up injuries, I'm ordering three hours' sleep for everyone," Matt called from the porch without looking back. "Everybody take three hours, and we'll meet up then. None of us are any good if we pass out." He lifted the brunette and quickly disappeared inside the sprawling ranch house.

Shane snorted. "Good plan." He eyed the boys sitting so quietly, surveying the ranch. "I'll show you guys to the bunk room." He started for the house.

Chance glanced at Jory, and he nodded. "I'll be in to check on you in a few."

The other two boys waited for Chance to start after Shane. The second he moved, they fell in step. Just like soldiers.

Jory rubbed his chest right where a pang hit. If it were the last thing Jory did, he'd figure out a way to make them boys again. Even if he didn't survive, his brothers would take care of the kids. Help them to be kids.

He wished he could be there. Help them overcome the training and pain.

The three hours weren't for sleeping—they were for saying good-bye. Just in case they couldn't deactivate the chips.

Waiting until his family had entered the house, Jory turned to Rachel. She hovered a foot below him, her face pale, her hands wringing together. Had he scared her by punching Brian? "Are you all right?"

She swallowed, her thin neck working. "Um, no."

Piper grasped her mom's arm. "Let's go inside, Mom."

Rachel drew back. "No. I, uh..."

Earl frowned and patted her back. "What's wrong, Rachel?"

"I shot you," Rachel said, staring up into Jory's eyes.

Jory rocked back. Why would the sweet woman make that up? "Excuse me?"

Piper released her mom and grabbed Jory's hand. "It was an accident. She didn't mean to shoot you."

He swung his focus to Piper. What in the hell was going on? "Excuse me?"

"It wasn't an accident. I infiltrated the people who had you, the PROTECT people, eased my way in by giving yogurt samples, found you, and shot you." Rachel patted his chest. "I'm the one. I'm so sorry."

Jory blinked, the world narrowing in focus. "Yogurt samples?"

"Yes, dear." She sighed. "I owned yogurt shops, and it was an easy way in when the commander blackmailed me." She frowned. "If it helps, he didn't know you were the target."

Jory grit his teeth, his brain flaring. "That doesn't help, believe it or not."

"I know." She rubbed her eyes. "He said he'd put Piper in jail, and since he'd set her up as a hacker, he could've done it. But at least I didn't kill you."

So much heat burned down Jory's throat, his larynx spasmed. "You didn't kill me? That's the upside here?"

Earl stepped in front of Rachel. "Leave her alone."

"No." Rachel pushed him to the side and visibly steeled her shoulders.

Piper touched Jory's arm. "I can explain."

Rachel rolled her eyes. "Sweetie, I'm a crack shot. If I'd wanted you dead, you'd be dead." Her sigh echoed through the morning, and she turned toward Earl. "I'm sorry about my past."

Tension vibrated around the group during the peaceful morning.

Earl rocked back on his heels. "That's okay." He grinned. "It's not like you killed him."

Jory's neck began to ache. "You tried to murder me."

Rachel's eyes widened. "Again, no I didn't. Crack shot here. Don't be such a baby."

His shoulders launched back in an effort to keep from striking. "Baby? I was in a coma for two years."

She pressed her lips together and nodded. "I am sorry about that, although not entirely sure that was a bullet problem and not substandard medical care."

He shook his head, his thoughts zinging around like a ricocheting bullet.

She patted his arm. "Listen, Jory. I was scared, and I did the best I could to keep my only daughter out of prison and not end your life. Not one of my shots was a kill shot."

Jory glanced from Rachel's steady gaze to Piper's worried one and then back. His shoulders settled, and his mind cleared. He'd been on missions before, and he understood trying to save family. And he loved the woman's daughter, which made her family. No matter what. "I guess you didn't try to kill me."

The relieved sigh from Piper eased over him and helped him the rest of the way. "I forgive you, Rachel." There went his big plan of revenge up in smoke. He still reeled from the information, but he did understand. "No more shooting people."

Tears filled her eyes. "I really am sorry."

"Apology accepted." For some reason, the woman needed to hear those words, so he gave them. Frankly, it was a fucking relief to know who'd pulled the trigger. Finally, he could concentrate on something else—namely, saving his brothers. "I'm sorry I've dragged you into this mess."

Her lips curved in a smile. "So long as Piper is away from that bastard, I'm fine here." She glanced around. "Where are we?"

"Montana." Jory slid an arm around Piper's shoulders and maneuvered her toward the house. "We have a few guest rooms and bunk rooms scattered throughout. Do you want one room or two?"

"One," Earl said firmly.

Jory bit back a grin. "One, it is. Follow me." He glanced down at Piper. "Have Laney patch you up, and then we're getting in three hours. I'd love for you to explain why you didn't tell me your mother had shot me."

Piper sat on the main bathroom counter and held her breath while Laney, Matt's girlfriend, slowly stitched up her shoulder. She'd removed her shirt and now tried to suck in her stomach. "So. You're a doctor?" Hopefully.

Laney bent closer as she worked, her brown eyes narrowed. "I was a surgeon. Now I'm a bartender."

Piper frowned. "Where?"

"Nowhere." She breathed in, carefully stitching. "You sure I gave you enough lidocaine?"

"Yep. Don't feel a thing." Piper gave up on trying to have ripped abs and sank against the mirror, which cooled her back. "It's probably difficult being a bartender while hiding out on a Montana ranch."

The door slid open, and Josie clipped inside, her hands full of glasses and a bottle of champagne. "I thought we should have mimosas, but we're out of orange juice. So champagne it is." She quickly poured three glasses. This close, she was even more petite than Piper had thought.

Piper accepted one and lifted an eyebrow at Laney. "*After* I'm stitched up?"

Laney grinned. "Fine. Spoilsport."

Josie took her glass and sat on the toilet seat. "How's the wound?"

"Not bad," Laney said, drawing out string. "She'll live."

Josie drank deeply. "Shane is so happy right now. Finally. We've found Jory."

Laney blew out air. "Thank God. Matt has been tortured for too long."

Piper bit her tongue to keep from spilling the truth about Jory's chip being unreachable. He'd want to be the one to tell his brothers. "It's nice to see them all together."

"They're quite the bunch, right?" Josie sighed, her fingers tapping on her glass.

Laney shook her head. "Don't get maudlin. We'll save them. We have to."

The door slid open again, and a pale woman walked in. The one who'd been throwing up. "Hi. I'm Audrey."

"Piper." She studied the woman. "Feeling better?"

"No."

Josie moved from the toilet seat and helped Audrey sit down. "Those rumors about morning sickness just lasting three months are plain wrong." She jumped up next to Piper on the counter.

Audrey sighed. "I know, right? This has to stop soon. Nate is driving me crazy with the hovering."

"Control freaks. All of them." Josie took another sip of her drink.

Piper swallowed. "Yeah. About that."

Laney snorted. "It's who they are. Live with it or not… but it's who they are."

Josie nodded. "I usually like the protectiveness, because it makes me feel safe. And we haven't been safe much." She chewed on her lip for a second. "Other times, I kind of want to shoot Shane in the foot." Her laugh was contagious. "I held a gun on Matt and Nate once."

Piper turned her head. "So that was you."

"Yep. Then I held one on Shane and Nate. But that time, Shane got it and threw the thing on top of the refrigerator so I couldn't reach it." Josie's lips curved. "Good times."

Laney laughed. "I held a gun on Nate and Matt once."

Piper stilled and glanced down at her new surgeon. "Why?"

Laney shrugged. "Long story, and it seemed like a good idea at the time."

Josie shook her head. "It rarely is, though. Don't pull a gun on these guys unless you mean to shoot."

Laney nodded. "True that."

Piper glanced toward Audrey. "Any gun stories?"

"Nope." The pregnant woman shook her head. "I don't think Nate would respond all that well if I pointed a gun at him." She shrugged. "Although I did hit him with an umbrella once, and it ticked him off because I didn't swing hard enough. He's a bit intense."

Laney nodded. "I'd like to think that once the chips are out, the guys will relax a little bit."

Audrey snorted, and the sound seemed forced. "You don't believe that, do you?"

"Not really." Laney leaned back to study her handiwork. "I appreciate everyone putting on a good face, but we're all worried and can show it."

Josie nodded, her eyes filling.

Laney cleared her throat. "So, Piper. What's up with you and Jory?"

Piper coughed. "We've only known each other a week."

"So?" Josie said, swinging her feet. "A week with a Dean brother is like a year with anybody else. You know. With the shooting, the espionage, the fighting for their lives."

"And the great sex," Audrey said, leaning her head back against the wall. "Don't forget the over the top, excellent, many times over... sex."

Laney nodded. "Amen to that."

Heat flushed up into Piper's face as all three women stared at her. Finally, with a shrug, she gave in. "The sex is phenomenal."

Josie sighed, a smile brightening her beautiful face. "I knew it. Yep. I called that one."

Laney rolled her eyes. "Yeah. That was a stretch. Not."

Piper shrugged. "We have some issues, though."

"Yes. I heard you're the commander's daughter," Audrey said.

Piper stilled. Would they hate her? "Yes."

"Dr. Madison is my mother." Audrey blanched. "She's crazy, and I think the commander might be right there in loony town with her. Ah, no offense."

Piper relaxed. "No offense taken. They're both scary nuts."

Audrey rubbed her chin. "So true."

Laney set down the needle and thread before taking up her glass. "Welcome to the gang, Piper. We have to stick together, and it's nice having one more woman in our court."

Piper lifted her glass in the toast, her heart warming. Friends. She'd just found friends.

CHAPTER
24

PIPER GLANCED AROUND the masculine bedroom after taking a quick look in the attached massive bathroom and tried not to think about her mother and Earl sharing a room. Nope. Not going there.

The door opened, and Jory strode inside.

She gestured. "Your room is nice." Lame line. Geez. The guy had seen her naked, rocked her world, and being shy was silly.

"Thanks. We built it after we escaped the Tennessee facility, and now I assume my brothers will build houses around the ranch. There's a master plan somewhere, I'm sure." Keeping her gaze, he drew his T-shirt up and over his head. "Did Laney patch you up?"

"Yes. I'm fine." Her mouth went dry. Hard, muscled, wounded—damn impressive, even with the scars. "What are you thinking?" she whispered, desire sensitizing her skin.

"That your mom shot me, and you should come over here and ease my hurts." Those eyes darkened to molten slate.

She smiled, her nipples peaking. "I like this commanding side of you."

"I know."

Her fingers tingled with the need to touch that amazing flesh, but her feet remained rooted to the hardwood floor. "Thank you for being kind to my mother about the shooting. Most guys wouldn't have quite understood."

"I'm not most guys."

No shit. Not even close. "I don't want to get hurt." Where the hell did that come from?

He leaned back against the door and crossed his arms. Even his forearms were masculine and sexy. "I can't offer you forever, Pipe. But I learned the hard way when I was young that life is full of moments, and if you get a good one, take it."

The words rang true. She lifted her chin, even as sadness threatened to swamp her. "You promising me a good one?"

Slow and sexy, his lips curved. A matching sorrow glimmered in his eyes. "Yeah."

What if they had forever? What if she could save him— give him longevity in life? The words hung on her lips, storing in her heart. Sometimes she was a damn coward, because she didn't want to ruin the limited time they had with the question. Or rather, with risking his answer.

So she kicked off her boots. "I don't have any other clothes."

"Then we should hang those up."

Why didn't he move? If he'd just kiss her, just take over, then she could get lost. "We should."

His chin lowered. "Come here, Piper."

The dominance in the tone, the order instead of request... all demanded her compliance. As if he wanted her to make the move, to cross to him. As if he needed it.

So she paused. Just how much did she want to push him? A part of her wondered how far he'd go, or how long she'd last. The other part wasn't as curious and wanted to just get to the overwhelming sex and power that was Jory. "Why?"

"Because I told you to."

She slowly tilted her head. "Maybe that's not enough."

He held her gaze, and no way could she move an inch. "You sure you want to play?" The Southern accent again, and this time it wound through her body as if he'd licked a path from her nipples to her clit. "One chance, baby. Come. Here."

Her body kicked into motion as if he held the controls. Well, at least she could drive him crazy as she followed his command. For the moment, she let go of fear and sadness to just feel. Grasping her shirt, she dragged the light cotton over her head to drop onto the floor.

His sharp intake of breath boosted her confidence, and she stepped toward him.

Her bra followed the shirt, and she took another step. Several more, and she could actually feel his heat. Smell his masculine scent.

Stretching up on her toes, she slowly brushed her mouth over the three bullet hole scars. One still had a fresh scratch across it. "Tracker?" she murmured.

"Tracker," he confirmed. One big hand tangled in her hair, and he drew back her head, elongating her neck.

Taking control.

"What do you need, Jory?" she breathed.

"You." He ducked his head and nuzzled her forehead. With a growl, he released her hair and lifted her, his hands flexing at her hips. "Wrap around me," he said, his mouth already at her collarbone, a desperation in his tone.

Like Josie had with Shane. Full abandonment and absolute devotion. Jory wanted that, too. At the thought, Piper's heart hitched.

She slid her arms around his neck, her legs around his waist. Holding him—surrounding him the best she could, even with his size. Trying to hold on when fate might rip him away. "I've got you."

The soft kiss above her breast, right over her heart, shot tears to her eyes.

Too much emotion. Way too much. She grabbed his hair and yanked back his head, pressing her core to his cock and her mouth to his. Hard and fast, she kissed him with her entire body.

He shuddered and then took over, as she'd known he would.

His tongue played with hers, his lips firm and demanding, his hands gripping her butt while she finally forgot about the danger. Need and want, lust and desire, hope and despair all collided inside her, creating a painful ache.

A desperate hunger only the man overtaking her could appease.

She rubbed against him, the rough planes of his chest providing friction to her sensitive nipples.

He moved easily across the room, holding her. When they reached the bed, he lay her down, his mouth continuing to obliterate any thinking.

Graceful hands removed her jeans and panties, and within seconds, they were both nude.

He sprawled over her, all delicious male hardness.

"I love your body," she breathed, running her hands down his chest.

"My body loves you." He licked the shell of her ear, chuckling when a shudder trembled through her body.

It was way much more than physical love, and an echo of sad need rippled through Piper. She fought back the idea and any emotion, trying to stay in the incredible moment. For once, she was with a good guy who gave a crap. Who'd step in front of her and any danger.

That was something to be appreciated.

"Hey." Jory nipped beneath her jaw, levering up to capture her gaze. "I lost you for a minute. Where did you go?"

Into fantasyland and lost dreams. "Nowhere." She caressed down his flanks to sink her fingers into his damn fine ass. His cock jumped against her, and she let out a soft whimper. "We only have three hours, so maybe you'd better get to work."

His gaze remained intense and probing, and then, with a small nod, he rubbed his nose against hers. "You're special, Piper. Don't ever forget it."

What he didn't say was as important as what he did. "You really don't think you're going to survive, do you?"

"No." He softened the word with a kiss to the corner of each eye. "Tonight, the chips are set to explode. We know the day—they made sure of that—and it'll be close to midnight." He kissed her, going deep and then keeping his lips on hers. "I'm sorry."

What if he was right and there was no way to deactivate the chip? "We have to do something. If we can't reach it, then why not just take it out? Maybe when the bullet damaged the chip, it actually deactivated it?"

"Maybe." He settled against her.

She wrapped her legs around him and played with his silky hair. Her heart hurt. "Have hope."

"I'd rather have you." Keeping his gaze, he levered back, and thrust inside her with one strong stroke.

Electric sparks flashed through her, burning her, taking over. She arched against him, gasping out air, her mind fuzzing. "I like it when you do that."

"I know." His hand flattened across her butt, and he lifted her off the bed, allowing him to go deeper. "You like this, too."

A ripple started inside her, and his chest hitched.

"That works for you," she murmured, smiling.

"Yes." He slowly pulled out and shoved back in.

Lights flashed behind her eyes. "I wish we had forever," she said, too much emotion rushing through her to hold back.

"Me, too." He slowly slid out and then back in, taking his time, desire flushing a dark red through his chiseled face. "Do you believe in love at first sight?"

She shook her head on the pillow. "Don't say it." God, don't do that to her. Not if he thought he was leaving.

He nodded and began to increase the speed of his thrusts. "Just promise you won't forget me."

She heard the plea behind the words and for the tiniest of moments could see the wounded geek behind the soldier's physique. "You matter, Jory Dean. I promise. I'll never forget you."

His eyes darkened, and his jaw firmed. "Then I have to say it so you have the words. So you'll keep them."

Tears filled her eyes, even with the devastating desire consuming her. "Okay," she whispered. Her hands unclenched in an effort to soothe him, to rub the pain out of him.

"I love you, Piper. All of you. The smart, the sweet, the lost. Everything you are and whoever you'll eventually become." His face softened in the way only a truly hard man could, and only for her. "You gave me a smile when I was in a cage, and you gave me a kiss when we were running through the woods. Now you're giving me you, and you're a gift I hadn't realized existed."

Her entire chest ached. One tear rolled down her cheek. When he gave the words, he found ones she'd never imagined. "Jory—"

"If I could, I'd spend every second of every day keeping you safe and warm. Totally loved without one concern." Still connected inside her, still pulsing, he breathed deep and leaned down to kiss her tear away. "Baby. I'll always love you."

"I want that." Her heart shattered. She tightened her hold as more tears fell. "The forever, and the safety, and the warmth." She wrapped her legs around him and held on with all her strength. Then she levered back and gave him the words. "I love you, Jory Dean. The tough, the sweet, and definitely the geek."

His lips twitched.

"Don't leave me," she whispered, her very soul in the plea.

He closed his eyes, and a tear actually rolled out.

She gasped. Jory Dean didn't cry. No way. Her hand shaking, she reached up to feel the wetness.

His eyes opened, full determination, full Jory. Then he slid out of her and back in. "Hold on, baby."

Her mind registered that he wouldn't lie to her, and he hadn't. He hadn't made the promise he couldn't keep. More tears slid down her cheeks.

"No more crying." He angled differently and hit her clit.

That quickly, her body went from sorrow to full-out passion. Hot, dangerous, so out of control she could barely breathe. Every sensation heightened with a desperate emotion, a fear that this was all they'd have. "Jory," she moaned.

"All yours." Holding her tighter, as if he'd never let her

go, he pounded faster. Harder, deeper, more intense…he took her over.

She matched his pace, her nails denting his skin. He lifted her higher off the bed, holding her, going deep enough he'd be there forever, like she'd promised.

Heat uncoiled inside her, sparks igniting every nerve she had. She caught her breath, holding on, trying to fall over. Even so, the explosion shook her so thoroughly she opened her mouth to scream. No sound emerged, all energy concentrated in the waves detonating through her.

The room flashed white and hot. She shut her eyes, bombarded by waves. By feelings too intense to identify or separate—love, hunger, fear, sadness, hope. Ripples shook her body, pounded against her core, and threw her into a second orgasm more powerful than the first.

She rode the wild, holding on, knowing he'd keep her safe. A small sigh escaped her as her body finally relaxed.

Jory stiffened, held tight, fully captured inside her as he came. Grinding against her, he dropped his head to the crook of her neck. When his body relaxed, his lips moved silently on her jugular in the shape of one word.

Love.

CHAPTER
25

JORY QUIETLY SHUT the bedroom door and shook out his freshly showered hair. Piper slept peacefully in the bed, and he figured she could use more rest.

Wandering through the house, he let the sense of home finally relax him. He'd loved this place when they'd had it built. Now, with Piper ensconced in his bed, it really did feel like home.

For now—while he still breathed. Holding information back from his brothers didn't set well, and as soon as he figured out their chips, he'd need to come clean. He reached the hidden panel near the fireplace and shoved it open to punch in the key code. His fake birthday. Even though he'd been gone two years, they hadn't changed it.

They'd trusted he wouldn't break and betray them.

His head lifted at the thought. His heart hitched and hard. Yeah. He'd never betray them.

A door slid open, and he quickly strode down a stairway to the hidden control room.

Finding all three of his brothers waiting wasn't much of a surprise. They'd showered and grabbed faded jeans and shirts. Just like his. But the hospital bed over to the side and fully stocked medicine cabinet caught him up short.

Matt nodded from one of many leather chairs. "You doing okay?"

"Yeah." The familiarity of his older brother taking stock felt fucking great. "You?"

"Getting there. We're ready to take out chips. The second you have the algorithm figured out."

Time to get to work, then. Those codes changed every thirty seconds, and he had to figure out how to manipulate the numbers. Jory grabbed the damaged computer tower and carried it over to the wide table holding a myriad of computers, hoping to hell the hard drive was all right. "Let's see how badly the PROTECT soldier broke this puppy." Then he told them about Dr. Madison being taken.

Shane cleared his throat. "Did she ever confirm she'd shot you?"

"She didn't shoot me." Jory reached under the table, plugged the tower into a large monitor, and then opened a drawer to fetch a power cord. His mind focused absolutely on the matter at hand and shoved all other distractions away, even while carrying on the conversation. "Piper's mom shot me." If he could just get the tower to take power, he'd be thrilled.

Matt coughed. "Excuse me?"

Okay. All plugged in. Jory pressed the power button on the tower and held his breath.

"Jory?" Nate asked, his Southern drawl breaking wide open. "Rachel shot you?"

"Yes." They had more important things to think about.

Dead silence pounded around the room. The hair on the back of Jory's neck rose, and he glanced up, truly perplexed. "What?"

Matt stared at him with no expression, while Nate frowned in his *about to be pissed* look.

Shane glanced at the two other brothers and then back to Jory before snorting. "Is Rachel psychic?"

"No." The monitor came on, and the tower hummed. Good. A sound, any sound, was good. Then he tried to focus again. Why was Shane trying to break the tension? Shit. Why was there tension?

Silence reigned for precious seconds. Then the tension dissipated in the room. Oh. He'd already moved on from the shooting and perhaps should've given his brothers a chance to process the information. Computers. So much easier than people.

"Why would Rachel be psychic?" he asked.

"Maybe she shot you to keep you from defiling her daughter in the future?" Shane chuckled. "One bad experience in bed, and a woman might never try again. Are you any good in bed?"

Jory sighed, his lips twitching with the need to smile. "You're an ass."

"Does that mean no?" Nate asked, amusement curving his mouth and the anger fleeing his eyes. "We could find you a *how to* book."

Jory rolled his eyes. "I liked you better cranky." Love had certainly given Nate a sense of humor. Shane had always been a smart-ass, so nothing new there. But damn, it was good being with his brothers again.

"Jory?" Matt asked, all business. "Care to explain?"

The hum increased in pitch, and he patted the tower with a bit of strength. "The entire situation with Piper was a setup, and the commander blackmailed Rachel into shooting me. The PROTECT people had me, apparently." He leaned down to listen better, his mind working calculations of the computer program.

The tower connected with the display, and a blue glow slowly emerged. Then widened. Finally, a cursor came up.

Shane cleared his throat. "So Rachel meant to kill you?"

"Not exactly. Apparently she's a good shot, and she did what she could not to kill me." Jory rolled a chair closer and dropped into it, his fingers already flying across the keyboard. The program came up.

Matt shook his head. "Wait a minute. If the PROTECT people had you, and boy, are we going to explore that issue later after we figure out the chips, then how did the commander get to you?"

"Rachel was wearing a camera. Funny thing is, once he saw it was me, he sent in troops to recover my body. Probably saved my life." Jory leaned back, cracked his knuckles, and started typing again. "I get Rachel having to shoot me— we all do. The commander is a master at blackmail, and the woman did what she had to do. We're all good now."

Matt growled. "Are you sure?"

"Yep." Code flashed across the screen.

Matt sighed. "I had such high plans for revenge and destruction."

"Me, too," Shane said sadly. "We can't destroy Rachel."

"No. I kinda like her," Nate lamented. "Plus, haven't you two wanted to shoot Jory at one time or the other?"

Jory chuckled and kept typing. "I don't think she enjoyed it much, but I'm sure she'll give you details." The program followed his instructions. "Fuckin' Eureka." Yes. He typed faster, his brain calculating more rapidly than his fingers ever could.

Matt was instantly behind him, hand on shoulder. "So much for revenge. Let's work on life. You got it?"

"Hell, yeah." Warmth, true and full, bloomed in Jory's chest. "The bullet failed to do any damage when the tower was shot." His memory clicked into place, and he automatically started typing in the program adjustments he'd watched Piper create. "Give me about an hour, and I'll have the codes by employing the alterations Piper wrote into the main program. We wouldn't be close if she hadn't had that access and an amazing brain. Who's taking out the chips?"

"Laney. She was a doctor." Matt's voice wavered just enough for Jory to notice. "I can't believe we're this close."

Without missing a key, Jory nodded. "I'll get you safe, Mattie. I swear to God you'll live through this. All of you."

The hand clenched. "We'll all make it," Matt said.

Jory kept his body relaxed as he added another line of code. "I might not, and I want you guys to know that it's okay. I'm prepared." There wasn't time for him to go into details or spend precious moments being angry with fate or holding on to regrets. "Thank you for being my brothers."

Silence ticked through the room for about two seconds.

Matt spun him around—hard.

"Hey—" Jory's fingers slipped from the keyboard, while his mind remained busy. So when Matt hauled him from the chair and put him against the wall, he didn't protest.

"What do you mean, *you're prepared*?" Matt levered in close, emotion riding his low voice.

Jory glanced to the side for Shane's help, but Shane had stood, his face harder than Matt's. Nate stood next to Shane, his chin down, tension all but falling off him. And they'd been having such a fun moment with his being shot and all.

"Jory?" Shane asked.

Jory exhaled. He hadn't wanted to go into this until his brothers' chips were removed, but apparently there would be no typing until they had this fucking discussion. "A bullet nicked my chip, sending it off-line. There's no way to reach it."

Matt stepped back. "Bullshit." His voice remained calm, but emotion seethed under the surface.

Jory had always seen beneath the surface—any surface. From day one, he'd seen the cost to Matt of being the oldest and of taking responsibility for the brothers. "I wouldn't lie to you." He grabbed Matt's powerful shoulders. "I'm all right. The commander had scientists try for months to reach the chip, and nobody came close. The thing is off-line, and it's going to stay that way."

Nate stepped up next to Matt. "So there's a possibility the chip has been rendered useless?"

"There's a possibility." Jory released his oldest brother. "Although it's doubtful."

Shane shook his head. "There has to be a way to reach it. To get it out." His hands clenched into fists.

"Sure. We can have Laney try to take it out without the codes and hope it's defunct." But Jory doubted it could be that easy. "Although she may detonate the chip at that point, and I'm not sure how much of a blast will occur." Just enough to sever his spine, hopefully.

"You. Are. Not. Going. To. Die." Matt spoke slowly and through clenched teeth. "So figure it out, genius."

"I need Piper," Jory said.

Matt nodded. "Later."

Jory couldn't help the small grin, even with tension destroying the oxygen around them. "Not for that. I need her on the computer next to me. Woman's a freakin' wonder."

"Oh." Matt nodded. "What about the rest of us?"

Jory shook his head. "Two of us are all I need to find the right codes."

"Okay." Matt stepped away and pulled Jory's chair out from under the desk. "Get to work. I want to check on the boys and then will get Piper. Shane, you get on the third computer and ferret out everything you can about the PRO-TECT group and where they took Dr. Madison. We need to find that bitch before she tells them everything."

"And me?" Nate asked, his gaze remaining on Jory.

Matt nodded toward the stairway. "Go check on Audrey and the baby before coming back down. Your mind has to be in this, Nate."

"It is." Nate crossed solid arms.

"Then go check on her for me." Matt turned toward the stairwell. "This is my first nephew or niece, and all of this morning sickness is scary."

Nate visibly relaxed. "Oh. Well, okay. I'll take her some ginger ale."

Shane rolled his eyes at Jory.

Jory smiled. "Just in case, I have to tell you guys—"

"No." Matt strode toward the stairs. "There's no thank-yous, no platitudes, no good-byes. No more fucking good-byes. I am so done with that shit and with all of us sacrificing our lives. We're fucking done, and we'll all fucking live. The first guy who tells me good-bye ever again, even if he's just going to the fucking grocery store, gets a fist planted in his fucking face." He disappeared once upstairs.

Jory retook his seat and glanced at Shane. "That went well."

Shane shook his head. "There's no Dean brothers without you, Jory." His gaze turned stark. Dark and unlike Shane. "So whatever we have to do...we do it. *Never alone.*" They'd lived and nearly died by the mantra from childhood. They didn't have a father, definitely no mother. But no matter what, they'd always have each other.

Emotion clogged Jory's throat, and he turned back to the computer screen. "Never alone."

Piper finished toweling off her wet hair and stepped into the bedroom, stifling a scream at seeing a man sitting on the bed.

"Sorry," Matt Dean said, not looking sorry at all.

Thank goodness she'd dressed in her jeans and one of Jory's shirts after her shower. Jory's big brother was made of solid muscle with a hard-ass face. Handsome but deadly.

He was the kind of guy who'd put you in the ground and whistle while doing so—if he felt like whistling.

"Can I help you?" she asked as evenly as she could.

"Yes. Can you save Jory?" Matt asked, all badass soldier and, she could admit it, Dean brother sexy. He sat quietly, but his hands clenched into fists on his thighs.

She took a deep breath. "I don't know, but I'd like to keep trying." Turning, she tossed the towel behind her onto the bathroom counter. "There are different frequencies still to find. But the risk is that the chip is dead, and what if I reactivate it?"

Matt rubbed his chin and stood to pace around the room. "The frequencies of the chips are too low for even us to discern, so first we need to find out if the chip is dead."

"Yes." This would all be so much easier to deal with if the chip had gone inactive.

"Okay." Matt stopped moving and towered. He probably didn't mean to tower, but with the serious expression and his size, he just did. "Your focus, no matter what Jory says, is to work on his chip."

Piper frowned, even while her heart gave a happy hop. It was nice to have an ally in saving Jory's life. "Jory wants to save you three and then concentrate on his chip."

Matt nodded, and granite had nothing on his jaw. Hell. Granite was Jell-O compared to this man's jaw. "Jory can keep working on the codes, because his brain is there now, and I can't pull him away from the puzzle if I wanted. He's motivated, and I understand that since I'd die for him, too, but you're motivated to save him, not me."

Actually, she'd like to save them all.

Matt cleared his throat, hard gaze softening. He shoved his hands in his pockets and rocked back on his heels like a kid unsure of himself. "Since your mother is the one who shot him and nicked his chip..."

Piper put her hands on her hips as her face heated. "There's no need to try guilt in motivating me."

Matt peered down a very long way. He blinked and seemed to hold his breath. "What does motivate you?"

She paused. He was damn serious. "Why?"

"Because I'll do whatever it takes. Money? Long life? Tour of the world? You ask for it, and I'll do it—if you save my brother." His voice cracked, and steel-filled determination glittered in his eyes along with a heartbreaking fear. Just like that, Matt seemed human. Frightened and determined.

Piper touched his arm, offering comfort. "I want to save Jory because he's Jory. But the second he realizes I'm working on his chip and not yours, he'll get pissed."

Matt moved a shoulder the size of a boulder. "Jory doesn't get pissed—he gets even."

Why did that sound worse? Even more, why did Matt sound so proud of that fact, even while in sorrow? "I'm not sure how to respond to that."

"No response necessary. Just saying that Jory will take action when he needs to...and if he's alive, you can handle him then, don't you think?" Matt clasped his hands behind his back, his lips twitching. "You love him, right?"

Her mouth opened and then closed. She swallowed. "I've known him less than a week."

"So?"

"So a week is too fast to fall in love." Her voice emerged way too wimpy to deal with a guy like Matt Dean, even as she told the lie.

"Ah." Amusement lit his eyes. "Our lives have been surrounded by death from the beginning. We faced it, we fought it. Hell, we've even dealt it. Time doesn't mean a damn thing. If you've got something good, fight for it."

She bit her lip even though she agreed with every word. "You're still trying to motivate me."

"How am I doing?"

"You're kind of impossible." She smiled. "But likable."

"Yeah, I get that a lot. I'm the nice one." He didn't crack a smile, but the irony was there. "For now, let me handle Jory the second he discovers what you're doing."

She lifted an eyebrow. "Jory's bigger than you."

"He's taller by one inch—I'm broader. Besides, I'm meaner."

She shrugged. "Maybe usually. But he's fighting to save his brothers—you—and I don't think you've seen *mean* yet."

Matt grinned. "Listen to you defending your man." He turned her toward the door. "Let's just hope I don't have to put him in another coma to save his ass."

She paused, facing the door. "I do love him," she whispered.

"I know," Matt said softly from behind her, his breath brushing her hair. "Welcome to the family, Piper."

The words slid inside her skin and pierced her heart. Home. She shut her eyes to shove down tears, and then lifted her chin. "Let's do this."

"Yes." He propelled her through the house to the kitchen, where they found a prowling Chance.

"Where's the passageway to the secured areas?" Chance asked, gray eyes curious.

Piper eyed the boy. Was he delusional?

Matt leaned around her and slid open a hidden panel before typing in a code. "Zero-eight-zero-eight," he said. "For future reference."

A panel in the wall opened, and a set of stairs became visible. Piper gasped and stepped back.

"What's down there?" Chance asked.

"Go and see," Matt said gently.

Chance eyed him and then glanced around the kitchen.

Matt's chin lifted, and understanding filled his eyes. "Our younger brothers are safe here, and you can take a moment to explore. You have my word."

They studied each other. Piper's breath quickened, while her heart ached. Matt and Chance looked so much alike—same eyes, same chin, same large frame. Those poor boys.

All of them.

Finally, Chance nodded. "Okay." Then he turned and cautiously made his way down the steps.

Matt let out a slow breath.

Piper turned toward the stairs. "It'll take time, Matt."

"I know." His gaze remained thoughtful.

She hoped they had time. Following Chance down, she emerged in a long cavern surrounded by solid steel walls. A bank of computers took up one side, while a makeshift hospital room took up the other side. Chairs were scattered throughout. "Wow. Quite the panic room."

Jory turned from one of the computers and flashed a smile that turned her insides upside down. He patted the chair next to him. "Come put that incredible brain to use, would you?"

She couldn't help smiling back, even in the intimidating environment. It was nice to be admired for her brain—as well as her ass. He did say he liked both. "Love to."

Matt dropped an arm over Chance's shoulders. "I'll show you the escape routes, the weapons systems, and the armory."

Chance stilled. "Really?"

"Of course. You're one of us now—all three of you are ours. There are no secrets here among family, and you need to know how to defend and protect your family, right?"

Chance swallowed, his Adam's apple bobbing. "Um, okay. Thanks." Bewilderment and hope slid across his face and broke Piper's heart. He nodded. "I need to go back to the compound."

Matt frowned. "Why?"

"My brother is buried there. I can't leave him." Chance's jaw hardened and looked exactly like Matt's.

Matt slowly nodded. "Your brother is my brother, buddy. We'll get him. I promise."

Chance bit his lip, and tears glimmered in his eyes.

Piper sat down, and next to her, raw emotion glinted in Jory's eyes. Swallowing, she began to punch in keys.

To save him. God. She had to save him.

CHAPTER
26

JORY KEPT TYPING away, trying to ignore the woman at his side and the emotion clawing at his gut. He'd seen the second that Chance had almost believed he had a family, one that would protect him, and he'd felt Piper's response.

The woman was all heart and brains...and he wanted her. Not for once, not for a moment, but for all fucking life.

Now he was pissed he didn't have one to give to her.

For months, he'd been fine with the thought of dying, so long as he could save his brothers. But that was before Piper had stormed her way into his heart, before he knew he could love a woman. The raw need to stay with her, to grow old with her, to protect her from the dangers he knew too well existed in life heated his very blood.

The commander wasn't done—not by a long shot. Dr. Madison was with the PROTECT group, and she knew every weakness of the Dean brothers. Hell, if the woman broke, she'd tell them everything.

Would she tell them about her unborn grandchild? Audrey was her daughter, and now she carried Nate's baby. If Nate was an aberration to the PROTECT group, was the baby?

Shit. Jory needed to be alive and protect that baby. And Audrey. And definitely Nate.

So when he'd realized Piper was working on his chip and not helping him find the codes, he hadn't stopped her. Her dedication and near obsession to save his life hit him square in the heart. Plus, he was minutes away from breaking the algorithm, and he didn't need help.

She typed away, her concentration absolute, her teeth worrying her bottom lip. She was perfect.

Sexy, smart, and dedicated.

A little wounded, but who wasn't? He could heal her. If he had the chance, he could show her that good men didn't leave. Good men protected people and kept them safe.

He could keep Piper safe.

If he lived.

His computer dinged.

He froze, his fingers over the keyboard. Matt glanced up from a computer down the way, where he'd taken over for Shane an hour ago when Shane had taken Chance outside to show him the perimeter. "Jory?"

Jory sat back, his gut clenching. "I've got it."

Piper stopped typing. "What?" She leaned over to view his screen. "Oh my God."

Fucking awesome. He grabbed her, lifted her right out of the chair, and whirled her around. "We broke the algorithm. There's the current code." He hugged her tight, his chest finally loosening. "Mattie—get your doctor. It's time to cut."

Piper hugged him and glanced around to the monitor. "You linked to Matt's chip."

"I did."

Piper struggled to get down, and he released her. She launched herself at his computer and quickly typed in commands. A countdown clock came up. "Eight hours. Oh my God." She swiveled to face Matt. "Your chip detonates in eight hours and three minutes." She paled and kept her eyes on the clock for several heartbeats. Finally, she breathed out. "Eight hours and two minutes."

Matt pressed a button on the desk. "Shane? Nate? Get Laney and get down here." He ripped off his shirt. "I'll be the guinea pig."

Jory's breath caught. He'd been so elated at finding the codes, he'd forgotten the danger in removing them. What if the codes were wrong? What if the commander had set safeguards in place? If he had, they weren't anywhere in the computer.

But still.

Shane ran down the steps with Laney on his heels and Nate right behind her.

Laney crossed toward Matt, all feminine, all grace. She placed her palm over his heart. "We have the codes?"

"Yes." He brushed her lips with his, and Jory fought the urge to look away.

Laney turned toward him, her eyes soft. "Thank you, Jory."

He nodded, his heart cracking with a fear he couldn't

afford to feel right now. "The second you get him on the table, I'll uncover the current code and will punch it in—it's active for thirty seconds. As soon as I find the deactivate option, it'll stop completely. I'll let you know, and you hurry."

She swallowed. Fear glowed bright in her stunning eyes.

Matt ran his hands down her arms. "If you can't do this, I'll have Shane pull out my chip. He's good."

Laney's shoulders went back, and she drew in a deep breath. "I was a surgeon, and my hands are quicker than Shane's. Smaller, too. I can do this, Mattie. I promise."

Jory frowned, doubt heating his lungs. "Maybe she shouldn't operate on you." There was a reason hospitals didn't allow doctors to operate on family members.

Laney wiped away a tear. "Are you sure you don't want anesthesia?"

"No—there's no need. You can do this." Matt smiled. "Right?"

She nodded. "I had a small problem with blood for a while, but now I'm okay. I can do this." She leaned in and kissed Matt's jaw. "Trust me."

He hugged her tight. "More than life, I do." Taking her hand, he led her over to the hospital bed and then turned to view everyone. "If this doesn't go well, take care of my Laney. I love you. All."

Jory swallowed. "Thank you, Matt. For everything."

Matt sprawled over the table. Laney hustled for the cupboard, while Nate and Shane followed suit. They all donned gloves, and Laney grabbed a scalpel.

She hovered over Matt's back, her gaze on Jory.

Jory turned back toward the computer. The code was 55yt#@$8tyz. He waited. And waited. And waited.

Nobody said a word. Shit. Was anybody even breathing?

The code changed to o998&%^*@!. He quickly typed in the connecting code, the computer searched, and then he was online with Matt's chip. He typed in the kill code, and commands came up. DETONATE or RESET.

No, no, no. "Crap. There's no option to deactivate. Detonate or reset." He shook his head. He had to take it off-line.

"Reset it," Matt ordered, his head turned to the side, his eyes firm and steady.

What if it didn't work? What if he'd waited too long? What if this was a trap?

"Now," Matt said.

"Wait—" Laney breathed.

"Now, Jory. Now!" Matt ordered.

Jory clicked RESET.

A bright red warning scrolled across the screen. "Shit. You have twenty-five seconds, Laney, or it'll reset again and detonate." He leaped to his feet and reached the bed, his hands shaking.

Piper stood next to him and slid her hand into his. He squeezed and tried to think of a prayer. Any prayer.

Laney leaned close to Matt's back and slowly drew down the scalpel. Blood welled. Then she cut the other way.

Shane held out a bowl.

"Get ready," Laney said quietly. She must've slipped into surgeon mode, because her hand remained steady, and her voice threaded with command.

She cut again.

Grabbing forceps, she leaned in. The instrument hovered above the chip. "God, it's in there but good," she hissed.

"Don't jiggle it," Jory warned.

"I know." She reached around, leaning down for a better look. "The chip is cylinder shaped, and it's…shit… dented."

One touch, and it might go off, code or not. Jory glanced back at the computer. *Fifteen* seconds. *Fourteen. Thirteen.* He couldn't lose his brother. Not now, not after everything.

Piper tightened her hold on his hand, and he focused on Laney. Should he take over?

She groaned and sweat dripped into her eyes. She blinked. Shane reached over with cotton to wipe her face.

"Thanks," she muttered. "The second I clamp this, it might go off. Everybody step back."

Nobody moved, but Jory did check the countdown clock. *Five. Four. Three.* "Now, Laney," he ordered, turning to watch her hands, panic ripping up his throat.

With a soft cry, she dug in and clamped. Sparks flew. Fast as a whip, she struck and yanked the chip from Matt's body.

The chip clattered into the bowl.

For a moment, they all stared at the quiet cylinder.

Laney staggered back. "It's out. Oh my God. It's out."

Jory glanced down. The rectangular chip was about two inches long and made of metal. Or some type of new plastic perhaps. Smoke rose from it. The device seemed pretty flat, but he didn't want to pick it up.

The computer dinged a warning.

Steam cascaded from the chip. A spark flew, and it jumped inches. Blades cracked open, unfolding from the base. Slicing hard and fast into the metal.

Everyone stepped back.

"Holy fuck," Nate breathed.

Yeah. That would've definitely severed Matt's spine and killed him. The smell of burned metal filled the air. Nausea filled Jory's gut. He couldn't go out like that. If he came close, he'd use a gun. He'd have to.

Matt turned his head. "Am I done?"

"Wait." Laney grabbed thread and quickly sewed him up. "You're good."

He turned and jumped from the table to grab her in a huge hug.

She sniffled against his chest.

Jory stood, so much emotion in him he thought he might explode.

Matt released Laney and leaped for him, grabbing him. "You did it. You fucking did it."

Jory hugged him. "We all did it." Matt was saved. Thank God.

For now, he forced a smile. "You're next, Nate. Hop up." God, hopefully Nate's chip was damaged less than Matt's. He'd figured getting the codes would be the tough part, but each cut into their backs was an invitation for death to attack.

He turned back to his computer and quickly linked to Nate's chip. "Seven hours and fifty-five minutes. It's on the exact same timer as Matt's. They must've set them all to detonate at the same time."

Figured. He could see the commander finding irony there.

Jory shook off thoughts of the evil bastard. Time to save his brothers. He glanced over at Piper, who had sat back down at her computer.

She'd paled again. For once, her fingers were silent on the keyboard.

"Piper?" he asked.

She swallowed. Tears filled her eyes. "I, ah, wrote a program that will identify any signals sent out from any device in the room. It finally just kicked into gear."

Yeah. Made sense. Even though the chips weren't sending out signals, they still had a frequency. "So you found the frequencies?"

"Yes." She swallowed.

The rock always in his gut expanded. He stood and walked around to view her screen. After ignoring computers and cell phones, he could make out signatures. Two very strong and one weak.

"Damn it." He ran a hand through his hair.

She nodded and pointed to the weaker light. "Your chip, Jory. We can't reach it, but it's active. I'd hoped when it was damaged it had just shut down. Stupid." She craned her neck to see his screen, and her voice cracked hard enough to fill the room with despair. "You have seven hours and fifty-four minutes until your chip detonates."

He nodded. "Let's get the chips out of Nate and Shane. One thing at a time." His solar plexus clenched as if hit with a medicine ball, hurting deep. He'd known somehow that he wouldn't make it out of this, but he'd had a goal, and as soon as Nate and Shane lived through this, he could relax and enjoy what little time he had left with the one woman he'd never thought to find.

His.

Piper glared at the computer screen, desperation tasting like sulfur in her mouth. She couldn't connect. No matter what she did, she hadn't found a way to connect to Jory's chip.

They'd taken out Nate and Shane's chips, and both had been dinged and dented enough that the procedures had been nerve-wracking. But they'd done it.

Afterward, they'd double-checked the kids to make sure they hadn't been tagged yet. They hadn't.

Now she'd spent another four hours logging in code in the computer with no damn luck.

Jory sighed next to her at the computer console. "Okay. What are we missing?"

Matt groaned. "There has to be something we can do." He sat in front of yet another computer that wasn't helping. Shane and Nate perched on chairs, waiting. For anything. All soldier hard, all emitting fury at their inability to do anything. The men were doers, and the tension in the room was choking Piper.

She leaned back and stretched her aching neck, her mind spinning uselessly. "We can't connect wirelessly." She halted. Waited a minute. Her heart stopped for a second. "We can't connect wirelessly."

"You're repeating yourself," Jory said, his gaze still on his screen.

She jumped from her chair and ran to the bowls sitting on the hospital bed. Holding her breath, she reached for Matt's chip.

Jory instantly halted her hand. She hadn't even heard him move.

"Be careful," he said. "The blades will slice your fingers."

"I know." She gulped down fear at what they'd do to his spine. Gingerly, she grasped Matt's deployed chip with two fingers and lifted it to the light. One way and then the other.

Matt appeared at her side. "What?"

She peered closer, and fire bloomed in her stomach. Nerves set to life. She gasped. "Look. There's an indent in one end."

Jory took it and studied the chip. "I'll be damned."

Matt grabbed one of the other bowls. "An indent? Oh God."

She nodded. "Yes. We can't connect wirelessly, but there's a port built into the device. Just like any electrical device. Phone, camera, you name it. We can connect manually." Hope filled her chest. They could do this.

Jory shook his head. "We don't have the right cord. We can't even see inside to find the right configuration."

They'd done a great job of building a cap to partially shield the port, so there was no way to get the configuration. Sadistic bastards.

Matt grabbed the chip, set it on the wood floor, and stomped on it. Then he picked it up. "Now we do."

Piper glanced over his shoulder. No, they didn't. Whatever the configuration inside the port was destroyed when the port was opened or exposed. "We can't create an attachment if we don't know what it needs to attach to—how many prongs should be there." They were so damn close, she wanted to scream. Loud and with frustration.

Matt nodded. "You're right." He glanced at his watch, and in a microsecond, he turned into the formidable soldier she'd first thought him to be. "Here's the plan. We have one hour to detail an attack, one hour to say good-bye to loved ones, and then one hour to reach Utah. We fight with no mercy, get to the infirmary, and then we have approximately thirty minutes to take out the chip."

Piper's breath stopped. Plain and simple, she stopped breathing. "Thirty minutes?"

Matt nodded. "If we plug in, we only need a few seconds, right?"

Jory shook his head. "Absolutely not. We are not putting all of us right where the commander wants us. Not for me."

"We're going." Matt nodded to Shane and Nate. "Right?"

"Yes," Nate said.

"Abso-fucking-lutely," Shane said, determination filling his eyes.

Jory shook his head. "No. Hell, we don't even know where the correct cord is. There might not even be one."

"Oh, there is one." Matt turned and loped toward the stairs. "You know the commander has one somewhere."

"He won't tell us where it is," Jory argued.

Matt turned back, all semblance of the good-natured brother gone. "Oh. He fucking will."

Piper shivered at the tone and backed away a step.

Nate and Shane followed Matt up the stairs, leaving Jory and Piper alone.

She reached out and ran a hand down his arm. "You'd do the same for them," she said quietly.

"I know." He stared at the now empty stairwell, his chest vibrating. "But I can't let them go."

She was pretty sure nothing would stop them. "I'm going, too."

"Hell no." He turned on her, grabbing her arms. "No way."

"Yes." She leaned up and kissed his whiskered chin. "If you're on the table, I'm needed on the computer. Just in case. You know it."

He shook his head. "I won't put you in danger like that."

"Thank you for caring." She recognized the order for what it covered. "But I'm needed." For once, she was going to give all for a man. One who might not even live through the next day. "I'm all in, Jory Dean."

The scrape of furniture over wood floors echoed down the staircase.

"Damn it." Jory took her hand and led the way upstairs to where Matt directed the boys in widening the table for several leaves and more chairs. It easily fit the fourteen people now in the room. Nate wheeled in an old-fashioned white board with markers.

Jory shook his head. "We are not doing this."

Matt focused on Chance, who was sitting between his brothers at the far end of the table. "We need the layout of the Utah compound."

Chance lifted his chin. "I'm going with you."

"No." Matt shook his head. "This mission is for brothers aged eighteen and over."

"You need me." Chance met his gaze head-on. "I know the place better than anybody."

The ex-senator reached out a gnarled hand and patted Chance's. "Just give the info to the boys. That'll be a big help."

Chance slowly turned his head to meet the senator's gaze. "Um, thanks, sir."

"Jim. Grandpop Jim." The senator patted his hand again. "I'm grandpop around here, so get used to it."

On the far side of Chance, Wade leaned over to see past

his brother. "We've never had a grandpop." Hope filled his dazed eyes.

"Two." Earl spoke up from next to a tousled-looking Rachel. "The senator and I make a great team, and I'm a grandpop, too." He scrambled in his pocket and drew out several pieces of butterscotch candy to push across the table. "See?"

Wade slowly nodded and then elbowed Chance in the ribs. Chance nodded, frowning. With a happy grin, Wade then took a piece of candy.

Jory cleared his throat. "I think I've lost control here. Listen, everybody—"

Rachel reached for a piece of candy. "I think I'm more of a Nana Rachel than a Grandma Rachel." She unwrapped a piece and focused on the kids. "What do you think?"

Kyle cleared his throat, his green eyes sizzling. "We get to stay?"

"Of course. We're family," Rachel said, glancing around the table for anybody to disagree.

Matt cleared his throat. "Listen up, gang. We're all family, and after we save Jory's as—I mean butt, then we're staying put. Building houses, hanging out, doing normal family shit people do. Nobody is going anywhere else—and we'll live happily ever fucking after. Freaking. Happily *freaking* after."

Piper bit back a grin. The crude words said with such impatience settled the kids as nothing else could have. Wade took another piece of candy—this time without waiting for Chance's permission.

And *that* . . . that was family.

Kyle smiled at Rachel. "I like Nana Rachel."

Rachel clapped her hands. "Excellent. Nana Rachel it is. I paint, you know."

Audrey pushed back from the table, her hand clapping

over her mouth. Nate was instantly by her side, helping her up. Turning, she ran for the back.

Rachel wrinkled her nose in a purely sympathetic gesture and stood. "Morning sickness sucks." She nodded at Jory. "Grab me a ginger ale, would you?"

Jory paused and then slowly, deliberately opened the fridge and fetched a soda can to hand to Rachel. With a murmured "thanks," she hustled out of the room.

Earl stood. "I'll go help."

The senator stood. "I should probably help, too. She likes people to make her laugh when she's down, so we should be funny."

The two men disappeared down the hallway.

Piper tried to enjoy the moment, but so much tension emanated from her lover that she found it difficult to breathe.

Jory cleared his throat. "Matt? I'd like to speak with you and Shane. Alone."

Matt turned. "Let's go back downstairs and plan. I'm not sure how, but I believe I've lost control of this briefing." He leaned down and planted a loud kiss on Laney's mouth. "I'll be back up in forty-five minutes to fight with you about your going into the battlefield. By the way. You're not." He pivoted and headed downstairs.

Piper opened her mouth to speak, and one look from Jory froze the words on her tongue. Scary, badass soldier back in serious form.

"Give me forty-five minutes," he asked. Well. He kind of asked.

"Fine." She turned to Josie and the boys. "How about we dish up something interesting for dinner?"

Wade's eyes widened. "I'm always hungry."

Jory gave her a half hug. "I'll be back in a few minutes."

CHAPTER
27

JORY WAITED UNTIL Nate joined them downstairs in the computer room, carrying the white board. They sat in top-of-the-line leather chairs, the four of them, everyone quiet.

Matt leaned forward. "Go ahead."

"I can't ask you to risk your lives. To give up what you've found." Jory shook his head. "It's too much—" He paused. With his senses, he could hear a heartbeat on the stairs.

Matt turned his head toward the sound. "Chance? If you're going to join us, do it. Please."

Chance loped down the stairs. "I, ah, thought I should join in." He kept his chin up and his voice level, but his heart beat hard enough Jory wanted to wince.

Matt kicked a chair the kid's way. "Have a seat."

Relief. It poured out of the kid. "I need to go on the mission. To end this. Please."

Jory rubbed his chin. "Nobody is going."

Nate set his elbows on his knees. "I have no problem knocking your ass out and throwing you on a helicopter, Jory. Just let me know if that's the path here. If not, shut the hell up and use that freaky brain to keep us safe."

"My brain isn't freaky," Jory muttered.

"We need you." Shane spoke softly and straight-up. "The last two years, not knowing if you were alive or dead." His voice cracked on the end. "We fucking need you."

He might as well have hit Jory in the chest with a sledge-hammer. "No—" Jory began.

"Yes," Matt said quietly. "Growing up, you were the

youngest brother, and I know that came with issues. We protected you, and I trained you until you must've hated me. I get it. You wanted to save us, to be a badass soldier like you think we were. But you already saved us, Jory. You definitely saved me—all through our childhood."

No, he hadn't. Jory shook his head.

"You did. Always made us laugh, always gave us something to hope for." Nate leaned toward him. "You hid your fears, and you hid your doubts. For us, you tried to be a kid. I get that, and I like that you're expressing yourself now. Probably because you found Piper."

A lump formed in Jory's throat. So big, he didn't think he'd ever swallow again. And Matt was right. He'd found himself because of Piper. "Right, and you have too much to lose now, Mattie, so I can't risk you."

Chance rubbed his eyes. "You guys always so girly?"

Jory burst out laughing. The tension dissipated. Matt shoved at Chance's chair, rolling him toward Nate. "Smart-ass."

Chance grinned. Then he quickly sobered. "I know the layout of the facility, and I've studied the troops."

Jory smiled. Smart kid. He eyed his brothers. "I can't talk you out of going?"

They met his gaze levelly, nobody saying a word. Sometimes there just weren't any words. "All right." He sat back, knowing he couldn't talk them out of the mission. They were his brothers, and they never went in all alone. "We need a good plan, then."

Chance sighed. "Hate to beat a dead dog, or whatever that expression is, but five of us don't stand much of a chance against the commander's troops."

Jory nodded. "We've been out for five years."

"So?" Chance lifted a shoulder.

Matt scratched his chin. "If you would've gotten out, what would you have done?"

"Run hard and fast as far away from the place as I could." Hollow hopes and killed dreams rode the kid's strong words.

Nate nodded. "What if you had kill chips embedded in your spine that would detonate in five years?"

Chance rubbed his nose. "Well, hmmm. I guess I'd spend nearly five years preparing for war. Just in case."

Jory nodded. "Welcome to Sins Security—the company of ex-soldiers we've built over the last five years." He rolled his shoulders. "I guess you're part owner now. You, Wade, and Kyle." He turned toward Matt. "Right?"

"Definitely. Every brother gets a share." Matt kept his voice level.

Chance shot a jerky hand through his hair and sucked in several deep breaths of air. He blinked rapidly, slowing his breathing. A mere moment later, the kid eyed them all, back in control. Tough, wasn't he? "Great. Let's go to war," Chance said.

Four matching sets of gray eyes all focused on Jory. Waiting.

He let his brain go through the problem, and their decision made no sense. So he let go of thinking and opened his heart. They belonged together, and when one was missing, they all hurt. Finally, he gave in. They had to save him as badly as he'd wanted to save them, and he was just as important to the family as anybody else. He mattered. "I get it. Let's plan for war."

Nate stood by the board, marker in hand. "We need to diagram the layout first."

Jory sat back, and within half an hour, they had a plan. It took fifteen minutes to put the first part in action—mainly, they called in their employees. The master plan would be risky and quite possibly involve treason and death.

He was already facing death.

Exactly an hour after starting to plan, they all trooped upstairs.

Matt paused. "One hour, and then we suit up." He faced Chance. "You're right about going, and I'm leaving it up to you. But make peace with Wade and Kyle just in case something goes wrong, they're okay. I'm not taking them—too young."

Chance nodded. "I don't want them to go. Neither has killed yet, and I'd like to keep it that way."

Jory didn't move and kept his expression blank. As did Matt. "Good," Matt said, shooting Jory a hard look.

Yeah. He'd killed by Chance's age, so it shouldn't surprise him. Yet something in his gut hurt. Bad. They'd have to deal with that if and when they returned. For now, he had to talk to Piper. To tell her what she meant to him.

He found her in his bedroom, staring out the sliding glass door at the darkened sky. For once, the night was clear. Stars dotted the night, showing hope, although midnight and death waited for him mere hours away. He opened the door and gestured her outside into an unseasonably warm night.

She stood in the moonlight and turned to face him. So damn beautiful his chest hurt. "Did you come up with a plan?"

"Yes."

"Which is?" she asked.

"To attack, find the cord, and take the chip out." He wanted to touch her, but he wanted to commit the moment to his heart. Of her in the moonlight, love and concern in her eyes.

She smiled, her lips trembling. "Sounds easy enough."

"I know, right?" He moved toward her, needing to touch. Gently, he ran a knuckle down the contours of her face. "I couldn't imagine anything more beautiful than you."

She slipped her hands beneath his shirt. "Oh, I can." A low hum whispered on her lips as she shoved his shirt up.

He ducked to help her take it off. "I'll do my best to get back to you."

"I'm coming with you." She leaned in and licked his right nipple.

He shivered. "No."

She nipped. "Yes. I'm the hero of my own damn story, Jory Dean. Protect me all you want, but this once, I'm needed with you. War or not."

If something happened to her, he'd fucking die. Well, if he didn't die in a few hours, anyway. "I can't do what I need to do with you there."

"I'm a hacker, Jory. Even with the right cord, we may need to hack into the chip." She nibbled up his chest to kiss under his chin. So gentle and so damn sweet.

"I don't want you to see me like that." To see the real him, the one that could turn off all emotion and kill so many damn ways.

She sighed, her eyes luminous. "I love all of you, Jory Dean. Every facet, the dark and the light. And I won't let you die. You need me there."

Worse yet, she was right. He might need a hacker.

His brothers could hack, but chances were they'd be busy shooting and preventing the commander's men from getting into the infirmary. With a jolt, Jory realized that not only was Piper needed on the mission, but so was Laney. Would Matt realize it? If not, they'd have to make do. Matt would have to cut out Jory's chip.

"Fine," Jory murmured, grateful for any extra moments with her, even spent in battle so long as she stayed safe. "But you'll follow orders. You'll be armed, and at all times, you'll be surrounded by guns. Can you handle it? Agree or it's off."

"I agree." She grabbed his hair and yanked his mouth down. "I'm glad you're seeing reason."

He ripped her shirt apart, nearly shocking himself at the raw need to keep her safe. To take her and make her his. No matter what—forever. "Remember how I imagined us?"

She gasped and glanced around. "Yes."

"Good." He stepped back. "Take off your pants."

Her eyes widened, and she shoved off the worn jeans. Her bra and panties were next.

Yeah, she was perfect.

He shucked his clothes, watching her watch him. With curiosity and need—and a small amount of trepidation. Good. He liked her off balance. Getting Piper out of her head, even temporarily, was a challenge he'd love to meet every single damn day.

So he tangled his fingers in her hair, effectively tethering her. A soft gasp whispered from her when he twisted. Then his mouth took hers.

No persuasion, no gentleness—just a hard and fierce claim. He thrust deep, tasting her, taking what he wanted. *She* was exactly what he wanted.

She pressed against him, her hands flattening on his pecs, trying to get closer. Accepting who he was, what he wanted, and giving even more. The woman gave everything.

He lifted her, laying her down on a settee on his patio. She reached for him, and he flattened a hand on her abdomen. A couple of kisses to her thighs were all the warning he allowed before tasting her.

She hissed out a breath and lifted her hands to her face.

He grinned and sucked her clit into his mouth.

She gasped and writhed against him. "Too much. Tooooo much."

"Nope." He spoke around the small bundle of nerves, knowing his timber would vibrate deep inside her.

She groaned, and a fine tremble cascaded through her spectacular thighs.

He licked her again. Spice and woman—his. Keeping up a quick rhythm without enough pressure to force her over, he pressed a finger inside her. Then another one. She gyrated against him, trying for more, but he kept it light as he played. As he enjoyed her.

Minutes passed. She moved against him, her hands now in his hair, trying to force him down.

He chuckled against her, and she ground out a threat or two. "What?" he asked.

"More," she demanded.

"Why didn't you say so?" Truly enjoying himself, he nipped her clit and crisscrossed his fingers inside her. She nearly shot off the lounge, and ripples cascaded through her abdomen.

He prolonged the orgasm as long as he could, finally stopping when she smacked him on the top of the head and went limp. Man, she was fun.

Then he stood, the ache in his balls nearly unbearable.

She glanced up and shoved her unruly hair from her eyes. Taking a look at his raging hard-on, she smiled. Slow and satisfied. "Well. What should we do now?"

For answer, he reached down and flipped her around to her hands and knees. She gasped and struggled to find balance. When she did, he grabbed her hips.

"Now?" He leaned down and nuzzled between her shoulder blades before standing back up. "Now we go with my idea."

Piper clutched the fabric of the lounge, acutely aware of the man grasping her hips. The fully erect, ready to rumble, man. She looked back over her shoulder. "Well?"

He pressed at her entrance and slowly—so damn slowly—entered her. She bit her lip against the exquisite pleasure. That quickly, that easily, he stroked the desire in her higher than before. Hotter than before. She pressed back against him, allowing him to lead. To take them both where he wanted to go.

One huge hand flattened between her shoulder blades and caressed down, touching every inch of skin. As if he wanted to know all of her. His hands roamed around and cupped both breasts, tugging gently on her nipples. Sparks of electricity zipped from her breasts to her core, and she convulsed once around his shaft.

He groaned and tugged again.

So much. Jory Dean was so much as to be too much. Yet she wanted him all. So she released her hold and leaned down onto her chest.

His sharp intake of breath made her smile.

His hold returned to her hips, and he slid out and then back in. So damn deep. Holding tight, keeping her in place, he began to pound. Fierce and hot...and so full. The slap of his skin against hers echoed through the peaceful night. Friction sprang alive inside her. She tried to move against him, to fall over the cliff, but he held her in place.

She'd never met a stronger man. Add in his intelligence, and Jory Dean was the full package. "I'm keeping you, Jory," she murmured against her arms.

He paused inside her, pulsing. "You've got me."

Yeah. She did. For how long? She gave him what she knew he needed. "You've got me, too."

The control she could always sense in him snapped. Hard and desperate, he started to pound. To take her—without his usual carefulness—without his usual containment. Jory Dean in full force. A completely delicious man.

Heat cut through her, a rapid fire of an electrical storm. She held her breath and promptly detonated. Everything inside her exploded out, around him, into him. He thrust harder, paused, and came against her. Waiting until the shocks stopped shaking her, he withdrew and turned her around, flattening her on the ottoman.

The chill of the night had nothing on the warm male sprawled lazily over her.

She pushed his dark hair away from his face. "Jory."

"I love you." He kissed her so gently, tears filled her eyes. "Keep that—"

"You aren't going to die." She tightened her hold while her entire body began to ache with dread. "You can't."

"Thank you for making this week the best of my life." Vulnerability and love glimmered in his mysterious eyes.

Well, if that didn't slice her heart in two, nothing ever would. She breathed out. "I love you, too." So he had to stay alive. She had him, and she'd meant it when she'd said she was keeping him. He was one of a kind, and he had to live. What if she couldn't save him?

He kissed her one more time. "Our hour is up."

CHAPTER
28

CHANCE DEAN GLANCED around the helicopter, his mind running through the plan. He'd adopted the family name the second Mattie had put stock certificates in his hands—equal shares in Sins Security for Chance Dean, Kyle Dean, and Wade Dean. Just in case they didn't make it back home, the younger brothers were protected. And kind of rich.

Just seeing the last name on the documents had almost made Chance cry like a little baby, and not the killer he knew himself to be. He figured his new brothers knew he'd killed—they had the same look in their eyes that he did when he looked in the mirror. They'd probably killed young, too.

Doing that changed a guy, and not in a good way.

But as he took in the two silent women on either side of him, he wondered. Could they find good in their lives? Was there a chance for happiness and that goofy, soft, love stuff?

Piper and Laney were super-pretty and so soft. Even wearing khaki combat gear with guns strapped to their legs, they had a delicacy that drew Chance. He'd never met anybody soft or nice. Ever.

Shane flew the copter with Nate in the passenger side. Jory and Mattie hung close to their women, sitting armed to the teeth across the aisle from him.

Chance frowned. "I don't need to be flanked once we go in. Not like you have planned."

Identical gray eyes studied him, but neither man said a word.

He tried again. "I'm not one of the women." Laney's eyes widened, and Piper opened her mouth to say something. He halted her with one hand. "I'm not saying it's because you're girls. It's because you're not trained like I am. Girls can be tough." He didn't believe that one for a second, and by the narrowing of Laney's brown eyes, she knew it. Piper just grinned at him like he was adorable.

Either way, he'd put his foot into it.

Facing him across the aisle, Matt leaned forward, his voice deceptively soft. "What's your job with your brothers?"

"To protect them." The words sprang instantly to Chance's mouth as his shoulders went back.

"Why?" Jory asked just as quietly.

"They're mine." Chance shrugged. "I'm the oldest, and well, they're mine."

Matt nodded, his gaze dark. "We're older than you."

Jory lifted his chin. "You're ours now. Like it or not."

Belonging. Chance had figured it felt like warmth and apple pie. It didn't. It was more like a wrecking ball to the chest that hit hard and burrowed right in.

"Never alone," Matt said. "It's our mantra—learn it."

He didn't need to learn it—he was living it. Finally. For the first time, he wasn't alone, and a hollow place in his gut, one he'd always tried to ignore, finally warmed and filled. He swallowed over a lump in his throat. "Okay."

Piper patted his leg. "I'll try not to shoot you today. With my being a girl with a gun and all."

He rolled his eyes while Jory grinned. The lady was a smart aleck, and she'd served to break the tension gripping him. So he looked at his brothers. "No matter what happens, I won't let either of them be harmed. You have my word."

Laney slid an arm over his shoulder and kissed him on the head. "You're a sweetie, Chance."

He stiffened. The gentle, natural affection nearly stole his breath. Plus, nobody who'd ever spent two seconds with him had ever thought him sweet.

Matt nodded, sympathy twisting his lip. "They say stuff like that all the time." He shook his head.

Well, if she thought he was sweet, Chance would fucking learn how to be sweet.

Piper slipped her arm between his. "You're ours, Chance. No matter what."

He leaned into her, allowing himself a brief moment to experience softness and acceptance. She was the first lady who'd ever shown him kindness, and he'd do anything to stay in her world. To be around soft and nice . . . and to protect her.

"You're a nice lady," he murmured.

Piper chuckled. "I'm no lady, kid. When I said I'm keeping you, I meant it. If anybody tries to mess with you, or tries to hurt you, you'll truly understand how much I'm *not* a lady." She hugged him close with the words.

His mouth dropped open and then shut. She meant it. He could tell, and she meant to keep him. "Thank you," he mumbled.

Then he leaned back.

For now, he needed to be the killer the commander had trained him to be. Nothing, and he meant nothing, would harm any of the people in the helicopter on his watch. No matter what he had to do. And once he got them safe, he'd do what he'd planned when he'd talked them into taking him back into hell.

As far as he was concerned, he had one job left in this life.

Piper tried to keep her hands still and not drum her fingers on her legs as the helicopter continued to cut through the early morning. She'd said a tearful good-bye to her mother and Earl, just in case things didn't go well. But she had to go, and her mom had understood.

The combat gear was surprisingly heavy—who knew a bulletproof vest weighed so much? The gun strapped to her leg felt weird, and she truly did hope she didn't accidentally shoot somebody.

"Two minutes out," Shane said from the pilot's seat.

Jory, Matt, and Chance instantly moved into soldier mode, drawing weapons and losing any semblance of the men she knew.

Piper's breath panted out, and her heart sped up.

Jory leaned toward her. "Deep breaths, and let the adrenaline do its job. Don't fight it."

"That obvious?" she asked.

"I can hear your heart and see your breath." He smiled without any humor. "We have special gifts."

Chance gasped. "Me, too."

Matt nodded. "Use them today. All of them."

Piper set her hand on her weapon. Special gifts? Just how special? There was so much she didn't know about Jory. Would she get the chance to learn, or had he been a dead man the second he'd been shot two years ago when the bullet glanced off the kill chip?

An explosion rocked the air. Gulping, she levered to see out the front window. Holy hell. They were about to enter a war zone. Fires lit the ground below and smoke billowed up. Several attack helicopters had landed throughout the compound, and the pattering of gunfire filled the morning. She turned back, wide-eyed.

Jory nodded. "We sent troops in a half hour ago to clear the way."

She swallowed. "How many troops do you have?"

Matt reached for the door. "A lot." He eyed Laney. "Everybody understand the plan?"

Everyone nodded.

"Good." The helicopter set down, and Matt yanked the door open. "Time to run."

A high-pitched scream rent the air, and another explosion rocked the earth. Piper jumped out, and the Dean brothers quickly herded her, Laney, and Chance into the center of them. Heat from fires blasted into them.

Smoke and debris stung Piper's eyes, and she tried to see through the pain. As one, they ran for the main building. The door hung by one hinge over the opening, swinging slowly. Shots peppered the ground before Jory, and he pivoted, already firing. A soldier in black dropped to the ground.

The Dean brothers returned fire, and soon they reached the opening.

Jory stepped inside and swept right to left. "Clear."

They jogged down the hallway. Piper kept to his heels, her heart in her throat. Or maybe that was fear. Either way, it took every ounce of concentration she had to keep moving and not panic.

Two soldiers in black ran around a corridor, and Jory fired along with Matt, neither man losing a step. They were scary and freaking amazing all at once.

Three more turns, two already-smashed open doorways,

and they emerged into the infirmary. Three beds and a myriad of medical equipment took up the room. Counters, basins, machinery, and tons of drawers covered every wall.

Matt nodded toward the two entrances. "Shane. Nate." The two men hustled to stand right outside. "Chance, cover Shane. I'll cover Nate."

Chance ran to stand on the inside part of the door near Shane, while Matt did the same with Nate.

Jory holstered his gun. "Drawers. Let's find that cord."

The firefight continued outside, and Matt issued orders with a com-link attached to his ear. Piper ran to the north wall and started yanking out drawers. Cotton balls...medication...syringes. Drawer after drawer, she frantically searched while Jory and Laney did the same.

Nothing.

Ten minutes later, they'd gone through every cabinet and drawer.

Jory turned toward her, no expression on his rugged face. "It was a long shot."

The simple words, the easy acceptance from him, pierced her heart. No. There had to be a way. She glanced at her watch. Fifteen minutes. He had *fifteen minutes* to live. Oh God.

Matt growled. "Lie down, then. We might as well try to take it out." Pain and fury radiated with his words spoken in a full Southern accent.

Laney nodded. "I'll be as quick as I can." Terror filled her dark eyes, but her voice remained steady.

Chance pushed off the door, panic across his face. "There's nothing we can do? Nothing?"

Jory shook his head. "This is it, I guess. Let's give it a shot." He reached out a hand to Piper, and she ran to him, burrowing into his chest. He patted her back. "It's all right. I figured the commander wouldn't just leave the right cord for us to find."

The commander. Find. Oh, shit. Where would he hide it? The room. His secret little hidey-hole of a room off his office. It had to be there.

Piper levered back. "I know where it is." She grabbed her gun and started for the door. "I know where he'd hide it." Maybe. Who the hell knew?

Matt yanked open the door, and Nate fanned out. "Where?"

"Left. Toward the commander's office." She hustled toward Matt, and Jory dragged her behind him.

"Stay clear," Jory ordered. "Chance, have her back."

A ruckus set up on the other side of Chance's door.

Nate dodged inside and went to help his brother.

Matt immediately took his position. "I'll clear the way. Jory, you take Piper and Chance to get the cord. Laney and I will keep the infirmary clear. Get back here now." He ducked a bullet and then fired three shots. No cry of pain echoed. "Clear," Matt said.

Jory took the lead. "Direct me."

Piper coughed out smoke-filled air. "Go left and then right at the end." Jory launched into action, and Piper followed with Chance protecting her back. They made it down two hallways before meeting resistance.

Jory fired before Piper could scream, instantly killing two soldiers in black. Running boot steps heralded behind them, and she turned in time to see Chance calmly fire his gun, hitting one of the commander's soldiers between the eyes.

She gulped down bile. Strength. She needed to be strong.

They kept moving and finally found the commander's office. Jory splintered the door open with one hard kick. He swept high while Chance swept low. Piper shut the door behind them, and it hung drunkenly from one side. Running around the massive desk, she felt for the button.

Click.

The hidden door opened.

Jory pivoted and took a defensive stance at the main door. "Piper, go through the room. Chance, go through the desk and this office."

Piper nodded and moved for the room, while Chance sprang into action. Piper stepped inside the quiet room and went still at the barrel of a gun pointed at her head. Her father grabbed her, held the gun to her temple, and yanked her back into the room.

Jory and Chance froze, their gazes on Piper.

Bubbles of energy rippled up her esophagus, and she bit her lip to keep sane. To think. "Please don't do this," she whispered.

Her father laughed an eerie, deep chuckle. "So. I get to watch a chip explode now. Nice."

Jory slid his gun back into the holster, calculating the exact distance between him and the commander. Chance remained quiet on the other side of the desk, his gun pointed down.

"Holster, boy," the commander ordered, keeping his focus on Jory.

Chance shoved his weapon home, his gaze direct.

Jory motioned him back. The smart move would be for the commander to take out Chance, but the commander had an ego, didn't he? Quite possibly he didn't see the kid as a threat.

"She's your daughter," Jory said.

The commander shrugged, his chest bumping the back of Piper's head and jerking it. "She betrayed me, which isn't surprising since she's a woman. However, Jory, your betrayal shocked me, and now it's too late to make amends."

Jory forced an eyebrow up. "Betrayal? How the hell did I betray you?"

The commander's dark eyes blackened further. "You followed Matt and not me. I *created* you." He pressed the gun harder against Piper's temple, and she winced.

Everything in Jory narrowed in focus by that one wince. "I love Matt. He's my *brother*." Without seeming to move, Jory edged closer. "You're *nothing* to me." Another movement.

"Hey—" The commander shook his head.

Chance cleared his throat. "Where's Dr. Madison? Did you get her back from the PROTECT soldiers?"

The commander swung his gaze toward the kid, his eyes blazing. "Not yet, but I have most of my forces out looking for her. We will avenge her, and she will be home soon."

Nice job, kid. Jory took another sliding step.

"Move again, Jory. Try it. I'll blow her brains out before you can take another step." The commander leaned to the side and glanced at his computer. "Looks like you have about eight minutes left before we watch you implode."

Piper hissed a small cry of distress. "Please don't do this."

"Now!" Jory ordered.

Piper jerked her head away from the gun and went limp. Chance shot forward and tried to grab her. Jory leaped for the commander's wrist and shoved as hard as he could.

The gun went off.

For the briefest of seconds, everybody froze.

Blood burst onto Chance's face.

Jory pushed the commander back and into a filing cabinet before punching the bastard in the wrist three times. Hard.

Bones cracked and cartilage smashed. Satisfying, but a rage rolled up in Jory that he'd never experienced. Too hot and too dangerous, the beast at his core finally roared.

"Chance," Piper breathed. "How bad?"

"Through and through on the shoulder. I'll live," the kid said. "Go find the cord."

Jory barely heard their interchange, so absolute was his fury. "You made my brothers' lives hell, and you made us kill." With a flick of his wrist, he threw the monster from his childhood over the desk and across the room. The commander impacted a wall of weapons and guns rained down to the floor. "You made us into something we didn't need to be." And he'd hurt Piper...badly. Without missing a stride, Jory flew across the room and picked the bastard up.

Blood dotted the commander's mouth. Jory punched him in the nose, and more red sprayed. "Matt wants to kill you, but I'm not gonna let him live with that."

"Neither am I." With a bloody smile, the commander dodged forward.

Jory pivoted to the side a second too late. A sharp pain lanced through his abdomen. He glanced down as red bloomed over his right side where a knife handle protruded.

The commander shoved harder. "Die, you worthless creation."

Jory's vision grayed. Digging deep, he covered the commander's hand with his and squeezed.

The commander's dark eyes widened, and blood flowed freely from his broken nose.

Using all the strength he owned, using all the training Matt had drummed into him, Jory pulled the knife from his side.

"No." The commander tried to reclaim his hand.

"Yes." All the rioting in Jory stopped and went silent. He grabbed the commander's neck and shoved him against the wall. Lifting the blade still dripping with his blood, he used every ounce of strength he had left to plunge it up into the commander's neck in a kill strike.

The soldier gurgled, his hands clawing at the bloody handle.

"I told you it'd be me." Jory leaned in until they were eye to eye. The life slowly faded from the commander's body. "For my brothers."

CHAPTER
29

Piper UPENDED THE last of the cigar boxes, and her heart leapt. A cord, tightly wound, lay in the corner. She grabbed it, her hand shaking. She'd found it.

Turning, she hurried out of the hidden room in time to see her father's eyes flutter shut. Jory dropped him to the ground and staggered back.

Chance stood to the side, his face white, his mouth open. "You killed him." Wonder filled the kid's voice as if he couldn't quite believe anybody could kill the commander. "He's dead. I mean, he's really dead." Hope now pushed away the wonder.

Jory turned around, blood flowing from his side.

Piper's feet remained rooted, and she held up the cord. "I found it." Her gaze went to her obviously dead father. *What? How?*

She blinked several times, and cold burst through her chest. Her vision fuzzed, and she swayed, disoriented. Dead. He was really dead.

Chance jumped for her and grabbed the cord. "How much time?"

She shook herself out of shock to glance at her watch. Death and freaking out would have to wait. "One minute. Please. One minute."

Chance shoved one end of the cord into the commander's computer tower. "We don't have time to get back to the infirmary."

Jory ripped off his shirt and smashed the cotton against

his bleeding rib cage. "Piper, you hack." He reached down and picked up one of the fallen knives. "Chance? You cut."

Chance backed away, his hands shaking. "I don't know how—"

"I'll cut." Piper took the knife. "Lie down." Leaning over, she quickly started the computer program and found the right sequence and algorithms from the server. "When that turns over, let me know." Then she shoved everything but the monitor off the commander's desk. They didn't have time. They didn't have enough time. Oh man. They needed time.

Jory knelt on the wooden floor and leaned over the desk, his chest against the oak. He turned his head to the side. "I'm sorry about your father."

She shoved hair from her face. "Not now."

"This may be all we have." A lock of black hair fell over his forehead, and she brushed it back. Her hand shook, and she tried to calm herself before she cut into him. She could do this. Hell, she had to.

"Hold really still." She eyed the scar next to his C4 vertebra. Pressing her lips together, she made a fast incision at one end, then another at the other end. Blood welled up. She squinted to try to find the opening, but too much blood was in the way. She couldn't touch the chip or it'd explode. Blood rushed through her ears, and her palms began to sweat. "I can't see."

Chance leaned over and spit onto one end. The spit pushed blood out of the way and revealed the opening in the chip. "There you go." His fingers flew over the keyboard.

Jory cut him a look. "Thanks."

"No problem." Chance's voice hitched, and his chest trembled. "Just don't die."

Piper grasped the free end of the cord. It had two long silver prongs with an intricate meshing between them. There was no way she would've been able to redesign it in time.

Using her free hand, she cut along both sides of the kill chip, careful not to touch or disturb the metal.

"Piper?" Jory asked, his cheek on the desk, his gaze on her. "I am sorry."

She nodded, her heart thundering. "I know, and you're forgiven. Truth be told, I like you a lot better than I ever liked him." The words were true, and the least she could do was reassure him. Just in case.

At the acceptance, Jory's body relaxed. He nodded. "Whatever happens, I love you."

She paused, so much emotion ripping through her, she hurt. Bad. "I love you, too."

"Kissy later." Chance hissed. "The chip detonates in twenty seconds."

Holding her breath, Piper paused. If she hit the device wrong, she'd kill him.

"You can do it," Chance whispered, hope and fear in his voice.

She had to do it. "Oh God, Oh God, Oh God." The mantra ran through her head as Piper inserted the prongs into the end of the chip. She froze in place, trying not to twitch. Nothing. Good.

Chance let out a shuddered breath. "You're connected?"

"Yes," she whispered, her gaze on the chip. Her muscles tensed, and her stomach cramped. "Tell me when."

"Wait...okay..." Chance typed in the commands. "We have a connection. Typing in the code, and...Now!"

Please, God. Piper grabbed the chip in the center and tugged. It popped and agony rippled along her fingers. The blades shot out, and she yelped, throwing the thing across the room. Matt was just entering, and he threw out a hand, sending the device spinning into the wall. The blades took hold, leaving the chip fully embedded. It smoked and hissed.

For a moment, nobody moved.

Jory stilled. "We done?"

Matt had him off the desk and in a bear hug within seconds. "You did it. We didn't think there'd be time, so we hurried to you. After running into some trouble."

Oh God. Jory was saved. Piper wiped sweat off her forehead with her good hand, her chest swelling. Her vision disappeared, and it took a second to realize she was crying. Then she fell back against the file cabinet. Her knees shook.

Jory turned and grabbed her hand. "I heard the chip detonate. You cut?"

"No. Burned." She glanced down at the bubbling skin alight with pain. "Well worth the result." Holy fuck it hurt.

Chance grinned, his eyes weary. "You're awesome."

"No. You're awesome." She grinned back, enjoying the moment.

"You're all awesome," Laney said from the doorway, her arms laden down with bandages. "What are the injuries?" Then she gasped and rushed Chance. "Oh, honey. You got shot."

Chance glanced down at his bloody shoulder. "Just a flesh wound."

"Oh." Laney helped him remove his shirt and quickly pressed a bandage on both sides. "I'll stitch you up in the air. For now, keep pressure on it." Leaning over, she frowned at Piper's burns. "I have salve at home." Then she ducked and slowly removed Jory's wadded-up shirt. "Eesh. Okay." Handing him a bandage, she bit her lip. "Keep pressure. You need stitches first."

"Once we're in the air," Matt said. "Nate and Shane have cleared a path. Let's go."

Piper nodded and tried to push the pain somewhere else while running into the hidden room and taking the laptop off the top shelf. There had to be a reason it was hidden. Biting her lip, she then shoved the picture of the Dean boys as kids under her arm. She hurried back out.

Tucking her head under Jory's arm for his uninjured side, she tried to help him toward the door. He instantly released her and shoved her behind him, pulling out his gun. "Stay behind me."

She rolled her eyes. "Okay, hero boy."

His blood-riddled back straightened. "Just do it. We're not to safety yet."

For answer, she held out a hand for a bandage from Laney and then slapped it over the hole in his back. "Your special abilities don't give you more blood, do they?"

"I don't think so." He stalked toward the destroyed hallway. "But then again, I'm not sure. Maybe."

She shook her head. An explosion sounded from outside. They were still fighting? Trying to keep her limbs moving, she drew her gun. Just in case.

Chance jogged next to her, scanning the hallway. Even injured, he was on full alert. Must be a Dean characteristic.

They ran through the hallways, twisting and turning, leaving trails of dotted blood. Finally, Matt cleared the way outside where Shane and Nate waited in the helicopter with the blades already rotating.

So close. So damn close.

Piper followed Jory and kept an eye on Chance. Both moved well, but blood marred the ground as they ran.

Finally, they reached the helicopter, and Jory all but tossed her inside. He turned for Chance.

Chance backed away. "I'm sorry. I can't."

Jory paused, having no doubt the kid would pull his gun if necessary, considering his hand remained on his holstered weapon. "Chance?"

"Sorry." Chance's jaw firmed, but his lips trembled. "I really am."

Two soldiers dressed in black ran around a burning Humvee, and Jory shot one in the neck while Matt pegged the other. One got off a shot, and it ricocheted off the helicopter, smashing the one remaining window in the main compound.

"Chance? Get in the copter." Jory could probably get to him before he drew.

Chance sighed, looking young and desolate. "I can't leave him. Can't leave Greg." He pointed to a graveside on the other side of a barbed wire fence. "Not alone."

Jory's head jerked up. *Never alone.* Glancing around, he spotted the construction zone. He didn't believe in much, but family he understood. Loyalty and going to the mat for a brother, no matter what. His chest settled. The fight continued around them. They'd chosen their employees with care, and so far, they were doing a stand-up job. For now, he had family to worry about. "You're right. Let's get him."

Chance coughed. His shoulders drew back. "Wh-What?"

"Let's get him." Jory pressed the bandage against his bleeding gut and eyed Matt. "Provide cover and then pick us up over there."

Matt's head jerked as he looked out at the gravesite. Then he glanced at Jory and finally at Chance. Deep and gray, emotion burned in his eyes. "Go."

Jory touched Chance's arm. "Run."

Hope flared across Chance's bruised face. "Yeah." He turned and ducked low with Jory on his heels.

They zigged and zagged toward an excavator. Automatic fire peppered the ground before them. Damn it. Jory glanced around. "Sniper on the far roof." Ducking, he dropped to one knee, focused, and shot.

The bullet impacted the sniper's throat, and his gun clattered to the ground a second before the body.

Jory jumped back up and followed Chance. They climbed the excavator, and Jory worked the levers. His gut had gone numb, which probably wasn't good. In addition, his right arm wasn't working all that well. "Duck, kid."

More bullets sprayed across metal. The sounds of gunfire echoed behind them as Matt provided cover. Jory drove the tractor around burning vehicles and scarred earth, holding his breath as he reached the fence. He had to shoot twice before they made it to the uneven field. The massive tires threw up mud and dirt clumps.

They reached the fence, and Chance tightened next to him. Jory drew up the boom and continued on with full power.

The fence drew taut and then let go with a loud PING. The sound of freedom had a beautiful ring to it.

They continued on, two wounded guys with the stars shining down on them, gunfire echoing behind them. Chance gurgled in pure joy, and Jory grinned.

"Fuck them," Chance bellowed.

Jory nodded. "Yeah. Fuck them." He paused and made sure his innards were still inside. "You okay, Chance?"

"Not really. You?"

"No, but I will be. So will you." The promise echoed like a vow, and that worked for Jory. "I promise."

"So long as Greg is with us, I'm good. I promised him."

Under the light of a full moon, they reached the grave, and both exhaled. The rounded dirt showed the path, and it was small. Too damn small for a grave site—kids shouldn't die. Jory worked the controls and slowly churned up earth. By the time he'd cleared the small casket, Matt was dropping the helicopter three yards away.

Jory jumped down. "We need to lift him out. If I use the tractor, the coffin will split."

"I'll pull out the coffin." Chance kept a hand on his bleeding shoulder.

Matt, Shane, and Nate all leaped from the helicopter and strode toward the open grave site, determination on their hard faces.

"Greg belongs to all of us now, Chance." Jory turned to help Chance down. "Let's get our brother."

Even wounded, even in pain, the brothers lifted the casket out with reverence and carefully placed it down the center of their transport. It rode the helicopter home in the middle of the aisle, where they all could touch and find comfort.

Laney worked tirelessly in crappy conditions to stitch them up, finally sitting back with a loud sigh. "This is why I became a bartender."

The second they reached Montana airspace, something in Jory relaxed. Completely. He had to talk to Piper and make sure she really was all right with his killing the commander, and he should probably debrief his brothers. But first, they all had something important to do.

Matt dropped down on the north side of the property near an outcropping of majestic pine trees just as dawn began to emerge from the east. "Here?" he asked.

"Here." Jory jumped out first, holding back a wince when his stitches pulled.

"I thought so." Matt stopped the engines. "I called Josie and the gang to bring shovels." He hadn't finished speaking when two SUVs drew up. Kyle and Wade jumped out and ran right for Chance.

Wade stopped cold. "You got Greg?"

"Yeah. We got Greg." Chance dropped an arm around Kyle's shoulder. "How about there?" He pointed up at a blue spruce about a hundred years old.

Kyle's eyes filled. "Yeah. That's good."

Grandpop Jim carried over shovels, his face somber. "We're ready to dig."

Jory reached for a shovel while Chance did the same. Within fifteen minutes, with almost everyone digging, they were able to bury the coffin.

"We'll get a nice marker," Matt said, his voice hoarse.

Jory leaned against a tree. "Chance? You want to say anything?"

Chance nodded and stared down at the fresh earth covering his brother. "Greg was a good guy. Smart with computers, crappy with knives, but good with guns. He was kinder than anybody else I've ever met." Tears clogged his voice, and he cleared his throat. "More than anything, Greg was a good brother. The best."

"The best," Wade said, tears on his face.

Kyle wiped his eyes. "We miss you, Greg."

They stood there in the early evening, a family made by blood, circumstance, and hope. One by one, they gathered up to head to the ranch for dinner.

Soon, only Chance and Jory remained.

Chance hadn't moved. Even now, his head down, his gaze remained on the earth. "You don't have to stay with me."

Jory pushed off from the tree so they stood side by side. "Remember our mantra?"

A choked sound came from Chance. "Never alone."

"Yeah." Jory dropped an arm around Chance's shoulders. "No matter what, you're never alone again. I promise."

"Do you think Greg's in a better place?"

Jory breathed out, his chest constricting. "I really do. He's in a good place now."

"Even if we don't have souls?"

Jory tightened his hold on his brother. "We have souls. From the beginning, I could see beneath the surface of everything. Everybody. We have souls because I've seen them move. Grow. Hurt. Love. I promise you, no matter how they made us, we have souls."

Chance stiffened. He coughed. Then, with a shudder of absolute defeat, he turned his head into Jory's good side and broke.

Finally. Jory held him as he let it out, watching over Chance, keeping him safe. His gut hurt, his heart hurt, and now, it was time for them all to heal. Chance would be all right. And he'd never be alone again.

CHAPTER
30

PIPER TAPPED AWAY on the commander's laptop while her mom bustled around with dishing out breakfast. Fragrant homemade cheesy egg casserole had delighted the two younger boys, who were digging in over by the grandpops. Her mind spun.

Now that the danger had passed, where did she and Jory really belong? Was it all the tension? Would he still want her now that he had an entire life to live?

How well did she know the guy?

After dinner, they really needed to talk. Her heart kind of hurt, and she couldn't keep questioning everything.

She nibbled on her lip, flipping through files. Many old mission notes, many contacts delineated in governments around the world, and several plans to grow the compounds and the military research facilities. The commander had been a visionary—and crazy. She'd never think of him as her father again. In the short time she'd known Earl, the guy had acted more parental toward her than the commander ever had. Before breakfast had been served, Earl had mentioned speaking to Jory about his intentions toward Piper.

Matt Dean had paused in grabbing plates for the kids. "Can I watch?" he'd deadpanned.

Laney had promptly elbowed him in the ribs. "I think we should discuss your intentions toward me."

Matt had turned to her, gray eyes softening. "Oh, we probably shouldn't discuss my intentions in mixed company."

Laney had snorted. "Perv."

The place felt like home, and the people felt like family. Piper genuinely liked Laney, Audrey, and Josie, and they seemed to like her. Piper hoped she got to stay with Jory.

Man, she wanted to keep him. In this amazing place.

A sense of finality and relief permeated the makeshift family meal, along with a strong feeling of freedom.

Finally, the Dean brothers were free.

She'd be forever grateful they'd destroyed the kill chips. The Dean brothers deserved to live.

Jory and Chance walked through the front door, chuckling about something. Chance's face was puffy, but his body was relaxed. She lifted an eyebrow at Jory, and he gave a quick nod. All was okay.

Her mother hurried toward Chance and led him to the kitchen sink. "Wash your hands, sweetie. Then we'll dish you up some food."

Chance blinked and then nodded, allowing her to lead him to the sink. "Thanks, Nana Rachel."

So damn sweet. Piper rubbed her eyes and went back to the laptop.

A hidden file caught her eye, and she clicked to open it. Secured. Hmmm. Her fingers all but flew as she hacked, the challenge rising in her. Within minutes, the file opened.

Jory dropped into the seat next to her with an overflowing plate of eggs and bacon. "I love your mom."

"So do I," Piper murmured absently, scrolling through documents. He said he loved Piper, too, but she needed to hear him say it in the light of day and not when death loomed over their heads. She stilled. "Oh, my."

"What?" Jory happily shoveled in protein.

She rapidly read the file. "I found a file on Matt."

Matt lifted his head from across the room. "What kind of file?"

"Everything." Piper lifted a shoulder. "Your early tests, your schooling, your psychiatrists' notes." She peered closer. "I'm not reading any of them...just listing them for you." She flipped through and then caught her breath. "The number of brothers created from your father's sperm."

Jory stopped eating and leaned to look, while Matt rose and crossed the room.

Piper started reading. "Oh God."

"What?" Matt asked, moving next to Jory.

"There are more...at the same time as you. At least three." Piper scanned the documents. "The maternal donors were, ah, *taken care of*." That could mean anything from bribery to death.

Matt slid onto the bench next to Piper. "More brothers our age?"

Piper swallowed and opened a word document. "Yes." She sat back, her mind spinning.

The computer dinged. Whoa.

A series of code scrolled across the screen. She started typing, trying to slow down the numbers to see what was going on. "Shit. The file triggered an automatic link." She reached for the OFF button.

Jory grasped her hand. "We can't be traced here, and we won't stay on long. Let's see who opens up the other side." He slid the computer more in front of him as a picture began to form. "Shit," he muttered.

Dr. Isobel Madison came into view, her face close to a screen. Probably a smartphone. "Jory! You little bastard."

Jory blew out air. "I'd hoped you were dead."

"Not yet. No thanks to you." Her gaze went behind him. "Is my daughter around?"

"No." Jory's expression gave nothing away. "Where the hell are you?"

She sniffed. "I do not know, and this call is being monitored. Come and get me. You owe me."

"Not a fucking chance. Why did this file trigger your cell phone?"

Madison snarled. "Oh, that. Well, I wondered if you'd ever get into those files. Which one did you find?"

"You tell me," Jory said evenly.

"I don't know." The nutty scientist giggled. Weird, that.

Matt reached for the laptop. "Do I have other brothers out there?"

Delight flashed across Madison's face. "Oh. That file. Yes, you do...and I know who and where they are. Of course, unless you rescue me from the PROTECT organization, I'll have to tell them everything."

Matt frowned. "You already did, or they wouldn't have let you answer this phone."

She leaned down and glared. "You killed Franklin. You will die."

Jory leaned closer to the camera above the screen. "Look in my eyes. I. Killed. Him."

Pain and then calculation filtered through her gaze. "I always figured it'd be Matt."

"So did Matt," Jory said. "You were both wrong. I'll carry that one. Easily."

Her lips pinched. "You'll die next, then. I may not agree with the PROTECT group, but they've vowed to help me avenge Franklin's death in return for information. I am going to bury you."

"Any time, any place. Come get me." Jory shoved the computer away.

Audrey had waited patiently across the room and now moved toward them, leaning down over Matt's shoulder. Nate was instantly at her side.

"Mother? Just leave us in peace, would you?" Audrey asked, her skin so pale as to be translucent.

Isobel's blue eyes narrowed. "Good Lord, you're pale. Morning sickness?"

"Yes."

Isobel snickered. "Not surprised. You don't even know what you have growing in you, do you? What they are?"

Audrey leaned down. "I know exactly who my son is and who they are. Come after me, and I'll take you out."

"Turn against your own mother, would you?" Madison shook her head. "Not a chance."

Audrey's jaw firmed. "Come after my kid or my family, and I'll kill you, Mother. I promise."

Piper smiled. Damn, she liked her new friends.

Nate tugged Audrey away. "Enough, baby. Let's forget about her and the past."

"Good plan." Jory typed away, and the screen disappeared. "No offense, Aud, but that woman is bat-shit crazy."

Audrey chuckled. "Yeah. I know."

Matt leaned back. "We need to find any other soldiers created by the commander and Madison before the PRO-TECT people get to them."

Jory nodded. "I'll send directives to our computer center in California and get our soldiers on it. They're regrouping after the fight at the compound, but it looks good. Several injuries for us, but no deaths."

Matt leaned back and smiled. "We trained them well."

Jory nodded. "We'll start investigating PROTECT and hunting down any soldiers or brothers we might have out there." He slid the computer away. "For today, let's just enjoy the moment. We're not going to die anytime soon."

Shane lifted his Bloody Mary from across the room near the kids. "To not dying."

The cheer went up, the idea somber but the sentiment almost gleeful.

Piper shoved curly hair off her head. If she didn't get Jory alone to discuss their possible future, her head was going to explode. They had to have a future. "The eggs were great. What now?"

Wade took his empty plate to the sink. "Um, I saw a bunch of baseball stuff in the back room."

Grandpop Jim nodded. "I bought that stuff off the Internet for when the baby comes." His dark eyebrows wiggled. "We should try it all out now."

"We have never played sports." Kyle hopped up. "When we watched shows about families, they played baseball outside together. Even the vampire families."

Matt rubbed his chin. "Well, I guess we could."

Jory scratched his arm. "Um, okay."

Piper frowned. "Why don't you guys want to play baseball?"

The Dean brothers all shifted in their seats, but nobody spoke.

Earl patted his belly, and his eyes widened. "You don't know how to play baseball?"

Shane shrugged. "We never really had time to learn."

Piper gasped. "What did you do for fun as kids?"

"Put together missiles?" Matt asked.

"Practiced grappling and hand-to-hand," Nate mused.

"Threw knives." Shane nodded.

"Hacked into the Kremlin," Jory said.

Piper glanced around. That was crazy. She'd never met anybody who hadn't played baseball at least once. Her heart broke a little, and she glanced at the women in the room. "Ladies?"

Josie shook her head. "Grew up in foster care with no money for sports. I've never played."

Audrey patted her still flat belly. "Boarding school. No getting dirty or playing outside—except for tennis."

Holy crap. Piper rounded on Laney. "Please tell me—"

"Nope." The graceful woman shook her head. "I was a lab nerd and played with chemicals for fun. No real sports."

This was unbelievable. Piper stood up. She owed her mother for giving her a wonderful childhood. "I played softball for eight years."

Her mom threw her apron on the counter. "I coached for several of those years."

Earl gave Grandpop Jim a hand to help him up. "I played baseball."

"Me, too." Grandpop Jim's eyes sparkled. "I guess it's time to teach these kids how to play."

"You cannot just create your own baseball rules," Piper muttered, plucking a string from the bedspread. She'd already showered after the vigorous game and had left Jory to help clean up.

He emerged from the attached bathroom, hair wet, broad chest damp. A fresh bandage covered his side. A towel hung loosely at his hip.

Her mouth went dry.

He grinned. "Why not?"

"Because. The rules are the rules, and the *Piper Carry* doesn't get you more points." He'd tossed her over a shoulder and jogged around the bases while the boys had chased him, declaring that if he touched home plate, he got two points. "You've played baseball once. No new rules."

He shrugged and grinned. "Shane liked the rule."

"Because he was on your team." Piper rolled her eyes. "Nate hated the rule."

"Only because he couldn't pick up Audrey and run around. She'd puke all over him." Jory leaned against the door frame, muscled arms crossed. "Now do you want to tell me what's wrong?"

The way he looked at her. Gentle determination and patient amusement. It ticked her off. "No." She lifted her chin.

His cheek creased. "Yes. Spit it out, Piper."

"We haven't known each other very long, and we jumped right into this." She wet her lips, not missing the flare of interest in his gaze.

"The circumstances surrounding us make time lines irrelevant. Together we've been through more in the last week than most couples get in a lifetime."

But what did that mean? Did he want to date? Have sex? Work on a life? "Okay."

"You love me, Piper."

She stilled, her head jerking up. "You are so arrogant." Although he was right, and she did love him. But how was he so sure?

"No." He shook his head, losing his smile. "Well, not in this case. I'm just sure."

"How?" she whispered. Yeah, the guy had her heart. But how did he know?

"I can see it." An odd vulnerability filtered through his stormy eyes. "One of those extra abilities I have? I can see beneath the surface . . . things I shouldn't be able to see."

"Love?" She tilted her head, her heart thumping, her mind whirling. "What does love look like?"

"A wisp of color." He stretched his neck, his gaze remaining on her. "At first, when I was young, I wasn't sure what I was seeing from my brothers for each other. But when Nate fell in love with Audrey years ago, I saw it and I knew."

"Nate and Audrey knew each other years ago?" Piper grabbed on to the one fact to focus.

Jory grinned. "Yes. You have a lot of family history to catch up on."

Now that sounded promising. "Does love look the same on, ah, everybody?"

"No. Different colors, or maybe different frequencies." He shrugged. "Masculine and feminine energies always look different."

She stood and faced him. "What does my love look like?"

His gaze softened. Warmed. "All encompassing and bright. Full of heat and determination. All mine."

Well then. She swallowed. "I'm stubborn. Sometimes reckless."

"I'm overbearing and sometimes possessive." He shrugged. "We all have issues. I like yours."

Man, he just wanted to own her heart, didn't he? She paused.

He faltered. "Um, we should talk about the fact that I killed the commander." The vulnerability darkening Jory's eyes hurt to see.

Piper shook her head. "There's nothing to talk about, and it isn't anything that's standing between us. I didn't know him, much less care for him, although I wanted to badly. You? I care about. You did what you had to do, and I'm with you." Saying the words released something in her. She was with him and would remain so. "Can you see your love underneath your surface?"

"Yep. Darker and more dangerous than yours. Protective and possessive. An absolute." He pushed away from the wall and reached for her arms. "Mine's tinged with your light now and has been since the first time I kissed you. No matter what, green eyes. You live here." He patted his chest over his heart. "I love you, Piper."

She faltered. "I've never trusted a man before."

"I know."

She lifted her chin. "I trust you." Moving where she wanted, she stood flush against his chest. "I love you, Jory." Stretching up on her toes, she slid her mouth against his. Life was too damn short for uncertainty or taking things slow.

A sound of welcome rumbled up from his chest. A sound of home.

He tugged her into him, a haven of warmth and safety. And electricity. Taking over the kiss, he delved deep, giving her everything she could ever want. Home. Security. Love.

Life was good...and they now had time to live it.

CHAPTER
31

SHANE DEAN SHOOK water from his wet hair and crossed into the bedroom, his heart thumping hard in a second. Josie sat cross-legged on the bed, her face scrubbed fresh in the shower they'd just shared. He'd taken her twice, and now, seeing her there, he hardened again.

"You're gorgeous, Angel," he said.

She rolled her pretty eyes. "You're insatiable."

"Yep. So are you." He tuned his extra senses into the sounds of the house, relaxing when everything came back familiar.

"Is Mattie okay?" Josie asked.

Shane rubbed his chin. "Yeah. He and Laney are chatting it up in their bedroom." Shane's hearing was strong enough when he wanted that he could actually listen in on their conversation, but he gave them their space. "Discovering we might have other brothers out there hit Matt hard. We'll have to track down the lead and see if it's true."

"What about you?"

He shrugged. "I'll get worried when we find out if the file was true or just Madison messing with us."

Josie nodded and rubbed a bruise on her arm. "The kids had fun playing ball."

"So did you." He reached her and studied the bruise. "But you got hurt." Damn it. How had he let her get bruised?

She rolled her eyes. Again. "It's a small bruise from sliding into second. You're just mad you didn't get me out."

Truth be told, he'd fumbled on purpose because she'd been so damn cute sliding. "You were too fast for me."

"Right." She smiled up at him—his perfect, stubborn, beautiful angel. "Having the kill chips out is so surreal, I'm not sure what to do with myself now."

He chuckled. She knew better than to open herself up like that. So he set a knee on the bed and flattened himself over her, careful not to squish her. "Well, I'll see what I can come up with."

Her pretty blue eyes sparkled, and she slid her hands over his bare shoulders. "You know what I meant."

He did. Having the chips out didn't even seem real to him yet. Having a house full of grandparents and kids didn't seem real, either. "You know how much I love you, right?"

Her smile softened, and her eyes darkened. "I do know. I love you, too." Amusement curved her lips. "According to Grandpop Jim, we're the only ones here not living in sin."

Shane chuckled. "We're an old married couple, are we?"

"Sure." She wiggled her butt in a way that enticed him. "Do you think we're safe here?"

"I promise we are." There wasn't anything he wouldn't do to keep her safe and happy. "Trust me." Years ago, when he'd met her on a mission, he'd promised her forever. The words were a cover, the meaning behind them absolutely true. Now, he had the chance to make it happen. "Forever, Angel."

Matt Dean leaned against the headboard, his arm around a snuggly woman. Laney placed her hand over his heart and her head on his shoulder.

Pure trust.

She caressed him. "Are you sure you're all right?"

He tightened his hold. "I'm fine. I don't mind losing a game of baseball, especially when Jory kept making up new rules."

Laney snickered. "That's not what I meant, and you know it."

He sighed. "I know. There was always a possibility of more brothers out there, considering we were created in a lab. Finding out that they might exist isn't a shock to me. Stop worrying, sweetheart."

"That's my job," she said lightly. "Now we have grandparents, kids, and a whole lot of brothers in love with pretty great women. I know you, and I understand how you take responsibility for everyone. For safety, for protection, for their lives."

Yeah, but he didn't *have* a life without them all. Not one he'd want. "This is the good stuff, Laney. The responsibility is part of what we want and need." Plus, it wasn't like he was alone in this. He'd trained his brothers until they'd nearly dropped, and they could take care of themselves and anybody they loved. "By the way, you were pretty damn amazing taking out those chips the other day."

She shrugged. "No biggie."

He loved it when her words were country and her infliction all Ivy League. "The best moment in my entire life is when you found me in that alley," he murmured, brushing her hair off her shoulder.

She patted his chest. "Mine was the first time you kissed me."

"That made you mad." He smiled.

"You're dangerous when you kiss."

Hell, he didn't know how to be anything but dangerous. "I appreciate your moving to Montana and putting up with my, ah—"

She chuckled and threw a leg over to straddle him, her

palms flat against his chest as her butt settled on his thighs. "Your possessiveness? Bossiness? Extreme need to keep me secure and safe?"

His lids half lowered. "Yeah. That." Reaching for her waist, he tugged her closer, moving her along his shaft. Fire shot through his skin.

Desire flushed across her high cheekbones. "Since the chips are out, do you think you'll relax now?"

Man, he wanted to reassure her. To even lie to her. "No."

She coughed out a laugh.

He shrugged. "We're safer, but I wouldn't say safe." And if anything ever happened to her, he'd be destroyed. "I'll give you everything I can in this life, Lane. I promise." While keeping her safe.

"Hmmm." She played with his chest. "How about a baby?"

They'd never talked about kids. Longevity hadn't seemed possible, but now with the chips out? "You want a baby?" The idea of a little girl with Laney's pretty eyes warmed his heart.

She shrugged. "Watching Audrey throw up constantly hasn't quite won me over, but perhaps? What do you think?" Her chest lifted, and he could tell she held her breath.

He ran his hands down her toned arms, nearly overwhelmed with emotion. "I think we should start trying right now." Her chuckle as he flipped them over slid through his skin and into his heart. Where she belonged.

Nate Dean tossed the pregnancy book across the room. "This thing doesn't make any sense."

Audrey kicked her foot while sitting on the edge of the bed. "Morning sickness is normal."

"Not all day." He scrubbed a hand through his thick hair. Feeling helpless pissed him off, and considering he spent tons of time pissed off, he was tired of it. "We have to fix this." Seeing her in pain cut him deep.

She shrugged, her stunning blue eyes sparkling. "I just finished eating dinner, and I haven't gotten sick. In fact, I feel pretty damn good." She patted her belly. "You're just worried about Mattie, and you can stop that. He's fine."

Nate paused and focused on the woman who held his world in her delicate hands. "He's fine?"

"Sure. You've known there could be other brothers, so it isn't a shock. Yes, Matt feels responsible for everyone, but you all do that. The chips are out, and there's time to find these other brothers before my psychotic mother gets to them." Audrey glanced toward the door. "Was there dessert?"

"You're sure? Matt's okay?" Nate studied her. The woman was a genius and read people better than anyone he'd ever met.

"Yes. Would I lie to you?" Amusement lifted her lips.

He narrowed his gaze. Nobody could lie to him, considering one of his gifts was to discern any falsehood. The woman was telling the truth. "You're a smart-ass, you know that?"

She shrugged. "Takes one to know one." Then she patted the bed. "Maybe you should do something about that."

He grinned. "You sure?"

She lifted a shoulder, pushed off, and bounced toward the door. "If you can catch—eek."

He easily caught her, wrapping an arm around her waist and lifting her back to the bed. "You were saying?"

She pouted even as he lay her down. "You could at least give a girl the idea she has a chance."

"Oh, baby. You definitely have a chance." He tore the shirt over her head.

She laughed, cupping his jaw. "I love you."

The words were simple, but for him, they dug deep and healed. Every damn time she said them. "I love you, too."

She shifted against him. "Prove it."

Now that he could do. His mouth took hers, promising everything he'd held inside for so long. Everything he was.

Jory tucked Piper closer into his side and tuned into the sounds of the house. He'd had to really block noises for a little while, considering there were many private celebrations going on for hours. They'd have to talk about building individual homes throughout the ranch soon.

Piper stirred against him and shoved curly hair from her eyes. "What are you smiling about?"

"I'm happy." For the first time in as long as he could remember, the rioting in his head, in his chest, had quieted. "You make me happy."

She grinned and caressed his chest. The woman liked to touch, and she did it naturally and without thought. So it meant more than he could express. Instead, he placed his hand over hers. "You're going to marry me, you know."

She stilled. "Marry?"

"Yep." Sure, it was too soon to ask, and he wanted to give her time to get on board.

"You're supposed to *ask*."

He smiled. "I will. When the time is right." Man, he'd probably have to ask Rachel for Piper's hand in marriage, or something like that. When he proposed, and he was going to do it right and big, he'd want an audience. The entire family, probably, so he could share the joy and the moment.

"Humph." She actually sounded disgruntled. "Did you have a time frame in mind?"

"Nope." Although they did have a couple of issues to discuss first. "Even though I'm comfortable on the computer, I'm still needed in the field. Especially once we find the other soldiers."

She blinked gorgeous green eyes at him. "I know."

"You're okay with that?"

She shrugged, and kissed his shoulder. "I'm in love with all of you, Jory. The computer geek and the soldier. Nobody says you can't be both."

Acceptance. He warmed head to toe. "True." He rolled them over and settled on top of her.

She wiggled to get settled beneath him. "You're a hero, Jory Dean."

Man, was she off base. But he loved the idea that she thought that about him. "I'll never let anybody get to you, Piper. Nobody will come close."

She smiled. "I know." Then she patted above his heart. "That darkness you try to hide so well? That keeps us safe and protected. It's time to stop worrying about whether you're good or not. You're great."

He studied her. "You don't mind the darkness?"

"Nope. Can't think of a hero who doesn't have at least a little bit."

Her way of looking at the world, of looking at him, eased a tension through his gut he hadn't realized had always been there. "You told me the truth," he said.

She ran her fingers through his hair, her gaze softening. "I did?"

"Yes. The first day we met."

She eyed his lips. "What did I say?"

"You said you were there to save me." He lowered his head, and his lips brushed hers. So much love slammed through him, he could barely breathe. So he lifted up and smiled. "You did."

EPILOGUE

Two Weeks Later

JORY CROSSED HIS arms next to his oldest brother and surveyed the living room. "I think we're closer to narrowing down the name or names of the other soldiers created by the commander." One may even be a brother, if the commander's intel was true.

Matt nodded. "Good." Then he sighed and surveyed the sprawling family room.

Riley barked and leaped over a pair of boots at Payton Manning, who caterwauled and flew across a table, scattering a candy dish. Grandpops Jim and Earl obsessed over the remote control of the television set and why the second screen refused to come up, while three boys wrestled on the floor in front of them.

Like boys should.

Audrey patted her belly while Josie and Laney flipped through baby magazines, filling out a sheet of paper on what to order on the Internet. If they kept going, the family would need to build two nurseries just for Audrey's baby.

A box of baby ducks rested over by the far wall with a

sunlamp on them. Wade had rescued them a couple of days earlier.

Matt shook his head. "Ducks. We have ducks."

An aromatic fragrance wafted from the kitchen, where Piper and her mother, the amazing Nana Rachel, cooked something delicious. Piper poked her pretty head out to give instructions on the remote control.

Earl clicked a button, and the entire screen went black. Both men groaned. Piper shrugged and winked at Jory.

Amusement bubbled up through Jory, and he smiled. She was here, she was his, and he wasn't ever letting her go.

She disappeared into the kitchen.

Shane tapped a hammer on the wall, placing one of Nana's paintings, while Nate walked by and checked him into said wall. Shane turned and was soon on the ground with Nate, rolling around. The three boys instantly jumped into the fray.

Audrey lifted her feet as they rolled by and then turned to flop her legs over the side.

The cat howled again.

"What the hell did I do?" Matt rumbled, his chin lowering, his gaze on chaos.

Jory shook his head. His gut settled, and his heart warmed. "You made a family. You promised, and you got us a family."

The dog barked and went after the cat.

"I sure as hell didn't mean to." Matt frowned. Warmth and determination filtered through his gray eyes—the look of protection and devotion he'd always worn for his brothers. He'd always have to hold on tight, but this was a good group to shield.

Jory grinned, his shoulders going back. He could accept the darker side of himself, the one he'd fought, because he was needed to protect and defend. He'd damn well do it on the computer as well as in the field. He may be a nerd, but he was a fucking dangerous one. "It is a motley crew."

Matt snorted. "And they're all ours."

Yeah. They were.

Piper poked her head back in to check on the television and give more instructions, Rachel popping up at her side.

The time was now. Jory crossed to Piper and grabbed her, his lips taking hers. He kissed her until she sagged against him, filling himself up with love and woman.

Matt cleared his throat. "Get a room."

Jory grinned and stared down at the very flushed, bemused, perfect woman. "Marry me."

Rachel gasped and clapped her hands together, and the rest of the room went silent with held breaths.

Piper blinked and then slowly smiled. "Yes."

He kissed her again amid hoots and hollers of celebration. Finally. Jory Dean was home.

Discover how Rebecca Zanetti's thrilling, sexy series began!

Please see the next page for an excerpt from

Forgotten Sins.

CHAPTER
1

Present Day

JOSIE'S HEELS CLICKED in rapid staccato against the well-worn tiles, the smell of bleach making her stomach cramp. Her mind spun. How could this be happening? It must be some sort of trick.

Someone had taped smiling pumpkins along the hospital walls to celebrate the month of October. Something about their jagged teeth against the dim walls creeped her out. Even as an adult, the sense of helplessness she'd felt as a child in the hospital caused her body to tense and brace to flee from the antiseptic smells.

Several nurses converged behind a wide counter, studying charts. Josie ignored them and hurried down the hall. She reached the last room on the left and ran smack into a uniformed police officer. Bouncing back, she struggled to balance herself in the heels she'd worn to work. The call had come in after dinner, and she was still at the office. As usual. A promotion to vice president was up for grabs, and she was going to get it.

The cop steadied her, dark eyes appraising. "You all right, ma'am?"

"Yes." She tugged her handbag strap up her arm, need-ing to get a grip. She was an adult and in control now. "A Detective Malloy called me to come down. I'm Josie Dean." Her breath hitched on her last name; she'd be changing that soon.

"He's inside with Mr. Dean."

"Major Dean," she said automatically, and then her face heated. "I mean, he used to be a major. He may have been promoted." God. She sounded like an idiot.

A voice over a loudspeaker announced a code blue. The officer straightened, listened, and then relaxed his shoulders as a room on the third floor was named. "You can go right in." He tipped his head toward the open doorway before flashing a smile at a pretty nurse pushing a book cart down the hall.

Yeah. She'd *go right in*. Easier said than done. Josie took a deep breath, steeled herself, and walked inside, her atten-tion instantly captured by the male figure perched against the hospital bed.

For the briefest of seconds, time stopped. Memories flooded through her mind, her body, maybe somewhere deeper until her lungs forgot their job. That quickly, she was helpless with the need to heal him. Coughing, she forced air down her throat and took a good look.

Several bandages were strapped across Shane's muscular torso while a splotchy purple lump rose from his forehead. His long legs were encased in bloody jeans, and he'd crossed his thick boots at the ankles. He sat bare to the waist, his scarred chest and packed abs betraying a life of combat. The new wounds would fit with the rest.

Those scars broke her heart all over again.

His gray eyes lasered in on her, and she fought the urge to run. Pain, need, and familiarity swirled through her brain. Her skin warmed. Damn, he looked good. Dark brown hair swept back from his battered face, and even with the bruises, his rugged features spoke of strength and masculine beauty. Fierce and dangerous like a wolf.

His hair had grown to his shoulders and added a wild new edge to the danger.

She had a lot of layers, and he'd appealed to her on each one by providing security and fulfilling her desperate need to belong. Until he'd abandoned her. She faltered and clutched her handbag strap until the leather cut into her skin.

A throat cleared. "Mrs. Dean?"

"Josie." She shifted her focus to a man in a rumpled brown suit who leaned against a poster depicting the inner ear. The room was small—examination table, smooth counter with sink, one rolling chair for a doctor. Yet she hadn't even noticed the other man until he made a sound. "Detective Malloy?"

"Yes." Shrewd eyes the color of his suit studied her, and he began scribbling in a notebook. "Is this your husband?"

The quiet power of Shane's presence yanked her attention back to him. Even after all this time, he commanded her body's responses. He cocked his head as if awaiting her answer.

She nodded. "This is Shane Dean." This couldn't be happening. The helplessness she'd felt as a frightened and hurting child in the hospital closed in on her. The need to flee made her knees tremble. She focused on the closest person she had to family, struggling to keep her lips firm. It was really him. Really Shane. "They said you have amnesia."

Shane gave a short nod. "I can't remember a damn thing."

The familiar rumble of his voice slammed into her solar plexus. Emotion washed through her edged with a sharp pain. Two years. Two long years since he'd left her. "What happened?"

The detective stopped writing. "We were hoping you

might provide an explanation. Where was your husband going today?"

She barked out a laugh. Seriously? "I have absolutely no idea. We're separated."

Shane stilled, the air thickening with tension around him. "We are?"

"I haven't seen you in two years." Her voice shook, and she fought to settle raw nerves. She would not let him affect her. "I didn't even know you were back in the country."

"What country should he have been in?" the detective asked.

Like she'd know. "He's in the marines based out of Pendleton. Call them." Wait a minute. "How did you know to call me if you didn't know he was in the military?" She took a small step back to study her husband. "And what are you doing in Washington State?"

Shane shrugged. The paper on the table crinkled as he moved. "Dunno. Probably coming to visit you from my home in Oregon? I have an Oregon driver's license as well as a card with your name and phone number in my wallet... along with our marriage license. Am I from Oregon?"

Her thoughts began to swirl. "Yes. I mean, I think so."

A muscle in his jaw ticked. "You don't know?"

"No. I didn't know much about you, Shane. We met in California and married there." Within three weeks of meeting each other—the one and only time in her life she'd taken a risk and been spontaneous. Of course it had ended in disaster. She had been so stupid. What had she been thinking?

The detective cleared his throat. "Your husband isn't wearing dog tags. He was found down by the river, which is miles across the city from your home. To your knowledge, does he know anyone else here in Snowville?"

"No." At least, she didn't think so. More than 100,000

people lived in the eastern Washington town. Shane might know somebody else who lived there.

Her knees began to tremble, and she forced them still with stubborn pride. She dug her nails into her palms to quell the urge to caress his bruises. Her romantic notion of being able to heal him, to show him love was possible, had earned her a broken heart. Rightfully so. It was over. *They* were over. Her body needed to freakin' remember that fact. As did her heart.

Shane's eyes sharpened. "When did you move to Washington?"

"Two years ago."

"When we separated."

"Yes."

He lifted an eyebrow in an expression she remembered well. "Did I know we were separated?"

Warmth flushed through her chest, just under the skin. "Ending our marriage was your choice." In fact, he hadn't bothered to officially end the marriage. He had just disappeared—leaving her alone after making promises he clearly had never intended to keep. Some people didn't get a family, and she should've remembered that before trusting him.

The detective clicked his pen, gaining her attention. "Please explain. Is it some religious type of deal? The separation?"

Josie tilted her head. "Excuse me?"

Malloy straightened his pose against the wall. "The separation instead of a divorce. Is it a religious deal?"

Josie blew out air. "No. We're getting a divorce. I didn't feel right requesting it in absentia, and I wanted to wait until Shane could sign the papers. It just seemed fair..." She'd wanted to face him, to end it right. Of course, there had always been that tiny chance he'd try to win her back— explain why he'd deserted her.

No such luck.

Now she'd had enough of waiting—the papers were ready. As was she.

"That was nice of you, to wait I mean." Irony clanged in Shane's tone and spurred Josie's vertebrae to snap to attention one at a time.

"Yes, it was." More than once she had thought about filing the papers, but she couldn't steel herself to end it one-sided. To divorce a soldier most likely in combat seemed wrong. Even after everything, to hurt him like that would hurt her more. "I sent the divorce papers to your base in Pendleton. You could've mailed signed copies back to me."

"Maybe I don't want a divorce." Shane's jaw set in the way always guaranteed to prod her temper.

She forced anger down. Way down. She would not argue in front of the cop. Her gaze searched Shane's bruised face. "Was he mugged?"

The detective began to write again. "We don't know. If so, the muggers might need medical help, as well." He gestured toward Shane's bloodied knuckles. "He beat the crap out of someone." Scribble. Scribble. "Ah, Mrs. Dean, would you know anyone who'd want to injure or kill your husband?"

Besides her? She'd have to know him to know his enemies—and she didn't. "No. But again, I haven't seen Shane in years. You really should contact the military. Or his brothers."

Shane's head snapped up. "Brothers?"

"Yes. You let it slip once that you had brothers." How could he not remember anything? For a control freak like Shane, it had to be hell. "Though I have no idea who they are."

He exhaled in exasperation, and his gaze wandered over her face in a caress so familiar she almost sighed. "Sounds like I didn't trust you much, blue eyes."

"You don't trust anybody." She'd given him everything she had, and it wasn't enough. Tears pricked the backs of her eyes, and she ruthlessly batted them away. He didn't get to see her cry now. Before he'd left, there was one night when she'd thought they were getting closer, she had thought he was finally letting her in. Then he'd disappeared.

His eyes warmed and a hint of a smile threatened. A tension of a different sort began to heat the room. Josie tugged her jacket closed as her traitorous nipples peaked. She'd forgotten his ability to shift affection into desire. Damn the man.

Shane glanced over his bare right shoulder. "Have I always had the tattoo?"

"Yes." Malloy leaned for a better look. "Nice symbol. What does it mean?"

"Freedom," Shane murmured, rubbing his shoulder. He swiveled his head to meet Josie's gaze, both eyebrows rising. "Right?"

"Yes." She swallowed. "You already had the tat when we met, and you said it meant *freedom*."

"I don't remember getting inked, but I know what the symbol means." Shane frowned, running his wounded hand through his hair.

The detective cleared his throat. "So, you don't know who'd want to attack your husband, and you haven't seen him in two years. Ah, Mrs. Dean, you've built a life here, right?"

"Yes." A good life with roots. Sure, she was alone, but she was secure.

The detective nodded. "Are you dating anyone?"

Heat rose into her face even as Shane's eyes sharpened to flint. She shook her head. "That's none of your business, Detective."

Shane lifted his chin. "But I believe it is *my* business, angel."

The man always could issue an effective threat with the mildest of words. She opened her mouth to tell him to stuff it when his words hit home. "You remember. You called me 'angel.'" He'd given her the nickname the first day they'd met at a small coffee shop in California.

He shook his head, giving a slight wince and then holding still. "No. No memories. You look like an angel—big blue eyes, wispy blond hair. My angel."

"Not anymore." She wouldn't let him do this to her. It'd taken two years to deal with the past, and she couldn't face the pain again. No matter how lost he looked, or how lonely she was. "We're over."

"Who are you dating, Josie?" As usual, Shane ignored her words and narrowed his focus to what he deemed important.

"We do need to know, Mrs. Dean," Detective Malloy cut in before she could tell Shane to go to hell. "Just to clear the suspect list, if nothing else."

She sighed. "I'm not dating anybody."

"Someone popped into your mind," Shane said softly. Too softly.

Icy fingers traced her spine, and her heart rate picked up. She shrugged off the sensation. The cop narrowed his eyes. Both men waited.

She took a deep breath, pulling calmness in. "I'm not dating anyone, but I do spend time with Tom Marsh. He's in construction, and the last thing he'd ever do would be to mug somebody. And we're just friends."

"What kind of friends?" Shane kept his focus solely on her as if the cop weren't in the room.

"None of your business." The panic that rushed through her veins ticked her off.

He grabbed a crumpled shirt off the flattened pillow and yanked it over his head, grimacing as he tugged down the worn cotton. He pushed off the bed—toward her. "Does Marsh know you're taken?"

Awareness slammed into her abdomen as Shane's unique scent of heated cedar and rough male washed over her. How could she have forgotten how big he was? How much taller than her own five foot two? She tilted her head to meet his eyes. "Tom knows I'm about to be divorced."

"You sure about that?" Shane grasped her arm, his focus on the detective. "Malloy, you have my contact information while I'm in town. I'll be staying with my wife. Call if you hear anything."

The firm hand around her bicep—so warm, so familiar— sent a wave of thrilling awareness through her veins. The one touch could set her back months, maybe more. The man had always been unreal and larger than life. Wanting him had nearly destroyed her once. Never again. She sucked in a breath. "Did the doctors release you?"

"Yes. I have a concussion, and once it's healed, my memory should be restored. Though"—his voice dropped to a rumble—"you'll need to awaken me every two hours tonight, darlin'."

The twang. That Southern twang that escaped when he was either tired or aroused—an idiosyncrasy he normally managed to camouflage. The mere sound of it ignited memories of heated nights and soft whispers from her brain straight to her core. It was an intimacy most people didn't know about him, and learning about it made her feel special. Her mouth went dry.

A visible tic set up underneath the detective's left eye. "You're not free to leave, Major Dean."

Shane smiled.

The air rushed out of Josie's lungs. She knew that smile. The detective didn't stand a chance.

Neither did she.

Shane lowered his voice to a purely pleasant tone that wouldn't fool anybody with half a brain. "Malloy, I was attacked and have cooperated with you. I unfortunately have no new information, nor am I under arrest. Thus, I'm going home with my wife. Call me if you have questions."

The twang was gone.

Malloy tapped his pen. "I could hold you as a material witness."

"Try me." Somehow the tone became even more pleasant.

Josie fought a shiver.

Malloy, to his credit, ignored the threat and turned bloodshot brown eyes on her. "Is there anyone who'd want to hurt you, Mrs. Dean?"

Josie sucked in air. "You think he was injured because of me?"

The detective shrugged. "I don't know. This might've been a random mugging, but we need to explore all possibilities."

She hadn't seen her husband in two years. No way was the mugging connected to her. "Nobody wants to hurt me. Besides, most of my friends don't know I'm married." Next to her, Shane stiffened, and her breath quickened in response.

The detective nodded, his gaze taking in them both. "Are you sure you want him with you?"

No. Though it was time to finish this. "Sure. We need to talk, and I have papers for Shane to sign. Thank you for your concern." Not for one second did she think Shane would stay away at this point.

"Are you sure you're safe? He may be dangerous." The detective appraised them both without expression. Cop face . . . soldier face. She'd seen it on her husband.

"Shane's dangerous as hell." He'd saved her from an obnoxious jackass the first day they'd met, his combat training obvious. She allowed herself a wry grin. "But he would never hurt me." Physically anyway.

Malloy cleared his throat. "Major Dean, what about your safety?"

Shane blinked twice and then chuckled. "Ah. You mean from the deadly pixie doll standing next to me?"

"Perhaps." Malloy's gaze probed Josie's eyes as he addressed Shane. "You're estranged and she has moved on. Statistically, it's possible *the pixie* hired someone to take care of you." He smiled. "No offense, ma'am."

She coughed out a laugh. "None taken, Detective. Though I assure you, if I wanted Shane dead, I'd do it myself." He'd tried to teach her some dangerous skills during their brief marriage, but she'd never had cause to use them.

The detective's eyes narrowed.

Shane chuckled even deeper. "Let's go, angel."

She allowed him to tug her from the room. They passed the uniformed cop and the many rooms, Shane's large form dwarfing her in a way she'd forgotten, in a way that made her feel safe—protected—and yet so vulnerable. The detective's concern filtered through her thoughts. Shane was dangerous before. What if he was even more so now? Where had he been the last two years? She didn't know him anymore. Heck, she'd never known him.

Maybe she wasn't so safe.

However, as the exit doors came into view, her stride sped up in an effort to escape the hospital. For her first visit, when she was seven, she'd been brought in by a foster parent who had hurt her. The second time, when she'd turned nine, she'd been carried in by a foster parent trying to save her. Different experiences, yet the result had been the same. She'd ultimately ended up alone.

Here she was again, leaving the hospital with someone who would soon leave. He'd abandoned her once. No matter how quickly her heart had leaped when she'd seen him again, or how lost he seemed right now, he wouldn't stay.

Shane wasn't a guy who stuck around.

He paused near the sliding glass exit doors, turning her to face him, tipping her chin up with one knuckle. The breadth of his shoulders, the narrowness of his waist, the strength bunched along his muscles promised power and danger. Warmth and the masculine scent of heated cedar wafted her way. "So, wife. Have you slept with this boyfriend of yours?"

Fall in Love with Forever Romance

A HOPE REMEMBERED
by Stacy Henrie

The final book in Stacy Henrie's sweeping Of Love and War trilogy brings to life the drama of WWI England with emotion and romance. As the Great War comes to a close, American Nora Lewis finds herself starting over on an English estate. But it's the battle-scarred British pilot Colin Ashby she meets there who might just be able to convince her to believe in love again.

SCANDALOUSLY YOURS
by Cara Elliott

Secret passions are wont to lead a lady into trouble... Meet the rebellious Sloane sisters in the first book of the Hellions of High Street series from best-selling author Cara Elliott.

Fall in Love with Forever Romance

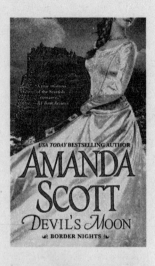

DEVIL'S MOON
by Amanda Scott

In a flawless blend of history and romance, *USA Today* bestselling author Amanda Scott transports readers again to the Scottish Borders with the second book in her Border Nights series.

THE SCANDALOUS SECRET OF ABIGAIL MacGREGOR
by Paula Quinn

Abigail MacGregor has a secret: her mother is the true heir to the English crown. But if the wrong people find out, it will mean war for her beloved Scotland. There's only one way to keep the peace—journey to London, escorted by her enemy, the wickedly handsome Captain Daniel Marlow. Fans of Karen Hawkins and Monica McCarty will love this book!

Fall in Love with Forever Romance

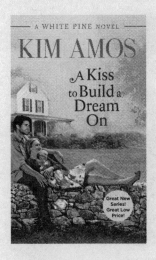

A KISS TO BUILD
A DREAM ON
by Kim Amos

Spoiled and headstrong, Willa Masterson left her hometown— and her first love, Burk Olmstead—in the rearview twelve years ago. But the woman who returns is determined to rebuild: first her family house, then her relationships with everyone in town...starting with a certain tall, dark, and sexy contractor. Fans of Kristan Higgins, Jill Shalvis, and Lori Wilde will flip for Kim Amos's Forever debut!

IT'S ALWAYS BEEN YOU
by Jessica Scott

Captain Ben Teague is mad as hell when his trusted mentor is brought up on charges that can't possibly be true. And the lawyer leading the charge, Major Olivia Hale, drives him crazy. But something is simmering beneath her icy reserve—and Ben can't resist turning up the heat! Fans of Robyn Carr and JoAnn Ross will love this poignant and emotional military romance.

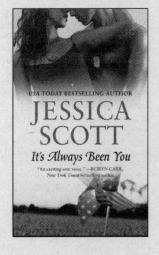

Fall in Love with Forever Romance

TOTAL SURRENDER
by Rebecca Zanetti

Piper Oliver knows she can't trust tall, dark, and sexy black-ops soldier Jory Dean. All she has to do, though, is save his life and he'll be gone for good. But something isn't adding up...and she won't rest until she uncovers the truth—even if it's buried in his dangerous kiss. Fans of Maya Banks and Lora Leigh will love this last book in Rebecca Zanetti's Sin Brothers series!